Maggie's MISSION

Rachel D. Muller

LOVE & WAR
Book Two

RACHEL MULLER

For Chris—my loving husband.
No one else could fill the shoes you do. Thank you for all your
love and support throughout this new phase of life.
For cheering me on when I felt like giving up.
For picking up where I left off.
I love you.

CHAPTER ONE

14 January 1945
Belgium, 238ᵗʰ General Hospital

Tremors of fatigue-driven adrenaline shook Maggie's skilled hands. Everything was going so well, until…

"Doctor, his blood pressure is dropping." Maggie clamped her hand over the unconscious soldier's wrist, listening to his failing vitals while he lay on the operating room table.

"I just need ten more minutes." The intensity in the doctor's voice indicated he would have ordered the patient to live if he could have. They'd lost so many men already.

Maggie listened as the numbers fell in the patient's pulse, her heart plummeting with each slowing heartbeat.

"Doctor?" She waited for his order as she exchanged a nervous glance with Lieutenant Vera Marshall, who stood at Maggie's side, monitoring the anesthetic liquids dripping into the patient's veins.

Then the surgeon's eyes bounced from Maggie to the patient lying on the table beneath the doctor's bloodied hands, concern etched into his tired eyes. "Come on, soldier. Hang in there. I'm almost done."

"Eighty-four over sixty—tell me what to do, Doctor." Panic wavered Maggie's voice. Her hands refused to still, no matter how skilled she may be. She was a good nurse—one of the best in the field. So why couldn't she, along with the doctor, save this boy's life? They were trying every avenue, and until this week, she'd never lost a patient. Her confidence dithered.

Lord, please don't let another one die. Please. He's so young. He's so young…

"Going into shock." Vera's hands strapped onto the patient as his body convulsed.

Without thinking, Maggie dropped her utensils and placed her hands on the young soldier's cheeks. Fire consumed her insides. She'd seen too many die this week—she couldn't lose another one.

"Don't you die on me! You hear me? You hang on!" In an instant, her demeanor went from the edge of calm to hysterical.

"Lieutenant, stand down! I need you to get him stabilized. Administer more plasma."

The doctor's crisp words registered, and she went to work, but her hands continued to tremble, making it difficult to change the IV. She was on her eighteenth straight hour of surgery, the third day of non-stop surgeries. She was already sleep-deprived, hungry, and exhausted from morbid sights of war. In an area far behind the front lines, the 238th General was unaccustomed to these types of visceral cases, and the task was daunting.

Beads of sweat formed on her brow as she made a quick job of administering plasma to the soldier on the operating table. His skin turned from gray to pasty white. His lips held a slight hue of blue as his life seeped from his body and drizzled down the operating table into a puddle on the floor. She knew the look. She knew the signs, even if the loss of blood wasn't enough to confirm her fears. Her heart leapt in bounds, slamming into her chest wall. The boy in front of her was losing his life and she had no control over it.

"Doctor, we're losing him," Vera announced.

Using his forearm, the physician wiped sweat from his hairline. He called for more clamps to stop the blood flow, but it was no use. Maggie's eyes grew wide, and tears formed in their corners. She checked the soldier's wrist again. "Doctor, there's barely a pulse." She was pleading with him more than informing him.

No answer.

"Doctor! I said there's no pulse! Can't you help him? Don't let him die!" As if stepping outside of herself, Maggie lunged for the doctor and threw her fists against his chest. "Don't let him die! Not again. Not again. Bring him back!" Her cries turned into sobs. She tore away from the doctor and threw herself against the dead patient. Deep inside, her logic knew they couldn't bring the young man back, but she hoped there was still a chance for a miracle.

Two sets of hands grabbed hold of Maggie's arms to pry her away from the soldier's body.

"Don't touch me! We can still save him. Help me." Her clenched fists beat against the soldier's chest, willing him to come to. "Don't just stand there, help me! You're a doctor, for crying out loud!"

The rest of the room grew deathly quiet and the other medical personnel in the surgery stared in bewilderment. Vera and two other nurses glanced among one another, unsure of what to do next. But none of them moved forward to help her. Not one. Hot tears spewed from her eyes. Why were they standing there, watching her instead of trying to save a life?

Too many wounded. Too many dead.

But she could push through this. There was still time for a miracle. She could save him—if someone would only help her.

"Fine. If no one will help, I'll do it myself." She started chest compressions then she slapped the soldier's cheeks. She—

Two more sets of hands—this time, stronger hands—clamped down on each side of her and grasped her arms. Her bewildered and betrayed eyes glared at the doctor. "Captain, what are you doing?"

"Lieutenant Johnson, you are relieved of duty as of this moment. Haines, Baker, get her out of here."

"Wait. I'll take care of her, Captain." It was Vera who then came to Maggie's side, gently laying her hands on Maggie's shoulders.

"Thank you, Lieutenant Marshall."

Once behind the wash room curtain, Vera pressed a damp cloth against Maggie's face. The cool against her hot skin felt wonderful to the touch, but the rest of her body was numb. Not even her fingertips felt alive.

"Come on now, honey. I know it hurts, but this is why we're here. We've done our best. You know how it goes sometimes. Most make it, but there are the few..."

"No, this is not why I'm here. I'm not here to care for soldiers so they can die. Vera, do you know how many of *my* patients have died this week? Three. Three! That's too many for a General Hospital, our hospital. That boy in there makes loss number seven for us today. We've never lost that many in one day, Vera. I can't..." Her words broke off as her breathing quickened. Tears clogged her throat. "I can't watch another young man die. I just can't."

Vera took a firm hold on Maggie's shoulders and stood unyielding as she ordered Maggie to snap out of it. "Look at me, Margaret Johnson. If you don't stop right now, they'll admit you—Luminal every four hours. Do you want that?" Vera threatened treatment by using a secondary name for the sedative, phenobarbital, for patients suffering from combat fatigue.

Maggie's watery eyes lifted from the floor to Vera's face and she shook her head. No, she didn't want that.

Vera's smile softened her features. "There now. You know, I wipe down soldiers day in and day out. I don't need to be wiping down your pretty little face too. Come on, you're all tear-stained, and your nose is running like a faucet. It's pretty nasty. You'll never land a man looking like this." Vera's sassy tone pulled on the corners of Maggie's mouth. "Is that a little smile I see?"

"I'm sorry, Vera. I don't know what's wrong with me." She wiped at her nose with the soft hanky Vera handed her.

Tears slid down the slopes of Maggie's cheeks. Vera's arms wrapped around her and held her close. Maggie's dear friend let her cry on the shoulder she so desperately needed. They all needed it once in a while, but today was Maggie's day.

"I'm so tired, Vera. I'm so exhausted I don't feel hunger anymore. I just want to crawl into a dark hole and stay there for a month."

"I doubt you want to climb into any dark holes in these parts. From what I've heard, mostly Germans occupy those."

Maggie leaned back and sniffed into her hanky. "I'm losing my mind. I'm the strong one, Vera. Nothing shakes me. I've been through so much. I can't let this war get to me."

"Maybe it's all just catching up to you now, honey. For a girl your age, you've been to the moon and back...*if* that's even possible."

Maggie's eyes drifted closed, and she tilted her head upward. Her eyes stung from the crying fit, and her shoulders ached terribly, but just sitting down and closing out everything else around her—even if for only a moment—lessened the evils around her. Sometimes just imagining her little flat back in Arbor Springs, Maryland with her best friend, Grace, was all the comfort she needed when the life of a nurse became stressful.

But those days were behind her now. She was a member of the Army Nurse Corps—a lieutenant to be exact. She had new obligations and duties that meant leaving behind all the modern comforts she was used to. Yes, Vera was right. She'd been to the moon and back in her journey through life...particularly the last three years.

15 January 1945

Sometimes the past revealed its cruel nature at the most inconvenient of times. It had no regard for her feelings and re-opened her freshly healed wounds. Today, it decided to pummel Maggie with vivid memories of Danny. His face barged into her thoughts with crystal clear mental images. The medical cabinet in front of her faded and her hands stilled. Her eyelids lazily fluttered, and Danny's boyish laugh resonated in her ears. A tremble infected her hand as she groped for the gold cross hanging from her neck. How she missed him. How she wished for that final good-bye.

For years she hid behind the robust façade that nothing could quake her. Not even Danny's MIA status shook her to her knees at the time of the letter's arrival. No, she'd learned to handle any impediment with her chin held high and her feet immoveable. That is, until she broke under pressure.

The truth was, Danny Russo's death crumbled her spirits, but she chose to mourn him silently while her friends and colleagues looked on in amazement and with a hint of pity. No one knew how badly her heart ached when she climbed into her bed at night, letting the silent tears of pain stream from her tired eyes.

Her teeth clenched together as her eyelids squeezed shut against the dull ache in her chest. It would subside in time. It always did. And when morning came, she would muster up the strength to start a new day and put on her best smile for the boys fighting to stay alive. She never had the chance to save Danny, but with each boy she sent home healthy and alive, she believed she was saving some other woman's Danny. In a way, the deed brought comfort to her own loss one piece at a time. One day, all those pieces would be put back in place, making her whole once again.

"Maggie! There you are!"

Brushing moisture from her eye, Maggie looked up from her tray of medical inventory and into the brilliant blue of the major's concerned eyes.

"Walt."

In one bound, his knight-like arms swept around her and pulled her close to him. She fell into his chest, thankful for the sphere of safety his embrace provided her.

"Are you all right, sweetheart? One of the medics told me what happened in the OR yesterday."

Her muscles recoiled and stiffened at the mention of her lapse in surgery. She backed away from his grasp, her smile fading from her lips. Her hands tugged on her blouse to right it. "I'm fine, Walt. Really. I just had a bad day that's all."

She knew that look in his eyes. Her explanation wasn't enough to convince him. "Maggie, are you getting enough rest, enough to eat? Darling, I'm worried about you. You're looking so thin and worn out. If you need time off, I may be able to arrange that."

"No." She raised her palm. "Walt, you can't give me special treatment while we're here. It's not fair to the other nurses who are working just as hard, or harder, than I am. We both know that'll cause trouble for the two of us. Lieutenant Harris gave me leave the remainder of the day and I slept it off. I got the rest I needed. I'll be fine."

His hands slipped around her waist and his fingers pressed against her back as he leaned in. His lips, soft and warm, gently rested against her forehead then a ragged breath escaped his chest. "Oh, Maggie…I don't know what I'd do without you. I worry about you so."

She listened to the beat of his heart. She loved the feel of his strong, muscular chest against her cheek. She felt safe and secure, as if dropping bombs and screaming aircraft didn't exist in their cocoon of affection. Moments like this didn't come too often since transferring to the General Hospital in Germany. However—

Although Walt did his best to shelter her from danger, his overprotective arm shielded her from the life she wanted to live.

"Don't fret over me, Walt. I'm a big girl. I know what I've gotten myself into."

"And I suppose that's why I've come to adore you so much. But I'm afraid that—"

"Hey, kid, do you have—Oh! Major Radford, sir. I apologize."

Walt and Maggie tore away from each other as Vera entered the supply room.

"Lieutenant Marshall. No apology necessary. I—" He looked between Maggie and Vera and his Adam's apple bobbed. "I was just leaving."

"You don't have to leave on my account, sir. My question can wait." Vera cast a coy eye in Maggie's direction and turned to leave.

"No. Wait, Lieutenant. We were just finishing up here." Walt turned to Maggie and lowered his voice. "Lieut—Maggie, we'll talk later?"

She nodded. "Of course."

After replacing his cap, he left the supply room.

Vera sauntered over to Maggie's side, clucking her tongue. A sly grin played on her lips. "If you needed time alone, I would have left. You know I'd cover for the two of you."

"I know that, Vera. You know how Walt is. He's always looking out for me."

Vera leaned her backside against the wooden table and crossed her arms over her chest. "You're not breaking any rules. So why act as if you're two kids afraid of getting caught?"

Maggie shrugged a shoulder, her eyes downcast.

"You know any girl would kill to have a man like that on her arm, Maggie. So why do you keep him at arm's length?"

Maggie busied herself with replacing bottles of alcohol back onto the shelf. "I don't know what you mean, Vera. You know I'm serious about Walt. I'm not some Dumb Dora who doesn't recognize a gem of a fella when she sees one."

"You're right about that. But you're usually not one to be so evasive either."

"Evasive? What have I been evasive about?" Maggie propped her fists against her hips, agitated by Vera's line of questioning.

"You hide like two teenagers who are guilty of sin when you're together. You're adults for crying out loud! Break radio silence and broadcast your relationship. Besides, if marriage is in your future, at least you'll be stationed together and not risk the separation."

"You're always ready to cut to the chase, aren't you, Vera Marshall?" Maggie spied the pile of olive drab army blankets that still needed placing on the wooden supply shelves. Lifting them in her hands, she marched them to the next room. Vera followed with a second pile.

"If you hadn't noticed, kid, there's a war raging over here. I'm sure the major has his own worries when he's not worrying about you. Don't you think he gets lonely over here? Why, I'm surprised he hasn't popped the question already and talked to the chaplain about his intentions."

Maggie cringed. Then her heart accelerated. Walt had made subtle hints about their relationship—a long term relationship. She knew his heart was growing fonder of her every day since their embarkation to Europe—and she felt fond of him too—but as the bond between them became stronger, so did Walt's fears. She suspected that he contemplated using his rank to transfer her back stateside just to keep her safe and out of harm's way.

But she *wanted* to be here. She put her name on the list of willing volunteers to serve overseas and charge the front lines. Saving lives is where she wanted to be. Where *God* wanted her to be. Marriage would alter all that. Her duties and priorities would change. Instead of focusing on the many men who needed her undivided attention, Walt would be the one who needed her undivided attention. Not that she minded pleasing the man she loved, but she couldn't divide her time in such a place as an army chain hospital.

No, it would be better if Walt didn't propose marriage. If he did, Maggie wouldn't be able to give him an honest answer.

CHAPTER TWO

21 January 1945
Oflag 64, Prisoner of War Camp, Poland

The barrack's wooden door banged open and Nazi soldiers barged into the crammed quarters, startling the sleeping Americans.

"Despicable maggots," the officer mumbled. "Get up!" The ruthless officer yanked a blanket from an ailing soldier.

Joe squinted as he fought the stinging in his eyes from a goon's flashlight shining in his face. A rush of frigid air swept into the room, but the prisoners alongside Joe ignored the freezing temperatures and scrambled to their feet. *The Commandant.* His mind registering who stood at his door, Joe pushed up off his burlap sack his captors called a bed and stood at attention. A swirl of dizziness clouded his eyes as he did.

Wearing a sly smile on his face, the Nazi guard opened his mouth to exercise his practiced English. "Everyone to the yard for *appell*. Today we *marsch*. Anyone who falls behind will be shot." He flaunted his pompous grin as he swept his eyes over each American prisoner, challenging them to protest, then he sauntered out the door and into the cold.

Joe's eyes glared at his captor as he walked away. The man's countenance reminded him of a serpent always in the strike position. The Nazi made Joe's stomach twist every time the officer—donned in his greatcoat—drew out the hiss of his "Ss."

The room was quiet except for the howl of blustery wind, but as soon as the Nazi left the prison cabin, fire flashed in each soldier's eye and low growls emerged from their weakened stomachs, which hadn't eaten a decent meal since—

Since...Joe honestly didn't know. He couldn't remember much of anything before his incarceration as a prisoner of war. Regrettably so, he couldn't recall *when* his last real meal satisfied his wasting stomach.

"If it's anyone who's despicable around here it's those good for nothin' idiots." Al Flemming turned to Joe, whose dark-haired head rested in his hands. "Hey, Joe, you doin' all right?"

"Yeah. I'm good, Al. What do you think Hitler has in store for us today?"

Al shrugged and pulled on his worn-out boots. "Don't know. It's odd they want to move us out so quickly, unless one of the guards discovered the tunnels. You heard the radio reports—the Russians are moving in. It's more likely they'll move us yet again. I just pray they don't stuff us into those death-trap boxcars again." Al paused and stared at the prisoner I.D. tags that adorned Joe's neck. "Sure wish your memory would return. If something were to happen while they're moving us to who-knows-where, it would be good to know who to send a letter to for you. You can't go on the rest of your life as the GI named Joe, that's for sure."

"Sorry, Al." Joe tapped his temple. "I try to figure it out and sort through the fog, but I always come up empty."

"Well one thing's for sure. With that dark hair and rough accent, you've got some thick Italian blood running through your veins. Brooklyn or New York ring a bell? Maybe Boston?"

Joe wrinkled his brow as he pulled on his outer layer of trousers. The chilled air sank deep into his bones. "Come on, Al. We've been through this before. Nothin' comes to mind." He sighed and pressed his backside against an old crate. "I guess I'll just have to get used to a new name and a new life." *Nothing seems familiar except for this rickety, drafty old prison home and those itchy burlap sacks used for beds.* "I don't even remember being thrown into this joint." He tugged at his worn-through, dirt-splotched tunic. He hadn't changed since the day he awoke in Oflag 64. With dirt and coal smudged into its threads, fleas and lice found his unwelcomed filth a pleasant abode.

"I remember it plain as I see you standing there. You were out cold when they dragged you in. Took you several days to come to. We didn't know whether you'd pull through or not. Tony said you most likely suffered a concussion from the size of the egg those scoundrels left on your head."

"At least they were kind enough to leave me with a gift." Joe touched the scar where a deep gash once blemished his temple. Thinking back to the day he awoke in the prison camp—not knowing exactly where he was or how he got there—brought back all the frustrating moments when he'd tried digging into his soul to remember who he was and where things had gone wrong.

He was a soldier. He knew that for sure. And he knew they were engaged in a war. But until Al informed him he was a prisoner under

German control just outside of East Germany, Joe hadn't even known he was in Poland. More importantly, how did he get to Poland, and how had he become a POW?

The wind picked up and a frigid draft squeezed through the barrack walls. A cold shiver made his upper body convulse, pushing gooseflesh through his thinning skin. Bread and water alone did little for his health. His hair had grown out longer too, and the scruff around his face was itchy and uninviting. Illness and diseases were already spreading around the camp like a shadow, slowly lapping at their heels. There was no warning when a man woke up to the symptoms that were feared and dreaded by the American soldiers. The anxiety of not knowing who would be next caused them all to take each breath with caution. At the same time, they were in this together, nursing one another back to health and some even giving up a meal so the ailing would regain strength from extra nutrition—no matter how small that nutrition would be.

The guards returned and hurried the men outside to line up for morning *appell*. They were ruthless when it came to the weak soldiers. Patience was not a practice in this camp, and if one wasn't careful, he could be shot for lagging behind. So Joe pressed on despite the ache in his bones from lack of nutrition, exercise, and warmth. Besides the long overcoat he was given out of a surprising issue of rations shortly after he arrived at Oflag 64, they hadn't given him anything more to warm his head or hands. So he flipped up the collar on the overcoat and clutched it tight beneath his chin, hoping the oversized lapels would protect his ears from the sub-zero temperatures.

Spying his sick friend, Joe grabbed the underarms of a stumbling prisoner. "I've got ya, Abe. Act calm and don't show weakness."

"Whatever they want us to do, Joe, I won't make it." Abe's voice was raspy and tired.

Joe kept his eyes straightforward, his tone even, and tried to look as if nothing was amiss. The Germans were like vultures, waiting for the weak to collapse then pouncing on them and finishing them off before having their meal.

"You've got to try. Maybe we're being transferred or maybe liberated. Who knows, maybe our side has struck a deal with Nazi Germany."

They fell in line, and when Abe had his footing, Joe released his arm.

"Thank you, friend," Abe whispered as he struggled to straighten his back at attention.

"*Ruhig!*" The Commandant's sharp tongue ordered quiet over the men. He looked them over with a stealth eagle's eye before going on. "Look at you—a pitiful sight for the *great American hero*. You are filthy swine!" The officer paused, a smile coming over his features. He tucked his hands behind his back and paced down the row and back again. "It seems the Soviets are fast approaching. You will all *marsch* to your new compound—"

Abe's deep, uncontrollable cough interrupted the Commandant's speech, and those snake-like eyes zeroed in on Abe.

Alarm filling his insides, Joe glanced at his friend. Abe was bent over trying to catch his breath. "Abe," he whispered above the coughs. "Abe, hold it in."

Wearied Abe reached for Joe's forearm as he stumbled to his knees.

The Commandant snapped his fingers. On command, a guard with a rifle in his hand hiked towards them with purpose.

Pulsating blood in Joe's feeble body rushed from his feet to his head, dizzying his mind. He glanced from the approaching guard to Abe, who knelt at Joe's right side. Joe's heartbeat quickened as he watched the German's angry eyes beat down on his friend. He knew what was coming. He could see the enjoyment of brutality play across the guard's face.

The sound of Joe's heart thumped in his ears over the sound of Abe's granular cough. His buddy's head was bent, preventing him from seeing the Nazi trooping toward him. The poor boy had no indication what was in his very near future—then again, maybe he did.

The butt of the guard's rifle swung up and aimed for Abe's head. Without thinking, Joe leaped in front of Abe just as the gun was thrust forward. Joe's leg buckled and pain radiated from his left thigh and seared up his spine. He held back a holler by clenching his teeth and clamping his eyes shut. But only for a moment. There would be more to pay. Then the strike of a leather hand stung his jaw.

"Ah. The no-name American. Trying to make a name for yourself?" The officer sauntered up to Joe and leveled his eyes on him. "You are a nobody, GI Joe." His voice hissed like a serpent. "You are nothing more than a ghost. Your company thinks you are dead, you're family thinks you are dead, and the world thinks you cease to exist. Maybe you want an escape, Mister…" He reached for the brown, metal I.D. tags around Joe's wrist. "102783?" He released the tags, and a devious grin spread across his face. "You are lucky this time. But maybe not so lucky next time you step out of line. And I'll be watching."

The officer turned his back and Joe released the breath he'd been holding, but he relaxed too soon. Before he could suck in another breath, a backhanded slap landed across his cheek. Joe stumbled back and bit back bile that threatened to force its way up his throat. He heard Abe yell out pain. Turning around, he spotted poor ailing Abe clutching his midsection and gasping for air. The Kraut had landed a boot on Abe's already debilitated stomach.

Joe couldn't do anything more for his friend. The morning roll call was already underway and guards hovered over them like the vultures they were. So the men stood ram-rod straight in the freezing cold for an hour while every prisoner in the camp was counted.

A little while later, when they were all heavy-laden with their packs and rations, they heard the words, "*Vorwarts, marsch!*"

All at once, the 1,400 prisoners started their trek to who-knew-where. With packs slung over their backs and bedrolls under their arms or slung over their chests, they marched through the frozen mud and snow. Without the protection of knit hats and gloves, the below-freezing temperatures would surely kill them before they reached their next destination unknown.

The German guards marched alongside them with their rifles and lugers ready at all times. The men were smart enough to know that if they "stepped out of line," the Nazis wouldn't think twice about popping them with lead.

Joe pushed his legs forward. The bitter cold shoved back. From the corner of his eye, a German soldier approached him. His stomach tensed and he averted his eyes.

"*Tragen.*"

Joe then looked at the guard. The man thrust a sled filled with supplies toward him.

"*Tragen!*"

"Carry? You want me to take?" he asked.

The guard pushed the cord into Joe's hand and turned back the way he came. Joe assumed it was his turn to pull the sled. He cast a glance in Abe's direction. The boy didn't look too well. He was in no condition to trudge through the light snow that had fallen and fight the bitter cold that penetrated their coats and worn-through boots. Abe was forced to drop his pack several miles back. His rations and extra clothing he needed were gone. Joe couldn't help but feel sorry for the young man. He was sure pneumonia plagued Abe's body by the sound of his raspy, chesty cough and the blood he spat on the ground.

"Abe? You still with us?" Joe called over his shoulder.

"Yeah."

But the shiver in Abe's voice gave Joe concern that hypothermia was setting in. He slowed his footsteps so Abe could catch up with him.

"Don't wait up for me, Joe. If they see you straggling behind, they'll leave you for the wolves too."

"I'm not gonna leave you behind. We're all in this together.

Brothers."

Abe's chest rose and fell as if a great weight was placed on it. "I can't...make it any longer, Joe. I'm gonna have to stop."

"No, don't stop. You can do this." Inwardly, he knew his comrade couldn't. "Come on, buddy, keep moving your feet forward. Push through the pain."

"I can't. I can't feel my feet. I lost feeling a ways back."

Abe started to look as though he was going to drop at any given moment.

"Don't you dare think of quitting on me."

An ear-piercing whistle screeched through the air.

"*Auszeit.*"

He didn't understand the order. It was a word he'd hardly heard his whole imprisonment. "What's he saying?"

Abe collapsed on the sled Joe pulled. "He said we get a break. And not a moment too soon."

"No wonder I didn't recognize it. When was the last time we were ordered a break?"

Al lumbered toward the two men and lowered himself to the frozen ground.

"I don't think the break is necessarily for us." Al pointed to a group of tired Germans. "I think this trek has worn them out as well."

"Thank the Lord." Joe let out a breath. "Al, you heard any word on where we're going?"

"Nothing definite. But we don't have much light left. I'd say we'll march on 'til dark then camp out for the night. We're heading west. Might be heading for Germany. But the thought of that doesn't settle too well on my mind either. They could be marching us straight into Berlin."

Al had a point. Rumors of extermination camps began to surface the last few months. Trains carrying cattle cars, packed with prisoners, transported innocent people to their deaths. Is that where he and his group were headed? Were they being forced to march to their death, whether it meant they froze on the roadside or executed by a firing squad? More questions blistered inside his mind. Yet, the sad thing was the Nazi officer was right. He was nothing more than a living ghost. No one knew of his existence, even himself. So why on earth did they keep him around?

March 1945

"Abe." Joe shook his buddy awake. "Hey buddy, come on. It's time to go."

Abe's eyes rolled beneath his eyelids as he fought to regain consciousness. The boy looked thinner—much thinner—this morning. The straw he lay on seemed to swallow his body whole. Joe waited as long as he could before arousing him again.

"You have to get up now. The guards are waiting."

"No." Gravelly and weak, Abe's voice was just above a whisper. "Go…without me."

"I'm not leaving you behind."

Just then, a guard ordered the men out of the barn and into the cold. It was time to move again.

Joe pleaded with Abe to fight harder and keep walking, but it was no use. Abe just wasn't strong enough to push off his bed of straw and continue the march.

Joe stood and watched Abe's eyes close. The boy wouldn't be coming with them.

"I'll send help as soon as I can," Joe told him. "I'm sorry, Abe. I'm sorry."

Abe's weakened state kept him from answering, and Joe feared this moment would be the last time they saw each other. So, with a burdened heart heavy enough to drag his wasting body through the mud, Joe turned to leave, glancing back over his shoulder only once to secure that final memory of a friend so dear.

⊰৵৵

Joe awoke from his grueling nightmare. Taking deep gasps of breath, he tried to calm his thumping heart. The march to Stalag VIIA had been harsh, brutal. Never before could he remember being so cold…if that even counted, considering the state his mind was in.

He closed his eyes. Even in the silence of night he could still hear the sound of metal scraping against frozen ground—like metal on metal. The ping and blunt thud of shovels hitting solid mud stirred defeat in his soul. They were told to dig a latrine. How was that possible in temperatures well below zero?

Even more defeating than scraping the surface that would not budge, was the guilt weighing heavily on Joe's mind. Many of the men from Oflag 64 were abandoned to freeze to death, were left to die in the barns of German farms because their bodies were too feeble to go on, or they were shot in the forehead because they didn't move fast enough for their German guards. There were no questions asked, just German orders to move out—without their dying comrades.

Joe pleaded with Abe to muster up the strength to make it through one more day, but it was no use. Abe just wasn't strong enough to get up. In fact, his condition had worsened. His head grew warm with fever and his cough rattled deep inside his chest. His breathing wheezed with each intake and exhale of breath. Joe worried that morning would be the last time he'd ever see his friend again.

Moisture pooled in his eyes when he said good-bye to Abe and the other men. Their eyes showed the uncertainty they felt. Uncertain as to whether they would heal from their ailments, or how long they would be allowed to reside in the barns of German farmers, or if they would live to see another day. Leaving a brother serviceman behind was not the American way. But they weren't in America anymore. They were in enemy territory, and the game had to be played by their rules.

Joe wiped the flashbacks from his eyes. Every time he closed his eyelids, he could see Abe's thin face peering up at him. How Joe wished he could have saved his friend. To see him this far. Now he was burdened with the guilt that he survived the march and his friend, potentially, did not.

Chapter Three

March 1945, 1 a.m.
Arbor Springs, Maryland

Through sleepy eyes, Grace Brady reached across the sheets to find empty space. Luke's absence awakened her. However, she wasn't surprised to find him standing at the bedroom window, staring aimlessly into the night.

Gently, she lifted her quilt from her legs and slipped out of bed. Her heart ached for him every time she caught him struggling for peaceful slumber. The war may have been over for Luke Brady, but some fragments channeled their way into Luke's soul as he left the European Theatre of Operations.

Her quiet footsteps were carefully measured as to not startle him as she drew near his silhouette form. Her eyes lingered on the stump of his arm a mere moment, and she wondered if brutal flashbacks plagued him tonight. When he was close enough to touch, she slipped her arms around his waist and peered up at him. The moonlight reflected off his morose eyes.

Luke glanced down at her and a smile softened his features.

"Can't sleep again?"

"Yeah. Sometimes…old memories resurface just when I think I've buried them."

"You thinking about Tommy?"

Luke stood silent for a few moments, and Grace knew he needed time to put his feelings into words. But when he spoke, only one word drifted off his lips.

"Danny." He bent over the window, leaned his left arm against the pane, and sighed.

Grace let him go, knowing they'd been down this road many times already in the last three months, and yet, perceiving there would be so many more nights like this one and the ones past. She rested her soft hand against his back and kissed his cheek.

"I'm sorry, sweetheart."

No other words were needed in a time like this. Danny's demise had hit Luke with intensity after his return to the States. A lifelong friendship ending prematurely.

"Sometimes it feels like he's not even gone. Nearly twenty years of friendship and not once did we part in separate directions until Danny volunteered for parachute school. I should have talked him out of it."

"But would he have listened, Luke? It seems to me, that's what Danny wanted."

She watched as Luke's eyes scanned the moonlit sky.

"He was always looking for the next adventure."

"Maybe he was saving you from his fate."

❧❧

The following afternoon, Grace greeted the mailman as she usually did. With the weather turning slightly warmer and Spring nearing, stepping into the outdoors and feeling the sun on her skin became the highlight of her day.

"Thank you, Louis." A stack of letters was placed in her hands and she hoped today would bring word from Maggie.

"Good day, Mrs. Brady."

Closing the door behind her, Grace flipped through the mail. Her breath caught in her throat when she spotted familiar script on a certain white envelope. She couldn't wait. Setting down the rest of her mail on the occasional table, Grace tore open the letter from Maggie and settled on the armchair.

Dear Grace,

We've made landfall in Europe. I regret I cannot give specifics, but you knew that already. Surprisingly, seasickness did not plague my body during the trip over the Atlantic. There were days it would have been nice to spot at least a small sliver of land. A feeling of isolation settles over the soul as you look out the sea deck and realize you're nothing but a tiny vessel amid a large ocean.

Good news, Walt's orders came when mine did, and we are making this trek together. I never imagined my trip across the Atlantic would be with someone other than Danny. In a way, it's surreal, but I'm thankful for the support and care Walt has graciously given me. I think I'm falling for him, Grace. I know it sounds crazy, especially so soon after Danny's death, but God's grace has washed over me.

There are nights I still mourn Danny. Times I miss him terribly and maybe more so now that I know he's not coming back. Those are the nights I cry into my pillow until I drift off to sleep.

Enough about me. I want to hear all about life with Luke. How was the honeymoon? Have you settled into your new house yet? Spare no details. I'll be looking forward to your next letter.

Love Always,
Maggie

Grace smiled at Maggie's probing questions. Could Grace put into a letter the wonderful advantages of marriage? If only Danny would have made it home to fulfill his promise with Maggie . . .

Then again, some things just weren't meant to be. But the Lord always knew when to fill those voids at the right time. And it seemed Major Walter Radford was the man for the job.

CHAPTER FOUR

29 March 1945
Belgium, 238th General Hospital

"**O**kay, ladies, start packing up. We're moving out!"
Enlisted personnel swarmed the camp, carrying crates of ammo, canvas bags, and large poles in their arms. Maggie and the girls began packing medical supplies and finished with discharge paperwork. The 238th was leaving Belgium.

"Where do you suppose they're sending us next, Maggie?"

"It's hard to say." Maggie glanced at Bonnie, who bit down on her bottom lip. "Good news is if we're moving further into Germany, at least we know our boys are hitting their targets."

"Oh, boy. I won't even have time to wash my hair before leaving this lovely place." Vera's roguish eye batted a wink at Maggie.

"That's one way to keep the fellas away."

"Thanks a lot."

"You're welcome." Maggie folded the box lid over and hefted it into her forearms. A strand of hair fell above her brow and she blew it from her line of vision. Today's task of breaking down camp would be arduous. But nonetheless, she plugged away like the soldier she was trained to be.

That is, until she turned and bumped into a solid being.

"Here. Let me take that for you."

Startled, Maggie blinked and opened her mouth but stopped short when she looked up into Walt's smiling face.

"Walt. Thank you." Her cumbersome load lifted from her hands and into his.

"I can't stay long. I made an excuse to leave HQ so I could see you."

Trying to look as though they were busy packing up camp instead of busy with one another, Maggie and Walt made their footsteps swift and purposeful. However, Maggie hung close to his side as they carried packs and crates from the triage tent to the supply trucks.

"Do you have any idea where we're headed, Walt?"

"I do, but I can't tell you here."

She deliberately halted her stride, dropped her pack, and crossed her arms in front of her chest. With her best effort to attempt sad, puppy dog eyes, she stared at Walt. Watching his jaw tick and his eyes bouncing back and forth, Maggie inwardly smiled at his undoing.

Walt's shoulders drooped and his head angled to the side. "Now, Maggie. Don't do this to me."

"I've missed you, Walt. It's been so long since we've had an evening together."

A sigh, transmitting his yearning, deflated his chest. "Believe me, I know it."

His hungry eyes settled on hers, bringing back those feelings she hadn't felt for a very long time. Her stomach somersaulted in a flurry of desire, knocking breath from her lungs.

She took a step closer to him, not caring if everyone in the outfit saw them wrapped in a private moment together. Inching her way toward his smooth baby-like complexion, she closed her eyes and whispered, "Just kiss me, Walt."

His warm breath blew against the coolness of her skin. Electrical pulses tingled in her chest the closer he came. She could almost taste the sugary sweetness of his kiss…almost.

"Johnson! In my quarters immediately!"

And the electrical current was broken. Like someone had flipped a switch, the magic was gone, the light doused.

"Yes, ma'am," she answered over her shoulder. Then sorrowfully, looked back at a disappointed Walt. "I'm sorry."

His thumb touched the curve of her cheek. "Me too. I'll try to stop by one more time before we move out."

A smile tugged up the corners of her frown. "I best be getting over to Harris' tent. I have a hunch I'll have some explaining to do."

"I'll be sure to clear things up with her. Maggie, I—I love…" The rest of his sentence was drowned out by the honking of a passing supply truck.

"Excuse me." "Coming through." Suddenly, enlisted men and women buzzed by them, interrupting their private exchange.

Knowing she'd get written up if she didn't make it to the lieutenant's tent on time, Maggie lifted her hand and waved a pathetic good-bye to Walt. His lips were still half parted and one side of his cheek was turned up in a pitiful half-smile. He was disappointed, she could see, but he tried putting on a positive façade for her benefit.

If she were truly honest with herself, she'd let Walt's words sink in. Truth was, she knew what Walt was trying to declare just before the supply truck cut him off. She could hear the sincerity in his voice. He loved...*her*. Not the Army. Not Germany. Not his rank. Major Walter Radford loved her, Margaret Johnson, Lieutenant. But that terrified her. Love just didn't last these days. She should know, she'd seen it first-hand since that terrible attack on Pearl Harbor. Boys were ripped from their family's lives and dragged into a watery grave. Girls—such as her best friend, Grace—became widows long before their time. And boyfriends went missing...boyfriends like Danny Russo, who wouldn't be coming back.

Maggie jogged the distance to the chief nurse's quarters at the ANC tent. When she stepped inside, Lieutenant Harris, Vera, Bonnie, and Helen all sat patiently in wooden chairs.

"So glad you could make it on such short notice, Lieutenant Johnson. Please, have a seat."

Maggie cast a glance at Bonnie and Vera as she lowered herself onto a chair. Their eyes held no indication of what was to follow.

"Ladies, General Patton's army is moving across the Rhine River. If his forces continue to secure ground at this rate, we'll be marching into Berlin in no time at all. We've reached a critical point in the war and our boys are closer than ever in breaking Hitler's regime.

"I've assembled you here because the 39th Evacuation Hospital has requested four able-bodied nurses. Four of their ANC members have been sent home after announcing pregnancies. It pains me to bring the four of you in here like this. I uphold each of you as outstanding nurses and I hate to lose you.

"The Thirty-Ninth EVAC is entering Bad Kreuznach." Pausing, Lieutenant Harris folded her hands over her desk and leaned forward. She pursed her lips together before adding, "Their camp is located just miles from the front, ladies. There is a strong surge of mortars, fighters, air raids, and there is always the chance the Germans will break through the line our boys have set in place. That front is continually fired upon. Word is their nurses are in surgery sometimes twelve to fifteen hours a day. It will be a physically and mentally exhausting job. If you feel you cannot handle it, speak now. They want only the best, and I plan to supply them with only the best."

Lieutenant Harris' eyes bore down on the four women seated in front of her. Maggie's heart thundered in her chest. She wanted to go. The call summoned from deep inside her—a call she couldn't ignore. The fire that was kindled one year ago was now a raging inferno, edging her to the point of no return. She *needed* to go. To not do so would be disobedience.

But what about Walt?

Volunteering for this job would mean separation from him indefinitely. How would that affect their relationship?

On the other hand, she was a good nurse, and she'd made a promise to God long before landing on Germany's terrain that she would follow His leading—even if it meant leaving her loved ones behind.

"I'll do it, Lieutenant Harris. I'll go." Maggie forced her eyes to meet her superior's.

Nodding her approval to Maggie, the chief nurse looked to the other girls. "Ladies?"

"I'll go."

"Me too."

"Yes, ma'am, I'll go."

The rest of the women quickly followed Maggie's lead.

"All right. Here are your orders." She handed each nurse a sheet of yellow paper. "You leave first thing tomorrow morning. The camp moved into the area this morning and should be open by the time you ladies reach the station. I'll find replacements for your positions immediately. Begin packing and be ready for departure at 0500 hours tomorrow. God bless you."

The girls gathered themselves and stood to leave.

"Lieutenant Johnson, a moment please."

Maggie lagged behind, and when the room was free of everyone except for herself and Lieutenant Harris, the chief nurse motioned for her to take her seat.

Lieutenant Harris removed her thick reading glasses from her eyes and blinked hard.

Maybe this would be her reprimand for her outward display of affection with Walter. She braced herself, waiting for the tongue lashing.

"Maggie. . ." The Lieutenant's informal approach took her by surprise. "I mulled day and night over my decision. After your fiasco in the OR back in January, I had my reservations about sending you to the front, but your skills are impeccable and your take charge attitude is invaluable. If not for your leadership abilities, we wouldn't be having this conversation right now. Do you understand what I am saying to you, Lieutenant?"

"Yes, ma'am."

"Very good. Don't disappoint me, Johnson. I have faith in you."

Maggie's head still swirled when a cool breeze nipped at her skin upon exiting the ANC tent. Slowly, her senses came back to her. Had she really just volunteered to take on the front? They were leaving the 238th for good?

Vera, Bonnie, Helen, and Maggie threw looks at one another like side pitches. The news was so sudden that it almost didn't seem real. Just where was this war taking them now?

❦

"It sounds like we're heading into the deepest, darkest jungle," Bonnie said as she stuffed her blanket into her duffel.

"All the more reason to pay full attention to our superiors," Maggie replied. "I can't believe I'm getting this chance. I've wanted this for so long."

"Why?"

"Because, Lieutenant Marshall, I am a skilled nurse. I think I'll be an asset to the Corps if I'm closer to the front. I know I can take care of those men while the doctors are busy performing procedures."

"You've got the confidence, I see. You're not trying to be a hero, are you? Make *us* look bad?"

"Of course not, Vera. Why would you even think such a thing?"

"You just always seem to be pushing yourself ahead of the pack. What about you, Helen? How do you feel about this?"

"Do I have a choice? I wasn't about to let you girls go off without me. If you want the truth, I'm scared to death."

Vera dropped the navy blue skirt she held in her hands and stood next to Helen. "Honey, there's no need to be afraid. Look out that window. You see that big ol' red cross on that white circle?" Vera pointed to the insignia on the tent tops. "We are covered by the Geneva Convention. No enemy will even think of attacking us. We'll stick together and we'll be all right. I promise. Now come on. The Army doesn't tolerate tardy nurses."

Maggie couldn't help but feel a little put out at Vera's earlier statement. "Do you really think I try to outdo you girls, Vera?"

"Look, kid, drop it. I didn't mean no harm by saying that. It was just an inquiry."

If it was just an inquiry, then why did Vera avoid eye contact with her? "An inquiry with a dash of disdain." Maggie stuffed her thick, olive drab army blanket into her footlocker. "Are you threatened by me, Lieutenant Marshall?"

"Threatened by you?" Vera's tightly arched eyebrows rose high into her forehead. "Of course not. I don't allow silly contests to fluster and cloud my mind."

Contests? Who here was entering themselves in a popularity contest? Maggie glanced at each one of her nurse friends as they packed. Was there just a hint of jealousy lingering in the air between them?

≪⌘≫

Maggie found Walt standing in the unearthed spot where HQ was formerly established. Looking across the camp as she neared him, the area sat naked of olive drab canvas and army station signs. The only signs of life were the doctors, nurses, and personnel who folded up the tent canvases, loaded the poles, and carried crates of ammo and supplies to the truck convoy.

It was all a reminder of the path she'd chosen for her life. It seemed she didn't stay in one place for very long before it was time to take up her bed and move on. But she'd lost far too much in her lifetime to stop and dwell on those things now. Losing sight of her mission and focus could cost her and the people around her their lives. So she would do as she'd learned to do—carry on.

Her nervous fingers tensed and relaxed as she wrung her hands in front of her while silently practicing her memorized speech. It was difficult enough facing the fact that they were going to be separated, but how to break the news to Walt that she'd volunteered for this mission? Her nerves spiraled her thoughts in every which direction.

Maggie stopped several yards short from where Walt stood. He was looking over his paperwork and occasionally looked up to answer a passing soldier. He was so handsome in his uniform and constantly her pillar of stone in her time of need. With the sun beating down on her face, warm memories flooded her mind as she recalled the day Walt showed up at her dormitory door. He swooped in like her knight in shining armor after the harsh reality of Danny's death was confirmed. His unwavering and patient affection is what drew her to him, but unexpectedly, his sheltering arms would always be the reminder of Danny's demise. It was because of Walt she'd learned Danny was killed in France. It was Walt's steady hand who held her broken frame as her tears fell on the green of his jacket. It was Walt who'd somehow managed to replace Danny's spot in her heart.

"Maggie? There you are. Sweetheart, you look as though you've seen a ghost."

Maggie shook out of her fog and blinked back the memories from her mind. Walt's long strides brought him through the mess of enlisted personnel and to her side in just a few short bounds.

His eyes searched hers, and his hands brushed back the stray hairs from her forehead. "Are you all right?"

In that moment, it seemed everyone else faded from sight.

"Um, yes. I'm fine. I—I was just...thinking." Too many thoughts swarmed her mind. Walt didn't deserve the leftovers of her broken heart. To force her past behind her, Maggie wrapped her arms around Walt's middle and held him close. Her eyes closed against the coarse material of his jacket and she inhaled the scent of musty canvases and spilled coffee on his tunic. "I'm so glad to see you." She savored the moment, the feel of his chin propped against the crown of her head and his protective hands cradled around her back. If this moment could only last...

"A man expects this kind of treatment when he's leaving for war, or just coming home."

She squeezed him a little tighter. He had no idea what she was about to reveal to him. Under the tautness of her embrace, his back muscles tensed beneath her hands. Then she knew he sensed it.

"You're not here just because you've missed me."

Her throat tightened, and she forced herself to pull away from the safety of his embrace. She willed herself not to cry. "I do miss you, Walt. But no, this isn't our regular rendezvous. We're pulling out first thing in the morning."

"I know that, silly. We all are. So what's this all about? Everything's okay between us, isn't it?"

"Yes. It couldn't be better. It's just—" she sighed—"Walt, I've been given an assignment."

"What kind of assignment? Did Lieutenant Harris punish you for being caught with me? If so, she's going to get a tongue lashing. We didn't do anything wrong. I may be able to get it reversed—"

Maggie lifted her palm to stop him. "No, no. Walt, you can't use your rank for everything around here. Besides, it's nothing like that anyway."

"Then what is it?"

"I'm being transferred to the 39th. Not just me. Vera, Bonnie, and Helen are going too. We leave first thing tomorrow morning."

Walt's jaw hinged open. His eyes drooped downward. His hand swiped across his forehead then raked back his dark, wavy hair.

"How could she do this?"

"The 39th needs skilled nurses. She thinks we're the best she has to send."

His head shook from side to side, and his knuckles pressed into his hip. "No. She's punishing you because of me. I can talk to her superiors, Maggie. I'll march right in there this very minute and demand they let you off the hook."

Maggie caught Walt's arm before he brushed past her. "Stop. Walter."

Her feminine touch must have been enough to bring his focus back to reason. He stopped. Then all at once, he scooped her into his embrace and covered her mouth with his lips. The heated passion he enforced on her burned through his grasp, crisping her skin.

Maggie went breathless. When had she ever been kissed like that? Never. Heat still radiated from her lips after he pulled away. Leaving him would be so much harder than she expected. He could never know she volunteered for the job. But he did need to know what her new orders were.

"Lieutenant Harris isn't sending me to the 39th for punishment. She truly feels I'm needed in Bad Kreuznach."

"Bad Kreuznach?"

"Mm hm."

His fingers explored her face, her cheeks, her neck. "What am I going to do without you?"

"Write me. I won't be too far away."

"I'm going to worry myself sick over you, Maggie. You know that, don't you?"

"Leave it in God's hands. If I learned anything from my best friend, it's that God has a way of working miracles." She smoothed her fingers over his lips.

"Easier said than done."

"That's what faith is."

His strong arms enveloped her all over again. This time holding onto her until time wouldn't allow any longer.

CHAPTER FIVE

30 March 1945

"It's so much colder here than I anticipated it to be." Vera's voice quivered as she tried to keep her teeth from chattering.

After finishing their breakfast in the mess tent, the girls slung their duffels over their shoulders and tried to act as though the forty pound load on their backs weren't a bother.

"I slept with three layers of clothing on last night—*not* including my coat! I haven't felt this cold since January." Maggie pulled her wool winter coat a little tighter around her neck and chest. She was ever so thankful for the extra thick gloves she'd packed right before embarkation.

"Okay, girls, hush the complaining. Don't want anyone thinking we can't handle this. Just load up on the hot coffee and biscuits until this winter spell breaks."

That was Vera's approach to handling life's situations. But the girl was right. They were here to do a job and do it well. If anyone overheard grumbling and complaining, it would be a sign of weakness and the lions would pounce to make their kill. No, they had to be strong in this masculine world and brave the fiercest elements—even if it meant coming nose to nose with death.

"Mmm...coffee." Bonnie groaned, and her lazy eyes closed. "I'd love to have some hot coffee right now—with two scoops of sugar."

"Hang in there a little longer, Bonnie belle. I'm hoping the Thirty-Ninth welcomes us with a hot meal right off the kettle."

All this talk of food, combined with cold shivers, made Maggie's belly growl. Their meal of grits and sausage hadn't filled her famished stomach. But she kept her grumblings to herself. Right now Walter was heading in one direction and she was leaving for the other. That alone was enough to hollow her stomach when the hunger bug hit.

A corporal stood behind a mobile supply unit as the nurses neared.

After chucking the girls' duffels into the back, he held out his hand and assisted each woman into the truck. Maggie settled herself onto the truck floor, and her gazed shifted to the bare ground of what was the 238th General. As her eyes raked across the mud and mounds of dirt, an ache burrowed in her chest. Her mind's eye snapped one final ghostly image of the threadbare camp. This place had been her home away from home. Where friendships were built. Where a second chance at love was gifted. Where her spirit was tested to its limit. Now God saw it fit to move her onward as this mission stood complete. But haunting images of the 238th and Walt's adoring eyes would stay with her always.

Promise me we'll always be together. Walt's request had startled her. He didn't realize the last time anyone spoke those words to her was the day Danny left—for good. His flat statement soured her stomach as she readied herself into the wee morning hours for her departure.

Sitting nestled beneath blankets in the back of the army supply truck, Maggie's eyelids fluttered. The rocking of the vehicle and warmth from sleeping bodies inside lulled her like a lullaby. With the girls fast asleep on each side of her, she drifted in and out of consciousness. Somewhere in the twilight haze, those final moments with Danny surfaced. This time she allowed herself to dwell on the sweet memory...

While waiting at the depot for the next train departure, her white and red polka dotted dress framed her knees as she lowered herself onto Danny's lap. His arms felt natural around her waist and she relaxed against his chest. Only a few minutes longer to enjoy this moment then Danny's train would pull out of the station and head for Georgia. People rushed past them in a hurry to reach their next destinations, but Danny and Maggie immersed themselves in these final few moments together.

"Hey, I've got an idea. Why don't we get married?" Danny's voice cut the silence between them.

"What?" Maggie's voice squealed.

"Let's get married. Right now."

He'd certainly taken her by surprise. What was this dark-haired Italian boy thinking? She tried to open her mouth to ask for an explanation but those words lodged in her throat and refused to budge.

His enthusiastic laugh helped her recover.

"Daniel Russo, please tell me what you're talking about! Your train leaves in ten minutes. There's no time for a ceremony and our best friends just parted in opposite directions...I can't..." Her mind spun in five directions. She held her fingers to her temples to balance her senses.

His masculine hands pulled her fingers from her brow and he held tightly to her hands. "We don't need a preacher or friends. Right here, right now, let's pledge our love to each other."

Was he crazy? Was she ready to give her heart to Danny? Completely?

"Booooard!"

Maggie startled. His train was ready to pull out.

"Maggie?"

Her chest rose and fell heavily with each breath she took. This was all so sudden.

She saw Danny's Adam's apple bob, and a look never before worn on his face appeared. He was actually...nervous?

"Maggie." His voice came out shaky. "I need an answer. It's time."

Her fingers softly brushed the back of his neck. Could she say it?

She inhaled and braced herself.

"I...love you, Danny."

He blew out a relieved breath. A broad smile came to his face and he pressed his forehead against hers, his large, Italian nose poking her eyelid. His hands grasped hers and he tucked them under his chin. "Maggie, I promise to stay true to you and love you to the ends of the earth until we can be reunited and seal this promise." He kissed her fingers. "Will you promise to wait for me to return?"

She nodded, unable to squeak out even a simple yes. Consenting to his leaving would only confirm those uncertainties swirling around in her mind. He was leaving. It was final. And the guarantee of seeing him again was bleak. Maggie studied his features one final time—his hairline, his square jaw, his skin tone.

The conductor gave the final boarding call and Danny glanced from Maggie to the train car and back to Maggie again. Worry lines creased his forehead as he ran his fingers through the mass of his hair and rubbed the back of his neck. "I love you." He ducked his head and leaned in for their last kiss, caressing her lips with warmth and his deepest affections. "I'll come back soon. I promise."

Maggie slid off his lap and he picked up his duffel. He slung it over his shoulder like a true knight unafraid of the war he was marching into.

Then he was gone.

Maggie's eyes misted over and the last memory of Danny faded away. He was her first true love. No one had stolen more kisses from her than Danny Russo. Who cared if he had a big nose, a loud mouth, and an overbearing family? She missed his fun loving humor, quick wit, and the times he made her laugh, even when she was mad.

Lord, I'm sure Danny's up there making a raucous in heaven right now. He always was good for that. If you could, please tell him I miss him. But also tell him I'm all right. Thank you, Jesus, amen.

The camp looked like any other camp. Drab green tents lined dirt paths on both sides. Red crosses painted in white circles adorned the tent tops, and enlisted personnel swarmed the grounds.

An all too cheery soldier bellowed to the girls in the transport vehicle. "Okay, Lieutenants. Welcome to your new home."

He lent a hand to the weary nurses as they hopped off the truck bed.

"Not quite as big as I imagined." Vera's hand lingered against the truck's side panel. "Is Harris sure there's enough room for us to even fit in here?"

"We're replacements, Vera. But don't get your hopes up about bunking together."

"Oh dear, I hope our new roomies are friendly."

Vera draped an arm around Bonnie's shoulders. "Don't worry, kiddo. Those gals will fall in love with your sweet, innocent charm."

"Or they may devour me."

"Lieutenants. Our replacements from the 238th?"

The girls snapped at attention as an officer addressed them. "Yes, sir. Lieutenants Johnson, Marshall, Fitzgerald, and Newman reporting for duty, sir."

"Very good. Follow me. I'll introduce you to your Chief Nurse, First Lieutenant McGee. She'll oversee you while you're here, and she'll be the one to assign you to your new living quarters."

As they walked along the dirt and mud pathway, the four women received curious looks. Passing soldiers eyed them as they made their way through the cluster of medical tents. Several nurses standing at the entryway of a triage tent eyed them with arched eyebrows. Their lips pressed into fine lines as Maggie lifted her hand in a half wave. To her surprise, the small group of women waved back.

"Maybe this won't be so bad," she whispered to Vera.

"Just act normal and confident. Like always."

Like always.

Was Vera getting another jab in? Maggie *had* to be strong and confident. No one else was ever the backbone in her life. Even her parents had succeeded in making sure she knew that if she wanted anything in life, she would need to be the one who worked for it. Who earned it. There was no emotional support in nursing school. Grace was the closest living person who came anywhere near a true family member. Her spiritual sister. How she missed Grace in times like these. Although her nursing friends were there to lift her up, they were also very good at letting her down.

Lieutenant McGee showed the women every square inch of the camp. The tents were set up according to order. Men's tents were on one side of the camp while the women's tents were set up on the opposite side of camp. The mess was a large canvas structure big enough to hold approximately seventy-five or so enlistees. The high-ranking officers' quarters were situated just down the pathway from the mess tent. Really, the set up was not all that different than the layout of the 238th. Adjusting wouldn't be an issue for the replacement nurses.

Finally, they came to the most important area of the camp—the wards. Wearied-looking nurses emerged from their posts with dark circles tinting their eyes. Litter bearers, burdened with cumbersome stretchers, carried wounded men from one ward to another. Inside, wounded and recovering GIs recuperated from surgery, broken bones, bullet wounds, and deep lacerations of the skin from flying shrapnel and other debris. Few were kept for illnesses such as pneumonia, dysentery, frostbite, and trench foot.

After the tour, and when she found her *address*, Maggie located Vera, Helen, and Bonnie to see if they were billeted close to one another. "I'm in tent twelve. Where are you three at?"

"Tent nine," Vera answered.

"Two. Wish me luck, girls. A snow bunny being thrown to the wolves." Helen slung her duffel over her shoulder.

"Be sure to save us seats at mess. That way we can at least catch up with each other," Maggie added. "Where are you, Bonnie?"

"Looks like you and me are roommates, Maggie. I'm in twelve too."

"That's a relief. I wonder who the other two women are." Maggie picked up her luggage and began heading in the way of tent 12. "Good luck, Vera. Will you be okay?"

"Oh, yeah. I'll be fine. It's an *adventure,* remember?" After giving the women a smile, Vera turned to the tent marked "9" and entered.

Off in the distance, echoes of explosions and deep *booms* traveled over the countryside. Maggie gazed toward the east where pockets of white smoke lingered on the horizon. She was as close to the front as she could get without being handed a rifle.

Moving along, Maggie and Bonnie walked the short distance toward their new home in distracted silence. So many scenarios entered Maggie's mind. It was like the first day of school. Would the girls like her? Would she fit in?

"Are you nervous at all, Maggie?" Bonnie's gentle voice smoothed the wrinkles in Maggie's nerves.

"Me? No. We're army nurses, Bonnie. We're the best of the best. Otherwise, Lieutenant Harris wouldn't have commissioned us." So she lied. Bonnie needed a strong anchor in times of rough seas. Maggie was determined to be that anchor and not let her own insecurities and fears be revealed.

"I'm a ball of nerves."

"And Jesus said, *Lo, I am with you alway.* Just remember that, Bonnie."

"I'm glad McGee grouped you and me together. I don't know what I'd do without you."

Maggie turned and smiled back at her meek friend. Poor Bonnie was a good nurse but lacked confidence, which held her back from the exceptional skills she possessed.

"Okay, tent twelve. Here we are."

Maggie pushed open the wooden door. It was surprisingly light and she about shook the whole tent as it flew open.

"Hey! Watch it. It's only made of sticks you know," a voice from inside the tent barked at her.

"I'm sorry. I was expecting the door to be heavier."

"Well, just be careful. If it falls down, we're out in the cold…literally."

Maggie mouthed the word "Oh" as she rolled her eyes downward. She and Bonnie set down their luggage. "Where do we bunk—"

The door flew open, interrupting Maggie's query.

"Not too bad out there today, Peg. I got through my hair wash without the water freezing up on me this time." The woman unraveled her scarf from around her face. When she spotted Maggie and Bonnie, she stopped. "Oh, hello. You must be the new nurses. I'm Linda Parker."

"Nice to meet you. I'm Lieutenant Margaret Johnson, or just Maggie. This is Lieutenant Bonnie Fitzgerald. I'm assuming you were expecting us?"

"They told us we'd get replacement nurses. When the other two gals packed, we knew they were going home. I guess you've already met Peggy."

"Well, not officially." Maggie glanced at the nurse who sat quietly in a corner reading a book. More than just cold air chilled Maggie's skin as her gaze brushed over the grumpy nurse.

"Oh, well, this is Lieutenant Peggy Blizzard. We've both been here over a year now."

"It's nice to meet both of you," Bonnie said with a courteous smile spread across her face.

"Where should we place our things so they'll be out of your way?" Maggie held up her duffel.

"These two bunks were Karen and Tina's. So now that they've left, you two can take them. We share the locker. We just have to make the best of it. I hope you packed light. We only keep our formal suits and dancing dresses hung in here." Linda opened the small locker closet and showed the two women the small, crowded space. "All our other clothes we mainly string up around the tent." She pointed to the field clothing that hung from twine tied from one tent post to the other. "We have to change frequently here. We get a lot of wounded into camp and the weather conditions keep us drenched and cold. We don't really have a chance to put away our clothing so we just keep it hung up."

"Doesn't sound too different from what we're used to. Right, Bonnie?"

Remain confident.

"Uh-huh."

"All righty then. If that's understood, then we'll get along just fine." Linda rocked back on her heels.

The tent was small, and the bunks were stacked to save space. Between the two bunks sat a nightstand with an oil lamp. At the other end of the tent, near the tiny locker, sat an oil burning heater. The small contraption was the only heat source for the small space.

Linda must have spotted Maggie staring at the heater. "We have to be careful with that thing. Our government sent those over to us to save gasoline."

"Yeah, but what our *government* didn't bank on was the fact that oil freezes in these conditions," Peggy gruffly added as she peeked over her book.

Linda turned back to the girls. "So we must be careful to keep it lit at all times. If we forget to refill the oil or if the light goes out, then we'll freeze overnight. We usually take turns getting up at night and checking it."

"That's fine with us. We'll do what we have to to help," Bonnie stated.

"Great. I think we'll all get by just dandy. If you have any other questions, just ask. Our shift doesn't start until nine o'clock tonight. It sounds like Lieutenant McGee is giving all of you the rest of the day off. Chow time is at five o'clock sharp. If you don't make it, you don't eat. Just to warn you. If you want to nap for the afternoon, we can wake you a half hour before chow time."

"That's very kind of you. Thank you."

Maggie began unpacking her belongings. A thump outside the door was followed by a light rapping sound. Bonnie reached for the door. Two, young privates stood in front of her, one wiping his brow and the other heaving an exhausted breath.

"Got your trunks, Lieutenant. Where do you want them?"

"Oh, thank you. Just set them next to the cots in those empty spaces."

Maggie let out a relieved sigh. She was thankful for the prompt delivery of her personal belongings. As she rummaged through her trunk, she cast a glance in Peggy's direction. The nurse's eyes met hers and Maggie smiled. But the response was anything but warm and inviting. Peggy harrumphed and buried her nose deeper into the book she was reading.

Maggie had that sinking feeling that her stay at the 39th was going to be anything but a picnic.

CHAPTER SIX

1 April 1945

Nothing was more peaceful then waking up to the pitter patter of water trickling into a brook. Maggie almost didn't want to force herself out of her restful slumber, but as her mind roused from sleep, she realized the camp wasn't situated next to a stream. She pushed herself off her cot and placed her feet on the ground beneath her.

"Ack!" The squishy, seeping feeling of mud and moisture immediately soaked through her socks. "Look at this mess!"

Bonnie groaned and wiped her eyes. "What are you grumbling about, Maggie?"

"There's mud…everywhere! Oh, dear. Our trunks will get water logged. Bonnie get up and help me get something under our foot lockers."

Bonnie stifled a yawn and stretched before fully opening her eyes. When she spotted the small stream of water traveling under her cot like a swelling river, she squealed. "Good heavens, Maggie! Why didn't you say so!"

"I did. Now come on and help me."

Their cots had sunk several inches into the muck. Their trunks were salvageable, but in need of a good cleaning. After saving their clothing and personal items, the girls dressed in their field uniforms and boots— with extra socks insulating their toes.

As they pushed open the door to the outside world, their eyes widened in amazement. The camp was a complete and sloshing mud hole! Deep ruts scarred the dirt pathways and the girls' already too-big-for-their-feet boots slurped and sucked as they trudged through the ankle-deep mess.

But they didn't complain. Oh, never would Maggie let anyone hear her whine about a little rain and mud—at least she tried to convince herself it was just a little rain and mud.

"Come on, Bonnie. We better check the roster. Don't need our patients drowning when they've already been saved from enemy fire."

The ward held six recovering soldiers. Private Lance was healing nicely from a bullet wound in his leg. Thankfully, the bullet only injured more flesh than muscle and bone.

"You'll be out of here in a few short days, Private. Just promise me you won't agree to play the target anymore. You're too nice a fella to get shot up."

"Yes, ma'am."

Maggie winked an eye and moved to the next casualty, a twenty-six year old tank operator who was healing from a broken arm.

"How's the mummy doing today?" She glanced down at the right arm casted with plaster and dressing.

"Aw, this thing is just awkward. Nurse, I gotta itch my arm so badly it's driving me nuts. Can you just cut a hole right here so's I can kill the itching?" He pointed to his arm just above the elbow.

"Let me see what I can do about that."

"Lieutenant Moss, I already told you nothing can be done about your arm." A gruff and rugged voice sliced the quiet atmosphere. Maggie turned on her heel to identify its owner. "You've endured weeks on the battlefield and artillery fire. You can certainly deal with something as insignificant as an *itch*."

Maggie's mouth hinged open. Her eyebrows furrowed in shock as she listened to Peggy Blizzard's abrasive manner.

"But Lieutenant, I—"

"That's enough out of you, soldier. Whatever I say goes."

Maggie held up her palm, unable to take the sting of her words any longer. "Hold it right there, Lieutenant Blizzard. That's enough out of *you*." Using force from somewhere rooted inside her, she grabbed Peggy by the elbow and dragged her to the linen closet. "I believe your shift was up..." Maggie checked her wrist watch. "Hm, a half hour ago. Lieutenant Moss is under my care now. From now until seven o'clock this evening, I will decide what care this patient needs. You are relieved of your duty, Lieutenant."

Peggy grumbled beneath her breath and folded her arms across her chest. Her eyes zeroed in on Maggie. They were sharp enough to kill...if looks could. "You are in no position to dismiss me, Lieutenant. I hold the same rank as you. And I will leave when I'm ready to leave. Just because you were assigned here to replace our good nurses doesn't mean you have the authority to take over. You're not above everyone else."

"And neither are you, Peggy. I'm here to do my job and take care of these soldiers. I'm not looking for a best friend to impress, and I'm certainly not looking to impress you."

"Then we understand each other."

"Clearly."

"Fine."

Maggie's eyes bore down on Peggy as their eyes locked momentarily. Without the hint of backing down, Peggy gave Maggie a once over then left the tent.

Maggie released the air that threatened to explode from within her. She'd kept her composure and wits about her. She wanted to fire on Peggy for the horrible exchange she had with the injured Lieutenant, but no, for the sake of her patients, she kept a level head and an even disposition.

Leaving the privacy of the linen closet, she returned to her patient. "I'm terribly sorry, Lieutenant Moss. Now let me see what I can do for that itch."

"Thank you, ma'am."

"I haven't done anything yet." She smiled as she adjusted the pillow behind his head and blanket covering his body.

"No, I mean thank you for getting rid of 'ol sour lips. She's a nasty one."

"So it would seem. I have to bunk with her." Maggie pinched her lips together, realizing her thoughts slipped from her tongue. "Excuse me, Lieutenant. I didn't mean . . ."

A sympathetic expression replaced the fatigue lines on the lieutenant's face. "Gee, I'm right sorry about that, ma'am."

"Well, I suppose both you and I have our own enemies and challenges to deal with. You know, I think I have an old wire hanger I can straighten and slip under this cast so you can relieve that itching. Can you give me a few minutes?"

"Well, I've waited this long. What's a little while longer?"

"All right then. Sit tight and I'll be back shortly."

After the rounds were made, records updated, bedding changed, and Lieutenant Moss's itch relieved, Maggie and Bonnie found themselves sitting in the comfort of the mess tent at a wooden table big enough for two—only Vera and Helen had squeezed into the small space, making their table setting a shoulder to shoulder experience.

"I'm telling you, Vera, I can't stand the woman. She hates me. She's mean, bitter, and couldn't care less about those boys in that ward. All I got to say is I'm glad we're on separate shifts. There's no way I could ever work with someone as pitiful as her."

"Never say never, kid. That's almost asking for trouble." Vera popped a forkful of kidney beans into her mouth.

"Well, I'll say this, I've always hated the way Walter wants to use his rank to protect me, but if the *Ice Queen* and I are ever paired together, you can bet I'll be writing Walt a letter, begging him to pull a few strings."

"Can't you just talk to her, Maggie? I mean maybe it's all just a big misunderstanding. She may feel threatened by us coming in on her turf and worry we're here to take their jobs away. Just explain that it simply isn't the case."

"Helen, I'm not so sure that'll work. If I even look her way, I can hear her growling at me. She's an angry Doberman, ready to attack."

"Ladies, I have to say that I'm proud of Maggie for sticking up for the wounded lieutenant like she did. I was there, and I heard the whole exchange. Peggy is not just any jealous fix. I do believe she's just plain nasty." Bonnie sucked in her cheeks as if tasting a sour lemon and pushed her eyebrows high into her forehead.

Maggie nodded her agreement.

While the assignment to the 39th seemed like a good idea at the beginning, Maggie wondered how long the outfit would keep her and the other girls around for—or how long she'd be able to cope with Peggy Blizzard's chilly and brash attitude.

Dear Walt,   *2 April 1945*

I'm writing you as I lay on my cot. I'm wet, I'm tired, and I'm cold. There's a small river running under my bed. My boots leak water and mud. The rain keeps falling, making it nearly impossible to truck in the wounded. The litter bearers are sinking ankle deep in the muck as they push on to get those needing medical attention to the hospital. It's not a pretty sight. Certainly not what I had expected. To make matters worse, the air in the tent is frigid and the cold is the kind that sinks deep into your bones. But it's not the kind of cold you're thinking of. It seems my roommate, whose name matches her icy personality, hates me.

Today she accused me of stealing her boots! Can you believe that? I was ever so thankful when she found them inside her locker. I assumed she left them there to keep them dry and forgot about them since we always keep our boots beside our cots. Nonetheless, she never apologized for accusing me of theft. In her eyes, I'm an outsider, a scavenger...an enemy.

On the bright side, the doctors are impressed with my nursing skills. The patients look forward to my shift, making me feel like their hero.

How are you? Please write back and tell me you're all right.

Sending All My Love,
Maggie

"A letter to the major, Maggie?"

In the dim light, Maggie could just make out the soft features on Bonnie's face. Bonnie was propped on her right elbow, a blanket over her, and her hair in curlers. Maggie was glad for the alone time in the evenings with Bonnie and without Peggy's grumblings. It helped keep her mind at ease enough to sleep.

"Yes. I haven't written him since we arrived. This was the first moment of peace."

"I'm sorry Peggy snapped at you this morning. I can't believe the way she talks to you sometimes."

Maggie shrugged her right shoulder into her chin. "It's not like I can't take it. I guess I'm used to it after the way I left home."

"What's the story with you and your parents anyway? You avoid talking about them like it's the Malaria bug."

Beneath the dark of her eyelids, Maggie groaned. On top of dealing with Ice Queen Blizzard, she didn't want to open the old wound to her heart that dealt with her parents. It would be too much.

"Maybe we'll save that for another day. Tonight I'm exhausted and cold." The cot creaked as she rolled onto her side and pulled the blanket close around her shoulders.

The rustling behind her indicated Bonnie was doing the same and willing to let the conversation go for tonight. Hopefully Bonnie wouldn't misunderstand her silence for anger.

"Hey, Bonnie?"

"Yes?"

"I'm not upset. It's just, tonight's not the night to talk about it."

"I understand, Maggie. Thanks."

The Lord always comforted her in these times. Right now Maggie was thankful for the one kindred spirit she'd found in Bonnie. Without the meek and small girl, she couldn't make it through this war.

5 April 1945

"All right, let's move it! Time to pack it up. We're heading out!"

The call to relocate had come in. Once again, the EVAC would move with the Army deeper into Nazi Germany. The good news was the Allied forces were placing the pressure on Hitler's regime and shoving his power further back into his own despicable corner. The 39th would move closer to the front lines while still sinking into ground sodden with moisture. With the muddy surfaces and foot-deep ruts, the camp was, in every shape and form, a mess.

"Hey kid, there you are." Vera draped an arm over Maggie's shoulder. "We've got patients to move out. Which ward are you working in today?"

"Triage. Those just coming in. I've got to decide where they go from here. There are a few who can be transferred to the 121st, others will need to be air-evacuated into England."

"I've got the shock ward today. Not too busy, but enough to fill an ambulance."

Two litter bearers carrying a recovering stomach wound patient passed by. The girls side-stepped out of the way.

"Well, I better get going. Time is not something we have at the moment. Good luck today. I hear old Blizzard is in triage too."

"What?" Maggie's jaw jutted forward. "I didn't hear this."

"Just assigned." Vera began her retreat. "See you later, Maggie."

Maggie's hand lifted in a sorry attempt to wave good-bye, but it only hung helplessly in the air.

Air deflated from her lungs. So much for her quiet work day.

With hard, deliberate steps, Maggie trudged through pasty mud, passing ward after ward until she reached the triage tent. Medical personnel called out orders to the nurses and technicians from all areas, directing the flowing traffic of wounded patients from one area to the next.

The canvas lip to the triage opening flapped in the breeze. She prayed Peggy wasn't already—

"Hold still and let me have your arm, Corporal!"

"You ain't touching me, you—"

Oh, dear.

Too late. Peggy was already in the ward terrorizing her patients. From the long string of expletives, Maggie imagined the greeting she'd get from the Ice Queen when she walked in.

"Buck up, soldier," Maggie told herself. "You're a big girl and can handle anything that comes your way."

With a deep breath and a roll of her shoulders, Maggie steeled herself against the harsh, barbed, and conflicting personalities she was about to face.

"Good morning, fellas." She made her voice as cheery as possible. "How are we today?"

With a jerk, Peggy turned a cool glare in her direction. Clearly, the girl was already annoyed.

"Oh, thank the heavens above! Nurse, could you please tell

Lieutenant Claws here to get her dirty paws off me?"

From the stance Maggie perceived, Peggy had been wrestling with the patient, who seemed very nervous. She had to tread carefully. Some nervous patients could be a handful and hard to restrain. Yet, she'd witnessed Peggy's brassy behavior toward her patients before and wondered if the resistance had to do with that.

"Corporal, if you would just hold still and let me take your vitals I wouldn't have to get tough with you."

The wrestling started again.

Maggie couldn't believe her eyes. Never were they taught to wrangle a patient the way Peggy was going about it.

"Get off me, you gorilla!"

"Hold it! Lieutenant, that's enough."

"Lieutenant Johnson, I have this patient. Go on to your other work."

Maggie watched as the corporal's arm turned bright red from Peggy's death grip. His eyes were a mixture of anger, pain, and fear.

"Not while I'm seeing this. This is no way to treat a patient."

"He's not your typical patient, Lieutenant Johnson. He requires strong restraint." She turned back to the corporal. "Now, sir, if you don't cooperate I'll have to call the MP's to hold you down while I give you a shot in places most unpleasant."

His eyes grew wild and his flailing arms fought back with vengeance.

Maggie grabbed a hold of Peggy's arm. "Stop it, Peggy! Let him go!"

Without warning, Peggy's hand whipped around and stung Maggie's cheek.

Maggie stepped back in shock and pressed her palm against the pain in her face. It seared and burned beneath her touch. "You—you slapped me."

"I'll do it again if you interfere with my work."

The patients' faces registered shock and disbelief. Maggie's cheeks flamed, not just from Peggy's steel hand, but from humiliation. How could that woman assault her in front of her patients?

In the next moment, a scream escaped the corporal's mouth, snapping Maggie's attention back to the altercation. Peggy had just thrust a shot of morphine into the patient's thigh.

"He'll be out in a few minutes. Then we can get him labeled and moved out."

Was this woman proud of herself? Acidic bile rose from Maggie's stomach to her throat. She'd seen some gruesome sights over the last year but nothing compared to the brutal treatment Peggy inflicted on her patients.

Angry tears blurred Maggie's eyes and she went on to the next soldier waiting to be seen. She blinked back her angst, remembering to be strong for the man in front of her.

Never in front of the boys...

She sniffed casually and went to work on a man who appeared to be in his early twenties.

"Where are you hurting, soldier?" Her voice was softer, more somber than usual.

"It's my hand. I think a bullet blew most of it off."

"Let me have a look here." She unwrapped the nearly severed hand, bloodied but at least still intact. "Well, it'll need surgery. You'll be on the next ambulance out. They're transferring us so we're unable to perform the surgery here."

He closed his eyes and blew out a ragged breath. "Will I lose it, ma'am?"

Could she tell him? It was her job to keep up morale and keep them comfortable. Not crush their spirit and put them in danger.

"It's pretty bad, but I'm not the one who decides what happens to your limbs. For now, be grateful you still have it, but understand that if it puts your life in danger at least losing it could save your life. I can give you something for the pain."

"Much obliged, ma'am."

After a shot of morphine, Maggie went to work wrapping the hand securely and pinning a record of his treatment and medication to his tunic. It was imperative that his hand remain stable through his ride to the next evacuation hospital and that the doctors in the next camp had some notation of his status and medical history.

Wrapped up in her duties, she thought the soldier had dozed off while she worked, so it surprised her when he called out to her.

"Ma'am?"

"Hm?"

"It wasn't right she slapped you."

Maggie's eyes darted across the way. Peggy's back was turned toward her as she filled out paperwork. "It wasn't right she mistreated your friend over there."

"Well, you didn't do anything wrong. Just know that."

Maggie patted his good hand and her lips pursed in a tight smile. "Thank you."

But deep inside, Maggie's chest ached as if a sniper had placed a bullet in her back. A war raged on.

CHAPTER SEVEN

5 April 1945
39th Move into Hersfeld

The ride along the autobahn was the smoothest ride Maggie had been on in a while. She could doze off peacefully without the jarring of ruts in the road to interrupt her peaceful slumber. Now awake, she stared out the window, taking in the panoramic views of morning. It was still early and she was still tired...and wet. While on board the personnel truck, she caught a glimpse of the long convoy ahead of and behind her. If not for the kind contribution of trucks from the 12th and 34th EVACs, the members of the 39th wouldn't be transporting the whole hospital in one trip. Thank goodness for friends in high places.

Although incredibly exhausted, Maggie couldn't convince herself to sleep. It didn't help that mud had seeped into her boots, and her socks were now soiled and cold. Her pants were also damp from the knees down, and her hands were dry with crusted mud embedded in the crevices of her palms.

The thought to put her down time to use caused her to pull out note paper from her satchel and begin a letter to Walt. Once they reached their destination, there was no telling when the next opportunity would present itself to reply to Walt's letter.

She told him they were on the move again, advancing into Germany, but didn't explain her current whereabouts as all that crucial information was strictly advised against and would be censored anyway. She elaborated on how much she missed him and her desire to be back in his arms.

That's where her thoughts halted.

For the longest time she paused and stared at the half-sheet left unwritten. Beyond what she'd already told him, it seemed there was nothing else left to say. Her letters were becoming repetitive—*How are you? I miss you. Write me soon.* The censorship disbanded all her true thoughts. She couldn't say where she was for sure or where they were headed, sometimes *she* didn't know where the Army would send her next.

Will my relationships always be so complicated?

Every man she ever dated always held some attachment to something else. She dated Harvey Thomas at the end of her senior year of high school, only he headed off to fulfill his commitment to college the following September. Then there was John. He enlisted in the Navy shortly after they started seeing each other and she never heard from him again. Although attracted to a few doctors she worked with, she never dated them due to her conviction of not pursuing anything more than a professional relationship with her colleagues. Throwing romance into the mix would only hinder their work together. Then there were the patients. Too many male patients to mention who made passes at her. But she made it a strict rule to not get involved.

Except for one patient.

She winced as a prick needled her heart. Danny was the exception. How could she resist the Italian charms of Danny Russo? Like his cute smirk when he was being ornery. His drawing personality. The way he could pull weariness from her body and chase away her bad moods. He had possessed qualities she'd not yet seen in another man.

Leaning her head against the door window, a smile crept onto her face. Danny's wide grin and big, Italian nose surfaced in her mind. He was so adorable. And for a moment, her trials and the world's problems melted away. Her cheek rested against the back of her hand and her eyes drifted closed. As plain as if she were awake, she revisited the day and place where her love for Danny was kindled...

He was recovering from his appendectomy. For over a week he'd been in her care and every morning she greeted him with his breakfast tray. Every evening she bid him goodnight with the promise of seeing him in the morning. But on the day he was to be released, she unattached herself to his appealing good looks and corny jokes. He'd been pressing her for a date for several days and her answer was always the same. "No. I don't date my patients."

But there was that night at the bowling alley with the girls. Danny Russo just happened to be there with his friends and he'd spotted her. Several weeks had passed since his hospital release, and she never thought she'd run into him again.

"How about that date you promised?" he asked over the commotion of loud music and tumbling bowling pins.

"I never promised you a date." Maggie slipped her three fingers into the bowling ball holes and tossed the seven pounder down the lane. The rattling and tumbling of pins were drowned out by Danny's voice.

"I think you're mistaken." He cut in front of her and folded his arms over his chest. "I specifically remember you saying you'd give me a date when you handed me that little tart thing, remember?"

Not even able to mask her laughter, Maggie giggled. "You're hopeless, Danny Russo. I did give you a *date*. That *little tart thing*? That was a date. You know, an exotic fruit? A friend of mine brought them back from a trip overseas. So I slipped you one."

Maggie bit back her laughter when Danny's jaw dropped. He looked as if he'd been duped, astounded. She brushed past him to sit with her friends, who giggled and blushed when Danny's gaze swept their way.

But despite his position, he persisted. "Why won't you go out with me?"

"Excuse me, ladies." She turned to Danny. "Because you were my patient," she whispered. "I try not to make a practice of seeing anyone who's been under my care. It's not professional."

"But what if it's love?" He captured her hand and brought it to his lips for a gentle kiss. "Look, Maggie, I'm not a tender, mushy, lovey kind of guy, but you do strange things to me. I get all happy and giddy when you're around and, well, I think you're the prettiest girl I've ever seen. I'd just like to hear you say that maybe there's a small, even a sliver, of a chance that you feel the same way."

Did she? She'd gone through the trouble of sneaking in a special treat for him while he lay in a hospital bed with strict orders. While Danny's nurse, she awoke each morning with a flutter in her stomach and a smile on her face. But she learned to shove those infatuations deep inside her for fear of falling for every man under her care. That was the type of person she was. Always changing. Always ready for the next adventure.

But Danny's sudden arrival at the bowling alley stirred something in her soul.

Her eyes—and her heart—softened and she folded her other hand over his. "That was beautifully said. How can I turn you down when you put it like that?"

"Is that a yes?"

On her nod, Danny's excitement exploded. He grabbed Maggie by her waist and twirled her in circles. Her skirt swished around her legs, making her feel like a princess in her prince's arms. To this day she could still hear his laughter ringing in her ears.

She startled awake when something dripped down her cheek. The collection of moisture beading on her finger surprised her. Tears had tiptoed, undetected, to the edges of her eyes and secretly escaped their barriers.

But they were just memories. Danny Russo was gone. Killed by German soldiers behind enemy lines. And Walt now filled that void left by Danny's death. She needed to move forward. Let Danny go for good. Her heart belonged to another man. A man who loved her. Guilt rushed into her mind and chased out those precious memories of Danny. A woman needing to get on with her life, must first purge the past from her heart.

⋙⋘

The tentage was erected without incident at the freeway junction. To the relief of the ambulance drivers, they wouldn't have to risk stalling in the mud. The road was close enough the litters could be carried on foot to the hospital. To add to the patients' benefit, the new Hersfeld hospital location was situated between several American/British airstrips. Air evacuation would not be a problem for those who demanded immediate attention at general hospitals, making their chances of survival that much greater…if the Luftwaffe kept their distance.

With the 39th's new location positioning them closer to the front lines, a larger surgery was put on the priority list. A storage tent was revamped and turned into a surgery. For protection against air raids, each corner of the camp was reinforced with antiaircraft artillery.

The nurses were the last of the personnel to arrive. Now that camp was established and the nurses on site, the 39th's new location could officially open. Within 6 hours, the hospital admitted its first patients. By the next morning, nurses were taking full shifts.

"We've got a problem." Captain Baker pulled Maggie aside. "Have you noticed anything suspicious about the hand, foot, and leg wounds we've seen in the last two weeks?"

"Nothing I can recall, sir."

"It seems maybe Lieutenant Blizzard's careful calculations were correct. I wasn't so sure, until now."

Careful calculations? What on earth did he mean by that?

"Sir?"

He lowered his voice and drew near so only Maggie would hear his words.

"General Patton made a visit to a neighboring hospital. He was not happy with what he saw. It's cause for us to take careful consideration of the types of cases that are coming in."

"I'm afraid I still don't follow you, Captain."

"Lieutenant, some of the cases we've treated were self-inflicted. In other words, they've shot themselves."

Her brows pressed inward. She was not at all happy about the accusations. How could he even have the gall to suggest such an idea?

"Captain, you're sure about this?" A twinge of irritation raised her voice a few notes.

"Shamefully, yes, Lieutenant. If it weren't for Lieutenant Blizzard's careful examinations I'd have overlooked it myself."

Careful calculations? Careful examinations? Had the Captain noticed the patients' tension when the woman entered the room? If *he* were paying careful attention to his own patients, he'd see that Peggy Blizzard's careful examinations consisted of threats and harsh handling. If any of the men had inflicted their own injuries it was to get out of her care!

"I don't know if I believe this rubbish, Captain—with all due respect, sir."

"Lieutenant Johnson, follow me. Let me show you something."

Maggie followed without complaint. If there were such accusations, better for her to see it for herself.

Captain Baker walked her to a sleeping patient. Of course, it was best to make an assumption while unnoticed. He pulled back the blanket and bandages that covered the soldier's legs.

"Look here, Lieutenant. See the angle the bullet went in? There's no way this fella saw hand to hand combat and got shot at that angle."

"Maybe he did, Captain." It just wasn't fair to place blame when the patient in question was sound asleep and unable to defend himself. "Did anyone press him for details? Is there a written report?"

"Lieutenant Blizzard tried, but he became upset."

"I can see why."

"Pardon, Lieutenant?"

Maggie furrowed her brows and took the liberty of covering the patient's wound and legs with the blanket. "I've witnessed Lieutenant Blizzard's methods, Captain. I hardly consider her handling of the men, *careful*. She's gruff, abrasive, and abusive to the patients. They all wince when she walks into the room. Surely you've noticed, Captain."

"Sorry, can't say that I have. Lieutenant Blizzard has been with the 39th for nearly two years. Even turned down her rotation stateside to stay with us. She's a dedicated worker. Maybe you caught her with an uncooperative patient. They come in from time to time. You know, shell shock, basket cases."

This was going nowhere. Of course her opinion wouldn't be taken seriously here. She was a new add on—a replacement. She'd have to prove her worth and disprove Peggy's methods.

6 April 1945

"More rain. That's all it does in this part of the world. Can't get away from it or leave it behind. It follows us."

"It's springtime, Vera. What do you expect? But I can't say I'm fond of waking up to rivers beneath my cot morning after blessed morning." Maggie rinsed out a washcloth in a ceramic basin.

"I miss a warm and dry bed."

"Won't that make going home all the more special?" Maggie bumped Vera's shoulder with hers and smiled. It was easier to make light of the situation than to drown in self-pity. Maggie should know, she'd seen it first-hand. That was all the more reason to push her relationship with Danny further from her mind. If she allowed her suffering to get the best of her, she would slink back into seclusion and lose touch with the tattered world around her. No, she was here for a purpose, to do a job. She wouldn't let self-pity drag her onto the front lines of self-absorption and risk killing someone else because of it.

Honking horns blared in the distance. Maggie and the girls glanced toward the autobahn. Within seconds, nurses and doctors emerged from the hospital's tents and triage area.

"Sounds like a convoy of wounded." Bonnie strained to see through the rain and fog.

Maggie's pulse quickened. It sounded like a bombardment of medical cases. A brief memory flashed through her mind and she tensed. The last time she was drowned in a sea of wounded, her mind had slipped into a psychotic state as she threw herself into a fit over a patient she couldn't save. And it was only because of Lieutenant Harris's grace that Maggie was serving with the 39th EVAC.

Don't disappoint me, Johnson. I have faith in you.

Harris's words echoed through her mind. She couldn't—no, she wouldn't—let her superiors down. She hoped the Lord had bestowed on her an iron stomach, impenetrable and solid. She prayed God would be merciful and give her only a finger-full of the bitterness that was sure to be rounding the camp's bend now.

Picking up their pace to a jog, the girls met the other nurses and doctors at the jeeps and ambulances. Wounded men were balanced on the hoods and rears of the vehicles. She couldn't keep her mouth from cracking open when men with missing and shredded limbs came into sight. Maggie tried to keep her eyes from lingering too long on the men who held their stomachs, arms, and legs, wincing in deep pain. She gulped and took a deep breath, willing the knot in her stomach to unbind and loosen to give her lungs air. It was all happening so fast.

Lord, make me ready for whatever's about to come. Give me strength.

She'd seen it all before, but never so . . . fresh. Ever since that day of her undoing, she feared large waves of casualties. But she was a good nurse and she paid careful attention to her patients.

"Lieutenant Johnson! Over here." An officer waved her to the next army jeep. She scurried over as quickly as possible. "What do you make of this, Lieutenant?"

Maggie waited as the tech unwrapped the bandage from a young private's stomach. Bright red liquid seeped through the already blood-soaked bandage and she immediately knew an artery had been hit.

When the wrap was lifted from his skin, blood streamed from an open, black hole in the private's side.

"Cover it back up," she said to the tech. "Get him to OR right now. It's an artery. He'll bleed to death if he doesn't get surgery now." Maggie grabbed the glass IV bottle and followed the tech into the Operating Room.

Her hands shook while she made the brisk jog with the litter bearers. In front of her, the young man's life was hanging by a very thin thread. Shooting quick glances at the boy lying on the litter, she willed herself to keep calm and remember what she was trained to do in circumstances like these.

She looked over her shoulder, wondering where Vera and Bonnie had gotten to. For the briefest of moments, her meltdown at the 238th invaded her mind and threatened her composure. She couldn't let that fiasco happen here. She could handle this.

"Status, nurse?" Captain Baker hurried to the patient's side.

"Bullet wound. Through the side. I think it's resting by the spine. A punctured artery, lots of blood loss."

"Let's open him up."

While the doctor prepped his instruments, a nurse sat down by the patient's head and administered the correct dose of anesthesia. Maggie covered her nose and mouth with a face mask then applied pressure to the gunshot wound, mentally willing it to stop bleeding.

She watched the patient's chest rise and fall rapidly until the anesthesia worked its magic and numbed the soldier's body. His lungs stopped their labored breathing and settled into an even rhythm.

"Okay, we're ready," the doctor announced.

Dear Lord, please help this young man. Guide the doctor's hands and help us to save his life. In Jesus' name, amen.

Maggie took a deep breath and braced herself for the moment she'd been preparing her mind and body for. Keeping her breaths even, she tried to keep her mind focused on what was at stake instead of the gory sight that lay open in front of her. She swallowed hard, feeling her stomach churning with each snip of the scissors.

"Clamp and some silk."

Grateful for the demand, Maggie handed a clamp to the doctor then prepared the thread and needle.

"How are we doing, Lieutenant Kelley?"

"Pulse is keeping steady, doctor. Everything is looking normal."

Maggie sighed in relief, thankful the soldier was doing all right for the time being.

She looked down at the man who lay unconscious before her. He was barely into his twenties. So young. So very handsome. His mamma must be so proud. What atrocities had he already witnessed? Was he frightened on the front? Did he have time to react? Did he fear death?

She was allowing her mind to travel beyond the limits she'd set for herself. If she kept it up, she would be chartering into forbidden territory. Unleashing her feminine emotions would be damaging to both her and her patients. She forced her mind back to the doctor's hands and wiped the bloodied area clean for the physician's line of sight.

Then something went wrong. The soldier's body began to convulse.

"Going into shock, doctor. Pulse is dropping." The medic began fooling with valves and wires.

Panic struck Maggie as swift as a bee's sting. This man couldn't die on her table.

"Doctor, what do you want me to do?"

"He's losing too much blood. We need a transfusion and a way to cork this artery. I can't do both. The clamp isn't working."

Her heart throbbed inside her throat and she swallowed hard. Putting her two fingers together, she pushed them into the gaping bullet hole and sealed the artery with the tip of her fingers. She closed her eyes, trying to think of nothing but saving this man's life.

"Nancy, get the transfusion ready. I'll stay here and try to stop the bleeding." When Maggie glanced back down at her hand, it was dripping with bright, red liquid. She sent up another prayer, asking God to seal the blood vessel and spare this young man.

The minutes that passed seemed like hours in her mind. Her patient's coloring had faded and was now a pasty white. The medic hooked up the blood bottle and let the plasma run down the IV line into the patient's body. The doctor instructed Maggie to slowly lift her fingers and allow him access to the area.

Amazingly, the blood had slowed its flow.

"Lieutenant," the doctor looked up at her. "I think you did it."

Rachel D. Muller

Chapter Eight

Stalag VII A, Germany

They were on the move again. Joe accepted his ration of bread—
one loaf—which he could have devoured in just a few bites. How
long had it been since he'd been given a whole loaf of bread to eat on his
own?

Since the last march.

His stomach rumbled as the faint smell of baked dough taunted his
nose. He'd eat just one small bite now and wrap up the rest for later. He
learned the hard way that this would be the only meal rationed to him
during their next voyage through the German countryside. The march
from Oflag 64 nearly killed all of them. Very little food was given out,
and when able, the men bartered their cigarettes for bread and jams from
the local farmers. Joe was thankful he wasn't a smoking man, but he was
grateful he had the brains to keep hold on his cigarette rations as their
value became the equivalent to money. Ironically, those cigarettes may
have saved his life.

Hearing his captors' voices outside the barrack door, Joe quickly
deposited his loaf under his jacket. He paused long enough to catch sight
of his thinning skin clinging to his ribs. Food. Some days he could
almost taste the sweetness of an orange or the juicy cut of meat. One of
the prisoners' favorite pastimes became the citation and explanation of
recipes from their mothers' and wives' kitchens. Although Joe didn't
have an inkling of what his mother used to cook, or if he had a wife to
cook for him, he took pleasure in listening to the other fellas tell their
stories.

But the nights were lonely. Instead of playful images running through
his mind's eye, only blank, open space consumed him. As far as he was
concerned, the boys in the flea and lice-infested beds next to him were
the only family he had.

A gunshot pierced the outside air, cutting through Joe's thoughts and bringing him back to the here and now. The Germans were either giving the men a warning shot or...they were making an example out of someone. Either way, Joe flung his pack over his shoulder and rushed out the door.

Stalag III A, Prisoner of War Camp
Brandenburg, Germany

Joe rolled onto his wooden plank cot with careful measure, his intestines shredding with another bout of dysentery. If he lived through this ordeal, he'd never eat another spoonful of soup in his lifetime. But the only way to prevent his body and spirit from succumbing to the horrid disease was to keep working despite his feeble condition.

With another day of working-to-survive labor put behind him, Joe lay still on the stiff board given for a bed, and crawled back into his dark, harbored abyss—a place his mind escaped to when his day's work was done. It was a lonely hideout. A place where no one could keep him company. Where his thoughts only allowed him to wander as far back as the day he awoke in this wretched state of mind.

Night after night, he curled up in the same spot, hoping the next morning would bring freedom. Freedom from his slave work. Freedom from the illness that plagued his body. Independence from the bonds that kept his memory locked away from him. The only comfort he found was closing his eyes and dreaming of the food he lacked and the sweet smell of independence.

His eyes rolled beneath the dark of his eyelids and his wearied muscles loosened as his thoughts traveled to his safe harbor where the state of his mind found rest. Maybe if he focused intently enough, he would catch just a glimpse of that beautiful dark-haired angel with the fiery red lips who invaded so many of his nightmares. She'd fought off the menacing evil's aggressive behavior then turned to Joe and put all fears behind him with her crimson smile. Once or twice she called out to him, but her words drifted on the mist and evaded his ears. With one curling, slender finger, she pleaded with him to follow her, but her hands vanished when his fingertips came within reach of hers. Then she was gone.

It all started while marching into Germany. The first night she visited his dreams he was so cold he convinced himself he was dying. But her angelic face appeared and brought a divine warmth, settling his blistered mind into sound sleep.

The face seemed familiar, but his brain refused to piece together the scattered puzzle, leaving him in the same confused state as he was the night before. Still he wondered, was there someone out there who was missing him? Did he have a whole other life waiting for him back home? And how would he go about finding it?

7 April 1945
39ᵗʰ Evacuation Hospital, Hersfeld, Germany

"Lieutenant Marshall. Lieutenant Fitzgerald. Lieutenant Edwards." Maggie saluted in good natured fun. "Ladies, are you ready for this mission tonight?"

"Yes, ma'am! Lieutenant, ma'am!"

"All righty then. Remember, no fraternizing with the enemy and those smooth, sweet talking yanks—or it's to the brig with you!"

"Yes, ma'am!" The girls giggled and jostled each other lightly.

"All right, nurses of the Thirty-Ninth Evacuation Hospital, it's time to board your chariots and ride into the morning sun!" Maggie's portrayal of a general in action made the girls giggle uncontrollably. That is, all the girls except for Peggy, who sat in the corner rolling her eyes at every joke and comment Maggie made that evening.

No matter. The laughter was music to Maggie's ears and she learned to ignore Peggy's grumblings. They all found a way to cope with the heartache and sicknesses of war in their own manner, but laughter didn't come as frequently as the wounded did. They *had* to relish in the good-humored moments as much as they possibly could. And what better way to spend the night off than going to the USO show?

The women, along with several other nurses and their guards, climbed into the back of an awaiting drab green supply truck. The conversations grew louder as the Jimmy made its way down the dirt paths leading to the next camp, which served as host for the latest USO show.

"I've deserved this night off for a long, long time, ladies." Linda smoothed her skirt.

She attempted to keep the lieutenant persona obvious by her prim actions, but Maggie noticed the girl couldn't keep a bubbling smile from skimming her face.

"I can't believe we're finding time to celebrate in Germany!" Bonnie's excitement burst from her throat.

Maggie feared the girl would choke on her own words.

"Well, I don't know about you kids, but I'm hoping to swoon over the one and only Bing Crosby. And while he's at it, might as well throw in Mr. Astaire too. My, my, that man can dance!"

The truckload of nurses squealed with feminine magnitude over

Vera's fantasizing.

Once they unloaded at the next camp, the nurses glanced around, becoming acquainted with their surroundings. Open jaws and cat calls greeted the ladies as flyboys and wise guys hailed them. Vera, however, didn't seem to mind. She flashed her saucy smile and fanned her fingers. The gal could certainly work her charm. Those poor boys couldn't hide from the red stains flushing their complexions.

Maggie threaded her arm through Vera's and together they caught up with the crowd. A sea of khaki and drab green poured through the front gates. Everyone was eager to get a glance at the big name Hollywood starlets who would serenade them tonight.

"I can hardly stand the anticipation," Maggie started. "I will finally get to see the Hollywood big names in action! My knees are shaking with excitement."

Helen adjusted her fitted garrison and applied a dab of red to her thin lips. "I'm just looking forward to seeing a slew of healthy, walking, dapper men." A grin nearly cut off her words mid-sentence, and howls yelped from the girls' mouths.

"Would ya look at that, girls . . ." Bonnie's eyes grew wide as if the stars had reached down and danced before her.

Red, white, and blue banners adorned the stage. War bond posters and American flags swayed in the breeze. Instruments glimmered in the evening sunlight, and swarms of military personnel infested the ground before the rostrum. The army band played swing numbers from left stage while uniformed men and nurses danced without shame in the isles and grassy patches.

"Hey, girls! If you want dessert I'm right here!"

A group of officers with hard liquor in their hands passed by as the girls weaved through the crowd.

Vera couldn't resist the temptation and barked back, "And spoil my dinner? I don't think so, bud!"

The ossified men exercised their obnoxious merriment, purposely drawing attention to their ruckus behavior, then staggered away.

"Oh, come on, Vera. He's just having a little fun with us," Helen said sympathetically.

"How old are ya, hon?"

"Nineteen."

Vera rolled her eyes and hugged one arm around Helen's slim shoulders. "Oh, honey. We've got a lot to teach you. Stick with us. We won't let them boys take advantage of you."

"Hey gals! Save me a dance! It's my last night in town!" Another passing lieutenant tried his luck with the ladies.

Helen flashed her brightest smile and started to yell something back. Vera clamped her hand over the girl's mouth and silenced her before she could say anything she'd later regret.

"Hey! What'd you do that for?"

"Trust me. It's for your own good, honey."

After grabbing a couple of club sodas, the girls sipped on their beverages as people bustled around them. The air at the soda tent was cloudy and stale from the constant cigarette smoke. The lack of lighting created a dim, but warm, atmosphere—at least as best as a tent could allow. Across the way, a row of young soldiers leaned against a plywood bar, consuming their weekend fill of liquor.

What an earful Maggie would hear if her mother knew the only place to find a decent drink was in a bar. There were some things best left unwritten in a letter.

Eager to get back to the show area, the girls started for the theater. Back at the center stage, the band switched tunes and played Benny Goodman's version of *One O'clock Jump*. The crowd bounced to its rhythm and the girls gazed in awe as one man tap danced on a staged, military-style table situated on the grassy dance floor. His legs turned from tall, straight, stick-like supports to wobbly branches as his feet kicked and twisted in amazing tap steps.

"I wish I could dance like that," Bonnie said with a sigh.

"Bonnie, you dance wonderfully. You got some moves."

"Maggie, you've never seen me take dance steps. I trip all over my own two feet. That's not counting my dance partner's either."

"Wait a second, that's not some regular Joe. Isn't it…" Helen's fist pressed against her lips and her eyes grew wide in amazement.

"Good golly! It's Fred Astaire!" Vera pointed and gasped.

"Hurry, girls, before he leaves!" Maggie led the way and the women sprinted across the grassy strip toward the dancing king. Several groups of men crossed in front of them, temporarily obstructing their view of Mr. Astaire as they rushed to find spots in front of the stage. Finally, they reached the crowd who'd gathered around the Hollywood hero.

"Oh, gee whiz. He's gone. Just like that. His legs are as fast walking as they are dancing. Go figure."

Maggie giggled, despite the fact she sympathized with Vera. However, it felt so good to have the night off. It was a well-deserved vacation.

"What are you tittering about?"

"You, Vera. Why I haven't seen you this disappointed about a man in the time I've known you."

"The first time I have the chance to throw myself at a man who has looks and money, and I blow it, because my legs aren't as fast as his—and you think that's funny."

The other girls chimed in. Vera couldn't help but let her own amusement join in the fun. Before they all knew it, they'd broken into tearful laughter.

"I feel like a school girl again." Maggie swiped at happy tears that gathered in the corners of her eyes.

Fred Astaire's unexpected appearance in the crowd was the perfect way to begin the performance. The air around them was light, and for a moment, the dangers of war faded far away. Maggie leaned back against a stack of tires and observed her small circle of friends. They were all so different but they got along undoubtedly well. Vera, sassy and to the point, was not interested in dating soldiers, although her flirting would suggest otherwise. She'd grown up in the city near Philadelphia, lived and learned the way of the streets. While her behavior labeled her a bona fide tease, the girl had the smarts of a street mind—smooth and convincing, bold and saucy.

Now Bonnie, on the other hand, was too shy to even look at a man. The slightest attention from a fellow singed poor Bonnie's cheeks. Conservative and proper, Bonnie's meekness was her best quality…and her greatest adversary. Once she learned the perfect balance between reserved and forward, the tiny woman would be able to charm any man she wanted.

And dear Helen was just beginning to try her hand at the dating scene. She still weighed in as a girl in a woman's world. Because of her alluring eyes, taunting blonde hair, and perfect smile, whistles and cat calls echoed down the halls of the hospital when Helen entered her ward back in the States. At nineteen, how was a girl supposed to handle that kind of attention?

And Maggie? She was dating the major…albeit long distance.

Someone tapped the microphone, drawing the crowd's attention. A man in a black and white striped suit, complete with a top hat, clapped his hands together and addressed the crowd with his energized tenor's voice.

"Hey, hey, hey! Welcome to the show, ladies and gents. How about our surprise dancer out there in the crowd this evening, eh? Was that a performance or what?"

Roars and cheers lifted into the night air. Elation bubbled into Maggie's throat and erupted as a high-pitch squeal. She hadn't felt this free in years. The drummer hit a couple half notes and clashed the cymbals. The announcer faked his surprise and everyone chuckled at his overdramatized performance. When the noise simmered down, their host grew serious and introduced the war bond hero for the evening.

"Ladies and gentleman, please give a warm welcome to our real, live hero, an American prisoner of war, radioman for the Eighty-Second Airborne Division, Michael Brewer."

Entering the stage upon the uproar of applause and whistles, a dark-haired man in uniform hobbled onto the stage with a cane in hand. As his eyes scanned the mass gathering, silence fell over the crowd, so much so Maggie could hear Vera's breath entering and exiting her lungs. But the very moment the war hero began his speech, it was her own breath, her own beating heart she heard growing steadily in the drums of her ears.

"My job for the Eighty-Second wasn't only about jumping out of planes. I was called for a mission to bring freedom to one nation and defend the independence of our own. I volunteered for the position. I became a United States Army Paratrooper. . . ."

Maggie stopped breathing and her throat tightened. Suddenly, the man standing on stage wasn't just any American soldier. He was the very picture of her lost love.

"Danny," she whispered under her breath.

⊰⊱

Her eyes could clearly see that war hero, Michael Brewer, wasn't Danny Russo. But her heart made an attempt to convince her otherwise. Or was it that her heart was trying to prove that Danny still held a large fragment of her shattered spirit? With eager eyes and ears, Maggie watched and listened in undivided concentration.

". . .My comrades fell beside me as we fought our way through the French villages. Then I found myself surrounded on all sides by German soldiers. From there, I feared for my life, hearing the horrors and atrocities the German Army committed against their enemy. But a fate worse than death awaited me on the other side of a POW camp where countless other soldiers like myself were held, beaten, starved, and humiliated. . . ."

His words brought goose-bumps to the surface of her skin. The hairs on the back of her neck stood on end as his speech struck to the very core of her heart. Hot moisture stung her eyes and she hung onto Michael Brewer's every word, knowing her mind took a dangerous turn to a past she'd recently buried. Still, she listened.

"But just when I'd lost all hope and the use of my leg, thinking I was a dead man walking, Uncle Sam came bursting through the gates. A knight, wearing red, white, and blue. Our brothers came to rescue us from the place only suitable for the devil himself. Suddenly, I found myself alive, breathing, and thankful for a second chance to come home. Freedom. It doesn't come free, but together we can win the victory. The purchase of war bonds helps make that victory a reality. . . ."

Maggie didn't hear another word. All noise faded and her mind entered another realm. If one man could come home alive, why couldn't Danny? Of anybody she knew, Danny would've been the one to survive a freefall without a parachute or a capture by the enemy.

Her hand subconsciously clutched the gold cross she kept hidden beneath her fatigues and blouse. It was all she had left of him. All she could cling to in times of despair.

∽∾

"So when they told me I would be using a flame thrower, I pictured three rings and a skinny man, wearing a diaper, blowing out a stream of fire from his mouth!" Laughter bellowed from the nurses and Vera continued. "So I asked my sergeant, *Are we in the Army Nurse Corps or the circus?*"

"You didn't! What did your sergeant do?"

"Well, Helen dear, he didn't take too kindly to my humor, so I got one hundred pushups and twice as many laps."

In between acts, Vera amused the ladies by telling the gals of her own miscues and misunderstandings upon her entrance into the Army Nurse Corps.

But as the ladies simmered down, and wiped happy tears from their eyes, the band beat out a swing number. Several moments later, a group of officers approached the circle of jovial women.

"You ladies wanna dance?" Five handsome officers stood with eagerness in their eyes. Maggie knew the women couldn't say no. Helen was the first to step forward and take the first soldier's arm. Bonnie, Vera, Linda, and Maggie followed close behind. The group headed to the dance floor and each girl followed their man's lead.

As soon their feet found the beat, Maggie knew these fellas were no strangers to the dance floor. They twirled, spun, and dipped the girls to the exact timing of the music.

"C'mon honey, dish it right back out to him," Vera encouraged Helen as they passed.

As if finding a new confidence in herself, Helen straightened, arched one eyebrow and curled one side of her mouth in a side grin. "Is that all you've got, soldier?"

Energy swirled around them as more couples stood to dance. Maggie's mind cleared and she found herself back in her rhythm. Her partner's dancing shoes kept well in step with her own. He didn't make passes at her except a wink here and there.

But as the young man's profile rushed past her with each dip and spin, she saw two men in front of her. Guilt crept in.

Danny's handsome face sometimes flashed before her. And tonight those sentiments were multiplied a hundred times over with Michael Brewer's testimony. But with Walter being her steady boyfriend now, she shouldn't be keeping company with other men, mentally or physically. And Danny had yet to defy Army orders and refuse death to make a reappearance into her life. Which meant Danny still slept in his shallow grave.

On the other hand, tonight was different. She hadn't enjoyed a night off in months. It was rewarding to kick off her boots and fatigues and feel somewhat feminine for a change. She was having the time of her life—away from Walt, away from the war. But shouldn't she feel miserable right now while away from her beau? Shouldn't guilt replace the freedom she felt by fleeing her protector's wing? Or could she live…without Walt?

CHAPTER NINE

8 April 1945, 2 a.m.
ANC Tent 12

Before Maggie could kick off her boots after dropping face first onto her cot, she was fast asleep. Linda and Bonnie had also retired to their cots upon returning from the night out, and Peggy was working the night shift. Thank goodness. There was no need to ruin a perfectly enjoyable and fun night. Peace and quiet settled over her mind, inspiring sweet dreams. Pictures, like slide frames, flitted through her mind's eye and recaptured those moments when her dancing partner twirled her around the dance floor. She threw her head back in glorious delight, then she was transformed into a woman in a satin dancing dress, escorted by a handsome fellow. The dream had taken a blissful turn, pulling her deeper into its illusory chronicle.

The man on her arm was not tall and sandy-haired like Walt. Instead, he was slightly shorter with a generous endowment of fabulous, dark hair and beautiful, cocoa eyes. They danced under a blanket of diamonds in the most pristine ballroom in Europe. Her eyes refused to turn away from his face and he seemed content to hold her gaze. A slight grin etched smile lines into his cheeks. The music faded, but he held her tightly against him. Slowly, he moved in closer, his eyes bouncing on and off her lips. She willed him closer yet, ready to explore what he had to offer. And gently, ever so gently, her lips brushed...

"Margaret Johnson! What are you trying to do, kill us all off?"

The bombardment of harsh, ear-splitting words caused Maggie to nearly jump out of her skin. She pushed herself up out of her sleep—and sweet dreams—and rubbed her eyes, trying to shake out of the fog. Aside from trying to grasp reality, the air inside the tent became icy and frigid.

Peggy stood in front of her, her face flaming red and her fingers pressing deeply into her sides. The chill cooling Maggie's skin sent a spine-tingling shiver down her back. She tugged her blanket up around her shoulders for warmth—and to hide the shudder induced by Peggy's presence.

"Well? Are you just going to sit there, or are you going to explain?" Peggy's foot stomped to the ground, reminding Maggie of an angry bull. Bonnie and Linda stirred awake and sat up on their elbows.

Wiping at the sleep in her eyes, Maggie found the strength to address her adversary. "Peggy, what are you talking about? What makes you think you can barge in here and scare us all to death?"

"You haven't figured it out? Boy, you got to be the dumbest gal in the camp! The heater, Maggie, the heater!"

Maggie gasped and pinched her eyes closed. *Oh dear, the heater.*

"It's *your* turn to refill the oil and check the flame, but judging by the temperature in here, you never did. Now it's probably frozen. You could have killed all of us. It was a good thing I stopped by for an extra pair of socks. I saved your sorry behind!" With anger peppering her eyes, Peggy went for the heater and checked the oil, probably to see if there was any chance of getting the wick lit again—or hoping to find the failure in Maggie's fault.

"Go easy on her, Peg. They've only been here a few weeks. Give the girl some slack."

"Lucky you, I got here on time. It's not frozen. I should be able to get it going again." Peggy went about her business as if she couldn't hear a word Linda said.

Maggie was not about to be bulldozed. She stood to her feet, fully awake now, and dropped the blanket from her shoulders. "Let me do it, Peggy. You're right. It was my night to tend to it and I forgot. It must've been all that dancing we did all night with those hunky officers."—Good way to stick a rose's thorn into the woman's side. "I'll refill it now."

Peggy jerked up the oil can. "Empty. That's great." The can fell to the ground with a hollow thud. "And they picked *you* as our skilled replacement?"

"Peggy, lay off her." Linda swung her legs over the edge of her cot. "She's been working hard. She was tired. We were all tired. Any one of us could've checked it before we crawled into bed and we didn't. Just slipped our minds."

"Working hard? You call dancing and carousing with officers *working* hard? Linda, she's gotta learn on her own how things work around here. If she's not competent then she's not staying here with us."

Maggie's nostrils flamed with torch-like air. How dare Peggy insult her name in front of all the girls! "Are you saying I'm an incompetent, stupid woman, Lieutenant Blizzard?"

The Ice Queen's arms folded in front of her chest and her eyes glared at her much like those of Vivian Leigh's in her role as Scarlet O'Hara—the most devilish of looks. "Are you, Lieutenant Johnson?"

Only Maggie's strong will prevented her from screaming. She was better than that and she certainly couldn't let Peggy see that her words were adding fuel to Maggie's fire. With a huff, Maggie pulled her heavy coat on. "I have more will, stamina, and brains than most women, Peggy. And incompetent I am not. I'm heading over to the supply tent for more oil."

"You can bet you're gonna be the one to go out there and get the oil. Maybe that'll teach you not to slack on your job." Peggy brushed past Maggie, bumping her shoulder.

If that's the way things were going to be, so be it.

While stomping to the supply tent, so many thoughts ran through Maggie's mind. It was just her luck that she was bunking with the most miserable soul on earth. And to make things worse, that woman was a soul who sought out to destroy Maggie's nursing reputation.

Love your enemies.

"I know what you're asking of me, Lord, but this is something too big for me to handle."

Loving an enemy was easier said than done. Especially in today's world. Look at what America's enemy had already done to so many. It wouldn't be easy to look a German or Japanese man in the eye and bestow love upon him. But a woman as cold-hearted as Peggy Blizzard? Her callous ways were just as erroneous as the men the Americans were fighting.

Trust me, Maggie.

"I just...*can't.*" Her tongue weakened on that last word. She'd never dealt with a situation she couldn't handle. That's how she'd come so far. Would God give her the strength to overlook Peggy's insensitive disposition? Could Maggie find room in her heart to forgive? She wasn't sure.

Even so, her mind kept hearing those three words, *love your enemies.*

9 April 1945

"How's the patient with the side wound, Bonnie?" Maggie stopped to catch her breath before entering the post-op tent.

"The young private you saved?"

"Yes, that's the one." Maggie waited impatiently with her fist on her hip. She heard he'd pulled through and wanted to check on his progress.

"He's recovering nicely." Bonnie's small, sweet voice sounded even sweeter with those words. Maggie closed her eyes and lifted her head toward the heavens, whispering thanks to God. "You know, Maggie, it's because of you that he's alive. You really did save his life."

"God saved him. I did what I had to do, Bonnie. Any of us would have done the same."

"I don't know about that. I think any of us would have blacked out over the thought of sticking their hand inside someone's abdomen like that. Nurse or no nurse, you went in blind. How did you do it, Maggie?"

She shook her head. "I don't know. It...the Lord took over." She smiled at Bonnie and let her words sink in. She was thankful for the strength to endure such a tragic ordeal and for the Lord hearing her prayers for the young man's life.

"Oh, Maggie, that reminds me. That patient was asking for you this morning. His name is Peter Carlson, twenty-three years old. He's up and waiting for you." Bonnie tilted her head toward the tent doorway. Maggie glanced in that direction, getting the hint, and smiled.

"I guess I should go in there and say hello." She pulled in a deep breath and squared off her shoulders. After a night of dancing and socializing, and the report that Peter was doing well, the good news put a bounce in her step. For a moment, the cold weather melted away and warmth entered her heart.

She pushed through the flaps on the post-op's doorway and looked through the rows of cots. Her eyes rested on a young man near the rear of the tent, thumbing through an old *Yank* magazine while lying on his back. As she neared his cot, she spied a few days' worth of stubble on his face, making him appear a little older than twenty-three. War seemed to do that to these boys—aging them and cheating them out of their youth.

Her feet stopped just short of his wood and canvas cot. She watched as his eyes traveled from the magazine and followed her figure up to her face. When his eyes met hers, he attempted to sit up in bed.

"It's you."

She sat down on the footlocker beside his cot and shushed him. "Don't try to sit up. Just rest. We don't want to start internal bleeding."

"You're the nurse who saved my life."

Pausing, Maggie glanced at her hands then back at him. "God saved you. I assisted."

He reached out for her hands and brought them to his lips. "I owe you my life. They told me how you plugged the damaged artery with your hand and stopped the bleeding. Even the doctor couldn't do it. You're a miracle worker." His warm lips pressed to both her knuckles.

Maggie squirmed and wished he'd give back her hands. She searched for words that would bring the conversation back to him instead of her.

"I'm glad you came through all right. I was praying for you through the whole surgery. You know, with that bullet lodged so close to your spine, it's amazing you weren't paralyzed. How are you feeling, Peter?"

"You know my name. Say it again, will ya? It sounded so nice coming from your voice."

He must be delirious from all the medications.

Maggie patted his hands. "Yes, they told me your name before I came in. I just wanted to check on you and see how you were feeling this morning before I started my rounds."

"My stomach is killing me, my back is mighty sore and I have to change positions from time to time, but the pain medicine helps with that. They said I'll be going home as soon as I can travel."

"I have no doubt you'll be home before summer is upon us. Best not to push it until we know you're well enough for travel. Don't want an infection to set you back a few weeks."

The smile he'd worn while closely examining her face faded until it pulled downward into a frown. His gaze shifted to Maggie's fingers, which still rested on his. Not realizing that she'd been holding onto his hands for so long, she discreetly slipped them away and onto her lap.

"What's the matter, soldier?"

"You're the prettiest girl I've ever seen. You're an angel. You saved me and I—well...I'm afraid I'll never see you again after they send me home."

His words tugged at her heart strings. It was one of the most beautiful things a man had ever said to her. Maybe too beautiful. Too personal. Almost as if he felt bonded to her in an intimate way.

"Peter, that's incredibly sweet of you, but I'm afraid life must go on. You have your mother and father waiting at home for you. What about a girl? Don't you have a girl back home who sends you letters and says she's holding out for you?"

"Rosie. Yeah, Rosie. But she's not nearly as pretty as you, and she certainly wouldn't have done what you did."

Oh dear. How was she going to get through this one? He was definitely an apple who'd fallen hard from the tree.

"Peter, why don't you rest a while? Sleep is good for the body and that's when it heals the fastest. I'll be sure to come back and check on you in a little while."

"You promise?"

Easing onto her feet, she stared down into his slate blue eyes. "Yes, I promise."

The poor boy. In the mess of warfare, all this young man was looking for was someone to love him in his impaired state. While Maggie could offer her support and kind words, she couldn't be that model of affection for Peter. Not the way he wanted her to be. Like always, she would be that beacon of hope, bringing those tossed vessels to a safe harbor.

CHAPTER TEN

10 April 1945

An easterly wind blew in more than just clouds. Waves of wounded soldiers spilled through the doors of the 39th. While the gale helped to dry out the mud hole the camp had sunken into, it also made working conditions more difficult. The kerosene heaters were unfairly matched against the smothering gusts. Maggie and the other nurses pillaged the camp for every available blanket to drape over sick and wounded soldiers who shivered from fever and shock.

"I can't imagine what it's like for the overnight nurses. I'm sure keeping the heaters going is a job in itself."

"You ain't a'kiddin' there, kid." Vera dropped her arm load of drab, military-issued blankets to the wooden crate-turned-table. She and Maggie buried their hands in the pile and pulled out individual blankets to fold.

"Has your love sick patient been around today?" Vera plopped a folded blanket onto a new pile.

"Not yet. I don't know what to do, Vera. Peter hovers over my shoulder when I'm tending patients in the ward. He's not supposed to be up and about too much, but he always finds an excuse to hobble out of his bed and end up next to me. Then I have to drag him back to his bed and threaten to tie him down just so he doesn't risk injury."

"You saved his life, kid. I think he feels deeply connected to you." Vera dropped her linens and examined Maggie's features. "You know, you're a very attractive female. Those are two very big problems while serving in this position."

"I know. But I don't know what to do about it."

"I don't think there's much you *can* do about it. How often do you think these boys see women?" She lowered her voice to a loud whisper. "They eat, sleep, talk, walk, and travel with men. The only time they see a female is on the streets of those devastated towns, or when they land in a chain hospital. Between that and your looks and charm, I'd say it's a lethal combination. But you can't hide your face from the world, so you have to deal with it. We all have to deal with it." Vera's eyebrows raised high in her forehead as she picked up another blanket and went back to her folding routine.

"Lethal to them or me?"

Vera shrugged. "Both."

Maggie let out a sigh. "Oh, you and your ideas, Vera. Honestly, I think I've heard enough."

She gathered her pile of blankets into her arms, but stopped with Vera's next sentence.

"You're not afraid of falling in love with someone like Peter, are you, Maggie?"

Her jaw dropped wide open. Stunned, Maggie slowly turned. "What is that supposed to mean, Vera Marshall?"

"Well, Peter is quite attractive. He's not a bad problem to have. Neither are those officers you danced with last night. Walter is somewhere over yonder and…well, I'm sure it'll get lonely while we're out here."

She couldn't believe her ears. Was Vera actually insinuating that she would break her promise to Walt and gallivant over these hills with another soldier?

Maggie shook her head. "No, I made a promise. I will always live up to my promises and I never break them."

"Isn't *that* a hard promise to keep?" Vera crossed her arms over her chest.

"Not when you're in love." The memory of Danny's anxious face reappeared in her mind—the day he left for airborne training. She'd never seen that look on his face before. A look that he was truly in love—with her.

"Are you saying Major Radford is your soulmate? Because your actions the other night may prove you wrong. You certainly didn't look like a girl in love with her one and only."

Vera's question poked in areas that were forbidden, and frankly, too uncomfortable for Maggie to discuss without consulting and sorting through her own thoughts first. "Walt—? What?" She rubbed her forehead with her free hand. This conversation was giving her the beginnings of a headache. "Vera, you're talking me in circles. I can't even keep up with who we're talking about anymore."

"You mentioned love. Who are you in love with?"

"I—I . . ." A gust of wind banged the door open and closed. "Let's talk about this later. I have to get these blankets to those poor boys over there." Maggie shoved her way into the next tent and tried to focus on her job.

But Vera's question bothered her. It carved an unsettling hole into her heart. What was Vera observing that was invisible to her?

Who was she in love with? Who *was* she talking about when she mentioned her promises and being in love? Could it be that Danny truly still held a place in her heart? In a place that she never knew existed inside her? A place that held promise and stability? Then again, she was *Maggie*. Maggie who changed with the tides, changed with the seasons, and changed with the wave of a hand. Until she'd fallen in love with Danny, she'd bounced from man to man throughout her adult life, able to handle heartbreak as if it were an old garment of clothing easily cast aside in the church donation box. Now that she'd lost Danny to war, was she afraid of recommitting her heart to someone else? Like Grace Brady, did fear itself prevent Maggie from giving her whole heart to one man?

"Maggie."

She blinked back her deep thoughts and side-glanced at the man she already knew was standing beside her. "It's Lieutenant Johnson, Private Carlson." Her eyes bounced from the floor to Peter's face—his charming, handsome face.

"Right. Lieutenant." His eyes lost a little bit of that spark. He stood there looking at the dirt floor while his right hand covered his left side. Maggie noticed he still stood half bent over.

Dismissing her own rules, and hating it, she lowered her voice. "Peter, how you feeling? Do you still have pain in your stomach? Back?"

"It's nothing bad." His lips curled upward. "You used my given name. I thought you wanted to use proper terminology."

Her eyes skirted toward the other patients. "I was just asking...as a friend."

His hazel eyes bore longingly into hers. She couldn't help but perceive he possessed the brightest slate blue eyes she'd ever seen. So very different from Danny's.

"You consider me a friend, Maggie?"

She needed to tread carefully. This would be her open opportunity to flirt back, let out a slight giggle, and toss her chestnut hair over her shoulders. But she didn't want to be that Maggie anymore. No, she wanted to grow up, and be one man's girl. Vera's words echoed in her mind, *Are you afraid of falling in love with a man like Peter Carlson?*

Her eyes momentarily closed and she heaved a sigh. "Yes, Peter, I consider you a friend, but that's all."

His thin frame leaned against one of the tent poles, and his eyes drooped in defeat. Maggie noticed the downward draw in his features and paleness to his skin. But if he was feeling unwell, he didn't let on. Instead, he continued, "I think you're the most wonderful girl in the world, Maggie Johnson. You mean everything to me. You're the reason I'm still breathing today. As the fellas would say back home, you're the bee's knees of nurses."

A doctor glanced in her direction. She shuddered under his scrutiny— or maybe from the cold that managed to seep through her fatigues. "Peter, can we take this discussion elsewhere? The doctor won't be happy about you being up and about this long. And if they hear you talking like that, you'll get a reprimand. Let me walk you back to your bed."

She dispersed the last of her blankets to the soldiers she passed as she escorted Peter to his cot. At least she was keeping an eye on him if he tripped, became dizzy, or decided to faint on her. She took hold of his right arm and assisted him to a sitting position on his cot.

"Don't you want to lie down?"

His hand grasped her fingers. "No."

A surge of electricity tingled up her arm at his touch. It was no ordinary touch. This man held strong feelings for her. The thought left her breathless and made her realize just how dangerous it was to be away from Walt for so long.

His hand swept upward and touched her brown locks. "I can't get you off my mind. I sit awake on this cot all day waiting for you to come in. My heart speeds up like...like a bee's wings on take-off when you walk through that doorway." He paused and tensed. His hand pressed against his side. Pulling her hands from his grip, she supported his back and chest. She discerned he was in pain, but before she could intercede he said, "I can't keep it all to myself any longer, Maggie. I had to tell you, and I hope you feel something for me too." His free hand reached for hers and he held her fingers close to his chest.

Maggie's head fogged over. Although she had no interest in Peter Carlson, the attention and closeness of a man felt wonderful. She and Walt had shared only a few intimate moments together, but she already missed the security that his companionship gave her. She had to keep her heart guarded. This was the place where too many girls fell into temptation and struggled to get out.

"Peter, as I said, I care for you. I really, truly care for you, but if it's a relationship you're seeking, I'm not the one for you. I think I'm just the one who is filling that void in your life right now. What about your gal back home?"

"Oh, I've already written her and told her I'm in love with you."

Maggie winced, pulled her hand from his grasp, and touched a finger to her brow. "Peter, you shouldn't have done that without talking to me first."

"But...I love you, Maggie."

How was she going to get through this? How could she make him understand that all he was feeling for her were feelings of indebtedness, not love?

"Look, Peter, I already have someone who I made a promise to. I can't just send him a Dear John. I keep my promises."

That sorrowful look entered his eyes again, and he released his breath. "Oh. So...you're already spoken for."

She nodded.

"I shoulda known. I think I'll lie down now."

Maggie eased Peter onto his cot and made sure his pillow perched comfortably behind his head. "Is that okay for you?"

He nodded, but kept his eyes from hers.

"All right then. I'll let you rest. Do you need anything for the pain? You look a little pale."

He shook his head.

She turned to leave but stopped when she felt Peter's hand reach for hers once more.

"I'll always remember you, Maggie."

A subtle smile spread across her face. "I won't forget you either, Peter Carlson."

After she left Peter's ward, she caved. Peter was a sweet man, and someone she could easily talk to and get to know, and crushing his spirit was not easy. The look of hurt in his eyes cut her deeper than inserting her fingers into the gaping hole in his side.

And what about Walt? The past few days she hadn't even thought of him, pined for him, or wished for his arm around her shoulder. She needed to make time to miss him, to think of him. She needed to remind herself that distance between herself and her patients was a constant struggle in her life as a nurse. A struggle for her sanity and virtue. But once free of that struggle, she'd rest in the safety of Walt's arms.

My Love,

Once again, I'm sitting alone at my desk while the men carouse about in town. The draw of night life and music hold no appeal to me for it's you my mind craves both day and night. So here I sit in the dim light of my lantern and kerosene heater, missing you. Your picture sits at the corner of this parchment as I write, imagining it's your sweet face I'm talking to.

The distance is too long for me to bear. I miss you more than anything else I've ever known. Even when I think of home, I can only imagine you going with me.

Please write back soon, letting me know I invade your thoughts as much as you bombard mine.

With All My Love,
Walt

Dear Walt,

The longer the war keeps raging, the more I long for peace to settle over the world. The 39th keeps us busy. Surgeries last all day, sometimes stretching my shift well into twenty hours. Some days my body grows numb to the sleep-deprivation and cold. Some of us look like walking corpses among the living.

The weather is still wet and dreary. However, I've come to sleep better when listening to the trickling brook of rainwater running beneath my cot. We learn to cope with the inconveniences of front line living.

I miss you too. But I know I'm where the good Lord wants me. With that assurance, I trust our reunion will be all the sweeter. Be safe, my knight.

Love,
Maggie

11 April 1945

Maggie stepped into the post-op ward to start her daily duties, but the solemn expressions on Bonnie and Vera's faces caused her to stop and wonder what caused the gray clouds to hang over their heads.

"What is it?" she asked when they put down their coffee cups.

"I'm so sorry, Maggie," Bonnie blurted out then stalked out of the room.

"What's with her?"

Vera stood and took hold of Maggie's shoulders. "Um, Maggie, there's no easy way to put this but…"

All at once, old memories flooded into her mind. The Western Union telegram she handed to Grace, news that her brother, Phillip, had gone missing in action in the Philippines, Danny's MIA notice, then Walter's sharp blow when he handed her the report telling her of Danny's death while on the Normandy mission.

Fear seized her heart and squeezed until she couldn't breathe. "Vera, out with it." Her voice shook. "Whatever it is, just tell me."

Vera let out a rickety breath. "It's Peter."

A few minutes later, a breathless Maggie knelt at Peter's bedside. He looked as though he was just resting, sleeping peacefully.

Her hand stretched out and rested against his arm that lay limp on his chest. His skin temperature confirmed that Vera's information was true. He wasn't just sleeping.

Tears sprang to her eyes as she recalled the conversation they'd had just hours before. She recalled those beautiful hazel eyes that sparked when she walked into the room. And she remembered the day Peter Carlson was carried on a stretcher into her life.

The pools in her eyes spilled onto her cheeks, and she rested her head against Peter's cold shoulder. She couldn't contain sobs she was holding back in her throat any longer.

Moments later, Vera's soft hand rested against her back.

"I saved him, Vera. He lived. He was supposed to live."

∾✯∿

Her food held no taste. Nothing seemed the same since Peter Carlson's death. Maggie pushed her oatmeal and eggs around on her tin plate.

"Maggie, I do wish you'd eat something." The tone in Bonnie's voice pleaded that she take just one bite of her breakfast.

Not even the coaxing of her close friends could alleviate the sting that left its nasty venom eating its way into her heart. The choking sensation of tears always clogged her throat and threatened to invade her mouth, making it difficult to talk about anything.

She kept one hand on her fork and the other she held tightly against her mouth, hoping the girls wouldn't see her quivering lip beneath her knuckles.

"Maggie, you've got to pull yourself out of this depression. You did your best. Some things we can't control." Bonnie's words were soft and kind, but it only brought back the painful reminder that it hadn't been enough.

Why did she care so much?

"Bonnie, he was doing so well. Maybe I didn't scrub my hands well enough. Maybe I missed a dose of his antibiotic."

"No, Maggie. The doctor checked the charts. You had everything written down. He had all his medications. The doctor said it was an internal infection, not visible to the human eye."

"But I should have noticed fever, paleness...something that would've given any indication he was in trouble." Maggie's fork dropped onto the table and she placed her hands over her eyes. "He just wanted to be loved." She couldn't keep the uneasiness from her voice. She swallowed hard against the knot that had attached to her throat, but her efforts weren't enough. Tears pushed their way into her eyes and spilled down her cheeks. "It's my fault. Once again, I wasn't good enough. I messed up somewhere."

Bonnie and Vera sprang from their chairs and circled Maggie, rubbing her back and giving her shoulders a knowing squeeze.

"Hey, kid, let it all out. The sooner you get it out of your system the sooner this wound will heal. Just know you're a good nurse and you did all you could do."

"Vera, it hurts terribly."

"I know. Believe me, kid, I know."

A commotion at the front of the mess caused everyone's heads to turn.

"The airfield's been hit! The airfield's been hit! Luftwaffe fighters just peppered the airstrip! Everyone to the hospital!"

CHAPTER ELEVEN

"Grab your helmets, girls. Something tells me this isn't going to be a regular convoy of patients." Vera snagged the girls' hands. Together, they ran from mess to the triage area where medics, surgeons, and nurses congregated. Urgency hung in the air like a haunting mist, closing in on the camp and generating tension.

Jeeps and ambulances pulled into the hospital grounds. Litter bearers sprinted with the weight of freshly wounded men on their litters into triage, their patients writhing with pain as they bounced on the tan canvas stratum. Airmen and mechanics, blackened with soot and oil splotching their faces, supported one another as they carried their compatriots on foot. The whites of their eyes stood out against the smudge of black on their skin and from the smoke that rose behind them.

In the distance, black, billowing clouds reached skyward. A high hum rose from the ground as American fighters hurried to get in the air and defend their home. Maggie spotted two P-51D Mustangs lift off and pull up with sharp precision, veering to their left. Back on the ground in front of her, more medics rushed to empty their load of casualties. An explosion too close for Maggie's comfort shook the ground beneath them, causing everyone to duck and stoop to the dirt beneath their boots.

"Get me out of here!" A patient writhed on his litter. "Just send me home. Please, just send me home!"

Maggie tried to turn her ear from the sounds of agony. The patient was clearly in shock and shaking violently. Like the others, soot, dirt, and oil caked his face, hands, and arms.

"Shh. It's okay, fella. You'll be safe here. Where does it hurt?" Her eyes scanned his body for evidence of damage or trauma.

"M—my leg. Help…me." His trembling hands clutched his left thigh.

"Let me have a look and see if we can't patch you up and get you back on your way." Maggie reached inside a pocket on her tunic and pulled out scissors to cut his pant leg. Once the wound was exposed, she could assess the significance of his lesion. "I need to pack it to stop the bleeding."

"Sign me a pass home, will ya, nurse?"

She looked down into his widened eyes. "I'll let you know what we decide. Just hang tight, soldier." She turned from him and grabbed a passing medic by the arm. "Wrap his wound then get this patient into the shock ward. He's suffered a bullet wound to the thigh. I fear the artery in his leg may have been severed. Have the surgeon look at him for further evaluation. I have too many other patients to assess."

"Yes, Lieutenant."

"Maggie! There you are. The airfield just radioed in. They're sending in another ambulance with two pilots and several men from an aircrew. All are badly injured. We've been ordered to meet them at the hospital entrance."

Aware of the urgency etched into the creases of Bonnie's wearied features, Maggie sprinted toward the camp's entrance without a second thought. Her feet slipped and slurped in the muddy contours of the ground. Her pulse quickened and she realized she and Bonnie were racing into the open. What if the German fighter plane circled and zeroed in on the two of them? No, surely the pilot wouldn't do that. Even in war there were still rules. She looked back at the red cross painted on the white circle of the tent tops. Bold and clear. Surely they would be safe.

But still, the hammering in her chest continued, and her breathing became labored and quick.

"You did say the patients were meeting us here, right Bonnie?"

"Yes. I'm positive."

"I don't see or hear anything." Maggie shielded her eyes and strained down the road.

"Wait. Maggie, I hear something."

Oh no. Could it be the Luftwaffe?

"Look! Maggie, here comes the ambulance!"

She turned her eyes toward the area in which Bonnie pointed. Sure enough, there were several jeeps and ambulances barreling down the road toward them.

Only...

Her ears pricked.

That humming sound. It wasn't coming from the road, nor did it sound like the thrum of jeep engines. It was coming from elsewhere.

For the briefest of moments, all sounds faded. Only the sound of blood pulsing through Maggie's ears, beating like bass drums, reminded her to breathe in rhythm. Her intuition whispered something was wrong.

Voices and shouts raised from the tents behind her, and she scanned the area. Every person in the evacuation hospital buzzed throughout the rows of aligned wounded. Their ears and eyes focused on the patients in front of them. No one else seemed to sense what she was sensing.

"Maggie?" Bonnie's hands tightened around her arm. "Maggie, are you all right?"

"No." She shook her head. "Bonnie something's not right. That humming sound, it's not the medic vehicles—"

Pat-ta tat-tat...

Blood-curdling screams shrieked from their mouths as the ground popped with 30-mm bullets whizzing at their feet. Maggie instinctively placed her hands over the helmet that covered her head. Then the dull ping of bullets hitting metal sickened her stomach.

The ambulances.

"Bonnie, he's attacking the ambulance! We have to get over there."

"How? We'll get ourselves killed!"

"Those men will die too if we leave them there."

Tears of fright rippled in Bonnie's eyes, but Maggie watched as Bonnie glanced from her to the roadside ambulances and the men struggling to get out. Her facial expression evolved from terror to anger to resolve.

"If we die, Maggie, just know that I love you like my own sister."

"Likewise, Bonnie. Ready?"

The girl took a shaky breath but nodded her consent.

"Let's go."

Maggie's pulse ticked loudly in her ears. Her breath came quick, and the reality of this moment possibly being her last taunted her. "I'm sorry, Walt," she whispered as she took Bonnie's hand.

Together they ran toward the men who hurried to get their wounded patients out of the damaged trucks.

"Let us help! Tell me what we've got."

The driver did a double take when he saw Maggie standing beside him. "Hey, what are you doing out here? Are you coo-coo or something? Get back to the tents where you'll be safe!"

"Excuse me, Lieutenant, but my orders were to meet your convoy here. Now let us in to help before that plane circles back around to finish us off!"

His eyes relayed he was too tired to fight her, so he nodded.

Maggie quickly analyzed the two litters emerging from the back of the ambulance. "Get these two over to OR immediately. Where are the pilots I was told about?"

"They're in the back, ma'am. We loaded them first."

Maggie jumped into the ambulance to tend to the pilots. Two other litters were still lying in front of the pilots. As she passed by them her eyes assessed their condition. It only took one glance at each to realize why these men still waited on board the ambulance.

"I'm sorry, Lieutenant. These two were alive…until the stinkin' German pilot fired at us."

She pressed her hand to her stomach. They were so close to life, and yet, death had already beat them to the gate. "Take them out and set them inside the gates." After taking a moment to compose herself, Maggie moved on to the other men still in need of care. The remaining two pilots were unconscious. Blood seeped through their clothing. Noting the areas soiled by blood, Maggie gathered that both suffered bullets to the stomach. They would need immediate surgery.

"Corporal!" Her voice sounded muffled in the stuffy ambulance, even to her own ears. "The pilots must get into surgery. Take them to OR!"

She hopped from the back of the ambulance and onto the ground. Bonnie looked up at her from another litter. Her head shook from side to side.

Maggie's shoulders drooped. Another one gone.

"Nurse!"

Another pleading voice cried out to them. Maggie feared her head would topple from her shoulders. There was too much happening at one time.

Breathe, Maggie, breath. She wouldn't have another bout of fatigue-driven shock. She wouldn't. No, she *couldn't.* She wanted this mission. She had to save lives. Filling her lungs with a heaping breath of air, she opened her eyes and turned toward the weathered voice calling out to her. Looking over her shoulder, she spotted two more pilots supporting a man between their shoulders.

"Can you help our friend? He's from our crew. We need him. Please? Can you help him?"

They looked as if they had just walked through the flames of hell. Their faces, hands, even the hairs on their arms and eyebrows appeared singed and were gritty and black. Their sullied hair clung to their foreheads as sweat dripped from their brows.

Maggie took pity on them. Their faces told a story no author could make up. Their eyes were glazed over with a haze unknown to those who didn't understand the cost of war. Defeat diluted strength from their arms. Maggie and Bonnie relieved them of their load and assessed their friend's condition.

"Is he gonna be all right, miss?"

Maggie glanced up. The tall, thin pilot chewed his lip while his fingers cupped his chin. The other pilot knelt by his crewmate, gazing intently from his friend to Bonnie, who was busy taking vitals.

While Maggie remained silent, Bonnie looked up from the patient to the querying pilot. "I think you got him here in time. Let's get him over to the shock ward."

"MEs coming straight for us!"

Another wave of panic assaulted the group. Maggie's initial reaction was to hit the ground and curl into the fetal position, but no, she couldn't play the coward. Forcing herself to mask her overwhelming fear, she followed in line with the men. Each one of them—including Maggie and Bonnie—struggled to carry what they could. The task pushed her to her physical limit and was daunting, but together she and Bonnie rushed toward the safety of the hospital's gate. Although the safe haven was within distance, it still seemed as if their feet couldn't carry them fast enough.

The buzz of a fighter's engine resonated through the air and slowly rose in volume. She nearly choked on her own saliva as her throat constricted and fear strangled her air passages. Another spray of bullets shot from the Messerschmitt's barrels, and Maggie prayed the Lord would spare them from further injury. God's protective hand was the only covering they had at that moment.

Bullets kicked dirt into the girls' faces as they pushed faster toward the gate. The plane's engine buzzed overhead as the aircraft outran them. At least for the time being, they were alive and they'd made it to safety as their boots crossed the camp perimeters. Two guards' firm hands tucked them into a shield of protection as they fell to the ground. They were alive. Amazingly, they survived.

❧❦

Maggie sat down with a tin of black coffee. Her eyelids slid closed when the warmth of its comfort tickled her tongue. The day was a blur as she tried to think back. It seemed like two weeks had passed since Bonnie and Vera broke the news of Peter's death. In reality, it had only been a day, his death overshadowed by the Luftwaffe attack and the airmen coming in for treatment. She didn't even have time to truly mourn for him or think back on what she could have done to save Peter's life.

Now caked with dirt and mud, and tired and hungry but alive, Maggie let her eyes roll beneath her lids. She'd come so close to her own death today. She and Bonnie both. But brave little Bonnie did Maggie proud. The gal put on the bravest face Maggie had ever seen. She didn't know the girl had it in her. But the most important thing of the day—all those wounded airmen in Maggie's care had survived.

This mission accomplished.

However, now that the air around her had calmed and her mind found rest, Peter haunted her thoughts. She knew he wasn't feeling well, but instead of insisting on getting the doctor on his case, she had assumed bed rest was the best medication for him. It wasn't. He was dying…and she let it happen.

Tears seeped from her eyes when Bonnie and Vera sat down with her. She sniffed and rubbed grief from her face as they joined her.

"You know, kid, the whole camp heard what you two did outside the hospital today."

Maggie took a deep breath, and she stared into her coffee cup. "I assume we could be reprimanded for leaving the gates."

"I don't think so, hon. If your act of valor gets to the high-ups, I'd say you'll be shimmering with medals."

"Oh, Vera, honestly." Bonnie batted a hand. "It's not like we charged the enemy or anything. We didn't even shoot him down. I hardly think they'll merit us for doing our job."

Vera's eyebrows rose incredibly high in her forehead. "You may get a surprise there, Bonnie girl." Vera's eyes darted off and her words lodged somewhere in her mouth because they weren't coming out. Something hooked her attention. "Speaking of surprises…hello gorgeous. Two tall, dark, and handsomes coming our way, ladies."

Maggie and Bonnie twisted their necks to view their visitors. Bonnie's nails dug into Maggie's skin. "Those are the pilots from earlier, Maggie."

"I know."

"What do they want?"

"I don't know, Bonnie."

The thumping of the pilot's boots halted when they stood in front of the girls. The nurses were in the presence of officers so they stood and saluted, to which the two pilots returned.

"Lieutenants, we just wanted to come by and thank you for all you did today." The tall, thin pilot stood a little taller and more erect. "Without you there today, Marvin would have died. We have you to thank for saving his life."

The second pilot stepped forward and took his turn to speak. "We'd like to thank you somehow, so would you ladies care to join us at the Red Cross dance next weekend?" He may have been asking both girls to the dance, but his eyes begged for Bonnie to join him.

Maggie watched as Bonnie's cheeks flushed. The girl smiled a grin much too large for her petite figure. "Why, sure, I—I'd love to, Captain .

. ."

"I'm sorry, Fred Gibbons." He removed his hat.

"Captain Gibbons, glad to make your acquaintance."

"Fred. Just Fred if you don't mind."

Bonnie's cheeks glowed pink under the Captain's courtesy, making her look even more adorable than she already was. Maggie was sure the pilot noticed too.

"All right—Fred."

Vera and Maggie exchanged a knowing glance and inched back so Mr. Gibbons could sit next to Nurse Fitzgerald. Vera leaned to whisper into Maggie's ear. "And so it has begun, Lieutenant."

"I think you are correct, Lieutenant." The two women leered at Bonnie and her newfound friend.

"They'll be engaged before the war ends," Vera stated.

"How would you know? They only just met!" Maggie exclaimed in a strained whisper.

"Believe me, Maggie, I know."

The tall pilot, standing with his jaw slack, cleared his throat and found his voice again. "Well, ladies, is that a yes?"

Just then, Maggie found that inner strength she'd been praying for. It was time to put her foot down and quit the foolishness.

"I'm sorry, Lieutenant. I believe my boyfriend would have something to say against me dancing with another man, but Lieutenant Marshall here is free."

Before Vera could protest, the pilot took her by the hand and guided her to another table to talk.

Maggie leaned her back against the tent pole and crossed her arms over her chest. She surveyed the exchanges going on between two of her best friends and their new acquaintances.

She always ended up alone.

Even surrounded by hundreds of people, she was isolated, separated from her true relationships. Her parents had severed the lines of communication when she left Pittsburg to make a life for herself as a nurse. The only times they ever bothered to contact her was during the holidays or to relay news about Phillip, her brother serving in the Pacific. But Danny was gone, and Maggie was separated from Grace by an ocean. Grace, the only true friend who knew Maggie through and through, was now spending her life with the man of her dreams. Somehow, Maggie felt left out.

If only she could talk to Walt. That would make all her insecurities go away. Hearing his voice would calm her soul and remind her of what waited for her just around the next bend.

She shifted her weight and started for the door. Pushing through the doorway at the same time was Peggy, who brushed her shoulder with coarse vengeance.

"Excuse me, Peggy."

"You know, Johnson, don't think that just because everyone else here thinks you're a hero today means that you're the best nurse to ever set foot on the grounds of the 39th. Anyone could have done what you did today, and maybe even better. Oh, and maybe if you'd kept a closer eye on your side-wound patient, he wouldn't have died."

Peggy's voice dripped with disdain and hateful mockery of Maggie's character. It was enough to push Maggie over the edge. With an echoing clap, Maggie's hand made contact with Peggy's cheek. "How can you be such a hateful, mean person and call yourself a nurse? I've never met someone more vile and repulsive than you, Peggy Blizzard. So how about you stay out of my way and I'll stay out of yours."

CHAPTER TWELVE

9 April 1945
Stalag III A

Joe was thankful for the meat clinging to his bones. Although he'd lost a considerable amount of weight, he wasn't on the brink of death like some of his prison mates. God had provided for him in this dark valley with provisions smuggled into camp and shared between prisoners. Extra loaves of bread with very little jam and soups helped keep his body going in this dreary and filthy prison camp.

In the tight confines of his quarters, cigarette smoke curled into the air. His pals settled at the table in the center of the cabin and played a round of poker. Several others remained in bed, too sick and weak to attempt crawling out of their bunks. If their liberators didn't arrive soon, Joe feared they'd all eventually die here in Stalag III A. His own will to survive was fueled by the determination to regain his memory and the life he once lived. He couldn't die without knowing the secrets that were still locked away in the blocked compartments of his head.

Joe scratched at the month old growth coating his cheeks and chin. It was too cold to bathe, and the extra hair on his face provided the warmth his body lacked—if only by a few degrees. He knelt down by Al, who stirred the few measly coals in the pot-bellied stove.

"It's no use," Al huffed. "Get used to colder nights. Our last resort for heat is about to bite the dust. Just like most of the prisoners here."

Al's head lung low, the wooden stick he used for a poker falling limp in his hand. Joe didn't have to be a genius to understand what Al meant. The men at Stalag III A were losing their willpower to survive the remnants of winter in possession of the Germans.

As the two comrades sat together in silence, the door to the barrack creaked open. Three dark shadows lingered in the doorway. They stood with authority and the very sight of their black trench coats and leather gloves struck fear into the hearts of their enemies.

"Here it comes again." Joe stood with Al.

"I can't take much more of this. We've been beaten and questioned almost every week since we got here. I can't take any more of the interrogations. Why won't they believe us already?"

"Because we're the enemy."

The prison guard heard their voices and stopped. In his thick German accent, he turned to them. "What is this? You two are volunteering for today's interrogation? The warden will be happy to see you." He gave a snap of his fingers, and two guards handled the men with force and shoved them out the door.

"Great. These guys don't let up." A fist to his stomach doubled Joe over in pain and silenced him.

"The warden will ask you to talk when he's ready for you to talk. I suggest you keep your comments to yourself."

Joe and Al were pushed into the interrogation room. Inside, a man dressed in black, smoking a cigar and sitting in the shadows, waited for them.

"Gentlemen," he began in his evil tongue. "Ah, once again we meet here. Do you wish to comply today? I will spare you the consequences of refusing to talk; all you need to do is, uh, give me the plan of attack your country has plotted against me. Where are the Americans planning to attack next and what form of force are they planning to use?"

"I will proudly give my life for my country. I will not comply with you." Al spat on the desk where the Commandant sat. A flash of anger sparked in the German's eyes.

"Stupid man!" The Commandant stood to his feet and pounded his fist into his desk. At the same time, the guard drove the butt of his rifle into Al's spine.

Blunt force trauma forced Al to his knees and knocked the breath from his lungs. Joe knew his friend would surely feel the excruciating effects of the blow for days to come.

"I *will* take your word for it. You say you want to give your life? Fine! Your life it is—"

"No!" Joe interceded as the guard thrust his rifle into Al's gut.

The Commandant glared at the no-name soldier. "So you do not wish to see your friend dead? Is that right?"

"I don't wish to see anyone dead."

The man sinisterly laughed in his throat. "Then why don't I kill you first then?"

"Do what you want, but I will not betray my country or my friends."

"Hmm." The harsh Nazi crossed his arms and leaned against his desk. "My patience is running thin, *GI Joe*. I don't have much time. Why don't we try some persuasion methods?"

A guard emerged from the dark shadows of the walls. He wheeled in a cart with shiny instruments and needles lying on its top.

"Do you know what I have here, gentlemen?"

As the Commandant continued his pompous speech, Joe eyed his surroundings. Two brown shirts guarded the door. The guard who brought in the torture tools left. The only other guards who stood in the room were the two who held their grip on him and half-bent-over Al.

On the desk lay a pistol. If he could somehow take out all five men and grab their weapons, he and Al could make a clean getaway. But how to go about it? In his weakened condition, he couldn't take out these healthy beasts of men.

Lord, help me. Please renew my strength and my mind.

He could do nothing more than pray. At least his remembrance of his salvation had not left him. No matter who he was, even if it was forgotten, God knew and He would take care of him.

Hurried footsteps echoed down the hall outside of the interrogation room, then the door swung open, blowing in the sound of alarm sirens.

"Commandant." A guard popped his head through the crack of the door. "There's been a prison break."

This was his chance. With a nod of his head to Al, the two men turned and shoved their guards into a back wall.

"What are you doing!" The officer ran to his desk for his pistol.

Joe rushed to the desk and rammed the commandant into a filing cabinet. Al was holding his own with the guards. How Joe regained his strength after such a hard blow to the back he couldn't decipher, but was thankful for the adrenaline rush to keep going.

Joe threw his fist into the Nazi's jaw, momentarily disorienting the guard. But in the next instant, an electrifying blow to his temple knocked Joe to his knees. His strength was quickly leaving his body.

Help me, Lord.

Although panting, exhausted, and trembling with pain, Joe found his footing and lunged at the guard who belted him with his rock-solid fist only moments earlier. Reaching for the lamp sitting on the end table to his right, Joe used every ounce of power left in his arms to thrust the lamp into the guard's back. The blow would be enough to briefly paralyze the Nazi.

"Joe? A little help here would be nice."

Joe threw a look at Al once he regained his footing. One guard lay unconscious on the floor but the other three were lunging at his friend like lions hunting their prey. He glanced at the desk. The pistol still sat there. He needed to get to the weapon *and* help Al.

Father, please, right now give me the strength of ten men as you strengthened Samson one final time. Amen.

Taking a deep breath, he rushed the men surrounding his buddy and slammed their bodies against the cold, hard block wall. When he turned, the commandant had him pinned. The pistol's mouth pointed directly at Joe's chest.

He raised his hands.

"You really are stupid men. You may be able to stop my guards, but a bullet in your brain will stop you."

His gun lifted to Joe's head, and the man's finger curled around the trigger when a loud shot went off behind Joe, darkening his senses until all faded from sight.

⋙⋘

"C'mon, buddy. Wake up. I know you can hear me. You have ears like a dog. C'mon, wake up!"

Moaning, Joe stirred and turned his head from one side to the other. "Stop patting my cheeks, man. You're not tenderizing a cut of steak here." He rubbed his hand against his forehead.

"Glad your sense of humor wasn't bruised. We've gotta get out of here. We can't waste any more time."

Joe's eyes fought to open and he winced when his eyelids lifted. "Al, I can't take much more of this. Why am I always the one getting the blow to the head?" He lifted a hand to the place where sharp pain ran down the side of his face.

"Easy, there buddy. You're a lucky man. That bullet just grazed you. Almost took your head off."

"Just what exactly happened?" he asked as he moved to sitting position.

"I'll tell you later. Right now we've got to get moving. There's been a prison break. All the guards are out chasing down the escapees. If we move now, we may have a chance of getting out."

Joe looked around the room. It was still dark and reeking of a pungent odor that reminded him of burning flesh and searing pain. The guards and the commandant were all lying on the floor, unconscious.

He pointed to the commandant. "You shot him?"

"It was either him or you, and it *wasn't* going to be you. I grabbed the guard's pistol and fired just as the warden pulled the trigger. The bullet hit him before he could zero in on you."

"Thanks, Al. I owe you big time."

"We'll settle that later. C'mon let's get out of here."

Al helped him to his feet and they quietly snuck out of the interrogation room.

The halls were quiet—an eerie silence. Until footsteps brought the men to a halt.

"Which way, Joe?"

"*Halt! Was geht hier vor?*" A German guard sharply turned the corner, taking the two men by surprise.

Joe and Al froze.

Beads of perspiration formed on Joe's forehead and dripped down the sides of his face. What would happen? He didn't know an ounce of German. While he searched his head for a plan, Al came to his rescue.

"*Wir haben Aufträge zur Prüfung der Hallen und Zellen.*"

Al speaks German?

The Nazi soldier carefully sized up Al. But the guard's eyes relayed disbelief. Before the German could reach for his luger, a terrible roar splintered the air and shattered the glass windows.

"Get down!" Joe pushed Al to the floor. Both men curled into the fetal position. Another blast shook the walls and echoed through the hallway. It sounded like the front lines had landed on the camp's doorstep.

Nazi eyes glared at Joe from across the floor. The man's arm made a reach for his pistol.

"Al, he's making his move."

Exhausted but not down for the count, Al crawled across the cement floor and wrestled with the guard, throwing punches into his enemy's jaw. Joe joined in the brawl and somehow managed to pull the luger from the guard's holster.

Another explosion shook the building, startling the men. That's when Joe used the butt of the luger to knock out his assailant. When the guard's body fell limp against the hard floor, Joe and Al, let out exasperated breaths.

Joe made it to his knees. "Where'd you learn German?"

Al glanced at him and smirked. "The Army."

"What did he say?"

"He asked where we were going."

Joe took a subtle side glance. "And you said?"

"We had orders to check the halls and…"

Gunfire pulled their attention to the nearby window.

"What's going on?" Al's eyes widened and he craned his neck to peer out the window. "Joe. The guards are swarming the gates and watchtowers. Do you think . . ."

"I'm praying . . ." Joe stopped and listened. "No, it couldn't be."

CHAPTER THIRTEEN

15 April 1945

Peggy's agitation toward Maggie seemed to intensify over the last few days. The woman's hard eyes cast wrathful glances in Maggie's direction. Peggy hated her from the very beginning. But what could have triggered Peggy's animosity in the first place?

There were some things that one simply didn't know or understand.

Maggie's weary hand brushed over her brow. Then her face rested into her palm. Sleep was hard to come by with the constant arrival of patients in need of immediate surgeries. With the constant rush of procedures and ward duties, she'd survived many days on one meal and blurred vision from late night surgeries. Her bed now beckoned her, waving its imaginary hand for her to enter its soft, warm cushion. Not her bed of sticks and canvas, her real bed, complete with sheets, duvet, and pillows. Maybe she'd splurge when she got home and purchase a second pillow for her bed. The longing for a soft cushion for her head and a mattress for her body was almost as strong as her longing for home. She eyed the khaki and wood cot, already showing signs of wear—funny, since she'd hardly used it.

The cot let out a small moan under her weight. "What are you crying for? I've hardly burdened you all week." She patted the cot as if soothing a child. "Ah, I miss my bed back home. I miss Grace. I miss…" Her eyes misted over. She chewed her lip, warding off the tears that brimmed her eyes. "I miss Danny," she said under her breath.

A sigh erupted when she tilted her head back to stare at the tent ceiling. Why had Danny's face haunted her this week? Her dreams were disturbed with his smiling eyes and boyish grin. He kept telling her, *wait for me*, just before he departed into the black of her mind's eye. She threw her body onto her cot and furiously rubbed her eyes. *Stop it, Danny. Just go away. Let me be.*

"What's this? Sleeping on the job?"

Just dandy...

"No, Peggy. I'm off the clock. What are you doing here? I thought you were out terrorizing the patients."

"I live here, you prune. You know, you really need to toughen up if you want to make it out here on the front. We don't leave room for pansies."

Maggie's eyes narrowed into slits, and she slowly picked herself up off her cot. "Who are you calling a pansy, Queen of the ice people?"

A sly smile played across Peggy's lips. Her nemesis' eyes turned cunning, as if wanting to dig under Maggie's skin and make her cower. But the cold-hearted woman wasn't going to get to her that easily. Peggy may try trickery and her devious play on words to add to combat fatigue Maggie was already feeling, but Maggie wouldn't go down without a well-fought fight.

"Lieutenant Johnson, one doesn't have to be that perceptive to learn that you and your nurse friends have no idea how this war game is played. For one, who was it who figured out the yellow bellies were inflicting their own combat wounds to go home? Who is the nurse who sees through those smooth talking idiots and reads into their true intentions?" Peggy pointed a thumb at her chest. "Well, it's me, I tell ya. I'm the better nurse. Not some floozy from the east coast who flaunts her red lips and swings her hips from side to side."

Fire ignited in the pit of Maggie's belly. She stood with force and stalked across the dirt floor to Peggy, wagging her finger all the while. "Number one, Peggy Blizzard—"

"That's *Lieutenant* to you!"

"I don't care who you are! Don't you ever call me names like pansy or floozy again. Number two, I've never claimed to be the better nurse. So maybe it's *you* who thinks I am, and that frightens you. Thirdly, *Lieutenant*, I've been through a world more than you know and don't you ever claim to know what I've endured. And lastly, if you call me a floozy again I will not hesitate to smack your shrewd, little face across this camp. Do you understand me, Lieutenant?" Maggie's breath came quick and her heart pounded from within her chest. Her whole body trembled but she fought to keep her voice deep, even, and steady. She would not let Peggy get the upper hand and flatten her spirit. "And furthermore—"

"My gracious, ladies, what on earth is going on in here? I could hear the two of you squabbling from two tents down."

Maggie froze. Lieutenant McGee stood with her mouth agape and fists planted firmly on her hips. Slowly, Maggie's hands came to her side and she straightened.

"Just a misunderstanding, Lieutenant McGee. But I think we have it all worked out now." She said the words carefully, hoping the slight quiver in her voice didn't give her away.

"There's been tension here between the two of you since Lieutenant's Johnson's arrival. I thought by now both of you would have found common ground and put this silliness behind you. You leave me no choice."

Maggie's breath stilled. What was the lieutenant getting at? Shaking returned to Maggie's limbs.

"Lieutenants, from this moment forward the two of you will eat, sleep, and work together. That should give you plenty of time to become well acquainted with one another and do away with this childish nonsense. I'm giving you three weeks."

Her eyes pierced both girls, pricking Maggie's pride. So she'd been given a new mission. Dread washed over her like a spring rain soaking through her coat. She thought she could handle anything...but this? This was a war not even *she* thought she could win.

❧❧

Walter's latest letter bounced in her hand as the army vehicle jarred Maggie's joints. The 32nd EVAC was only 10 miles from the 39th, but Peggy's lead foot punched the gas as if they were traveling cross country.

"I think you missed a pot hole back a ways." Maggie side glanced. "Could ya take it easy, Peggy? My insides feel as though they're detaching."

"See? Told ya you were too soft. Besides, we've no time for fooling around. We need those meds and supplies now."

Maggie couldn't argue with that. For several days the 39th boiled used bandages for re-use, and the pain medications were running dangerously low. Inwardly, Maggie thanked God that the 32nd was just down the road and willing to share supplies.

"Well, just watch the ruts, will ya?"

Peggy mumbled something under her breath. Maggie didn't care to strain her ears to hear what she said. Instead she tried to focus her eyes on Walter's words.

Darling Maggie,

This war just isn't the same without you. Not a day goes by when I don't think about you. My arms ache to hold you close and safely wrap you in my love. I've been too careful with our relationship. If I could do it all over again I wouldn't hold back my true feelings from you. I've been a fool and now I'm regretting ever letting the Nurse Corps take you somewhere away from the protection I can give you.

As soon as I can convince the Army to move you back to the 238ᵗʰ, I will come for you myself and see you safely back where you belong. Then I'll be sure to guarantee the Army never separates us again.

Marriage, Maggie. I know this is the most unlikely place to wed, but I'll see to it that you have a fine wedding, complete with bridesmaids, flowers, a cake, and wedding march. Think about, won't you? Be ready to give me an answer when I come for you.

I love you to the ends of the earth,
Walt

Sweet Walter. Always looking after her and ready to come to her rescue. But marriage? She wasn't ready to consider marriage to Walt. And him wanting to use his rank to bring her back to him…

Shaking her head, her eyes closed. It was the same charade he'd played for months. Only Maggie wasn't sure she wanted to play by his rules.

You can't keep me close when I'll only volunteer again, Walt.

"What are you squawking about? Can't you keep your protests to yourself?"

"What? So now I'm not allowed to think out loud? It's a good thing this camp isn't far. I can't stand to sit here with your bitter silence a moment longer." Maggie crossed her arms in front of her chest with great emphasis.

"Just remember, I'm driving. Give me any trouble and I'll make sure to turn so hard it'll tumble your pretty little behind right off this ride." Peggy's right eyebrow arched high, making her almond-shaped eyes look all the more narrow and hateful. She'd most certainly pass as a perfect Vivian Leigh in her most rigid of roles.

Maggie gave Peggy a subtle side-glance. Maybe that's just who Peggy was. Maybe the woman didn't know how to be soft and gentle. Either no one had taught her how to love or something terrible must have happened to callous this woman so.

Why hadn't that thought ever crossed Maggie's mind before? Perhaps, God truly wanted Peggy in Maggie's life for a purpose. Not just for tribulation.

After a guard at the gate checked their paperwork, the jeep rolled to a stop, and Peggy killed the engine. "Let's get this done and over with. That way I don't have to be—"

Maggie held up her palm and finished for her. "You don't have to be crammed inside a small vehicle with the likes of me. I know." *At times, I feel the same way, Peggy.* Maggie hefted an empty box into her arms and started for the supply tent.

✐✐

"We can't thank you enough for the supplies, Captain. If you need anything at all don't hesitate to come see us." Maggie couldn't keep the enlightened smile off her face. The 32nd's Captain Sawyer was more than gracious enough to supply the girls with everything they needed and more. The old Maggie would've kissed the man, but instead she checked herself and settled for a warm smile and a handshake.

"No trouble at all, Lieutenants." The captain hoisted the box of supplies into the jeep and helped Maggie into the passenger seat. Peggy saw herself into the driver's side before any assistance could be offered. "Be safe getting back." He tipped his cap up with his thumb and tapped the hood. "So long, ladies."

"Bye, Captain Sawyer, and thank you!" Maggie called out as Peggy drove off.

"You need to stop flirting with the men, Johnson. It's unprofessional and I will not put up with it."

"What now, Peggy? I can't do *this* and I can't do *that* when I'm with you. And for your own information, I was not flirting with that man. A woman can be friendly without trying to land a man for keeps, you know. It wouldn't hurt you one bit to try to smile. It would improve your impoverished appearance."

"At least my *impoverished appearance,* as you put it, isn't as coy as your floozy personality."

"That's it! I've had enough! Pull over, Peggy. I'm walking the rest of the way."

"You're what?"

"You heard me. I warned you about calling me a floozy. This is the last straw. I'm walking back to the 39th—without you."

Peggy continued to roll down the road, but Maggie struggled to stand.

97

She would jump off this army vehicle if that's what it took to get away from this devilish woman.

"What are you, Johnson? Crazy? You're not going to jump."

"Oh, you just wait and see." Maggie's words tumbled out in a low growl. She stood to her feet and firmly gripped the back of the seat with her right hand while her left clutched the front window frame.

The jeep slowed.

"Oh, no you don't." Peggy jammed the jeep in park. "I see what you're doing. You're gonna make me return without you so you can prove me to be the bad guy. I see right through your tactics, Johnson. Well, McGee isn't gonna fall for it. She knows me better than you. She knows my dedication to this outfit and my career. It'll take more than one missing nurse to get me booted outta here and shipped stateside. No sirree, if you're gonna walk, then I'm gonna drive right alongside you. Either that, or you get your little hide back in this seat."

"You know what, Peggy, I—"

That familiar sound of low-droning engines stopped Maggie mid-sentence. Shielding her eyes with her hands, she glanced upwards and searched the skies. Her heart rate sped up as flashbacks of a Luftwaffe pilot strafed the camp. An eerie chill drizzled down her spine.

"Peggy?"

"Yeah, I hear it too. That's not good. Those aren't our planes."

"No, they're enemy planes." Maggie hopped back in the jeep with one bound. "Hurry, Peggy, back to the 39th! Those are bombers!"

The jeep's wheels spun before finally gripping the dirt and mud path. The girls bounced and jolted with each rut and hole they hit. But Maggie hardly let the jarring of the jeep affect her. Her heart beat too wildly and her adrenaline raced too quickly through her body to compute anything else besides the fact that enemy planes were heading straight for them.

She glanced back and jammed her steel helmet onto her head. Reaching back for Peggy's, she saw them. The dark, V formation of German Luftwaffe planes tailing them. She placed Peggy's helmet on her head.

"Thanks."

"Don't mention it."

The drone was right overhead. Maggie's breathing trembled with each breath. She'd never felt so scared or alone in her life. What if the planes attacked, and she and Peggy were thrown from the jeep? Or worse, what if they…never mind. Would someone be able to find them?

A deafening explosion caused the vehicle to veer. Peggy slammed on the brakes, sending Maggie into the windshield.

The crack she heard wasn't the sound of breaking of glass—it was her head colliding with the window frame. Momentary blackness darkened her vision, and immediately, her stomach lurched with overwhelming nausea.

"Maggie! Maggie, are you all right?" Peggy's gruff hands shook her shoulders in attempt to force Maggie out of her fog.

"My head. I hit my head." Another explosion jarred Maggie awake. "Peggy...get us out of here." A cold trail of liquid dribbled down the side of her face. The jeep's window frame must've gashed her forehead. Queasiness returned to her stomach.

"We can't drive on, Maggie. They'll see us and open fire. We've got to take cover." Peggy's voice wavered like a tattered garment on a windy day.

Maggie gasped. "Peggy! The hospital! We've got to go back!" She clutched Peggy's fatigues at the arm.

The ground quaked with another round of angry bursts. Peggy glanced from Maggie to the direction of the 32nd.

"Peggy?"

When Peggy's almond eyes found their way back to Maggie, tears pooled in their corners. "I don't know what to do, Maggie."

For the first time, Maggie witnessed something change in Peggy's appearance. For the moment, gone were the hardened features that warded off any chance of someone venturing in for friendship. In its place, a tender, almost feeble, expression rinsed away any callous traits fused to Peggy's personality. She looked...scared.

Maggie's hands pushed her up onto the seat. The bombing had ceased for the moment, and the hum of bombers were fading into the horizon.

"I think they're gone. Let's get back to the hospital. There're bound to be casualties."

Peggy sat there, staring into nothing. Her face a stony white.

"Peggy? Peggy, snap out of it. I said we've got to go." A shock of pain barreled through Maggie's head and she winced.

"I can't."

"You have to. *We* have to. Peggy, there's so much more to our lives, but we won't get to experience that if you don't push that fear back in its place and overcome it."

Finally. Peggy's eyes found Maggie's. Slowly, the nurse pushed herself upright and placed her hands on the steering wheel. "Let's go home."

CHAPTER FOURTEEN

15 April 1945
Stalag III A

An uproar of cheering men rang sweetly in his ears as he and the other prisoners raised their arms to touch the outstretched hands of their liberators.

"Where have you guys been?" Joe called up to a burly faced man with a cigar protruding from his lips.

"We sort of got hung up in the Ardennes."

Most of the men in the tanks and trucks looked as if they'd come straight from the front. For all Joe knew, they could have! Dirt smudged their faces, the hair beneath their helmets stuck to their foreheads, and grime had built up under their fingernails and embedded itself into the crevices of their hands and forearms. It dawned on Joe that they weren't the only ones living in filth and sludge.

Food and drink were quickly distributed, but most men soon tasted it again. Dysentery did that to the men infected by it. Even Joe found real food hard on his healing stomach, but nonetheless, his insides warmed at the thought of nourishment soaking into his intestinal wall.

After a brief evaluation by the medics, the men in the most critical conditions were boarded into the trucks and jeeps for evacuation.

Just a little nourishment from the K-rations was enough to lift Joe's spirits and a bit of his strength for transportation to the next hospital. The trucks he and Al hustled into felt liberating. He was saying goodbye to the wretched camp that stole so many months of his life.

Before the private secured the tailgate to the supply truck, Joe took one final glance at Stalag III. He scanned its wire fences, large gates, the watchtower, and the rows of cabins where all of them were locked away inside. His eyes squeezed shut. He may not have a past, but what he could remember of the camp would become a vital part of him. A story written in the pages of his life.

Hours passed, but by late afternoon, the convoy of wounded found refuge at an EVAC hospital. By now the group had grown weary with exhaustion. Conditions were not the best with the threat of rain, but they had a roof over their heads, food to eat, and were in the company of their own allies. Their bodies were finally able to rest after such a long and horrid imprisonment, but sleep only became a restless recollection of haunted memories.

Nightmares of his imprisonment, and vile treatment of his fellow servicemen, plagued him. Starvation, torture, which sometimes resulted in death, and the persistent beatings of prisoners were forever etched in his mind. Would the images ever go away, or would he be troubled with those visions for the rest of his life?

But—where would he go? Without his dog tags, without his knowledge of who he was, where would the Army send him next? Suddenly, the thought of being liberated was a terrifying consideration. All that he could recall was a life shared with a few thousand other men, in walls that leaked cold air in the winter, and humid heat in the summer. A place where lice and fleas burrowed into the fibers of his clothing and the strands of his hair. The only food he knew was a watery stew with small chunks of meat and potato skins, the occasional loaf of bread, and tea or water. What would life be like after he was sent back to the States? Would someone be able to identify him? Could the doctors work some miracle drug that would bring back his memory?

As his mind clouded with more unanswered questions, his eyes drifted closed and he fell into a deep sleep.

18 April 1945

"Hey, buddy. Your ugly mug looks better than it did a few days ago." Joe said as he sat up in the cot next to Al.

"I think those miracle pills the nurse keeps popping me is doing its job. Able to hold down food and water now." Although Al still had a long way to go, his cheeks were fuller and his skin was no longer dull colored or pulled tight around his limbs. "And you, Joe, looks like you have a little more strength in those bony knees."

Joe's eyes swept over his arms and body. For the first time in months he was able to compare himself next to the healthy bodies of other American soldiers. The men who liberated them seemed like giants compared to the walking skeletons that wandered through the stalag. But the sensation of his belly feeling full with wholesome food—even if it did come in a can—tasted like a full dinner menu. Joe's body hadn't quite filled out yet, but he could feel the nutrients clinging to his sickly bones. His black, wavy hair was now cut and combed, his shoulders were not quite so sunken and hollow, and his coffee colored eyes no longer bore the stain of dark circles. The only visible signs of abuse and neglect were the scars that remained on his forehead, cheek, and arms.

Joe flexed the muscle in his right arm and grinned. "I even started working out a bit this past week. They said I could go home, but I requested to stay and see this war through. I'm not giving up that easily. They also told me that my dental records should be able to identify me. For all I know, my family thinks I'm gone. Boy, will they be surprised to hear the news. Right now, I'm a ghost."

Al listened intently while Joe spoke. The two men bonded over the span of their imprisonment together.

From time to time, Joe still wondered about Abe and if he was still alive, if someone had nursed him back to health.

"I'm glad to hear you're on the road to recovery. Are you sure you want to stay longer than you have to?"

"I'm positive. They can't murder our boys like that and get away with it. I'll fight for them, for our country, and even you, Al. You saved my life in that prison."

Al let out a sharp, rigid sigh. "I just did what they trained me to do."

"I owe you, Al. I mean that. When I get back to the States, I'm gonna look you up."

"I hope it won't be too long until I hear from ya again. I'm heading out with the next hospital ship. I leave in a few days. I've had enough of this war. I want to go home. See my family—Momma, Pa, my sisters. Pick up where we left off." He waved a hand. "Before all this happened."

Silence fell between them, each one lost in his own thoughts. They'd become more than just friends. They'd become a part of the brotherhood. No man who left the front lines left unaffected. The men they served beside for months or years were all a part of the brotherhood of soldiers. Leaving each other behind was like walking without a limb.

"May God be with you, Al. It won't be the same without you." Joe reached out for Al's hand in a right-handed grasp. "My orders are to stay here. I can still receive the medical attention I need and work on light duty until I'm fully healed and my papers get sorted out."

"That's good. You need the R&R."

The two sat with their elbows on their knees as they perched on the sides of their cots. When Al stirred, Joe turned his attention to him.

"Joe, while you were in therapy, something turned up. I don't know the credibility of the story, but one of the men here at camp seemed to recognize you and said to give you this. He mentioned the name Danny.

He was pretty adamant about the suggestion and wouldn't let me go without giving me this to hand to you. I tried to get more information out of him, but the nurses whisked him away. He left on the last flight out. I'm sorry I didn't get any more out of the fella." Al pulled a book from the inside of his coat and surrendered it to Joe.

Joe's stomach twisted, but not from the dysentery he was healing from. No, this sensation rooted itself deeper than physical afflictions. It dug into his soul. Would the small book contain the secret to who he was inside?

Joe reached for the small booklet and studied its leather-worn cover.

"It's a Bible. Look at that." Amusement filled his eyes and a tight-lipped smile penetrated the darkened thoughts of his mind. "Thanks, buddy." He paused, swallowing back his apprehension. "Wow. I—I don't know what to say. I'm half afraid of what I'll find inside."

His fingers ran over the letters inlaid with gold ink. He held the key in his hand, why was he hesitating to open the cover and unlock his past?

"Okay, boys, the pow-wow is over. Time for meds." A tall, blonde nurse with eyebrows arched in near semicircles and lips plump and full appeared at the end of their cots with a clipboard in hand. She didn't seem to pay them any mind so Joe shook his friend's hand and whispered, "You won't be forgotten, my friend."

"I know."

"All right, first here is simply—" those eyebrows arched even further into her forehead. "Simply, *Joe*?" She looked at his dark, wavy hair then to his face. She wasn't their regular nurse, hence the confusion.

"That'd be me, ma'am. A case of amnesia is plaguing my mind. So the fellas just call me Joe."

She glared at him as if contemplating his integrity. After a moment's thought she gave him a nod. "Joe it is then. I'm Lieutenant Marshall and I'll be taking care of you this evening. Let's start with your vitals."

With her back turned to Al, the nurse felt for Joe's pulse. Then she took his temperature and asked him a few questions. After recording all his information and results, she administered his anti-biotics and sleep medicine.

"Okay, next we have Private Allen..." Her clipped voice dropped off and her face turned a pasty white as her jaw hinged open.

"Lieutenant Marshall? Is everything all right?" Joe asked.

She had trouble speaking. Finally her eyes lifted from her clipboard and slowly wandered to Al's face.

"Allen?" Her voice was dry, low.

Joe looked between the nurse and Al, trying to figure out what caused her reaction.

Al's own face was drawn tight with confusion, yet wonder.

"Allen? Allen Flemming? From York County High?"

Al's eyes glared at the woman for a moment then they sparked. "Vera? Little Vera Marshall from math class?"

"Y-Yes. It's me, But I—I can't believe it's really you. Here. In Germany. In this ward. Under my care."

She'd succumbed to stuttering and for the present time, both pairs of eyes settled on each other. Joe became invisible. Yes, a ghost would well fit his description for now. The ghost of a man that once was.

৵৵৵

With permission from his nurse, Lieutenant Marshall, Joe set out for a walk in the outdoors. A free walk. A walk not bordered with electric fences nor Nazi machine guns. He hoped the stroll would clear his mind of the ravages of war and maybe lead him to a path that ended where his life had cut off. Just looking over the darkened canyon of his heart would bring some comfort that he was somebody. Somebody that someone loved, and somebody that someone was waiting for.

He came to the edge of camp where trees, budding with new sprigs of green, lined the fence. Seating himself on a protruding rock, he pulled the Bible from his back pocket and flipped through its worn pages. He stopped when he came to Daniel chapter three.

Shadrach, Meshach, and Abednego stood before the king. They were facing charges for their disobedience to the law concerning the worship of the false image. Their sentencing was to be cast into the fiery furnace.

As Joe read on, verse seventeen of chapter three caught his attention. *"If it be so, our God whom we serve is able to deliver us from the burning fiery furnace, and he will deliver us out of thine hand, O king."*

Wasn't he in a fiery furnace right now? Wasn't he fighting for what was good and right and put through the tribulations of his actions? It warmed his heart to know that although he'd gone through severe punishment and brutal mistreatment, God was there with him all along. God had put Al there in his cell to be a friend and an encourager. Al had nursed him back to health, and God had given the two of them the strength to survive the prison camp and make it back to the American side.

They still possessed their lives. It hadn't fallen to the Germans. Joe breathed a prayer of thanksgiving to his Lord and Savior for the trials he'd been brought out of. He also prayed for the continued safety over Al as he would soon travel back to the States, and for Abe—wherever he may be.

As he finished his prayer and flipped through his Bible, a small picture and a letter slipped from between its pages. "What's this?" He held the photo up and squinted. It was worn and bent. He tried to iron out the creases with the heat from his hand. When he'd done his best to smooth out the parchment, he held the photo between his fingers. It was a picture of a beautiful brunette with an inscription on the lower left hand corner: *In my thoughts and prayers, Maggie.*

"Maggie," Joe whispered. Something about the woman seemed familiar. Was this her? Could it be he had a wife? A gal?

Tell me she's not my sister. He grimaced at the thought.

The letter crinkled as he unfolded it, and again he used his palm to iron out the creases.

Dear Danny,

You've been gone for a long time. Too long. My arm still aches because in my heart, I'm forever waving good-bye to you. It seems as though you left me a lifetime ago. Although I can still vividly remember our last dance together at the armory, it also seems to fade into the background as if I only dreamed it.

I made a promise to you and I intend to keep it. I'm still waiting for you to return. I'll always wait for you. You're the most handsome man I've ever laid eyes on—even if you do have a big nose...

Joe subconsciously raised his fingers to the slope of his nose, probing its structure.

I don't really think that, but I love the way your eyes look at me when we banter back and forth. You understand me. My family. My thoughts. And my fears. And although I think you're a nut for volunteering for the most dangerous job in the Army, I'm proud of you and I'm praying the good Lord will keep his hand safely around you until you come home. I love you.

Love,
Maggie

The beautiful face of an angel stared back at him and he glided his thumb across the photo's surface. What if she wasn't really his girl? What if he wasn't this Danny spoken of in the letter. What if—wait...

His head tilted in thought. A memory stood on the outskirts of his mind, taunting him. His eyelids slid closed and he concentrated on that memory. It was…just out of reach.

He threw a frustrated glance at the mysterious letter he still gripped between his thumb and forefinger. If only he'd been present when the man gave the Bible to Al. If only he hadn't been burdened by disease and malnutrition.

Picking up a stone and chucking it into the thicket with force, Joe breathed out an agitated grumble. He'd been so close. So. Close.

Chapter Fifteen

Dear Sister Maggie,

Forgive me for not writing you sooner. I hope this letter finds you well and out of harm's way.

I realize we never had the chance to become as close as most sisters do, so I'm hoping that by sending this letter maybe it will bridge the gap between us. I recognize we aren't true sisters and maybe you hold me accountable for taking away your only sibling, but I do hope that over time we'll become friends and the family we're supposed to be. I love your brother, Phillip, with all my heart and I know how much he loves you.

Maggie, as your sister-in-law, I want to be there for you. So please, if you can find room in your heart for another sibling, I'd like to be that sister you never had.

With all sincerity,
Libby

Maggie clamped down on her beans. Through bites of her supper, she read through Libby's letter. It came as quite a surprise. She never pictured Libby as the type to reach out to her and lay the foundation for a friendship. Libby had made it clear she wanted Phillip all to herself and that he was to cut the ties to his family as soon as the vows were said.

But her letter seemed sincere. Almost desperate.

Another forkful of potatoes and she gave Libby's letter a second glance.

"Maggie! There you are!" Vera rushed around the table and plopped herself down opposite Maggie.

"Gracious, Vera. What's eating you tonight?"

"Maggie, you'll never believe it. It's like—like God's angels just dropped him from the sky!"

Maggie rested her fork on her tin plate and held up her palms. "Hold it. Slow down, fast Freddie. Who was dropped from the sky?"

"Allen." Vera's hands clenched in front of the smile she couldn't hide.

"Allen, as in…"

"The Allen I told you about. Remember? I saw him on the big screen at the movies all those years ago. He's the reason I'm here, Maggie."

Maggie mouthed the word *oh* and leaned back. "He's here? In this hospital?"

"Yes!"

"Why, Vera, that's nothing short of a miracle, is what that is!"

"You ain't a'kiddin', kid!"

"So, go on, tell me details."

A slamming tin tray halted the girls' conversation. Both heads swung upwards to the owner of the meal.

"This is the Army, gals, not some middle school lunch table. Don't spoil my meal."

Vera sucked in her cheeks and folded her arms on the table. Maggie gave a slight roll of her eyes. "Really, Peggy, a little girl time would do you a world of good. You just rained on Vera's parade. She has some perfectly marvelous news to share and you just dampened the mood. Would you kindly allow her to finish?"

"That's okay, kid. I'll catch ya some other time—maybe when the weather *isn't* calling for showers."

Vera pushed herself up from the table and sauntered off. Maggie watched in disappointment as she left. Irritation grew like a fungus in her soul. Peggy struck again, putting a lid on her friend's happy moment.

"Peggy? What happened in the time between the other day and today?"

"What are you griping about now, Lieutenant?"

"What I mean is, we worked well as a team the day of the hospital bombing. And today, you're back to your mean and cruel self. When is enough, enough?" Maggie pushed her food away from her.

"What I don't understand is why you gals have a problem with me. I don't like noise while I eat, and right now…you are noise."

"Fine. Then I'll leave you to yourself and your gloom, little world." Maggie's fork and tin cup rattled on her tray as she lifted it from the table and marched it to the tub. As far as she was concerned, Peggy the Ice Queen could eat, sleep, and work by herself, despite their orders.

Maggie tromped from the mess tent as hard as she could. Her hands were still balled into fists as she recounted her tête-à-tête with Lieutenant Blizzard. A few questioning glances were cast her way as her angry steps put her further away from the subject of her fury.

"Maggie! Maggie, wait up!"

It was Bonnie's voice. Maggie's footsteps slowed, but her nostrils fumed.

"Maggie, what's wrong?"

"Nothing."

Bonnie fell silent and Maggie felt ashamed for snapping. "I'm sorry, Bonnie. I'm just...*mad*."

"Peggy again?" Her voice was small.

"Oh yes. That woman just lives to crawl under my skin and get to me any way she can weasel into it."

"Don't be so hard on her, Maggie. Linda says she has good reason to be the way she is."

"Linda, huh? Well, Linda hasn't told me anything. As a matter of fact, I don't even see Linda now that Mother Winter and I are working together. What could possibly be so bad that gives Peggy the right to treat people the way she does?"

Bonnie's small shoulder raised in a shrug. "Maybe you should ask Peggy about it."

Maggie growled. "Come on, Bonnie Belle. Don't tell me you've taken their side."

"I'm not on any side, Maggie. I just don't want to see you two at odds. I think it's all a big misunderstanding. Peggy—well, she might...need you."

Maggie huffed. "Yeah, a slap across her face is what she needs from me all right."

A sigh escaped Bonnie's lips. "You know, for someone who claims to have the love of Christ, you sure have a funny way of showing it."

Maggie stopped. Is that how her attitude looked to other people? Is that how they perceived her? As the problem?

"You *do* think I'm the hindrance here, don't you? Why Bonnie, I never thought that you'd turn on me. I'm hurt—deeply hurt by that."

Before Bonnie could offer up an explanation, Maggie spun on her heels and stormed off, bumping into a passing soldier.

"Hey, there, sorry 'bout that ma'am."

She turned and glared into his dark eyes. He shuffled backward and his eyes grew wide.

"I'm sorry, I meant Lieutenant." He examined her face.

Maggie halted. Goose-bumps showered her arms, and her encounter sent an eerie shiver down her spine. The hand the soldier used to steady her arm felt all too familiar, but she shoved the feeling away.

The corners of his mouth tipped upward. Was he finding enjoyment in her displeasure or merely drinking in the sight of her? Either way, her uneasiness turned into irritation.

"What's so funny, soldier?"

"Uh, nothing, Lieutenant. You just, well, you look like you've never seen a soldier with guns before."

Maggie blinked. The remainder of her anger drained from her face and she looked carefully into his puppy dog, brown eyes. "What did you say?" A whoosh of breath collapsed her chest.

"Guns, you know…" He flexed his biceps and pointed, clearly enjoying the chance to show off his physical features—even if they were depleted of nourishment.

Unexpected tears sprung to her eyes, bringing back a flood of very vivid memories.

"Danny?" she whispered.

His eyes flickered in the sunlight. "Everyone calls me Joe." He thrust his hand forward.

Not sure what to do, Maggie hesitantly reached for it. "Oh, I— I…excuse me." She bolted before her voice gave way to the tears that clogged her throat. Running as fast as her legs could pump, she raced for her quarters, gasping for breaths between the sobs she worked so hard to hold back.

Once inside her tent, she threw open her trunk and rummaged through her personals, hoping to find the one thing that she'd tried to detach herself from.

"Socks. Gloves. Note paper. More socks! Oh, where is it? Danny, where are you?"

Large, round tears dripped from her eyelashes and into her trunk. She paused to swipe at her eyes and cheeks, and she sniffed back the sobs from her throat. Her fingers combed through the rest of her belongings until they scratched against something metal.

Slipping her fingers around the corner, she pulled out the gold-colored picture frame that held Danny's photograph. Her hand brushed against the smooth glass surface. She could almost feel his skin beneath her fingertips.

More tears brimmed her eyes and fell down her cheeks like a dam giving way beneath flood waters. She rocked back on her heels and clutched the frame tightly against her chest. How could things go from bad to worse to horrible in a matter of minutes? First Peter, then Peggy, and now this. The threads that held her life together were unraveling fast, and her heartaches were exposed to the elements. Maybe she wasn't as robust as she thought. Maybe she *did* set herself and her nursing skills on a pedestal and flaunt her confidence. Now she was hallucinating and seeing her deceased boyfriend in the flesh.

She was a mess. How could one man bring back so many happy memories but create an ache the size of a crater in her heart? Another sob jolted her shoulders and caused her body to shudder. She pulled the frame back enough to see Danny's face.

No, that man couldn't have been Danny. He was too thin. Scruff shadowed his jaw and chin, and he looked as if he hadn't had a bath in ages. Danny Russo would never allow himself to grow shaggy and dirty. No. Danny was dead.

But still...

His grin. His playful banter...

No!

Maggie shoved the frame back inside the bottom of her foot locker and covered it over with her gowns and personals. She'd decided months earlier to move on with her life and not pine for the love that could never be.

But still...those eyes . . .

❧❧

Joe wasn't sure what happened, but by the look on the woman's face, she appeared to have just looked into the face of death.

His hand rubbed against the stubble on his chin.

Those wide, round eyes. Those red lips. He knew he'd lost weight and hadn't had a shower, but he didn't think he looked all that bad. He watched as the startled brunette rushed away from him. What had frightened her?

"Danny?"

Had he imagined it or did she whisper the same name written in the Bible and addressed in the letter? Her voice was barely audible, but he caught the tremor in her voice.

Coincidence? If his weakened body would allow him, he'd run after her, ask her the burning question searing his mind. By the way she fled from him, he guessed he wasn't the only one who felt a linking connection. His heart pulled as if it wanted to leap from his chest and chase after her. In the next moment, his feet pressed forward, following her footsteps. If she thought him to be this Danny, he needed to find her, and fast!

CHAPTER SIXTEEN

His hunt turned up empty. The nurse disappeared into a sea of olive drab housing. Worse yet, her quarters would be in the restricted area—no men allowed! Shoving his hands deeper into his loose pockets, Joe trudged back to the hospital ward with his head hung low.

Something about her sparked a vague memory, but it just wouldn't surface. Frustration and fatigue swept over him. Why was his journey to figuring out who he was always taking him on a wild goose chase or leading him to a dead end? He raked his fingers through his hair. It was time he got back to his hospital bed. His legs were starting to grow weary from the extra walking he'd done in search of that captivating, brunette nurse.

On his way back, the mail call went out and a surge of military personnel swarmed the currier. Joe's feet slowed their pace and he watched as letters from home were distributed into the eager hands of waiting soldiers. A pang of loneliness stung his chest. He hadn't received one piece of mail since gaining consciousness the day he awoke in Oflag 64. What would it feel like to hold a missive addressed specifically to him and read words only meant for his eyes? Knowing the currier wouldn't be calling his name today, Joe carried on down the path toward the hospital ward where his cot awaited him. It was the *only* thing that awaited him.

That nurse...

Her face lingered in his mind. Her expression. Her look of surprise. What raced through her mind as she stared into his eyes? What had she seen that sent her barreling into hiding? The only person in this camp who may hold the key to his existence, and she ran from him like a squirrel up a nut tree, disappearing into its branches.

After his strange encounter with the nurse, Joe returned to his hospital cot and picked Al's brain about the man who delivered the Bible into his friend's hands.

"Did he say who he was?"

"No. He just said he recognized you and was holding your belongings for you. Said he knew you couldn't be dead. The great Danny Russo, he said. Little Italy, he mentioned." Al paused and brought his finger to his chin. "I'd say though, by the patch on his jacket, he was part of the 101st Airborne. Does any of that ring a bell, Joe?"

His brows furrowed, creating deep creases in his forehead as he thought long and hard on Al's query. His head hinged from side to side. "No. I can't say I recall anything like that." His face fell into his palms. "A paratrooper, huh? You think that's what happened to me? A jump gone wrong?"

Al shrugged. "Anything's possible, fella."

And that's where the conversation ended. Now Joe found himself slumped against a pile of old tires. He was alone. Again. Why? Why was God holding out on him? Why couldn't the Great Physician reach out his all-healing hand and return to Joe what was lost?

His eyes lifted to the gray sky above and he pleaded with his Maker. "Father, I don't know what kind of guy I was in the past. But if I was so bad that you had to take my memory from me, I understand. But God, please, give me some indication that I exist. That I have a family, a home. Please."

Just After Midnight, 13 March 1945

What was that?

Joe forced his eyes open. His breath came fast and his pulse quickened. Hadn't someone yelled out? After a minute of contemplative silence, he assured himself it was another nightmare.

Go back to sleep, your mind likes to play with you.

He relaxed into his blanket and pillow, closing his eyes when the drumming of his heart simmered. But no sooner than his eyes closed again, the noise reached his ears a second time. Joe sat up in his cot and shook the sleep from his mind, his heart pounding in his ears as he startled awake. "Al, you hear that?" he mumbled through sleepy jaws.

"Hm? Man, what are you doing? We're trying to sleep here."

Joe ran his hand over his forehead and through his hair. He blew out a sigh then pulled one leg back onto his cot and eased down again, determined to wipe the war from his mind.

"Incoming!"

He stopped. There it was again, but this time it was clearer. He sat up on his cot, giving Al a smack on the shoulder. "Al."

"What!"

"Come on. Someone's outside."

"Joe, it's just the MPs horsing around. Now can I go back to sleep?" He pulled the blanket over his head and nestled against his pillow.

Joe pulled on his boots and grabbed his outside attire. Just as he was finishing up with the buttons on his shirt, a loud boom vibrated the ground, shaking the sleeping soldiers out of their slumber.

"What was that?" This time Al startled awake, alarmed.

"I told you. Something's going on out there."

"Incoming! Incoming wounded! We're being bombarded!"

All at once, panic spread through the ward. Those who could move attempted to jump out of their cots. Others, dazed and perplexed, mumbled unintelligible sentences. The scurrying of night nurses and doctors rushed from the back quarters and out the ward entrances.

"Gentlemen, please!" Several nurses rushed into the area, trying to calm the patients. "You'll be fine, gentlemen. Just some explosions in the distance. We're safe here. The ambulances will be bringing in wounded so just sit tight a bit. If anyone needs help sleeping just let me know." Her mouth smiled, but Joe noticed it didn't reach her eyes, which meant she didn't believe a word that came from her own lips.

Machine gun-fire and droning of plane engines hummed in his ears. An air raid was imminent. His eyes skimmed over the ward of patients. Men too sick to fight or help themselves out of a dangerous situation lay in rows. They far outnumbered the medical personnel.

Another explosion shook the dangling lights overhead and the canopy above them. Joe prayed that the good Lord would prevent disaster from striking the most vulnerable spot on the front.

39ᵗʰ EVAC, Tent 12

Another explosion quaked the tent, this time feeling dangerously close as Maggie shoved her feet into her combat boots.

"Don't forget your helmet, Johnson. Those rounds aren't far off." Peggy jammed her steel helmet over her head and pushed out the door. Maggie didn't have time to button up her field jacket so she let it hang open and followed quickly behind Peggy.

After a rush job of scrubbing and grabbing medical supplies, the men started pouring in. The events taking place outside the tent was pure chaos. Men were being directed in all different directions. Wounded writhed and screamed out in pain, nurses barked out orders, jeeps, trucks, and ambulances were coming and going at alarming speeds. And more shell detonations sent mild concussions over the camp, causing the doctors, nurses, and patients to shudder and duck their heads.

"This is the first wave, ladies. When those trucks return, there will be more wounded right behind them. It will be a long night."

Maggie's heart raced with each thundering burst and each new litter carried into the ward. Her chest ached with compassion for each moan and cry from injured soldiers. But the time had come to put her feelings aside and put her expert nursing skills to the test.

Taking a deep breath, she rushed to the side of a soldier who still awaited an examination. "Hey there, soldier. I'm Maggie. I'm going to take care of you, all right? I just need to take a look at you."

Trembling from loss of blood, he didn't say a word. He only looked at her with half-hollow eyes. Eyes that seemed to say he understood what she was saying—at least she hoped.

She pulled back the compresses on his abdomen and examined the wound. He was going to need surgery. Shrapnel had sliced deeply into his stomach, and infection would set in fast if he didn't receive immediate medical attention. She administered a shot of morphine to ease the pain. Within minutes, the young man relaxed and fell out of consciousness. Shortly after, he was rushed into the OR.

"Father, have mercy on him," she prayed aloud.

She wiped perspiration from her brow with a blood-soaked sleeve and looked around. The ward had filled with torment. Blackened and bloodied bodies lay helplessly on the wooden tables. Supply cabinets were emptied of their contents and turned on their sides to serve as make-shift hospital beds.

And they just kept pouring in.

Maggie's chest constricted. More shells dropped, and the sound of enemy bombers and fighters loomed overhead. A shudder ran down her spine, and she looked precariously at the tent ceiling. The dim lights flickered overhead and swayed back and forth on their cords. Her hands began to perspire and she realized she'd been standing in one spot for far too long.

"Johnson! What do you think you're doing there? Get your rear end in high gear and do your job!"

Jutting her jaw forward and giving her head a shake, Maggie blinked and groped for a wad of gauze. She marched to the patient furthest from Peggy and closest to the door. After quickly assessing her patient's condition, she bandaged up his exposed leg. She prayed as she worked, begging God's merciful hand to reach down and heal the broken.

A burst of cold air filtered into the room and she glanced over her shoulder. A tingling shiver prickled down her face and arms, sliding down her spine, and numbed her legs.

Standing next to her was that haunting face. The picture of a man that was branded into so many of her private memories. A rush of blood drained from her face, causing lightheadedness to assault her senses. It wasn't him. No, it couldn't be Danny. Dipping her chin and closing her eyes until the moment passed, she scolded herself for letting one lone soldier break her concentration. When her eyelashes swept upward again, she glanced back in his direction.

He hadn't seen her standing there. His eyes took in the carnage set before him, but after blinking back the gruesome scene, he back-tracked to the door.

Her pulse quickened.

He was leaving. Why should it bother her? Why did this mysterious man draw her curiosity so?

"Wait!" She didn't know why she called out to him, but the words were already out of her mouth and he was staring at her. "Don't go. I need your help."

∽͡ͽ

The sincerity in the nurse's eyes shot him from behind. Call it a sneak attack, he was stupefied by her beauty. It took him a moment to recover, but when he did, he was awestruck that she was the same nurse he'd encountered just hours earlier.

"Uh...sure. Just tell me what to do." There wasn't time to think about his problems at the moment. The ward was overfilled with wounded and dying men, and the look on the nurse's face disclosed the pressure she was feeling at the present time.

"I need bandages and scissors. I don't care where you get them from, just get them now. And hurry!"

Stumbling across the triage tent, he searched for a medical cabinet, or a tray, or something with the requested supplies. Spotting a large roll of gauze on a nearby tray, he snatched it up and rushed back toward the nurse, trying hard not to catch a glimpse at a gaping stomach or burnt flesh. But the smell he couldn't mask as he weaved his way through the ward.

"Here. I've got the bandages."

"Good. Where's the scissors?"

"Um..."

"You didn't get the scissors." Her shoulders slumped.

"Wait. I've got a knife in my back pocket. A good soldier never leaves it behind." He plucked an army knife from his pocket and unfolded the blade. "Just tell me how much you want and I'll cut it."

He worked side by side with her, helping her bandage the injured, talking her through the ordeal with gentle words.

"You have gifted hands, Lieutenant. Steady and unfaltering."

"Thank you. I'm afraid I don't feel gifted at the moment. I'm a mess on the inside."

Her eyes stayed focused on her patient at hand. Joe studied her profile. Her skin was so smooth, nearly flawless. Her eyes were beautifully shaped with long eyelashes and perfectly placed cheekbones that added to her beauty. But her eyes were also darkened by stress and fatigue. She was most likely awakened by the air raid and rush of wounded soldiers.

Hearing a hushed sniffle from her brought his mind back to the present.

"Come on. Don't die on me, Private." Just above a whisper, her voice pleaded with the young man on the table who'd grown unconscious.

Sensing her panic, Joe spurted out words from scripture. He didn't know where the memory of passage had come from, but he didn't care. "The LORD is my shepherd; I shall not want. He maketh me to lie down in green pastures: he leadeth me beside the still waters. He restoreth my soul: he leadeth me in the paths of righteousness for his name's sake. Yea, though I walk through the valley of the shadow of death, I will fear no evil: for thou art with me; thy rod and thy staff they comfort me. Thou preparest a table before me in the presence of mine enemies: thou anointest my head with oil; my cup runneth over. Surely goodness and mercy shall follow me all the days of my life: and I will dwell in the house of the LORD for ever."

Upon finishing the prayer, her gaze met his. Tears swam in her coffee-colored eyes and she bit on her lip, probably fighting back more emotion. Without thinking, he took her hand in his and smoothed his thumb over her knuckles.

A sharp exhale escaped her lips, but the next sentence out of her mouth knocked him to his knees.

⟡⟡

Was she going crazy?

She was on the brink of another meltdown. Flashbacks from Belgium shrouded her mind, causing panic to seep through the sealed walls of her heart. She couldn't watch another soldier die in her hands. Not on her watch.

But he was dying. The young boy on her table was losing the battle for his life and there was nothing she could do to save him. This was her job. Why couldn't she heal the dying? Just as her mind flooded with overwhelming stress and frustration, the voice next to her began reciting the 23rd psalm. Tears stung her eyes as she fought her best to stop the bleeding on her mortally wounded patient. Like a lullaby, the calming effect of God's words recited to her by a perfect stranger took over her will.

She couldn't do it.

Who lived or died wasn't her decision to make. God was the ultimate healer and sustainer.

Her hands stilled and the young soldier on the table took his final breath. She closed her eyes in a moment of silence for the fallen and when she looked back up again, she was met by the kind and oh so familiar eyes of the man she'd met earlier.

"What are you, a spirit? Were you sent to haunt me?" She shielded her pain by squeezing her eyelids shut.

His hand tightened around hers.

"Miss, I don't know what I am. I've been searching for that very answer, but I'm just as dumbfounded as you are. Perhaps I am a ghost."

Something in his voice seduced her to look up at him. She studied his chiseled and hollowed face, his wavy hair, his slender jaw.

"You look so much like him, and yet, so different."

When his hand reached up to wipe away the tear that trickled down her cheek, she couldn't help but turn into his palm and concentrate on its warmth. So much like Danny's—so much.

It had been so long.

"Your eye. What happened?"

She touched the gash caused by the jeep's window frame. "It's just a scratch. It'll be fine." She avoided his manly, caring gaze.

"You mentioned a certain name yesterday." He hesitated and waited for her eyes to meet his. "Am I...who is Danny?"

Her heart leaped so far from her chest and up her throat she pressed her hands against the curve of her mouth in hopes it wouldn't escape.

She wanted this man to be him, but...

"The Germans have broken the line! We need any able bodied men to the front. Pronto!"

Maggie's nerves vaulted when the officer stormed into triage, instantly breaking the contact between she and this *apparition*. She snatched her hands back and ran them up and down her arms, warming the chills that settled into her bones.

The officer shot a glance at the dark-haired GI standing in front of her and pointed a finger. "You. Are you well? Grab a rifle and get to the jeeps."

Alarm swept across Maggie's face. "No! He's a patient. He can't go."

The soldier's face jerked her way and he touched a hand to her shoulder. "I'm well enough. I have to go, ma'am. I'm better than most in here and they need my help."

He turned to follow the officer, but Maggie bounded for his arm. "Wait! Don't go. What about all of them?" She gestured to the triage ward.

"I'll return. But will you do me a favor? Will you tell me your name so I know how to find you?"

"Come on, man! There's no time for blabbering idiots!" The officer nudged him from behind.

He looked as if he didn't want to leave any more than she wanted him to. Without speaking, she shook her head, pleading with him to stay as he neared the door, but his feet carried him through the triage doors, finally breaking the eye contact between them.

She barged out into the night and called after him. "Maggie! It's Maggie! Maggie Johnson!"

CHAPTER SEVENTEEN

"Soldier! We need back up!" The sergeant on foot strained his voice above the barrage of bullets to call out to Joe as they rushed into a field screened with smoke. The Germans made a surprise attack on the camp and the surrounding areas. Shells dropped and cratered the ground beneath and in front of them. Men were hurt, and more troops rushed in to aid. With his body still wasted and starved, Joe shouldn't be charging into battle, but who said war was fair? This platoon was short-numbered and when asked to help, how could he say no? His brothers in arms dropped like flies all around them. As feeble as he may be, Joe could still stand. So he was back in the Army.

Joe positioned himself in a trench and fired his gun on the enemy. The battle carried on back and forth for some time. Their radio technician put in a call for help, and they waited for reinforcement from the Royal Air Force.

"What's it look like up there?" he asked a passing soldier as he reloaded his gun. Funny. His memory of his personal life may be gone, but his soldiering skills came to him as if they'd never departed him.

"I can't see a thing. We don't know these parts like they do. That's what worries me. We're shooting blind."

"Everybody down! I've got the big guns right here!" From behind, one soldier barreled to the front with a flame thrower slung over his shoulder. He marched forward, launching fiery liquid in front of them and sending a burst of heat and smoke into the air. "Someone cover me. I'm going in!"

"No!" Joe called out from the trench. "The flame will give away our position! Get back here!"

The poor idiot ignored the order and kept walking forward. Soon a barrage of gunfire splintered the air and pounded the trenches, somehow missing the man altogether. A rain of dirt and rock sprayed the men.

"Stanley, you idiot! You're gonna get us killed!"

"Spread out. Go either way. Some to the right, some to the left. We can make this work. If they think we're directly behind Stanley, we can surprise them on both sides." They quietly tiptoed their way closer toward the enemy's front line. As long as they could see the flash of German's guns, they knew where the enemy took cover.

"There's one right there." Joe's words carefully limped off his lips in a tight whisper. He pointed to a large rock covered with greens. "He's under the brush. You can see the shine of his rifle from the moonlight." The second soldier nodded and the two men jumped the German and gagged him to keep him quiet. They couldn't afford a gunshot tipping off their positioning in a mess of Germans.

"There now. You keep quiet, you keep your life." The man next to Joe, named Duke, growled at the young German. After tying the soldier to a tree and taking his weapons, Joe and Duke advanced further into enemy territory.

"If we get out of here alive, I'm going to get our heads examined. It's just the two of us here, man. This is crazy." Joe kept a keen eye out for more snipers.

"We'll be okay. If I remember correctly, there's a foxhole here somewhere. Most likely there are a few of them hiding inside."

"That's great. Now I gotta look out for a foxhole full of Germans. I can't even see where I'm going."

Duke breathed a shaky laugh. "You'll know when you've stumbled upon it."

Before the two men could go any further, the dull hum of aircraft thrummed in the distance.

"I hope that's a friendly."

The hum grew louder. "It's friendly, Duke. Oh, no." There was one problem. Joe's face dropped. "Duke, we're in front of the line."

"Shoot! Run!" They shuffled back the way they came before the planes dropped their bombs. Just as the American line came into sight, the whirling of a shell whistled above them.

"Duke, pick up your speed and dive."

Joe ran for cover under a patch of trees and brush, and covered his head in the fetal position. He felt Duke dive in right behind him. As they hit the ground, the shell exploded, and debris flew into the air, followed by a deafening roar and a storm of rock and dirt. Then another shell exploded, and another. They stayed under the cover of brush until the ground stopped shaking and until the planes left the region. Minutes that could have passed for hours slipped by.

"You okay, man?" Duke asked.

"Yeah. I'm good. You?"

"Not so much as a scratch." Duke sat up and removed his helmet as he wiped beads of sweat from his brow. "That was a close one."

"Yeah." Joe took a few deep breaths before standing to his feet. "Let's head back. See where the guys are."

But another wave of explosions knocked them to their knees—this time the horror of the shells' explosions sent a chilling fright through Joe's body as he looked westward.

"The hospital!"

✎✎

"Lieutenant, we have two ambulances out back, but they won't transport this number of men."

Maggie winced at the driver's conclusion. "Of course not. They're out bringing more in. What about the supply trucks?"

"They're still outside."

Maggie looked at the GI, her eyes straightforward and serious. "Do you think we can load the men into the back of the trucks? If we set them together and cover them with blankets, they should be able to keep warm enough to make it to the next chain hospital."

"I'm on it, Lieutenant." The private hurried a salute then turned and rushed out the door. Pushing away from her own station in a rush, Maggie went in search of others to help.

"Vera, Bonnie!" By the time Maggie found her friends, she was out of breath and her hair was in disarray from tending to the wounded. "There you are. The ambulances are out back, and we need to use the supply trucks to transport the stable patients to another evacuation hospital. What do you think?"

"We have no choice. They keep pouring in."

Maggie nodded in agreement and rushed off to get the patients ready for transport.

She walked to a young soldier who watched the scene from his bed. When Maggie began unhooking his IVs, he grabbed for her arm. Her fingers relaxed against the small hose and glass bottle and her eyes skirted down to him. He was just a kid, maybe no more than eighteen. Her eyes locked with his for the briefest of moments, but she saw evidence of fear and pain embedded deep inside them. "It's okay," she told him. "We're going to transport you to another hospital. You'll be more comfortable there and away from all this." She swept her free hand over the chaotic scene.

"Will I recover?" The young man asked. Maggie stooped down to his bedside and rubbed his hand.

"You will. In time. But it's going to take some strong medications and a strong heart. We'll do our best to take care of you and get you home." Her voice was soft and calm. Like a mother speaking to her child in a comforting tone. The young soldier's eyes filled with moisture and he looked away from her. "Would you like me to say a prayer for you?"

His head swung around, nodding slowly.

"Okay." Maggie bowed her head and grabbed the boy's hand as she prayed. "Father, we thank you for your tender mercies. I ask that you will please be with our boys tonight. Please heal the sick and wounded and allow them full recoveries and safety as they make their way home. Please be with...with..." She opened her eyes and checked the clipboard for her young patient's name then went on, "Please be with Michael, ease his pain, Father, and comfort his soul during this time. In Jesus' name, amen."

"Thank you, ma'am." His lips smiled with a weakened effort. Maggie patted his head.

"You're welcome. I'll be praying for you."

From across the room, Maggie caught Peggy's indignant glare, but underneath the surface, Maggie knew Peggy's blood boiled. Maggie's eyes shot back a questioning look. What was the deal this time? Was a simple prayer for healing not acceptable now? With a sharp jerk of her riled head, Peggy turned her back to Maggie and concentrated on her patient.

Maggie finished unhooking Michael's IVs and prepared him for transport, calling the litter bearers to remove him from the ward and board him in the supply truck. Then she moved to the next patient until all the men they could fit in the trucks and ambulances had reached full capacity. Exploding shells in the distance reminded her how precious time was right now. These men needed to be evacuated as quickly as possible before another surge of wounded overcrowded the hospital. With heavy barrage of artillery clapping a mere six miles to their east, more soldiers were bound to flood their gates.

And there was still more wounded to tend to. She wiped her brow and moved down the line. Men treated with morphine syrettes had the tubes pinned to their shirts to prevent overdosing. When Maggie saw the syrettes, she examined their wounds then was burdened with the daunting task of making the decision to move them into surgery or the shock ward. That was the routine Maggie found herself in for the time being.

Reading off checklists and pinning medication notes to the soldiers, Maggie found her mind traveling back to earlier in the evening when that mysterious soldier arrived to help. His face continued to inhabit the corners of her mind, plaguing her with haunting hallucinations.

Her eyes blurred from exhaustion. She squeezed them shut and rubbed the sleep away. At least that's what she told herself. Her legs ached and her feet longed for a break. A shudder ran through her body. Her chest became heavy, and she gasped for a breath. What was going on with her?

Air. She needed a breath of fresh air away from the stench of burned skin and open wounds.

She pinned the last medical tag to the last patient in the triage tent and made haste for the tent door flap. Her fist compressed against her midsection, begging God to calm the thrashing sea in the pit of her belly. When was the last time she'd eaten? Too long, she couldn't remember.

"Lieutenant Johnson, I'm glad you're here." A doctor caught the crook of her arm. "I have an amputation to do, I need your help. It's an emergency."

"Amputation?" Maggie's eyes grew wide. Although she'd seen open chests and stomachs, she had yet to assist in an amputation procedure. Her face paled, stealing the last of her strength. She wasn't ready for this.

"Lieutenant? Are you coming?" His eyes were impatient.

From the other side of the table, Linda took one look at Maggie, identifying right away what the problem was. "Maggie, you can do this. I'll tell you a little trick. They taught us this in training. Don't watch the initial cut. Wait until after the doctor is finished with the first cut to look. If you watch you'll faint. Okay? Do you understand?"

Maggie nodded, but her head still swam as if she bobbed on the sea.

"Come on, I'll walk you through it." Linda led Maggie to the operating table where the doctor and patient waited. "Okay, doctor, we're ready."

Maggie's hands became wet with perspiration. Tonight, the thought of sawing off a limb made her sway. But she resolved to stand firm and focus her attention on the patient and his needs. She took the advice Linda gave her and didn't watch the first incision. Although Maggie cringed at the sight and sounds of the procedure, she stayed alert and listened carefully to the doctor's instructions.

"All right, time to close him up. Nurse, needle and silk."

"Yes, doctor." Maggie handed him the supplies. "Needle and thread."

Another nurse came to the operating table and removed the limb from the table. As she walked off with it, Maggie felt flush and breathing became difficult. A low buzzing sound muffled her ear. Her eyes wanted to roll and her eyelids were closing on their own. Before she fell to the floor two nurses grabbed her by the arms and dragged her out of the OR.

"Come on, Maggie. It's time to snap out of it." Linda slapped Maggie's cheeks with cold, wet hands.

Maggie's eyes fluttered open. "Oh dear," she squeaked. "Linda?"

"Yup. It's me."

"Did I—"

"Went out like a light, honey."

Maggie's hand went to her forehead. "How embarrassing. I've never done that before. I'm so sorry."

"Don't be sorry, honey. It happens to the best of us."

"At least you made it through the amputation." Bonnie found her way to Maggie's side.

"I was fine until the nurse took—" Maggie choked. "I—it away."

"You're tired, exhausted. We all are."

It was easy for them to say. She was the unmovable Maggie Johnson. Able to handle any crisis. But her body had committed treason against her, showing the whole surgical staff that she wasn't invincible.

The women helped Maggie to her feet and took her into the shock ward for soda crackers and water.

"I'm feeling better now, girls. I think I can get back to work."

Linda's head shook side to side. "Oh, no. I think it may be best for you to stay put a while. Getting up so quickly may flatten you."

"Really, Linda, I'll be fine. It's been quite some time since I've had anything to eat. I'm just famished."

A screaming whistle tore through the sky above their tent. All three girls bounced looks one to another. Maggie's eyes widened, but before she could speak her warning, an ear-splitting burst pushed their bodies into the dirt floor. The ground rumbled and shook and screams pierced the night from outside the tent.

Sore from the tumble, Maggie pushed herself up with an unsteady balance. No longer did she feel dizzy and lightheaded—her pulse throbbed too hard to be short of blood. "Linda, Bonnie, are you all right?"

The girls nodded, but were slow to make it to their knees. Another round of eruptions and blasts forced them back down on their stomachs and caused them to press their hands over their ears.

Dread swallowed Maggie whole. "We're being bombed!"

CHAPTER EIGHTEEN

Maggie struggled to her feet, her hands attempting to block out the piercing resonance of detonating bombs. When she exited the supply tent, her eyes looked on in horror as the OR tent she'd just left moments earlier was in ruins and flaming.

"NOooo!" Her scream shrieked into the night air, and her legs pumped as hard as they could, carrying her to the wreckage of burning timber and canvas. She shielded her face against the heat. It prevented her from pressing closer to the bombed-out operating tent. Tears rolled down her face as she cried out for Vera and Peggy. She searched through the fire and haze with fervor.

No one answered.

"Maggie!" Two female voices called after her. She felt their presence pull up beside her and two sets of shivering arms wrapped around her shoulders.

"They're gone." Linda's broken speech was salted with unspeakable sorrow. Behind her, Bonnie only whimpered from the folds of her hands.

Members of the camp wandered around like sleepwalkers, taking in the devastation and moving on. They too weren't able to believe what they saw in front of them.

Linda sniffed and raised her chin. "There's nothing we can do here, ladies. Let's get to where we *can* make a difference."

"B—but what about Vera?" Bonnie wailed into the collar of her jacket.

Although it pained her to say it, Maggie urged Bonnie to follow Linda. "She's right, Bonnie. There's nothing we can do." Two large tears fell from her eyes.

The trio turned and started for triage, knowing that's where their work awaited them. From the shadows, two silhouettes limped toward them.

"Maggie? Linda, Bonnie? Is that you?"

Maggie's chin jerked up and she squinted into the dark, hoping that familiar voice was who she thought it was. The closer she came to the two figures, the more distinct their faces became.

"Vera? Peggy? You're alive? Is it really you?"

"It's us, kid. A little banged up, but we made it out before the bomb exploded."

A thrill launched Maggie into Vera's arms. She laughed and cried in hysteria over the miracle that her friend was spared. "Oh, Vera, I was so worried. I thought that—"

Vera clutched Maggie close. "I know. I was afraid I'd died and the Lord kept me here for punishment."

A bittersweet laugh escaped Maggie's chest. Releasing her hold on Vera, she turned to Peggy. "Are you all right, Peggy?"

A flash of relief flitted through Peggy's darkened eyes, hinting that for an instant she was glad for the inquiry on her health. "I'm fine," she answered. Then it was back to her short, brash manner.

Although Peggy's words were clipped, Maggie was thankful for the bark. She and Peggy may not be on the best of terms, but she certainly didn't wish death on any of the gals of the 39th.

The gals . . .

Alarm surged inside Maggie, and her eyes darted around the burning camp. "Ladies, where's Helen?"

"I—I don't know," Vera answered.

All four women paced back and forth as their eyes scanned the carnage.

"I don't see her." Linda wrung her hands in front of her. "Triage. She must be in triage."

Vera pointed to the wards that weren't on fire. "Over to triage, ladies."

"Oh, wait." Maggie stopped and the others peered over at her. "Let me grab some supplies. We were running low before they swept me in for surgery. And I can look for Helen over there."

Vera waved a hand and cast a worried glance up at the sky. The sounds of war hadn't halted and still kept everyone on high alert. "Don't worry about it, Maggie. Someone else probably already replenished the cabinets. We have to stick together."

"I'll just grab some extras, just in case. It'll save time if no one hasn't, and we'll cover more ground while we search for Helen." Before the others could discourage her further, she bolted through the fiery paths of tents and bucket lines of soldiers who worked tirelessly at putting out the flames. Rounding a corner, she rushed into the medical supply tent where Captain Baker was already emptying the shelves of its contents.

"Lieutenant Johnson, what are you doing here?"

"Apparently the same thing you came here for. Let me help you." She dug her hands into the cabinet and scooped up bottles of pain killer and antibiotics. Then she stuffed bandages and gauze into her tunic pockets.

"Get some plasma too. We're gonna need lots of it."

"Right away, Captain." She stuck the bottles into the pockets of her trousers and jacket and sidestepped the large desk in front of the second medical cabinet full of plasma. She grabbed handfuls of those too.

Time marched forward. It seemed an eternity passed as she clawed at the medicine cabinet to empty its contents completely into the medical bag she'd pulled from a nearby table. There was no concept of time. It seemed to suspend itself in mid-air, nagging her that any moment could be her last. She was living on borrowed time. Replaying the events of the day over in her mind, it was difficult to determine fact from fiction or how long ago she'd said good-bye to that emaciated soldier lurking in the shadows.

Another explosion brought her mind back to the present.

"Okay, got everything I can take, Captain. I'm heading to triage."

She drove her legs forward, shoving aside anything that stood in her way, but another whistling screech stopped her in her tracks. Her eyes widened in fear as the scream grew louder until...

An angry wave suspended her in the air like a rag doll tossed against a brick wall. A roar louder than anything else she'd ever heard pounded into her skull and darkened her vision.

In one second, everything around her shattered and she faded into a dark and terrifying abyss.

≪৯৶≫

The exploding shell was a direct hit!

Joe's body went numb when he saw the big, red cross painted on the hospital tent fly into the air along with everything under it.

"Please, God," was all he could say as is legs carried him faster toward the burning inferno. "Let them be okay, Father." But he was thinking mainly of one petite brunette nurse as he breathed the silent prayer.

His eyes widened as the camp came into view.

Not the hospital tent. All installations bearing the red cross were protected by the Geneva Convention. They were not to be hit by enemy fire. And yet, here it was, obliterated.

Several foot soldiers followed behind him, all hoping to find the same thing—survivors. But when he reached the sight, he was sickened by the gore before him. A doctor and two nurses were among the dead.

Stooping down he checked their faces, hoping among the casualties he didn't find the nurse who'd captured his attention.

A few tents over, patients were still being evacuated. But the individuals moving the wounded out seemed to walk a little slower, seemingly dazed. Moans and bellows cried from men's mouths, causing a deep-rooted chill to sink far into Joe's bones. Men blackened by burns and dirt wandered like living corpses across the tattered camp. Forcing his concentration to the pile of twisted medical tables and supplies, he began digging through the rubble for any possible survivors. His hands cupped over his mouth and he called out, listening for any response, even a moan, to answer him. He turned over pieces of wood, metal, and cloth, looking desperately for someone who may need him. But it was difficult to see anything with the orange glow of fire shining in his eyes. Shielding them, he squinted and tried refocusing his gaze into the mangled mess before him.

Sweat beaded on his forehead and he wiped the perspiration from his brow. His hands stung from minor burns he received while lifting smoldering debris from the ground. He'd been digging for nearly an hour now, praying someone would answer. Each time he spotted a limb he hoped he'd found a survivor, but once uncovered, it was too late. More litter bearers answered his casualty call and pulled bodies from the wreckage. Draping his elbows across his knees, he sat and sipped water from his canteen. His arms and legs had grown weary. He needed a moment to recover, but he wanted strength to press on. He had to.

"Lord, please let there be a survivor. Anyone. I pray not all were lost."

He allowed silence to settle over him. He waited for God's peace to take over and still his wearied mind and body.

That's when he heard it. A faint yell for help. He cupped his ear for better listening. The tiny cry came from a spot about thirty feet from where the hospital tent once stood. Joe rose to his knees, concentrating. Then he gathered his feet under him and ran toward the meek sound.

Her eye sockets hurt, her head throbbed, and her throat burned with fierce intensity. Maggie gasped for air but sharp pains shot through her back and chest causing her to cough painfully. Breathing was more than difficult, it was unbearable. She took quick, short gasps of breath. Her ears felt stuffed with cotton. When she could open her eyes, she realized what pinned her down. A large, metal medicine cabinet lay on top of her, trapping her beneath its heavy exterior. Her body was cold, numb, and drained of all will power. Her mind wasn't her own and her body overpowered her will to stay conscious.

Oh, if she could only open her eyes longer than a few seconds.

Through the mental haze, she tried to comprehend what just happened and how she got into this awkward position. A few moments later, grogginess started to dissipate and her thoughts cleared.

She was on the floor, pinned. Something forced to her to the ground. Oh yes. She remembered now. The explosion sent the tent, and everything in it, soaring into the air. The shell's concussion washed over Maggie and made her head feel as if she were going to explode when she was thrown into the air and pushed backward. Everything was muffled and seemed unreal as the incident unraveled. It all happened so fast, yet she felt every excruciating second. But to her astonishment, she never felt herself hit the ground.

Blinking back shock, Maggie looked from side to side. When she looked to her right, she met Captain Baker's vacant eyes staring back at her.

"Captain Baker? Can you hear me, sir?" It came out raspy, and pain shot through her chest, causing her to choke.

The captain didn't answer her. She closed her eyes and tried to blink out of her blurred vision. When her sight cleared enough to make out Captain Baker's facial features through the orange glow of embers, Maggie let out a scream. The captain was dead and his cold eyes focused on her. A frightening chill raced up her back and raised the hairs on her arms.

"Help me! Please, someone help!" Pain pierced her body like hundreds of needles penetrating her every layer of skin. Screaming for help would be of no use. The agony was too much.

And no one was coming.

The moments slipped by. Her nerves trembled from fear and the uneasiness of being in extreme discomfort and left alone...with a man who was dead and whose icy glare was glued to her face. A whimper escaped her mouth, but even that hurt. She couldn't even cry.

"Lord, help me. I'm so frightened. Get me out of here, please."

Her eyes clamped shut and she called out in quieter tones, hoping someone passing by would hear her and rescue her from this death pit. But each call for help became weaker. The stabbing pain in her lungs and chest cavity wouldn't allow her to continue much longer. Her eyes fluttered and she fought to maintain consciousness.

Don't close your eyes, Maggie. Don't succumb to the dark.

She was about to give up when she heard a man's voice. "I'm coming. Keep calling out."

A thrill of hope bounced in her heart. "Here! I'm over here! I'm pinned down." Maggie yelled out as much as her body would let her before a coughing fit overcame her. Finally she could hear the man throwing debris off of her. Little by little small slivers of light began to rain down on her.

"I see you. I'm here. Hang on. I'm going to lift the cabinet off you. Can you move?"

"I don't...know. I can't...with this thing on me. I'm so cold...and numb." Her voice came out desperate, shaky, yet relieved.

The cabinet's weight lessened then her rescuer groaned. Single handedly, he managed to toss the mangled, metal body off her. Immediately, she gasped for air as if she'd been holding it for the whole duration. But then coughing, caused by pain, strangled the air from her lungs.

"Thank you, God. Are you okay?" Her hero knelt down beside her and searched her face. His hand prodded her cheeks and forehead, his eyes probed her facial features.

"I feel much better with that off of me. Ooooh." Maggie made an attempt to move but fell back when more pain shot up her left arm and side. "It hurts too much."

"Just take it easy. There's a lot of blood and I'm not sure where it's all coming from. I'll help. Just let me know if it hurts too badly. I don't have a litter. So I'll have to lift you myself." Gently, strong arms lifted her to a sitting position. Her eyelids fluttered open and closed under the intensity of the pain, but instinctively, her arms wrapped around his neck for support. When her eyes opened again she gazed into the familiar eyes of Danny Russo.

"Danny? You came for me."

CHAPTER NINETEEN

"I need a medic over here!" Joe caught a glimpse of the last ambulance being loaded for evacuation. He cupped his hands over his mouth. "Hey!" He watched with frantic eyes as the ambulance driver ducked inside the vehicle and hit the gas. "Wait, you numbskulls!"

Joe's arms waved through the air, but it was no use. They were gone. And so was his last hope of saving the individual trapped beneath the rubble. Heaving a frustrated and defeated breath, he went to work and lifted debris from the collapsed tent.

To his surprise, a familiar face searched out his from beneath the carnage.

As soon as Lieutenant Johnson's brown eyes peered up at him, relief deflated Joe's lungs. She was alive. But she wasn't out of the woods. Blood stained her face that was smudged with dirt and grime. Her fatigues bore holes, and droplets of blood seeped through the outer layer of her uniform. He must be gentle while prying her out of the rubble.

An army doctor lying almost face to face with her stared on in a mangled mess. How long was she lying next to him? Surely a horrifying sight for the girl. Thankfully, the weight of the cabinet and desk wasn't too much for him to heft on his own. He wasn't sure where the extra strength came from, but he had a hunch the Lord had something to do with it.

As he assisted the nurse, he noticed the tight grimace on her face and the tensing of her muscles. Her thinned lips seemed to bite back yelps that pooled in her eyes instead. Then with her first good glance at him, she stilled and a ghastly expression shadowed her beautiful face.

"Danny? You came for me."

Joe's breath caught when her fingers stretched out to touch his face. Her light brush, like silk sweeping across his skin, made him turn into her touch. Something stirred in his gut, causing his heart to palpitate.

"Is it you? Or am I caught in a dream?"

He wished he knew.

"Lieutenant, I don't know if I am or not, but I sure wish I could find some answers—for you *and* for me." Her hand fell to her side, but he caught her arm and assisted her to a nearby crate. She kept her right arm tucked into her abdomen. "Sit here a minute and catch your breath. Then tell me where the pain is."

"It's in my right wrist. I think it's broken. And in my side. It's a sharp pain that shoots right back to my lungs."

Joe peeked at Maggie's back. There was no blood and no protruding bones, so the pain was from inside. "We need to get you to another hospital."

"I think the convoys have left. I don't know how long I was under that mess. We were getting all the wounded men evacuated. Then the explosion...oh, my head is pounding." Her head rolled back and a sob worked its way from her throat.

Joe sat and thought a moment. How was he going to get her to a medic? All the medics were on the front lines and the rest of the hospital had retreated, not to mention the medical personnel who were killed in the explosion. "Hey, stay with me. We may have to stay here a while until another ambulance comes through. We could walk, but then we'd risk enemy fire and I don't think you should make that kind of a trip." He looked over his shoulder. The camp was destroyed. Nothing was left but tattered tents and a few standing poles. And the dead. Unfortunately, not everyone had made it out alive.

"How long do you think it will take until another convoy comes through?" Her voice was interrupted by another dry, painful cough.

"Take it easy there." Joe moved to her side. He placed one hand on her back and the other he placed on her arm, as gently as possible. She kept her head down, whether it was from the discomfort and difficulty breathing or just the shock of being bombed, he wasn't sure he knew. But as he studied her profile, something familiar generated a sudden swell of protectiveness in him. Just being this close to her created a wholeness to his person. He couldn't explain the feeling nor could he pinpoint what prompted this reaction from him, but somehow he knew this woman held information that would bring him answers.

A moan, quiet as a mouse's cry, slipped from her lips. "It hurts everywhere."

His eyes scanned their surroundings for a spare cot, but found nothing near. "I'll do everything I can to keep you comfortable." While studying her profile, he realized his hands still lingered against her back and arm. Not sure if he was adding to her discomfort or his, he removed his hold on her and reached for his canteen. "Here. It's not much, but drink as much as you want. Maybe the water will help."

"Thank you."

She didn't seem too interested in talking at the moment—and for good reason—so Joe stood and studied the sky. The camp fell quiet with the exception of crackling flames at the edge of its perimeter. More battle sounds boomed in the distance and tracers lit dotted lines across the skies. Other than that far-off confirmation of life, the air around Joe, and the girl suffering beside him, stilled. It seemed everyone had moved out while he was still digging. Most of the foot soldiers had returned to the front while the hospital retreated. The poor girl was probably considered dead.

Hm. That was an interesting thought. He too was most likely considered Killed In Action. Now it seemed he wasn't the only one among the walking dead. For some strange reason, the notion brought comfort to his perplexed mind.

∽∾

The after-midnight temperatures were falling fast and the low-tone, thundering booms of shells still resonated in the air. Thankfully, the sounds were moving east—away from them. Joe knew they couldn't stay under a blanket of stars, so he needed to find shelter fast. His survival instincts took over and before thinking twice, he scrounged the camp for a few supplies to build a make-shift shelter. However, something above ground, visible to enemy, was not a good idea in the event Germans stormed into the camp.

Finding a broken spade, he cut into the earth. If he could build a shelter half above ground, he may be able to pull off a camouflaged dwelling. He set out to search for the shallow trenches that outlined the place where tents once stood, knowing the already dug holes would be his best covering of protection.

Periodically, he checked on Lieutenant Johnson, making sure she was comfortable and hadn't succumbed to sleep just yet. He was too afraid to move her in the fragile state she was in, not knowing what other injuries her body suffered beneath the covering of her clothes.

Two hours later, when the smoke had lifted and revealed a sheet of stars that stippled the dark canvas of space, Joe completed their temporary shelter for the night. Among the wreckage of tattered tents, bent metal, and splintered wood, he'd also found enough medical supplies to rig up a tourniquet and splint for Lieutenant Johnson's wrist. She'd hardly spoken a word, too overcome with pain and shock.

Sweat dripped from his forehead and trickled down his back. When he reached Lieutenant Johnson, she lay half-awake against a wooden crate. The extra blanket he'd found for her was draped across her shoulders and chest, and she shivered beneath the wool covering.

"Lieutenant? Are you able to move?"

Her eyes fluttered open, but they stared far away as if unaware that he was standing next to her.

"Lieutenant?" He drew to his knees and tried to pull her attention from whatever it was that held her gaze.

"I've never been one to believe in apparitions."

His brows creased, but curiosity made him look over the deserted camp. However, haunted by images no one should ever have to see, he was half afraid of what he'd see as his eyes turned across the horizon.

"I don't see anyone or anything, Lieutenant."

Her chestnut hair fell across her forehead as her head swiveled to look at him. The slightest of smiles pulled on her lips. His heart skipped at the beauty he saw within—even with dirt and blood smudged across her face, a physical attraction was growing inside him for her.

"I was talking about you, soldier."

"Me?"

"You're not real, are you? I hoped and wished that it was so, but really this is all a dream. I'm actually lying somewhere beneath the rubble, unconscious—perhaps dying." She paused to look out across the field one more time before turning her eyes back to his.

The soft moonlight and occasional glow of exploding shells illuminated her face in a gentle light. Her eyes glistened in the midst of all the hurt and turmoil of the night. But somewhere, she gathered the strength to lift her hand and brush her fingers against his cheek. So soft and endearing was the gesture he couldn't help but grasp for the warmth of her hand and hold it close to his jaw.

When she spoke again her voice was barely a whisper. "Are you here to torment me? To remind me of all the things I never said that I should have?" The glisten in her eyes now stemmed from tears. "That I should have waited for you?"

Questions and confusion swirled in Joe's head. What was this woman blabbering about? Talk of ghosts and hauntings...what did it all mean? Who did she think he was?

"Lieutenant, tell me more about this Danny."

Maggie could feel him, see him, and talk to him, but he was so different than she remembered. He talked as if he didn't know her. There was no humor in his voice.

But he was familiar.

Tears brimmed her eyes as he looked at her with hollow perception. Not once had he called her by her given name. And not once did he react to her calling him Danny. Instead he only stared back with confusion clouding his dirt-stained face.

She was going crazy. She didn't know what to believe. Why couldn't she decipher what was real and what was simply an illusion? Her head still pounded from the bomb's concussion, and every ounce of her body stabbed with pain. Oh, how she wanted to sleep and wake up to find herself alive in a hospital bed somewhere, but her hero wouldn't let that happen.

"Here, Lieutenant. I found some codeine tablets. I was hoping maybe that would help with the pain."

He'd been so kind, preparing a shelter for her, making sure she had medical supplies, and ready to bandage up her broken wrist and cuts. He'd also made sure he found pain killers to help with her discomfort. Yet, she couldn't do a single thing for him in return.

"Thank you." She accepted the offered water from his canteen. "I'm not accustomed to being on the receiving end of medical aid. I'm sorry if I've been a difficult patient."

That sentence came out right. She sounded a bit more like herself, not like the lethargic Maggie from a few hours before.

"Not at all, Lieutenant. I'm thankful the Lord led me to you."

His words caused her to study him while he finished tying closed the flap on the small tent. He'd found a flashlight that survived the air raid and now used it to secure the ties to their housing.

She watched as the muscles in his back flexed beneath his shirt. She considered the way he stooped and balanced on his feet and the way his dark, black hair curled around his ear. Why was she being tormented like this? Her heart wanted to believe it was him. That Danny lived…and was the one stooping beside her.

"What's your name, soldier?"

His face acknowledged her for a brief moment then he tapped the flashlight against his palm as he sat back against the ground and faced her. "I wish I could tell you that. But I told you once, my friends call me Joe."

"What about your last name?"

"I couldn't tell you, ma'am."

"I've never heard anything so absurd."

"Lieutenant, it's not that I can't tell you—it's just that—I *can't* tell

137

you. I don't remember a thing before June eighth, nineteen forty-four."

"Amnesia? Are you telling me you have amnesia?"

"I guess so, ma'am. The Army hasn't acquired my dental records as of yet and ain't got a clue as to who I am. *I* don't know who I am, and the enemy don't know who I am. So maybe your allegation that I'm an apparition is correct, because…I don't have an identity."

"But what about your dog tags? Surely you've checked those."

He was shaking his head. "No, ma'am. When I awoke in the prison camp, they were gone. Everything I'd had in my pockets were gone. The Germans took everything I would've had on me. Funny thing is I don't know why I was the only man in the camp without an ID. Well, they gave me a number anyway, but there was no name to go with that number. So I became prisoner number 102783."

New pain jabbed Maggie's stomach. Not for herself, but for the man who sat across from her. Tears stung her eyes. She couldn't say anything but, "I'm sorry."

"Don't feel bad for me. I've done enough of that to last the lifetime I don't remember."

"So your buddies nicknamed you."

"The GI named Joe. It sounds more like a joke, doesn't it?" He twirled a twig between his fingers then snapped it in half with the pressure from his thumb.

"No. I don't think there's anything funny about it."

For the longest time he avoided her gaze and wrestled his fingers. What must he be feeling right now? Here he is a liberated prisoner of war who had a history—most likely a story to go down in the text books—and no one knew he existed. No one except for her.

The longer he stayed silent the longer she allowed herself to take in his appearance. The resemblance was uncanny. If she could get him to smile then she'd know. If she could get him to laugh, she'd be certain.

"You never answered my question. Who is Danny, Lieutenant?"

Had he been reading her thoughts?

She shifted uncomfortably under the blanket that kept her warm, but a shiver still ran down her spine when he mentioned Danny's name.

"He was someone very dear to me."

"*Was?*"

Her head bobbed up and down, too afraid to voice her answer for fear of caving into her already shaken and emotional state. But her strength returned, if only a little, and found the words to go on. "Just before Danny left me for the final time, he asked me to wait for him. He told me he loved me and wanted to get married when he came home, but…"

"But he never came home."

Again, she nodded. "We couldn't even have a funeral. The whole thing was a mess—the way I found out he was killed, then there was no body to ship back to the States. They—the Army never found him. He just vanished from the earth, from my life."

"I'm sorry, Lieutenant."

"It's funny, Joe, at first I was upset, then life went on and I was okay with what happened. He was safe in the arms of Jesus, but now...now I'm plagued with his image following me everywhere I go. Ever since I transferred to the thirty-ninth, it's like little reminders are planted wherever I go. Then you—well, you're the spitting image of my Danny."

With that confession, she wanted to throw herself into his arms and nuzzle against his neck, imagine the smell of his musty cologne, anything to put her mind to ease and rest in the assurance that Danny had come back from the land of the forgotten.

But she couldn't. The man sitting in front of her didn't know her. Didn't know himself. So as she told herself, he was an apparition.

❧❦

It wasn't easy to pull her eyes away from the man sitting across from her, but at some point, the two of them grew weary enough to rest comfortably amid the *rat-a-tat-tat* lulling them into a fitful rest. Maggie's eyes had just drifted closed when Joe jumped up with fierceness and swiped viciously at his clothing. Her eyes burst open and her heart pounded beneath her chest cavity. But when she spotted the dance he'd concocted while attacking his offensive pursuer, a smile tugged on the corners of her lips.

"What's wrong, Joe?"

With one final stomp of his foot he fell back on his heels with an outbreath. "Spider. I hate spiders."

A burst of giggles protruded from Maggie's mouth, bringing a barrage of prickling pain to her lungs.

"Gee thanks. I'm glad I've enlightened you in my terror. After I rescued you and all."

Her laughter grew louder, then she grabbed her side when pain shot through her chest, returning the cough to her lungs in between spurts of giggles and moans.

"You all right?" Joe rushed to her side.

"Don't make me laugh anymore. It hurts too badly." But enlightenment still lived in her eyes.

"I wasn't trying to in the first place. I was simply trying to save my life from an eight-legged attacker."

With great effort she tried to hold back the snicker that wanted to escape.

"I see you haven't recovered from my near death experience."

She shook her head, trying to look sympathetic, but knowing she only looked pathetic with the attempt. Then it happened. For the briefest of moments under a dim lighting, he smiled. That broad, familiar smile.

Maggie's smile fell from her lips and her heart detached from her chest.

Without warning, the firing and shelling began again, this time closer since the initial hit on the hospital. Joe pressed his weight against her and his hand forced her head to the ground in protectiveness. More grueling pain shot through her chest and lungs, robbing her of her breath. Then again, maybe having this handsome GI so close to her was what stole the air from her chest.

"I've got to get you somewhere safe."

The shelling stilled and the drizzle of rocks and dirt hitting the canvas tent came to an end. Joe slowly released his firm hold on Maggie, enabling her to breathe again. He rolled to his side and let out a deep breath. For the first time, she could trace the outline of his jaw and face and his…his large nose.

Suddenly, a feeling emerged from the pit of her stomach. A sensation that exalted excitement, attraction, and—love.

CHAPTER TWENTY

How could one feel such a mix of passion and fear all at once? One minute Joe was running for his life then he was racing against time to save another's. Now he sat in a crammed shelter, alone, with a woman who magnetized him to her with her cautious charm and beautiful laughter. Now in the assortment of fear and relief, he found himself just inches from Lieutenant Johnson's lovely face.

His breath came quicker, deeper. He wanted to touch her face, brush her lips with his, and feel like he belonged somewhere. If he read her correctly, she sensed the attraction between them too. Her eyes bore the same mixture of fear and excitement. He'd like to think his presence gave her that reaction.

But it was too soon. It was just the height of the war pushing them together, forcing them to bear the company of one another. If not for the shelling of the hospital, they'd not be in this situation—a situation he shouldn't take advantage of.

'Whatsoever things are pure...think on these things.'

Another shard of memory pushed its way front and center. Now, what part of scripture was it taken from?

"Philippians 4:8"

"What?" Maggie's voice penetrated the silence of his audible thoughts.

"I think I remembered something."

Her eyes sparked and she attempted to sit up. "What did you remember?"

"Philippians 4:8. It must be a verse I committed to memory. It just...came to me."

"I knew you were a fellow believer. I could feel it when you talked of the Lord."

"Then you believe too?"

She nodded, her eyes revealing the amazement she must've felt. "So the good Lord was looking out for me after all. Who else would have sent you to my rescue at the time I needed you?"

"His ways are perfect."

"Yes. Yes, they are."

The wonder of the day and the joy of one smidgen of a remembrance was enough to set Joe's heart aflame. If God had planned all this from the beginning, then what did He hold in store for him next?

"Rest, Lieutenant. I'll keep watch and douse the light so the Germans don't pillage the camp and find us for souvenirs.

⧸ଚ⧹

Joe crawled back to his side of the tent and turned his back to her. She figured he was gentleman enough to give her privacy while she slept.

The air around them stilled and all was quiet—at least for the time being. Maggie wanted to close her eyes and quit fighting the codeine tablet she'd taken earlier, but she was enchanted by Joe. She was mesmerized by his story, but more importantly, his similarity to Danny. He may have given her the privacy she needed, but she couldn't pull her gaze away from the shadowed form of his body in the darkened tent.

She finally willed herself to get some rest, but her broken bones were making themselves known. To add to her discomfort was the chill that settled over the broken camp. The thin army blanket was not doing the trick. She was thankful for the thin layering, but she couldn't sleep while shivering, and she certainly couldn't sleep with cold feet.

So Maggie lay there in a quake—awake and exhausted. No matter how hard she tried to keep from shaking, the tremors wouldn't stop. She tried to close her eyes and imagine warm thoughts. Memories of her and Grace walking down Main Street toward the diner in the heat of summer. Summer nights dancing at the Armory and serving cold beverages to the uniformed men of the county. Warm July evenings on the porch swing, talking with Grace. That was back when life didn't seem so complicated. When it wasn't affected by war, and when loved ones were still close enough to hug.

A sense of someone hovering over her caused her to look up. She startled when she saw Joe standing over her.

"I'm sorry, Lieutenant. I couldn't help but hear your teeth chattering, so here, take my blanket."

His kindness warmed her insides. "I can't take this. You need something to cover up with too. You can't do me any good in the morning if you freeze to death."

"You're right. You *are* a difficult patient."

142

"So I've been told; we nurses are the most stubborn. But that's how we stay alive." She offered up a weak smile.

He looked as if he wanted to say something, but hesitated. Finally, he appeared to have made peace with his resolve and opened his mouth. "I have an idea, but I'm afraid it would come across as immodest."

Her stomach twisted. Dare she ask?

"What is it?"

"If we sit together and drape both blankets over both of us, we may be able to stay warmer. You know, use each other's body heat."

Although the tent was dark, she could sense the discomfiture in his stance. It was a forward request, but he was right. To survive, their body heat together would keep them both from freezing.

"All right. But no funny business or it's out in the cold with you."

"I give you my word, Lieutenant Johnson, nothing but a gentleman."

She considered him a moment. "I trust you."

⁕

Feeling the need to protect and watch over her, Joe carefully pulled Maggie closer to his side. She willingly obliged. He feared the cold had settled in her bones, leaving her vulnerable to illness and disease. But even up against his side, she still shivered. Each time a chill ran through her body, his arm tightened around her and he rubbed her arm gently with his hand. However, she still trembled and her teeth still clattered together.

Joe scooped her up as gently as possible and set her on his lap. She let out a squeak, but then eased her muscles and laid her head against his chest. He covered both of them with the wool blankets, tucking the inner blanket securely around her shoulders to prevent heat loss. He wrapped his arms around her frame and tried to offer up enough heat to take the chill from her bones. Warmth immediately soaked into his body. But was it the science of it or the fact that she was so close to him?

His heart thumped harder against his chest. She fit so comfortably in his arms, and if he guessed right, she felt the same way.

While lost in his thoughts—and trying to keep his emotions under control—Joe stroked the crown of her head softly, slowly.

Her body relaxed and before long, he heard her breathing even out. She'd fallen fast asleep in his arms. A deep sigh lifted his chest and his eyes closed. She was a featherweight compared to some of the other nurses in her unit.

He realized something in that moment: protecting this girl became his number one priority. What if this was the reason he'd been held captive? What if his amnesia was the only way to get him to this spot, under a German sky, in this tiny shelter, saving this woman?

Strands of hair tickled his nose. When he opened his eyes, he was surprised to find his lips resting against the crown of her head. When had his thoughts led his mouth to her soft, chestnut hair?

He squeezed his eyes shut and tried blocking out all images and thoughts that could lead his heart astray. This was war. He'd been a prisoner, sleeping on wood boards and a cold floor for months on months. Before that, he couldn't recall sleeping in a bed, or holding a woman this close. For all he knew he had a girl waiting for him somewhere in the world. Then thinking of Lieutenant Johnson, he presumed she too had a fella who'd already staked claim to her heart.

He'd been her hero today. That was all there ever could be. Joe tried to ignore the stabbing truth that pressed through his back and into his heart. Feeling guilty and turning a watchful eye and open ear to the outside war, he put all his night's woes to rest.

∽ⲟ⌘

"Danny, come with me."

How had he gotten to this field of roses? Its fragrant scent wrapped around his senses. But the voice…where was it coming from?

"Over here, Danny. Can't you see me?"

"No. Where are you?"

"I'm right under your nose, silly. I've been waiting for you. For a long time."

His gaze swept over the field, but he found no owner to the voice. That sweet, feminine voice.

"Who are you?"

"You know who I am, Danny."

"Danny. Who's Danny?" He wanted to scream the question. Everyone kept calling him by that name, but no one would tell him who Danny was. If someone would just answer that one, simple question, maybe he could start putting together the missing pieces of his shattered life.

A vibrant, white glow appeared out of the corner of his eye. He jerked his head in the direction of the light and squinted, shielding his eyes from its sheen.

It was *her*. It was his angel girl with porcelain skin and dark, coffee colored hair. And her lips…those familiar, red lips beckoned him to come closer. It was the same beautiful female who visited him in his dreams.

"You know the answer to your questions. It's all right in here." His heart skipped as the mystery woman extended her hand and pressed her fingers against his chest—the area above his heart. Then just as quickly as she appeared, her image faded.

"Wait! Don't go."

"Wait for me, Danny."

When the last ray of her beauty vanished, the scream of a train whistle resounded in his ears.

Joe's eyes opened in a panic. Where was he? A soft moan drifted from the sleeping body against him. He shook the slumber from his head, and rubbed his eyes with his dirt-stained fingers.

"Another dream. Why?" he whispered out of desperation.

"What's wrong?" Lieutenant Johnson squirmed. Still in the warmth of his arms, her head rested against his chest. "Oh dear. How did I get here?" She painstakingly brought herself to a sitting position and scooted back from him.

Joe ran a hand over the back of his stiff neck. "I feared you were getting a chill last night so I gathered you up in effort to keep you warm. It must've done the trick because you fell asleep within minutes."

Her good hand wrapped around her injured side. Her jaw tightened in discomfort.

"I need to get you help. Now that it's morning, we have a better chance of getting you to safety." His boot scraped against the dirt as he got to his feet. That screeching sound reached his ears once more. "Did you hear that? I thought I'd dreamt it, but now..." He poked his head out the tent flap and scanned in the direction of the road. He couldn't think of any railroad tracks in the area, but then again he could be wrong. He couldn't remember much of anything.

But the sound came again. Only it wasn't a train whistle...

⤜⤞

Maggie was glad for the distance put between them. With his back now turned to her, she could finally catch her breath. Her chest constricted when she awoke nestled into her rescuer's chest. But it wasn't her sleeping situation that stole her breath. No, it was waking up and looking into familiar eyes that she'd seen a thousand times before.

But he'd denied any accusations that he was her Danny. Sure, he looked different. His body was thin—much thinner than Danny's muscular build—and his hair was much longer than Danny would normally allow it—despite what his mother said. And his face, it was much too narrow and sunken in, but those eyes, his voice, even the hint of an Italian accent…

A tear slipped from her eye and she moved quickly to brush it away. She must be sicker than she thought. Either that or she was going crazy. Last she heard, Danny was nowhere near Germany. Then he ceased to exist at all.

"I think I hear military vehicles in the distance." Joe ducked back inside then grabbed for the rifle he'd picked off a dead GI. Before he headed out from their little shelter, he shot her a glance and caught her eye. "Stay here. Don't move or make a sound until I determine it's safe. If it's a convoy of our guys, I'll flag 'em down and come get you."

"Okay." She nodded with eyes wide and round.

"You promise you'll wait for me?"

Her face fell, her jaw hinged open. She was speechless. Suddenly, she was back in Arbor Springs before Danny left her on the train station platform.

"Lieutenant?"

"Yes." A shaky answer was all she could muster for the moment. She fought an inward battle against her mind. He wasn't real. He wasn't Danny. He just…wasn't.

The thrum of engines and the squeal of brakes quieted the voices that shouted at once in her head. She stilled and strained to listen to the conversation going on outside. They were too far away. All she could hear were the muffled voices of men then the slamming of a metal door.

Another minute later, her soldier poked his head back into the tent. "Good news. We've been rescued."

CHAPTER TWENTY-ONE

Maggie gasped when Joe lifted her from the hard bed of blankets. "I'm sorry," he said, his apology embedded in his expression. Maybe he misunderstood her struggle for air as pain shooting through her side again, but in reality, being tucked in his arms stole her breath away. Of all the places she'd looked for love, she never guessed a dirty, war-worn soldier in the gray, German countryside would sweep her off her feet.

With careful strides, he walked her toward the open door of a jeep. His footsteps seemed shaky, and she knew with his condition that his strength was fading fast. Still—somehow—he found the vigor to carry her to safety.

"Careful, she's pretty banged up." Joe set her down in the bed of the army transport where she would be most comfortable then took a seat opposite her.

She was glad for the space put between them. She didn't know how much more of his knight-in-shining-armor persona she could handle. So strong was the allure and mystery of this man that her eyes always seemed to find themselves lingering on his face.

The thought put a weak smile on her face. This life-altering experience would certainly be a great story to tell her grandkids someday.

The convoy started down the road with the promise of getting them both to the nearest EVAC hospital. Each bump and bounce jarred her insides and shot new needles of pain into her chest and side. Nausea added to her troubles, and this time she couldn't keep her moans from working their way through the open gap of her mouth. She prayed this trip wouldn't take long.

As she lay there on the bed rolls the men packed for her, she thought of Vera and Bonnie, and Helen, and even Peggy. Had they all made it to safety? From what she'd stolen a glance of in the ruined camp, there wasn't much left behind.

Father, I pray you've kept my friends safe. Even Peggy, dear Lord. I know we've been at odds, but I still wouldn't wish death on anybody. And Lord, help me. Help me determine what's real and what's a figment of my own unruly imagination. Help me see past the similarities and move forward. In Your name, amen.

Silence was the filler from the time they left the bombed-out camp. From time to time, Maggie stole a glance in Joe's direction, but he kept his head down and looked to have dozed off. The nurse inside her began to mull over his condition. He'd run out from the hospital tent so fast before the explosion that she didn't have time to call the MPs to bring him back to his hospital bed. Not that he was on constant bed rest, but he was nowhere near healthy weight for a man. To add to the confusion, he didn't have a legal name, no ID. The only background the Army picked up on this man was the affirmation that he wasn't a spy. But still, he could easily slip through the cracks and disappear from camp.

And from her life.

❧❧

Voices barked out orders as the truck rolled to a stop. A door squeaked open and slammed shut, and rushing footsteps against the ground grew louder.

"What have you got here, Corporal?" a man's voice asked.

The canvas on the truck was pulled aside and the tailgate let down. Joe jumped up from his nap, awakened by the ruckus.

"Got a wounded nurse and some guy—our side of course. I think he said his name was Joe."

The other man ordered them to get Maggie out first, but before the litter bearers could get to her, Joe was at her side.

"I'll get you out. They don't know where you're hurt."

Maggie warmed at the thought that maybe he liked being her protector. A mischievous smile played across her lips as Joe reached down to lift her.

"I think you like carrying me around." Her eyes searched out his, and her good hand came around his neck.

He hesitated at her approach, and his expression took on that I've-been-caught look.

"I was only jesting." She was so near his face she could feel his breath against her skin.

"I intend to see you safe until I'm convinced you're in good hands."

His baritone voice, smooth and soft, matched hers.

"Right now I *am* in good hands."

His eyes bounced to her lips, where they lingered for the longest second of her life. Would he kiss her right there in the back of the supply truck, in front of all these men?

Not today. He cleared his throat then eased her off the truck and carried her to the triage tent. The muscles and veins in his neck strained and she wondered how much longer his body would hold out without rest.

"You need a doctor," she whispered against his face.

"Right now, *you* need a doctor. I'll be fine."

"You're not fine. One of the others can carry me the rest of the way. You need rest and an evaluation." Now her tone grew stronger, direct.

"Lieutenant, you have far more waiting for you than I do. At least let me have the satisfaction of being a hero just this once and see that you'll be okay."

His words struck her like a sack of bricks tossed into her abdomen. He truly was lost and alone in this wretched war. But before she could say anything more to him, an army of medical personnel appeared all around them. A sea of questions flooded her from both sides. *What happened? Where've you been? Where are you hurt?* A nurse pushed a thermometer into her mouth to take her temperature. Another nurse appeared at her left side and took Maggie's pulse. Then the doctor examined her injuries thoroughly, poking in areas most severely wounded and making her wince in pain—she knew the routine, she'd done it hundreds of times before. But she'd never been the recipient of such care.

While the doctors and nurses rushed around her, each working with concern etched on their faces, Maggie found a visual pathway to Joe. He'd settled in the corner of the tent, leaning his back against the pole, his arms and his ankles crossed, watching her. Worry was etched across his face, but his gaze never left her. She tried to give him a reassuring smile, but that was the time the doctor decided to press against another broken bone, causing her to yell out in pain. Pretty soon her eyes blurred and her forehead beaded with sweat from the examination.

"All right. Let's get you to x-ray. I'm pretty sure we're dealing with broken ribs, a broken wrist, and who knows what else."

Joe caught her arm before the doctors led her out. "I'll be waiting to see how you do."

"Thank you, Joe—for everything."

After an intense gaze, he nodded and she left.

"Wait!" His sudden outburst startled her and she turned back.

"What's your name?"

"You know my name, silly." The look on his face was anything but humor. Fear? "What's the matter, soldier? You look as though you've seen a ghost."

When his mouth didn't move, and when he didn't answer, her smile faded. Something wasn't right. So she struggled for a deep breath and answered, "Maggie. My name's Maggie."

❦

In the next moment, a flurry of crying nurses surrounded her, blocking out his view of the girl who fit the shape of the missing puzzle piece in his heart. He was too dumbfounded to speak or press toward her.

Was it even possible that she was the angel-girl in his re-occurring dreams?

"Excuse me. Are you the fella who arrived with the nurse?"

Joe turned toward the officer addressing him. "I am."

"You got a gun?"

"Sure do." What did this guy want?

"Great. The lieutenant you came in with on the convoy lost a man. He's requested you to come along."

"Where to?"

"Back to the front. They need to supply the front with more ammo."

Resting his hands against his hips, he gave one final glance at Maggie. The letter that was pressed between the pages of his pocket Bible burned a hole through the leather covering and torched an ache in his chest.

Should he leave her? She was in the company of her friends and colleagues. She would be fine now. But would he?

He didn't have a choice. It was war. He needed to go where danger beckoned from—even if it meant leaving behind the key to the door of his past.

Joe followed the officer to the tent entrance, but stopped when that familiar voice called out to him.

"Joe?"

In an instant, his legs carried him back to Maggie. He shoved aside the medical staff as he fought to get to her. As soon as he reached her, his hands grasped hers. "Are you all right?"

"Broken ribs. Where are you going?"

"Back to the front."

"Joe, you can't. You're not strong enough."

"They need me. I can't stay here." But he wanted to.

"Don't leave. Please."

She wanted him to stay? He swallowed hard against the lump that suddenly worked its way up his throat.

"I have to."

"How will I find you again? To say thank you."

Unable to resist the urge, he reached up and smoothed a stray hair from her face. "I'll come back to check on you. Maybe we could—"

"Hey you! Time to pull out...now!"

"I have to go." Quickly, but reluctantly, he rushed away. As he slammed his steel helmet onto his head, he made a vow . . .

I'll find you again, Maggie.

≪⌒≫

Maggie was admitted. She'd earned a private room and hospital bed all to herself. So in the midst of all this grand treatment, why did her heart ache and burn so?

"Maggie!" Three blotchy-faced, red-nosed nurses shrieked and scurried to her.

Like clouds blotting out the sun on a clear day, her mental view of Joe was once again obscured by relieved and hysterical friends.

"Oh, Maggie we thought you were a goner!" Bonnie wrapped her arms around Maggie's neck.

"What happened to you? Where have you been?" Vera placed a kiss on Maggie's cheek as she leaned in for a gentle squeeze of her own.

Maggie shuddered as she recalled the bombed hospital and being trapped under the carnage...having the doctor's cold, dead eyes staring back at her.

"It—it was awful. Utterly awful." Tears stung and flooded her eyes.

"Oh, Maggie, we're so sorry. They whisked us away almost immediately with the wounded. We tried to tell them, Maggie. But they shoved us into the vehicles and...when we got here and couldn't find you..."

The gals glanced at one another as if they had something to tell—something dreadful.

"Go on, Vera," Bonnie began. "You know her best."

Maggie's brows furrowed and her lips thinned. The nervous tick of her heart started up again.

"Honey," Vera swallowed hard. "There were quite a few of the medical staff injured in the bombing. I'm afraid that...well, our Helen, she didn't make it."

Tears pooled into Maggie's eyes. "Helen?"

The nurses huddled together in solemn silence. Fresh tears slipped from Maggie's cheeks and her sobs shook her broken ribs, making her mourning difficult. But mourn she did.

⧯⧯

She was never so happy to see the girls and to be in their company. But under the object of their empathy, two new holes burrowed into her life. First, she'd lost a friend. Sweet Helen. So young. So full of life. A life much too young to end so violently. But then she'd spent the last 24 hours with a man who was hauntingly familiar. A man who'd saved her from a dreadful fate.

I'll come back to check on you. That's what he promised her before he hurried out of the ward. She hoped it was true, but in this battleland, finding one person was like sifting through sand for a diamond. Even if he did come back for her, it may not be in the form she hoped. Too many men who visited the hospital did not come out of want, but out of need— it was for the saving of their lives. And now she knew what it meant to be on the other end of the spectrum.

Instead of being the caregiver, she was now a patient like so many of the ones she'd taken care of in the past. Now she understood a little better how hard it was to stay in bed as instructed when her body ached to get up and flex. She couldn't do anything without the permission of her *nurse* first. At least in her case she was admitted to a specific ward completely separated from the men. The special treatment of her fellow nurses made her feel like royalty.

Now several days into her recovery, word came that her nurse, and Vera, and a few of the other ladies were down with an upper respiratory condition and confined to their cots.

A cool breeze blew into her tent as soon as the frame of a woman darkened the entrance. She inwardly groaned when the face of Peggy Blizzard became visible in the shadows.

But instead of a snarl or a sneer, Peggy calmly walked to the medicine shelf. Keeping her eyes lowered, she said, "Don't worry. I'm just a fill in. I know how much you despise me."

Although the words weren't harshly spoken or overly abrasive, Maggie still sensed apprehension in Peggy's voice.

Who could blame the woman?

Maggie hadn't been a good citizen to her fellow colleague. When she should have acted in love and humility, she'd reacted in hate and revenge. Of course Peggy would think she hated her. She'd confronted Peggy in irrational shouting matches. She struck as a serpent would—quick to react with damaging results. She'd slapped Peggy when she should have walked away.

Grief replaced the irritation Maggie felt. Her eyes closed in humiliation. Where had her love of God disappeared to? When did her compassion for others slip away? While she was busy accusing Peggy of being callous and misunderstanding, she was treating the nurse with the same cold-heartedness. And her life-threatening ordeal taught her that life was too short to allow hate to consume one's own heart.

Lord, forgive me for the way I've behaved. Please forgive me of the terrible things I've said and done to Peggy. Help me to love her, Lord. In Your name, amen.

The heaviness of her burden lifted from her chest as if Jesus himself reached down and lifted the chains from her guarded heart. She could think a little clearer now. As she glanced over at Peggy, who stood quietly, looking over patient records, she took on compassion. Maybe there was more to this woman than just ice and bone.

"Peggy?" Her mouth moved on its own. She didn't know what to say or how to say it, but words kept flowing from somewhere deep inside. "I don't really despise you." Peggy's eyes flickered. Maggie thought she saw her glance over once, but she couldn't be sure. "There's so much war going on right now and I know everyone's tired of it. So why allow another war to brew between us? Can you forgive me for the awful things I've said and done to you?"

The ticking thud of Peggy's thumb against the wooden shelf was the only sound piercing the quiet. Just when Maggie thought Peggy would ignore her all together, the woman turned with a jerk.

"You've got some nerve, Margaret Johnson. You think you can just waltz back through that door, expecting everyone to jump for joy at your safe return. Then you act as if you've had some epiphany while stranded at that camp, and now you want forgiveness? What do you think, you're better than everyone else here?"

Maggie opened her mouth to answer, but her rebuttal was cut off.

"You may have everything in the world, Lieutenant, but it doesn't last. Friendships don't last. Boyfriends don't stay. Wars never end. And prayers are never answered."

Maggie sucked in a sharp breath. "What did you say?"

"You heard me, Dumb Dora. I heard you praying with those boys. How could you sit there and give those boys false hopes. God doesn't hear prayers or answer them for that matter."

Maggie was appalled. "How can you say that?" Her heart ached for Peggy. What had been so terrible in her life to make her doubt the sovereign ways of God? Surely she could see the peace that took hold of those boys' hearts when Maggie breathed those words of mercy and faith in their presence.

"I can say that because I know! God doesn't care about us. If he did, why has he allowed so much chaos and war into this world? Did your prayers save that boy you prayed with that night, *Miss Goody-two-shoes*? What was his name...Peter? And what about the other fella? I saw that man who brought you in. I saw the look in your eye, but did he stick around to see you're okay? No. He left just like the rest of them. Don't pretend to have the perfect life, because deep down I know you're just as miserable as I am!"

"Don't say such things, Peggy. God does care about us. All of us! You wouldn't even know mercy or compassion when you saw it. How many times have you even offered to be a friend to someone or genuinely help your neighbor out because you cared?" Without a reply Peggy glanced around the room then stomped her way out the door.

Maggie almost missed it, but there was a glint of tears under Peggy's calloused mask. She was sure the girl applied layer upon layer of impenetrable armor until her face was veiled, screening all emotion and love from the contours of her face.

"Oh, Lord, I've done it again."

She hadn't expected a tongue lashing for trying to make amends. She knew she should say something, but the words lodged in her throat, unable to move to her lips. Her jaw hung slack like the empty porch swing at her mamma's house.

"By the way, *Magg-ee*," Peggy peaked her head back inside the tent just enough to issue her pointed glare. "I thought you already had a beau from your last assignment. A pity it would be for him to find out his girl is two-timing him while he's off fighting."

"Peggy, you wouldn't do such a thing. That's not true and you know it."

"But your boyfriend doesn't know that."

Every feature on Peggy's hardened face pulled tight. Then with a sinister grin, she left. No wonder all those girls in *Gone with the Wind* wanted to slap Scarlet O'Hara's face.

There you go again, Maggie, thinking ill thoughts. Grace. You must extend grace.

Something was eating at Peggy. Maggie didn't know what it was exactly, but she'd find out.

And Walt.

What was she going to do about Walt?

CHAPTER TWENTY-TWO

Arbor Springs, Maryland
April, 1945

Grace stooped alongside Luke in her old coveralls and red checked blouse with her hair tied up in a scarf. The weather had turned warmer and they would soon no longer need the warmth of the fireplace during the day. So together they cleaned ash from the mouth of the stone hearth. Luke shoveled the ash, while Grace held the dustpan and disposed of the cinders into a brown paper bag.

She loved helping him. With the loss of Luke's right arm, his capabilities were limited. So Grace became that missing right arm.

Metal scraped against the brick hearth and Grace scooped the remaining residue from the fireplace. As she did, Luke leaned in. Always ready to receive his tender love, she met him half way and their lips met.

"You're the cutest little chimney sweeper I've seen." His finger tapped against the tip of her nose.

"And you're the most handsome handyman I've ever laid eyes on." She leaned her forehead against his, and her eyelashes swept against her cheeks.

She loved the way he nuzzled her neck and tickled her senses, even if she did look a mess in her cleaning get-up. A squeak of laughter escaped her throat as goose-bumps skittered down her arms. It was all the encouragement Luke needed to take her into his arm and kiss her as if they were still on their honeymoon.

But then an unexpected knock at the front door interrupted their passionate moment.

"Just my luck. Looks like I'll have to take a rain check, Mrs. Brady."

Grace's smile broadened and her fingers curled around his neck. "I can issue a rain check, Mr. Brady." Her lips pressed into his cheek one last time. "Now, if you'll dispose of this dusty bag, I will see who's at the door." They both pushed to their feet. "Oh, gracious. I must look a mess."

"You look beautiful."

She cast a glance at Luke's retreating form. How she loved him. Oh, how she could never live without him.

As she pulled the scarf from her head and ran a hand through her hair, she peered out the window and caught glimpse of a young woman standing at her door.

Grace's brows pushed together as she wondered who would be calling at this time of day. No one had called, and Luke wasn't expecting any business guests. Slowly, she opened the door to a tall brunette with pursed lips and tense knuckles that curled tightly around her purse handles. Perhaps the woman was distraught. But her eyes were familiar, and her hair was colored the same shade of chestnut as Maggie's.

Maggie's . . .

"Libby? My heavens, what a surprise."

◈◈◈

Libby Johnson didn't know why her legs brought her down the street to this cute little house, but it seemed her heart led the way. Now she stood at the threshold of Grace Brady's home. She tried to paste on a brave smile as the door opened and a tall slender woman greeted her.

"Hello, Grace. I'm terribly sorry to intrude without calling first. I, well, truth is I didn't expect to pay any visits while in town."

"No trouble at all, Libby. Won't you come in, please?"

Her shoulders relaxed at Grace's warm hospitality. No wonder Maggie took a liking to this woman.

"Have a seat anywhere you like and I'll heat up some tea. Or maybe you prefer coffee?"

Libby removed her white gloves from her hands. "Tea is fine. I still haven't acquired a taste for black coffee."

"Neither have I. Tea it is."

While Grace busied herself in the kitchen, Libby's eyes wandered around the living room. The house wasn't any bigger than the old house Mrs. Lafferty had just shown Libby. The Brady's living room was quaint, but inviting. A small fireplace stood front in center along the side wall. Lace curtains hung freely from rods and Libby found herself yearning for a taste of home—her home. She hoped the sale of the house down the street would work in her favor, which was the whole reason for her trip to Arbor Springs.

"There now." Grace carried a tray of cups and saucers, teapot, and a bowl of sugar and two spoons to the coffee table. "Take all the sugar you like. This is a bowl I keep specifically for occasions like this." Her friendly smile relieved any other lingering tensions Libby had from her day's journey. "So tell me, Libby, what brings you here? I thought you and Phillip had a flat in York."

Libby's fingers stirred the spoon in her cup, dissolving the scoop of sugar. "Oh, we do, but well, I heard of a place coming up for sale in the area and thought I'd check it out."

"Is that so? How exciting. Tell me, which house?" Grace's lips sipped daintily from her teacup.

The Crebb's house. Their daughter, Mrs. Lafferty, showed me the place just this afternoon."

"I saw in the newspaper that the house is due for sale. Isn't that the house across the way from the Gregorys?"

Libby stared into her teacup, waiting for the appropriate words to say, and not wanting to stir up ghosts of the past. "It is. Grace, I suppose that's why I'm here; to tell you that it has nothing to do with the fact that it *is* across the street from your…well, your…"

Grace reached out a hand and gently placed it atop Libby's. "It's all right. I buried those memories a long time ago. Jack is in a much better place now and my life has moved forward in the most beautiful way. Luke and I are very happy. We no longer live in the past."

Libby nodded and smiled. "I know Phillip and Jack went way back, and I know Phillip still misses him terribly. So while I think my husband will like living somewhere familiar that holds very dear memories, I truly don't know what his reaction will be when I wire him. If the Laffertys take my offer, I'll go ahead and release the funds for purchase on the house. But I wanted to make sure you know that I'm not trying to rub salt in an old wound."

"I appreciate your concern on my behalf, Libby. Do you like the house? It began falling into disrepair several months back."

"Very much so, I love it. I know it's not the least bit attractive on the outside, but I saw its potential as soon as I walked through the door. I've lived within city limits far too long now, Grace, and I want—no, I *need*—a place to call my own. To call home."

"You poor dear. Libby, are you lonely? Is it hard living up there in the city all alone?"

Tears swam in her eyes. She didn't realize how long it was since she had another woman to share her thoughts and secrets with. But Grace's charm was too inviting to pass up this one chance to sort through her feelings. "I'm sorry, Grace. I didn't know it bothered me this much."

"Take your time, Libby. We all need moments like these once in a while."

Her nose stung like crazy, and she only allowed two tears to drip from her eyes, but it felt so good to release even a smidgen of bottled up emotion.

Delicate fingers pressed a tissue into her hand. "Thank you," she whispered. Dabbing at her eyes, she ignored the embarrassment that stained her cheeks. Surely her eye make-up would be running by now. But she pushed through the pain and found the words that needed escape.

"I need to get my life back. Lonely isn't the word to use. Seclusion is more like it. The first thing on my list is to restore my relationship with Maggie. We never got the chance . . ." Tears clogged her throat, and she brought her slender fingers to her mouth.

Grace must have understood. Patting Libby's knee, she changed the subject. "Any word from Phillip? How is he?"

"As best as can be expected, I assume. His letters have become so spread apart. So...distant. It seems as if his thoughts travel somewhere beyond the layer of the atmosphere. Sometimes it's like reading a riddle when trying to decipher his letters.

"I don't know where he is other than the fact he's somewhere in the Pacific. On an island surrounded by thousands of Japanese soldiers. He talks about the weather, the food, the mosquitoes, the water. But his words of love and homesickness for home have become non-existent. I almost feel as if I'm writing to a long lost brother, not my husband."

"Libby, war is an unkind element in today's world. Everyone is being affected. I know Luke still has nightmares about the invasion. Sometimes I can hear him whimper in the night, calling out for his men, particularly Tommy Hines. Poor Luke, he promised to bring Tommy home safely, but instead he brought him home in a casket. He has times where he blames himself, but we must always remember that God is in control, and even though we fight for a will to survive, it's God who chooses the outcome of our trials." Grace sipped her tea. "Phillip's been away for years, unable to make it to the east coast for time off, maybe he's feeling the same way you are, Libby."

"It's very lonely, Grace. I never once thought of Phillip leaving for war. In my own little newlywed mind, I thought he'd take an industry job and build war machines here, not use them *over there*. We were just married, barely months, before he came home with the paperwork in hand. He hadn't even discussed it with me first. Just decided on his own that I would understand he had a duty to his country to fulfill. I was so angry with him."

"I'm sorry, Libby. It was quite a shock to us as well, but if it's one thing I've learned from Luke, it's this: sometimes there are things a man has to do or else he'll spend a lifetime regretting what he didn't do to make a difference. And I truly believe—because it's evidence in my own life—that these situations arise to lead us down the path chosen for us. It's the only way to get where God wants us to go."

"I just don't understand why that path has to be so painful."

"Oh, Libby, none of us do. But in the end, we become so much stronger because of it."

The warmth of Grace's reassuring hand smoothed over the creases in Libby's heart. She didn't know why she felt compelled in the first place to pay the woman she barely knew a visit, but she was certainly glad for the prompting from God.

"If this situation does indeed work out, Grace, I'm sure glad I'll have someone like you for a neighbor."

Grace's flawless smile brightened the room. "Anytime, Libby. Come as often as you like, you're always welcome here. Tell me, have you heard from Maggie lately?"

Her cup clanked on the saucer as she set her half-empty teacup back on the coffee table. Then she smoothed out her skirt and settled in for girl talk. "I've written her and apologized for being selfish. I don't know what I was thinking in the beginning. I'm so ashamed of the way I led Phillip away from his family. I thought that if we stayed in Pittsburg, that his overbearing mother would surely run our lives. I don't want that. When I said *I do,* I was branching out on my own to start a new life, not get corralled under another woman's wing. I saw how Mr. and Mrs. Johnson ran Maggie out. The poor girl didn't have a leg to stand on. Why, if it wasn't for you, Grace, I don't know where my sister-in-law would've ended up."

"The Lord knows what He's doing. If Maggie hadn't shown up in my life, I don't think finding Luke would have been possible." Grace paused as her teacup rose and stopped mid-way to her lips. "Hm. Maybe the Lord is working right now in your life, Libby. I think maybe you're going to find something more awaits around the bend for you too."

York, Pennsylvania

Libby walked to the photograph taken on her wedding day. Phillip stood tall and proud and she held tightly to his arm in a formal pose, smiles beaming from each of their faces. Although the photograph only depicted a black and white shadow of the day, it still played across her mind as real as she could see everything today. It hardly seemed possible that three years had gone by so quickly, yet so incredibly painstakingly slow. And in so many ways, she felt cheated out of her youth as a young bride, indulging in the happiness and bliss of the married life. She knew she'd come to forgive Phillip for leaving her so abruptly, but the hole in her heart was missing its other half.

Maybe that's why she wanted this house so badly. It would fill up her time she spent longing for Phillip by preparing a lovely home for him to come home to. Between her hours at the cannery, she'd earn enough money to buy little materials for repairs here and there. Maybe Luke Brady could help her open a savings bond until all the arrangements could be made and set in stone. It would take everything she earned, and the money Phillip sent home, to make it all happen. But it just might work.

Just then the telephone in her apartment rang. She set the wedding photograph back on the occasional table and went for the phone.

"Hello?"

"Libby? This is Mr. Johnson."

Oh, dear, what did he want? Was something wrong?

☜☞

Her hands were still trembling when she hung up the receiver. Nothing could have prepared her for this. It had been months since Phillip's parents contacted her, and when they did they usually wanted something or had something tragic to share. But after the long conversation she'd just had with her father-in-law, she didn't know whether to cry or to be on her guard.

He sounded different. Talked different. But to offer funds to buy the house?

Libby pinched the pale skin above her wrist to be sure she wasn't dreaming. She'd asked Mr. Johnson three times to repeat his message. Surely she'd heard wrong or misunderstood. Phillip's father was far too stingy with his money to give it away, especially on something as extravagant as a house. Then again, maybe Grace was right. Maybe the Lord was working something out. Maybe the bend in the road held brighter days in her future.

She could only wonder at this point what caused the change in Mr. Johnson's heart.

CHAPTER TWENTY-THREE

Days had passed since Joe left Maggie in the safety of the doctors and nurses at the relocated hospital. His ammo-delivering venture had turned into a nightmare. For five days they were pinned down by enemy fire. Joe prayed that God would open up a small window of opportunity for escape. There was no way he was going back to the prison camps—no way.

His belly groaned its disapproval at the lack of nutrition. He'd known starvation at the stalag. His stomach's moans echoed back the agonizing sounds of death, disturbing his sleep and making every waking moment miserable.

In the confusion of all the week's misgivings, his paperwork wasn't processed, neither was he issued a weapon, rations, or ammo. He was grateful for the spare C-rations the corporal shared with him for the last few nights. But a forkful of beans and a bite of canned ham were not enough to sustain him. Not in the weakened state he was already in.

"Say, you don't look to be in the best of health there. You diseased or something?"

Joe quirked an eyebrow at the man sitting to his left. "Nothing wrong with me. Just came from Stalag Three is all." He kicked at a rock with his boot.

"Stalag? As in a prison camp?"

On his nod, his comrade tapped his cigarette and its ashes fell to the ground. "So why aren't you on your way back to the States?"

"It's complicated."

With the cigarette butt pinched between his lips, the GI took a long drag then released its smoke from his lungs. "Complicated. You running from the Army?"

"No. If anything I'm trying to find something."

"I ain't got time for riddles boy. Either you's runnin' or you got problems."

"All right." This time Joe turned his full attention to the man beside him. "I don't remember a thing before waking up in a cold prison bunk. My dog tags were gone. Any pictures on me were gone. My weapons— gone. Everything that could possibly tell me who I am was taken from me—and I don't know by who. After nine months in the Krauts' camp, an armored division barreled through and liberated us. Hospital says to stay until I recover and get some paperwork done, but it was bombed. Then I find one person who may know who I am and where I come from, and Uncle Sam comes calling again. So here I am...with nothing to show for my efforts."

"I'm sorry, fella. If I'd known..."

"Don't worry about it. I'm sure there's a reason for all of it."

With a lazy, glassy look in his eye, the man seated next to him eased back against the truck wheel and stared up into the sky. "I'm not a religious man, but I know there's a God. And I know He works mysteriously. Maybe you think you're the one who needs to be saved but what if you're here to save someone else?"

He hadn't thought of it from that angle before.

What if that *was* true? Did God have him here for underlying reasons?

Joe's thoughts reversed back to Oflag 64 where he met Al and Abe. He'd become more than just cell mates with those men—they'd become brothers. If he hadn't stepped in at various times to protect Abe from the German's iron fists, would Abe have made it to the little farm on the wintry landscape of the German countryside? Was his efforts to protect his friend for Abe's future?

And Al. Al asked Joe on more than one occasion to pray for all of them. They'd made it as far as the 39th together. If all had gone as planned, Al would be seeing his way across the Atlantic by now. To home. To safety.

Then Joe's muscles tensed and his stomach twisted as Maggie entered his mind. He'd turned the scenario around and around in his mind for days, and although he already knew what contents the letter contained, he couldn't bring himself to open the parchment that he left pressed between the pages of his Bible.

Was it fear that kept her memory at a distance? Was he afraid that the woman in the letter was not the woman he suspected?

The rest of the men droned or nodded off due to the lack of sleep. They'd kept watch around the clock for five days and were exhausted. Even the constant *rat-a-tat-tat* of machine guns couldn't keep these guys awake.

Joe took that moment to disappear behind the supply truck and put his mind to rest. He pulled the small Bible from his back pocket and flipped through its pages until he came across the yellowing parchment stuck in its folds. His fingers fumbled with the edges until the letter separated, allowing him to smooth out the wrinkles and read the script that flowed from a woman's heart.

Dear Danny,

You've been gone for a long time. Too long. My arm still aches because in my heart I'm forever waving good-bye to you. It seems as though you left me a lifetime ago. Although I can still vividly remember our last dance together at the armory, it also seems to fade into the background as if I only dreamed it.

I made a promise to you and I intend to keep it. I'm still waiting for you to return. I'll always wait for you. You're the most handsome man I've ever laid eyes on—even if you do have a big nose.

I don't really think that, but I love the way your eyes look at me when we banter back and forth. You understand me. My family. My thoughts. And my fears. And although I think you're a nut for volunteering for the most dangerous job in the Army, I'm proud of you and I'm praying the good Lord will keep his hand safely around you until you come home. I love you.

Forever Yours,
Maggie

Was it crazy to think that he'd stumbled on the woman who wrote him this very letter? Was it crazy to think that Lieutenant Maggie Johnson was the same woman who…loved him?

He flipped to the front of the Bible and pulled the photograph from its folds. Straining his eyes through the dark, he could barely make out the woman's facial features. But his heart knew…it was *her.*

His heartbeat quickened. He had to get back to Lieutenant Johnson somehow. He had to know.

"Incoming!"

That loud thud reverberating in his ears wasn't just the sound of his heart. All at once enemy planes swooped in for the kill, unleashing the wrath of Hitler's hate on the convoy. The men ducked for cover. Rolling on their backs, they aimed their rifles at the monstrous birds flying above them.

More men fell. But the most terrifying moment was when Joe spotted his cigarette smoking buddy wandering into the open field, his arms spread.

"What's he trying to do? Blow our cover?" Joe hollered.

"Someone get that idiot back here...now!"

When no one volunteered, Joe sprinted into harm's way. The planes made a turn and now aimed their guns at the man who apparently just lost his mind.

"Get down! Don't crack up on us now!" Joe pushed past the pain in his legs and pumped them harder before lunging at the soldier. Their bodies collided and crashed to the ground. Then the crack of a rifle went off and Joe's head slammed against a protruding rock. A sharp, blunt pain shattered his mind and his vision turned gray until all faded into nothing.

It was now a week since Maggie found herself under the ruins of the bombed camp. It'd been five long days since she last saw Joe. To keep unwanted thoughts from entering her mind on his condition, she focused the majority of her attention on her Bible. She'd gone too long without the reading of God's word. There was too much to be thankful for to neglect it any longer.

"But I say unto you, love your enemies, bless them that curse you, do good to them that hate you, and pray for them which despitefully use you, and persecute you;" The words of Matthew replayed in her mind. She certainly was surrounded by a world of enemies. Enemies on both the opposing and allied sides. God wanted her to love them...all of them.

"Hey, Maggie." Bonnie sauntered into the tent with a broad smile adorning her rounded face.

"Well, Bonnie. If this isn't a pleasant surprise." Maggie gently closed the front cover of her Bible and set it on the stand next to her cot. Sidling up beside her, Bonnie leaned down for a much overdo squeeze. "Are you on lunch break?"

"No, I'm working. But the mail just came through and you've a few letters here. Quite a nice stack." Bonnie's petite hand held up a thick bundle of tied up letters—all for her.

A smile pushed up against her cheekbones. "It feels like forever since I received anything. Thank you, Bonnie. Can you stay a while?"

Bonnie threw a glance over her shoulder. Convinced the coast was clear, she settled on a chair by Maggie's bedside and sighed. But it wasn't the average worn exhalation from the day's tasks. No, that grin playing on Bonnie's lips suggested something else was on her mind.

"What is it? What has that radiating beam on your face?"

Bonnie sported her pearly whites and straightened her skirt.

"Remember Fred? The pilot?"

"Yes."

"He wrote back."

Maggie inhaled. She felt like a school girl again, waiting for the juicy details of the newest high school sweethearts. "Heavens, Bonnie! What did he say?"

The young nurse's eyes took on that faraway look—the one that doesn't need words to describe the elation in her mind. "He's thought of me every day since we landed in Bad Kreuznach. He heard the airfield was strafed and he worried about me. I know this sounds crazy, but I think I'm falling for a guy I barely know."

Maggie tried to hide the grin that wanted to break out on her face. Hadn't she heard that line somewhere before? It wasn't all that long ago when Grace found herself loving a man she'd only met once.

Maggie nudged Bonnie's shoulder. "No, Bonnie, it doesn't sound crazy at all."

"I just—I've never felt this way about someone. I can't stop thinking of Fred either. When I looked into his eyes, I didn't see just another man. I know this sounds like an old fairy tale, but I saw forever in his eyes."

Maggie reached out with her free hand to clasp Bonnie's, a gesture only true friends could share. "That's wonderful, Bonnie. I'm so happy for you. You deserve a good man like Fred."

The girl's endearing smile warmed Maggie's heart.

"What about you, Maggie?"

"What about me?"

"Who are your letters from? I'm sure your beau has written most of those letters. Major Radford sure does take a shine to you."

"Oh, Walter. Right." Maggie's eyes dropped to the bundle sitting on her lap. "I'm sure you're right. I haven't written him in quite some time. He must be worried."

"What's the matter, Maggie? You look sadder than a puppy who's been told not to roll in the mud."

"Just the blues I guess. From everything that's transpired over the last week, I feel like I've spent an entire lifetime in the span of these last few days."

"You were looked after, Maggie. If that soldier hadn't come when he did...well, we were all afraid we'd lost you."

From closed eyes, Maggie felt Bonnie's warm hand grab a hold of hers and give it a tender squeeze.

"I better get. They'll be wondering where I've gone off to."

"Thanks for the visit, Bonnie."

They exchanged smiles and Bonnie started for the door. "Oh, and

Maggie? If you don't have peace about Walt, it's better not to string him along."

Maggie's heart stilled. How did Bonnie know that was the very thing going through her mind? Maybe it was written across her forehead. Maybe she was talking in her sleep. Whatever it was, she hadn't done a good enough job masking her confusion. Now she had the daunting task of trying to untangle the web she'd become caught up in. She certainly didn't want to hurt Walt, especially since he conveyed nothing but kindness toward her. But something deep down inside drew her to Joe and his visage. Deeper down, she hoped...she wanted to believe . . .

Maggie lifted the first letter in her hand and read the return address. It was Walt's letter all right. She opened the envelope and read its contents.

As usual, he told her how much he missed her and couldn't wait to be reunited with her. He wrote about the war and the relocations the 238th had made. But it was the last line that grabbed her attention.

Just give me the word, Maggie, and I'll send for you.

With his rank, she knew he meant it. He *would* send a replacement for her if she asked. She tapped the letter against her chin in thought. Her life was in complete disarray. Nothing seemed the same since she left the 238th. Before reassigning to the 39th she was awed by Walt, she was free of the danger she so desperately wanted to be a part of, and she was the go-to nurse. Now she didn't know how she felt about Walt, she'd been bombed and counted as another war casualty, and she couldn't keep peace within the walls of her own tent.

A longing ulcered her gut. A sudden ache for Grace and the people of her hometown pricked at her heart. Would going home prove any consolation?

Willing away the sorrows of her melancholy, she flipped through the other letters. Her fingers halted their rapid search when Grace's handwriting caught her eye.

Grace!

Bursting with relief, Maggie pulled the letter from the envelope and gushed over the latest news.

My dear friend, Maggie,

I'm glad to know you're moving across foreign lands unharmed. Luke and I pray for you every morning before we sit down to breakfast. I know you must be dying to hear what's been going on in town so I'll catch you up.

Mrs. Sullivan (or should I say Aunt Norma) is a regular Sunday dinner guest at our home. She and Luke have bonded rather quickly. I love how Luke's eyes light up when he and his aunt speak of his parents. The Lord has certainly blessed us.

A few of our local boys have come home. I can't say they've come home unscathed. All of them have some disability or another due to combat. I heard the college is looking to launch a program for the men coming home to help them earn their degrees and get them back into society. There's talk of the possibility of building housing for the troops enrolled in the program. The committee has been holding meetings with Luke since he's taken the position at the bank. So this is privileged information.

Luke is getting by well. The freshly healed wounds still ache from time to time, but his heart is still bruised. Between Tommy and Danny's deaths, I know Luke feels he's failed in some way. But then morning comes, and God's grace chases away those dark shadows of the past. Then Luke holds me in his arms, and I know everything will be okay. Thank the Lord for his tender mercies and a wonderful husband. I couldn't be happier, Maggie, and in time, I know this war and its atrocities will just be a memory.

That's all the news I have for this time around. I hope this letter finds you well. I'm wishing every day for your safe return. I miss you dearly. Be safe, my friend.

Love always,
Grace

Maggie stared blankly into the scripted ink of Grace's letter. Sometimes a strong longing for home gripped her soul, and she wished she could hop the next hospital ship out of port. She longed to see Grace and missed those special moments when they talked well into the night.

But life goes on. The war still raged. And Maggie's mission was still left unaccomplished.

CHAPTER TWENTY-FOUR

7 April 1945

The last of the patients were driven out from the camp. Maggie rubbed her eyes with her uninjured hand as she finished up the mound of paperwork. While having the option of being transferred to a general hospital in Belgium, she requested to stay on. Her injuries would heal in a matter of a few weeks. Her ribs still gave her trouble from time to time, but she was breathing easier and now walking. The only handicap she found bothersome was having her arm casted and hung about her neck in a tourniquet. To be of use to the outfit, she offered to fill out and file the paperwork no one else cared to do.

Now, with the hospital closing, they were all just sitting and waiting for the word, telling them to move.

Since her return to the 39th, she didn't feel the same. Somewhere between Belgium and Hersfeld, she'd lost her zest for life. Where had the adventurous, perky Maggie Johnson run off to? It didn't help she was constantly surrounded by gaping stomach wounds, torn flesh, puddles of human blood, and moans that could awaken the worst of nightmares. The stench alone was never easier to bear. But she pushed onward, reminding herself there was no one else to care for these poor souls. It was her job, her mission.

Needing to give her head and eyes a rest from medical files and numbers, she carefully stretched the muscles in her back and stood. She crossed the nurse's office and stood in the sunlight which the drab green tent kept hidden from her. The rain ceased falling, leaving behind a path entrenched in mud. Across the way, a large Caterpillar chugged along, pulling army vehicles, filled with supplies and tents, through the mud. Men were ankle deep in the muck, and the larger vehicles were digging further into the softened ground, lodging their tires into the slippery mess. Their engines revved higher as they fought against the elements. *Those poor boys...having to work against every hostility.*

Then she thought about Joe. He'd promised to come back. But it had been nearly two weeks since the Army whisked him away. Would she ever see him again? Would she ever find peace of mind and realize he most likely wasn't the Danny she so desperately wanted him to be? Could she love him if he wasn't?

"Hey there, kid."

A welcome voice turned Maggie's ear. "Vera. Hello."

"You look like you're in a thoughtful mood today. Come on, walk with me." Vera linked arms with Maggie, and the two strolled through the camp, skipping over mud holes and crates. "What happened to that spunky, care-free spirit of a girl I once bunked with at Walter Reed?"

"I think she grew up."

Their boots sloshed in the mire, and for a few seconds, they walked in silence.

"War changes people." Vera stopped and took in a full view of the field stretched out in front of them. A beautiful hillside staggered the horizon with rolling crests and budding trees.

"It steals their innocence." Maggie took in the beauty of Europe's canvas for the first time. There was so much to this foreign land, and she'd missed it.

"I suppose you're right."

"Vera, before we arrived, can we honestly say we knew anything about the fragility of life? I have nightmares and flashbacks of the bombing. One minute I was working alongside Captain Baker, talking and emptying the cabinets of medicine to take to triage then in the next second—the very next—I was staring into his cold eyes. His life was snatched away just like that." She snapped her fingers together and closed her eyes against the awful memory. "I was the last person to see or speak to him. And I was spared."

"It was a devastating day for all of us. Poor Helen. So young. Just spreading her wings to leave the nest." Vera side-glanced and gave Maggie a once over before continuing. The news of Helen's death in the bombing was a shock to all of them. A true loss for the 39th. "But we're all so thankful to have you back." Maggie smiled her thanks and Vera inhaled. "Since we're just waiting around for our next orders, some of us are heading to the USO show back at the 109th. Want to join us?"

"Do I? That sounds like fun. Of course, not sure how much dancing I'll be able to do with this thing around my neck." Maggie gestured to her casted arm.

"All the more reason the men will flock to you. They'll want to hear your story. We'll meet up at Tent Six around two o'clock. That should give us enough time to have dinner out there, see the show, and give the gals a chance to dance with some fellas." Vera grinned and winked, showing off her long eyelashes.

"The gals? And what about you?"

For the first time, Maggie watched as a blush stained Vera's cheeks.

"Despite what I've said in the past, I've been bitten."

"Ah. Allen."

"He asked me to start a long-distance relationship before he left."

Maggie smiled her surprise. "That's wonderful, Vera."

When the lunch hour had passed, Maggie found herself rummaging through her trunk while Bonnie settled herself into a chair. Linda was "putting on her face," and Peggy sat in her corner with her nose lodged in a book.

"I only wish I could go with Fred. That would make the day just perfect." Bonnie smiled and stared up to the peak of the tent as if in a day dream.

"You two are such saps." Peggy's resentful tone cut through the mild air.

Maggie thought it a shame that she, Bonnie, and Linda had become all too familiar with Peggy's growl and shrugged off her grumblings.

Ready to try something drastic, Maggie turned with a sharp jerk, but instead of letting her tongue run the show, she did something that surprised even herself. "Peggy, why don't you join us?"

"What?"

Ah...surprise replaced umbrage.

"Yes. Join us. You have the weekend off too. Why don't you come with us tonight? You can dance, eat some good food, mingle with the girls. You'll have fun."

The tent grew awfully quiet. Bonnie sat as if frozen in place, and the sound of Linda's compacts ceased its clicks and snaps.

"Why would I *want* to spend time with girls like *you*? You'll just make fools of yourselves in front of those men. Why would I want to be associated with a bunch of floozies?"

The sound of make-up slamming onto the wood vanity splintered the air. The girls looked over to find Linda gathering her things in a huff. "I've had about enough of this, Peggy. I tried to have compassion on you and live with your miserable ego, but now you've crossed the line." Linda's eyes, angered and fuming, flashed to Maggie. "I'll be at Tent Six where I can get ready in peace."

Bonnie soon followed, her meek frame skirted out the door with barely a sound, leaving Maggie and Peggy alone. With one final attempt, Maggie found the words her heart lacked in the previous months.

"Come on, Peggy, you know that's not true. Let's put our differences aside for one night and just have a good time. You could dress up for once—"

The clap of Peggy's book slamming closed made Maggie jump. "What are you saying? That I look too homely? That I don't dress pretty?"

"No, I was—"

"No, what you were thinking is look at poor Peggy—she doesn't have anyone. She's a grouchy old maid. She doesn't know how to have fun. Let's take pity on poor ol' Peggy and fix her up and make all over her. Well, let me tell you something honey—" Peggy now stood face to face with Maggie, pointing an accusing finger at her nose—"I don't need to go out with a bunch of heathens, with a bunch of men-seeking nurses just so I can have a good time! And I don't need a man to make my life happy. I'm happy just being me! You hear me? I'm just me!" With a good pound on her chest, Peggy stepped back and challenged Maggie's large, brown eyes.

But Maggie looked deeper. Past the anger, past the disdain. To her surprise, Peggy's eyes softened, showing hurt and neglect. Then she seemed to back down from the challenge and took a step in retreat, falling onto her bed and burying her head into her arms.

Maggie didn't know what to do or what to say—if she should say anything at all. The intensity that hung in the air suffocated Maggie.

There really wasn't anything else she *could* say or do. She took out her cosmetic case and began applying her make-up. Then she slipped on her formal, army green uniform for the outing. Peggy hadn't moved for those few minutes and Maggie still didn't offer up a word.

But as Maggie reached for the door, she stopped. Her chest heaved a heavy sigh and she contemplated her next words. "Peggy, I don't have anything against you, but I sure wish you would tell me what I do that upsets you so. I'm sorry I made the comment about no one loving you. I was wrong. You could be loved, by anyone. More importantly, God loves you no matter what. But you have to let someone in." She took another breath. "Will you come tonight?"

Peggy sniffed. "Just go, Maggie. I don't feel like partying anyway. I'll never feel like partying ever again." She never looked up from her bed and she never moved. Maggie left the tent, but something inside her told her to stop and wait. From a hidden spot, she stood at the tent door and peered inside.

Peggy wiped her tear-streaked cheeks and stooped over her footlocker. She lifted the lid and pulled up the top drawer. Her hands rummaged through the contents, but under her clothes, tucked away safely, she pulled out a picture frame. She held the photograph close to her chest and the tears she kept hidden from the other girls resurfaced. A shudder shook her shoulders and she cupped her mouth with her hand.

Maggie's heart ached for Peggy as she watched sobs overtake the poor girl's frame. There really was a reason Peggy kept herself hidden behind the façade of books and her profession. She was hiding from something that had mortally wounded her soul.

Maggie was almost to the rendezvous location when she realized she couldn't take this trip. Right now there was someone who hurt and needed a friend. When she reached the meeting point, she pulled Bonnie aside. "Bonnie, I don't think I'm going this time."

"What? Don't let Peggy get you down, Maggie. She's just a spoil sport."

"It's not that. There's something I need to do. I'll tell you all about it later. Have a good time tonight."

Maggie hated giving up her day off to spend it at the mud-infused camp, but she couldn't let Peggy stay behind all alone and go on believing no one cared.

She prayed the whole way back to her tent. She needed the Lord's guidance and His words to fill her mouth if she wanted to get anywhere with Peggy. When she opened the door and peeked inside, she found Peggy curled up on the dirt floor, clutching something to her chest.

"Peggy?"

She jerked up, and with aggression, began wiping her eyes. "What do you want?"

"To help. May I sit?"

"Aren't you missing the bus out?"

Maggie lowered herself to her knees, not caring if a little dirt smudged her skirt. "Yes, but I don't mind. I can't leave you here like this."

Peggy brought herself to a sitting position, but kept her eyes averted from Maggie. "Why not? I mean no one else seems to care." Her dark head lowered to hide the remnant tears that dripped down her cheeks.

"Well, I'm not everyone else." Glancing at the picture tucked securely against Peggy's chest, Maggie pointed and asked, "What do you have there? Is that him? The man who broke your heart?"

The girl's eyes flickered between the floor and Maggie's face. "Someone's been talking behind my back."

"Well, Linda said something to Bonnie some time back, but I put the rest together on my own."

A snort squeezed from Peggy's nose. "Figures. That girl has a mouth the size of the *Titanic*."

"Want to talk about it?"

"With you? Not really."

"Why not? If no one else will listen, why not talk to me? I promise not to blab. I'll keep it between us. Our little secret. If you tell me, I'll tell you something I haven't mentioned to anyone else."

That seemed to pry Peggy's attention from the floor to Maggie. Her shoulders relaxed and her head rested against the center tent pole. "What could you possibly have to say that is the least bit interesting?"

"Well, why don't you open up to me to find out? What do you have to lose?" Maggie shrugged her shoulders.

She could see Peggy contemplated the deal in her mind. The girl wanted to open up to someone, needed to, but fear held her back. Maggie had seen the same defeated look on Grace's face after Jack's death. It was the fear of opening her wounds up to someone and allowing the hurts to puncture her heart all over again. It seemed too unbearable.

While Maggie waited and prayed, Peggy opened her mouth. It seemed she was ready to confide in Maggie, but then her lip quivered and her eyes turned a shade of red, watering with tears once again.

"Oh, Peggy, come here." Maggie reached out and hooked her arm around Peggy for the first time, holding the woman as she cried out all her tears, fears, past, and pain.

They sat on the floor of the tent for over an hour while Peggy released all she'd held inside for so long. When her eyes drained of all fluid, she slowly composed herself and found her voice.

"We were in love. We were both eighteen. We were seniors in high school. He played on the football team." To Maggie's disbelief, a smile touched Peggy's lips. "He was so handsome." Her finger ran across the face in the picture. "His name was Richard. He chose me out of a whole high school of girls who were after him. He made me feel special, like a woman. I loved him for that. I never felt good enough, I never thought I was pretty, but he made me feel important and beautiful."

"Peggy, you *are* a beautiful woman."

"After high school, I went on to nursing school, and he became a plumber's apprentice. It was going to be a very secure job, you know. But then Pearl Harbor happened and he was one of the first to enlist." Peggy paused to stifle a hiccup and sniffed. "I was so mad at him for enlisting. I knew he would be shipped out as soon as the Army released him from boot camp, but he didn't care. He wanted to get revenge on the Japanese for what they did to our boys and our country. Anyway, he promised he would marry me when he returned. He sent me letters every day and I did the same. Then one day, all the letters stopped. I thought at first that he was moved out. Sometimes the mail is slowed down when the troops are moving. But that wasn't the case. Almost a year after he enlisted, I got the phone call from his dad that he didn't make it."

"Peggy, I'm so sorry," Maggie whispered. Her hand softly ran across Peggy's back.

"I didn't want to believe it, but one day a courier brought his mother what I never wanted to see—Rich's tags. Then I knew the Army wasn't mistaken. I was crushed all over again."

"But you bottled up all those feelings, didn't you?"

"Yes," Peggy whispered. "It hurt so badly, I couldn't stand it. I thought I would die. I found that if I stayed away from people who would ask about Richard, then I wouldn't feel the pain anymore. When they did ask, it made me angry. I never let anyone see me cry, so I lashed out at them. Soon enough, everyone kept their distance. I was fine inside my own little cocoon. If Richard wasn't there with me then I wanted no one. No one at all."

"I can relate a little to that, Peggy. I lost someone too. Like you, I left him with the promise of marriage when he returned. I was so annoyed with him for volunteering for the most dangerous job in the Army. He jumped out of airplanes.

"Anyhow, he parachuted into Normandy and that was the last anyone heard or saw of him. The telegram came saying Danny was missing. I refused to believe he was dead, so I decided to get in touch with a friend in communications back at Walter Reed in D.C. Then my friend delivered the heartbreaking news that Danny was killed. But you want to know the funny thing? His body was never found. I was crushed like an ant under the weight of a man's heel. I cried for days.

"After the Sunday service that week, I stayed at the church all day. There was something I needed to do. I needed to think, to pray. You see, it would have been so easy to get mad at God and everybody, but what would it have benefited? I'd just lose all those around me whom I loved dearly. I couldn't risk losing anyone else. I needed them. So right there, in the church, I prayed that God would heal my heart and soul. Then I made a promise to Him."

"You made a promise to God?"

"Yes. I promised that I would live the rest of my life trying to save and help others. I gave Jesus my life and let Him take the wheel and steer my soul in the direction He wanted me to go. An enormous weight lifted from my shoulders. And it happened right there and then. Peggy, you could have that too. You can have the peace of God and have all this hurt and pain lifted from you so you can live again. Do you want to live again?"

"I do, Maggie. You don't know how much I want to. But I can't. I'm scared and just—just…afraid." Another tear slid down Peggy's cheek.

"You don't have to be afraid, Peggy. Just believe. I can help you. Do you want my help? God's help?"

Maggie stayed focused on Peggy and refused to allow her gaze to fall. Peggy's eyes slid closed and she knew the woman was trying to find resolve in her mind.

When her eyes opened, she looked to Maggie and nodded. "I'm ready. I need to do this. I've been doing this too long."

She wanted to bounce and shout for joy! Maggie's greatest adversary had just torn down the walls and allowed God to penetrate her soul. Peggy bowed in prayer with Maggie and repeated the prayer Maggie led her in. It was the first step in her new life. After the prayer for sanctification was said, both women cried, but these tears were not tears of sorrow or pain, they were tears of joy.

CHAPTER TWENTY-FIVE

20 April 1945

It felt so good to flex her elbow again. Maggie admired the work of the doctor who removed the old arm cast and replaced it with a shorter one. Now she could move her arm freely without feeling awkward and clumsy. Once the stiffness worked out of her joints she'd feel almost normal again.

"How's the pain in your ribs, Lieutenant?"

"Much better, Captain. Once and again I get a spasm, but a few deep breaths knock it out."

"As long as you don't over-do it, I think you'll be fine. We'll keep an eye on that wrist, though. It was a pretty nasty break. Best to make sure it heals correctly without the threat of surgery. I see the head wounds have healed over nicely too."

"Yes, Doctor. Thank you."

Maggie hopped off the examining table and started for the door. She was due at triage to take vitals and a little inventory. It wasn't her *normal* job, but it beat being stuck in bed with a thermometer shoved down her throat.

She ran a hand through her wavy curls. Her hair needed a wash. Oh, how she missed the days of taking hot baths in the apartment.

"Maggie! There you are. Wait up."

Maggie slowed her pace and waited for Peggy to catch up with her.

"You and I have orders to pick up supplies at the 107th. Our escort has a jeep. If we can talk Lieutenant McGee into letting a few of the other girls tag along, we can have dinner at the Officer's Club."

Maggie's lips curled into a broad smile. How good it was to hear Peggy talk of venturing out with the girls. Her last few weeks of rejuvenated life had caused quite a stir in the camp. All noticed a remarkable difference in the woman. Peggy's rigid eyes and hard expression softened immensely.

"Are you going along, Peggy?"

With a smile on her face, Peggy confessed, "Who do you think thought up the idea? I haven't been out for a night of fun and dancing in a long, long while. It's about time I got back into the swing of things again."

"In that case, it sounds like a date to me. When do we leave?"

⤙⤚

With some much plot-out convincing, Lieutenant McGee finally permitted Bonnie, Vera, and Linda to take the ride to the 107th. They were issued a driver, and in no time were on their way with Peggy.

It didn't take very long to figure out where the Officer's Club was situated. Soldiers in uniform and pretty ladies poured into and out of its German-made doors. Under escort, the girls crossed the cobblestone street and were just about to enter the club when a group of spiffed up GIs intercepted them.

"Hiya, ladies. You here for a dance or two?" As he pulled off his beret, the young GI flashed a gorgeous smile and thick head of dark hair.

"Hey…" Vera's sharp, city tongue swung into action. "That's Lieutenants to you, fella." She tapped the insignia pinned to her collar.

The officer held up his hands and backed up. "No offense, Lieutenant. I wasn't thinkin'."

Linda pushed through Vera's protective perimeters and held out her hand for the taking. "Well, tonight I'm not gonna let rank interfere with my fun. I'm Linda, and it's a pleasure, boys. Hopefully you're free for more than just a dance or two." She winked at the group of dashing young men and pressed a hand into her soft, blond curls.

"If you need partners, we're just the fellas you've been waiting for. My name's Albert Davis."

"Linda Parker. These are my friends." She gestured to each woman as she introduced them by name. Taking Albert Davis' offered arm, she glided into the Officer's Club and the gals followed along behind them.

Maggie stopped and looked back at an uncertain Peggy, who stared with wide eyes as Linda and Albert walked off.

"Peggy? You all right?"

"I haven't danced with a man since…"

Maggie nodded in understanding. "It's okay. You don't have to dance if you're not ready. They'll understand."

"I want to. I need to get on with my life."

"Then go and have fun. Don't feel guilty. Richard would want to see you happy." Maggie used soft tones, careful that she didn't embarrass Peggy.

"How do you know that?"

"Because I was in love once, and I know Danny wanted to see me happy. Richard loved you. He, too, would want you happy no matter what."

❦

Peggy watched as Maggie easily slipped her arm into the crook of Harry Thornton's—her dance partner for the evening. Peggy stepped inside the club and admired the way Maggie laughed at something Harry said to her. She seemed to carry on without hesitation or fear.

Could I ever be that woman again?

There were so many things about Maggie that Peggy admired. She was pretty, a good worker, a good friend, she carried a warm smile and seemed to get along with anyone. Everything she loved about the girl became the reasons for hating her. How had Peggy let herself get so far away from that kind of personality? She once was vibrant like Maggie, but the black hole she lived in sucked the life from her until all that remained was a cold skeleton. But Maggie somehow revived her and brought her back to what really mattered in life. It was time to let go of the past and get on with the future she was promised.

"May I bother you for a dance, miss?" A tall, blond-headed officer removed his beret and bowed. His English accent gave away the fact that he was a British officer.

A shimmer of hope glinted in her eye. It reached the corners of her mouth and prompted her hand to enfold in the warmth of the man requesting her presence with him.

A shy smile extracted a chuckle from his throat. "Forgive me, but you've got to be the most beautiful girl I ever happened upon."

He'd hooked her. Their eyes met under the dim light of the club and she found herself wrapped in the arms of a man. A swell of lighthearted emotion bubbled in the pit of her stomach. She'd spent too long holed up in her hatred and despair.

❦

Maggie's dancing partner, Harry, was a delight on the floor. He punched out more moves than Maggie knew existed. She tried her best to keep up with him, but he jitterbugged her into the floor.

"You'll have to quit showing off or I'll be leaving the dance floor early," she warned him in her teasing voice.

"We can't have that," he answered. "So, do you have a fella back home?"

"No."

"Lucky me."

"I have a boyfriend here in Germany. And a major at that."

"Not so lucky me. I better treat you with the best of respect then. I sure don't want to upset a major." His darling eyes gave her a wink.

"We would both appreciate that." A few more dance steps brought them to where Vera and Bonnie danced with their partners. The girls exchanged grins and winks then passed without bumping into one another.

Maggie watched Bonnie. The girl was enjoying her time away from work and camp. She was young and just testing her wings and freedom. Life exploded inside her and she couldn't keep her laughter from her eyes. But then something—or someone—caught Bonnie's eye from the darkened corner of the room. Maggie watched as she stopped and stared at the back of the tent where a young, handsome, and familiar pilot stood with his hat in his hands.

"Fred!" Bonnie shrieked. She broke free from her dance partner's embrace and rushed to the place her heart led her. "Fred!"

This time Fred found the owner of the voice—Bonnie's voice. His eyes lit with surprise and joy.

Bonnie leaped into his arms and laughed when he picked her up and twirled her in the air.

Maggie and Vera exchanged a knowing glance.

"Fred, I missed you so much. I didn't know you were here." Bonnie smoothed back the hair on the sides of his head as she cradled his neck.

"You can thank the censorship for that." He took a moment to drink in her facial features. Not once did Bonnie flinch or blush—a first for the girl. It must be love.

"It's so good to see you."

He brushed a stray hair from her face and placed it behind her ear. "You're a sight for tired eyes. Just beautiful."

"I was afraid I'd never see you again."

Fred ran his finger along her cheek and replied, "No, I'd make sure I saw you again." His gaze deepened. He lowered his head and she closed her eyes as he gently placed a kiss on her lips.

"Would you look at that," Vera said with a tilt of her head.

Maggie leaned toward Vera. "Looks like our little Bonnie is in love."

"Those two have a future together."

The music changed tunes and a slow number hung in the stale air. Harry placed his hands around Maggie's waist and held her in a gentle embrace. Maggie placed her hands around his neck and stepped into his lead. She glanced back at Fred and Bonnie as they danced in each other's arms.

Could they really be meant for each other?

They seemed happy. Such a sweet romance. Two young kids falling for each other while on the front battle lines. How romantic can it get? Then again, how tragic could it get? These times were uncertain and lives in enemy territory were not guaranteed a ticket home.

"Lieutenant?" Harry called out to her.

"Hmm?"

"Are you still having a good time?"

She made herself look him in the eye as she answered. "Yes. Very much so." She wrapped her arms around his neck and closed her eyes as she thought about Walter. Their relationship wasn't the same when she left. She was different now and she knew that Walter sensed it. Maybe that was why he tried so hard to keep her close to his side. Did she really love him or was she hanging on to him to replace what she'd lost in Danny?

✑✑

The women gathered for breakfast at mess and got their coffee fix for the long shift ahead. They'd returned to the 39th well after midnight, and 6 a.m. came in way too early.

"So girls, how was everyone's evening?" Vera asked playfully.

Linda sipped from her cup then inhaled deeply. "Divine. Albert was a perfect gentleman and easy on the eyes too."

The women giggled. Vera asked about Peggy's night. "Well, I was a little hesitant at first, I admit, but when Kenny led me to the dance floor, I felt like Cinderella at the ball. I think I want to do it again."

An *aww* arose from the quartet of women sitting at the table then they all smiled at Peggy when a blush stained her cheeks.

"All right, Miss Bonnie. What about you, dear? You were the last person to board the truck." Linda crossed her arms and leaned her elbows against the table as if ready to hear the juicy details of the night.

"I was having a good time just like the rest of you." Bonnie's eyes remained on her food.

"Ooh!" All three women exclaimed simultaneously.

"Aren't you a foxy little thing," Linda said. "You and your first partner didn't make it too long, but you and that cutie of a dark-haired fella sure romanced the night away."

Bonnie's cheeks flushed and she shifted uncomfortably in her seat. She brought her hands to her cheeks to cool them. "Fred is a nice guy. I happen to like him very much."

"Oh, he likes you too, honey. He didn't let you out of his sights all night." Vera added.

"I was so surprised when he walked in. I didn't even realize I was rushing up to him. Then, there I was being scooped up in his arms and twirled around."

"And just like that, girls, we've lost her," Maggie said as she placed her arms around Bonnie's shoulders.

After a time teasing back and forth, the women finished their meals then started for their stations.

As Bonnie walked with Maggie back to triage, she fumbled with her words. When she finally gathered her thoughts she asked, "Maggie, what do you really think of me and Fred together?"

"I think it's wonderful, Bonnie. Why do you ask?"

"I really like him. How do I know if it's real or not?"

Was Maggie really the best person to pose this question to? Because at the present moment, Walter was the furthest thing from her mind, and Danny was lost somewhere between life and death. "Actually, Bonnie, I'm not sure where Walt and I stand right now. I don't know for sure how you know someone is the one for you, but I know with Grace, she just knew. That's how she explained it to me. She just knew. There were no questions, no strings attached. I think if you really love someone, you'll do whatever you can for them and do it without thinking of yourself."

"I think Fred feels that way. At least he acts like it, but my heart does funny things when I see him, and I get butterflies in my stomach. But when I look in his eyes, I see more than a man wanting to impress a girl and take her out for the night."

Maggie nudged the girl's arm. "Hang in there. Time will tell. You only met a short time ago. You have to let your relationship grow."

"Maggie, that's the problem. I'm not so sure about time."

Maggie swiveled her head to face Bonnie.

"He's a pilot, Maggie. Do you know what the life expectancy of a pilot is?"

Maggie shook her head.

"Just a few hours in the air." Bonnie paused to let the words sink in then started again. "I'm afraid for him. I care so much for him and I don't want anything to happen."

Maggie reached over and covered Bonnie's hand with hers. "It'll be okay, Bonnie. If God wants it to be, it'll be. We don't have to fear the future, He holds it for us."

CHAPTER TWENTY-SIX

23 April 1945
Weiden, Germany

The camp was quiet, the women were quiet. Even the men seemed quiet. All was still. "It's kinda eerie, isn't it? The quiet, I mean." Bonnie folded another blanket and placed it on the shelf.

"Yeah. It hasn't been this quiet here in months." Linda entered triage at that moment and placed new bandage wraps in the supply cabinet.

"It's only the quiet before the storm," Peggy added. "Not that I'm trying to be a downer, but, well, you know how it goes."

"Golly, I sure hope you're wrong, Peggy. I'm already knee deep in paperwork as it is. I don't know what the docs were thinking giving me the paperwork to rest my wrist. All I ever do is use my hands!"

The girls unsuccessfully held back giggles. "Oh, Maggie. Getting you to stay off your feet is like forcing a horse to sleep lying down—it simply can't be done."

"Ah, unless you knock out the horse with sedatives first."

"Are you saying we should slip some codeine sulfate into your coffee?" Peggy grabbed alcohol and thread to stitch up a patient who'd just come in suffering a laceration to his arm.

"If you're passing out free samples *I'll* take some."

The girls stilled and looked to the private who quietly slipped into the tent and sat on the examining table waiting for his treatment. "I'm no sissy, but this kinda hurts somethin' fierce." He gestured to the gaping hole in his arm.

Maggie and the girls bit back giggles and went back to their work. Peggy went to stitching up the private then sprinkled sulfa powder on the affected area to ward off infection and sent him on his way with orders to come back that evening to change his dressing.

The unit's latest move to Weiden, Germany—a very little town inside

Bavaria—put them closer to the front lines. From her seat at the triage desk, Maggie gazed out the tent flap and into nothing. Leaving Hersfeld was difficult. She kept chiding herself for having the thoughts she was having, especially when she'd given her heart to Walt, but leaving the camp and the airstrip was like closing a chapter of her life forever. Every day she kept watch for Joe's return, and every night she laid her head down to disappointment. Whether the man knew it or not, he'd left with a small piece of her heart. Now she wished she'd fought to take it back, to stop him before he'd stolen something that wasn't his for the taking.

Maybe he truly was just a hallucination.

Her job pushed her past expectations. She was forced to adapt to sub-zero conditions and rural living arrangements. She'd given up the luxuries of home. She sacrificed sleep and exposed her body to foreign diseases. No wonder it was easy for her to slip into a delirious state after such a deadly attack. Shock itself most likely toyed with her mind.

She subconsciously fingered the gold cross that hung around her neck—the cross Danny had given her. Was she a fool for keeping it so close all this time?

A bang against the tent pole startled Maggie from her deep thought.

"Incoming wounded, Maggie, get ready."

Peggy immediately rushed out the door and Maggie began clearing the desk and examining table. She went for the glass bottles and syringes, knowing the wounded would need blood and fluids.

Then came the honking of horns and the pounding of doctors' and nurses' feet against the ground like a stampede of cattle. She listened to the sound of doors unlatching and swinging open in a barrage of hurried activity to get the wounded out of the vehicles and into the hospital.

She couldn't stay in the tent and listen to the moans and morbid cries for mothers from the men. She needed to get out there and do her job. Giving the room one last glance, she trotted out the door and went to assess patients.

"This one needs morphine!" "Amputee right here! To the OR!" "Chest wound. Get 'em into the surgery."

Familiar sights and sounds engulfed her, but it was the silent orders that always bothered her the most. That look of regret and sympathy followed by, "Don't worry, we're gonna make you as comfortable as possible." Nothing else could be done but administer morphine for the pain and call the chaplain for last rites.

Litter bearers invaded the moment—to her relief—and waited for her instruction. A boy, barely twenty years old, stared fixated on her and convulsed uncontrollably.

"What have we here?" She scanned his clothing to the exact source of bleeding. When she found it, she cut away his tunic and exposed his chest. "Someone gave you a souvenir, I see." She reached for the alcohol and gauze strips she'd placed in her pocket and cleaned around the wound. The patient gritted his teeth against the sting. "I'm so sorry, but it's needed." While she applied pressure to stop the bleeding, she eyed the litter bearer. "To the surgery right away." Then she lowered her voice to a whisper. "He's critical."

"Am I gonna die?"

The boy's quaking voice ripped at her heart. How she hated answering that question.

"Let me just tell you, I refuse to let anyone die under my care." She hoped he didn't sense the uncertainty behind her eyes when she smiled down at him. Young Peter Carlson swept into her mind and threatened to weaken her stance. But she held her own and maintained her composure for this young man's sake. As the litter bearers took him to the OR, she whispered a prayer for the young man whose life hung in the balance of eternity.

⊱⊰

More paperwork needed recording, and her mind needed rest. Although Maggie's injured wrist ached, she pushed past her inconvenience and took up the pen in her hand.

The wounded never stopped pouring in. Mountains of paperwork waited on the desk for completion and filing. So she went to work. One folder after another she opened, and one page at a time she completed.

Soon the job fell into routine and she needed not to think so much on the task at hand. Instead, she dreamed about going home. She could have agreed to leave this wretched camp and everyone in it when she returned with broken ribs and wrist. But that wasn't who she was. Although she longed for the comforts of home, her mind would never allow her rest if she didn't see this war through.

"Lieutenant Johnson?"

She snapped her head up and met the eyes of a corporal. "At ease, soldier."

The corporal's chest fell and stepped forward, presenting her with another file.

"From the major, Lieutenant. I have orders to get the signature of the nurse and physician who took on this case."

Maggie took the file and opened it, scanning its front page. It wasn't uncommon for the major to request signatures on questionable cases.

They'd sent so many home or back to the front on self-inflicted injuries that needed a doctor's signature, confirming the soldier-in-question's care. Or with so many going MIA and returning again, more authorizations were needed.

Her eyes drifted to the inside cover of the folder and caught sight of the ID photograph taken by the Army.

Her eyes bulged, and she re-read the name on the paperwork.

"Danny!"

The file fell from her hands and landed on her desk, wide open. Her hands pressed firmly against her mouth and a shock tingled every muscle, every nerve coiled in her body. Danny was alive!

"Lieutenant?" The corporal still stood at her desk, and she waved him away.

"Dismissed, soldier. I'll have the file ready in an hour."

Once the messenger left the room, she blew out a frazzled sigh. Her stomach twisted as if a fist landed a blow to it.

Maggie mulled over the file, reading every note.

"Physician on duty requests a dental record search be performed on unknown patient. According to account given by patient, patient was detained in a stalag for nearly one year. Patient has been diagnosed with amnesia, upon a mental examination. Patient now answers to the name, Joe."

A yellow slip of paper was paper-clipped to the next page. It was the Army's dental records.

"The United States Army dental bank confirms the existence of inquiring physician's patient. Patient #5246987 dental transcripts matches existing records and is therefore confirmed to belong to Lieutenant Daniel Emilio Russo of the 101st Airborne Division..."

She stopped reading.

Squeezing shut her eyes, two tears seeped from their corners. She couldn't believe what she saw. But there it was, in written confirmation.

Danny, indeed was alive. And he'd rescued her.

She knew it! In her heart she knew. Joe was her Danny.

And he'd left her again.

⋦⋐⋑⋙

"Johnson! I've a critical one here. I need your assistance."

Glad for the distraction, Maggie took swift steps toward the doctor and his patient.

But her nerves inched her toward disaster. How could she handle a needle or surgical utensil when her hands shook vehemently? Her life had just made a sudden and drastic turn.

"This guy has no ID or anything else indicating who he is, but he's suffering from a severe stomach wound. It's a mess, looks to be a few days old. I don't know how he's made it this long without help."

Maggie made notes on her clipboard then peeked past it to the patient.

The board and her notes slipped from her grasp and crashed to the floor. Her heart cried out a most mournful bellow and she gasped for air.

"Danny?" Tears sprung to her eyes. "Dear Lord. Oh, no." Her trembling hands reached for his face.

"Lieutenant, you know this man?"

She could hardly speak over the lump in her throat. "Danny?" A sob wrenched her chest and her hand pressed to her mouth as she looked to the doctor. "We have to save him."

"Ma—gee?" His voice was pitifully weak. "Is that your...sweet voice?"

"I'm here, darling."

"Lieutenant, we have to move to surgery now." The doctor turned to a passing technician. "Thompson, get me another nurse over here, pronto."

While the doctor hurried them toward the OR, Maggie kept her head tilted toward Danny and clung to his pale hand, already weak, and exhausted of strength. A fresh tear trickled from her eye, slipped down her cheek then dripped from her chin.

"I can't believe it's really you." Her hand tightened around his. She sniffed back her disbelief.

Danny's eyes struggled to open against the sun's rays. "See? I...told you I'd come ba—" A tortuous cough rattled his chest.

She fought to keep her tears at bay but nothing could stop her voice from wavering. She had no control over either. The seriousness of his condition frightened her. His body trembled uncontrollably and his complexion was a ghostly white. She couldn't lose him again. She couldn't.

Maggie studied his face. The shape of his high forehead, his cheeks, the slope of his nose . . .

She could see it all now. For weeks she'd worked to convince herself that this man couldn't be Danny, but now, there was no question. No question at all.

"You're all right?" His pained eyes rolled upward to meet her, but his query came out strained and barely audible.

"Thanks to you, yes." She smiled down at him, but he grimaced and closed his eyes. "You were always my hero." Leaning down, she pressed her cheek to his.

Surgical utensils clanged together, and the nurse who oversaw the anesthesia settled down at the gas valves, ready to prep Danny for his life-saving surgery.

"Maggie..." A slight smile reached his lips as he spoke her name. Then it faded. "I'm sorry, Maggie. I'm sorry. It hurts. It hurts real bad."

Between elation that he was alive and heart-wrenching fear that he would die—again—Maggie's throat flooded with tears. She swallowed hard to fight them back. "I know. Shhh. Just rest. I'll take good care of you." Her fingers smoothed back a lock of hair that had fallen across his forehead, and she leaned in to press a kiss against his brow. "I love you, Danny Russo." The nurse turned on the anesthesia while Maggie prepped her patient.

Although his eyes refused to open, his lips smiled his approval. All at once, the affliction of her heart withered away and hope re-entered her soul. Danny Russo—*the* Danny Russo—lay right in front of her.

"Lieutenant Johnson, are you capable of helping with this case?"

She shouldn't have been surprised to see the doctor ready for surgery but she was. Taking a deep breath and willing her nerves to calm, she answered, "Willing and able, Doctor."

All the months she spent looking for him. All the time she mourned him. And all the odd similarities she'd noticed over the past few weeks. He was alive. Her heart knew all along that his life hadn't ended like everyone said. Was that the reason for the nightmares and the nagging ache in her heart for him?

As the doctor began his patchwork on Danny's damaged skin, muscle, and inside tissue, she prayed. Like she'd never prayed before, she prayed hard. She and his family had suffered his loss once, she was not about to let it happen again.

Maggie kept the surgical area clean of blood and dirt as the doctor performed the procedure. After wiping away at his torn skin, her fingers brushed against his appendectomy scar. Memories flooded her mind. But now wasn't the time to walk down the road to her past. She needed to stay focused—for Danny's life depended on it.

"Doctor," the tech spoke up. "Heart rate is dropping."

Rachel D. Muller

Chapter Twenty-Seven

Buzzing thrummed in Danny's head, and his eye sockets throbbed. The overwhelming stench of sickness and burnt flesh turned his stomach in unpleasant ways. But the sweet memory of his Maggie being close enough to touch wiped away all graying shadows of the past year. He was never so glad to be out of the POW camp. Never happier to not have to jump out of another plane as long as he lived. All those terrible images of fiery C-47s crashing into the Normandy coastline, dead paratroopers hanging from trees, and the stench of trailing Germans—all those memories escaped his mind like a caged lion freed of its captivity. All those bottled up memories that begged to be unleashed exploded into twinkling embers of his life's past.

He touched a finger to his temple, unsure if he was living in a dream or truly dead this time. Could it be true? Was he really remembering everything that his mind had lost?

Danny. The angel-girl in his dreams. The Bible. The Letter.

Everything made sense as he lay there, lethargic on the outside, but fully aware on the inside.

He was Danny. Danny Russo. The man mentioned in Maggie's letter. And Maggie Johnson was his girl. Somehow, God allowed him to keep his promise and make it back to her. Although, now, he was scarred and knew his prognosis was bleak.

The explosion of memories ran each moment of the war through his mind like ticker tape, but when Maggie's voice called out to him, his eyes flew open, and he struggled to sit up in his cot.

"Maggie," he huffed, but his body refused to cooperate, sending another wave of nausea crashing against his stomach wall and draining his body of all strength. His eyes fell behind a black canvas where his mind found peaceful slumber.

"Maggie, your patient came to while you were gone. He's back out again and resting comfortably."

A stab of disappointment pricked at her. She was hoping to be present with Danny when he awoke. But her duties prevented her from spending every waking minute with him. Now that her shift was over, she could spend the rest of the day at his side. Not even food could pry her away from him. He came home...to her.

"Hey, kid."

"Vera." Maggie leaped into Vera's outstretched arms. "He's alive."

"I heard. News spread through the camp like wildfire. You're not one to keep your love life private, are ya?"

A subtle laugh softened Maggie's eyes. "I guess not. My heart's been telling me who he is for weeks now, I was just too stubborn to believe it."

"Then believe your heart now."

"That's why I have to be there when he wakes up. There's so much to say. So much I have to tell him. So many unanswered questions in my mind."

"Then go, Maggie. Put all those wonderings to rest."

Quietly, she stared down at him. He was so handsome—even after just coming from surgery. Maggie's fingers rustled a lock of his hair that fell over his brow. Wavy and coarse just like she remembered. It was amazing how much weight loss and hair growth could change a person's appearance. But as she studied every contour and crease of his face, she could picture his filled out and broad build. She could hear his quirky jokes and his chipmunk-like laugh. How could she not see that it was him all along?

After almost two years of separation, she sat reunited with the man she vowed to wait for. This time she wouldn't let him leave her sight. And when he recovered, she would see to it that he made the next ship home.

Danny stirred under her touch. She held her breath waiting for him to open his eyes and focus them on her, but he only groaned and slipped back into deep sleep.

Danny slept for two straight days. Maggie wondered if he would ever wake up. She considered the extent of his injury and the trauma his body underwent. It wasn't abnormal for someone with a bullet to the stomach to sleep days without waking.

She kept his wound clean, changed his blankets regularly, and kept the fluids running through his IV. When she wasn't tending to her other patients or resting, she faithfully stayed by Danny's side. Most importantly, she prayed for him without ceasing.

She found herself gazing at him, memorizing every wrinkle and crease of his face, longing for him to look at her, hoping he would see her for the first time and make ready to take her back in his arms and cover her in kisses. During those intimate moments inside the walls of her mind, she thought her heart would pound right out of her chest. The anticipation of that first meeting, post-op, both excited and frightened her.

She glanced down at her wristwatch. It was time to check his vitals. Maggie placed two fingers under his wrist and counted each heartbeat. Then she carefully took his temperature with the thermometer. All was normal and she blew out a thankful sigh. She went for her alcohol, water, iodine swabs, gauze, safety pins, penicillin, and cutting instruments.

She would take every precaution in cleaning his wound. Those ten terrifying moments when Danny's heart rate plummeted on the operating table were the worst ten minutes of her life. What could be worse than being handed a slip of paper, saying her loved one was dead? Losing him again.

She prayed until droplets of sweat beaded on her brow. Then, as if God had granted her request, Danny's heart rate raised—a true miracle.

"Peggy, I'm going to need help in a few minutes with the Lieutenant's dressing. Can you roll him for me?"

"Sure thing, Maggie. Give me the signal when you're ready."

"Thanks, Peg." Maggie took her tray and set it down next to Danny's cot. He slept peacefully. She started by giving him the injection of penicillin. He never flinched. Next, Maggie unfastened the pin that held his dressing together and cut through the fabric, taking extra care not to nip his skin. After discarding the old dressing, she cleaned the wounded area with water and alcohol then rubbed down his skin with iodine to kill any existing germs.

"Did you get all of the Lieutenant's paperwork in order?" Peggy asked as she disposed of the old bandages.

"You can bet your life I did." Maggie winked.

"I can't believe it. I just can't believe it." Peggy clucked her tongue and shook her head from side to side. "I mean out of hundreds of thousands of serving men, you end up stumbling upon your boyfriend who was dead. Isn't that one for the books?"

"That's how the Lord works, Peg. I can't explain it either, but I'm sure glad He worked it out that way."

"Do you think I'll learn to love again, Maggie?"

Maggie's eyes jumped to Peggy's face. "Why yes, of course, Peggy. I look at how far you've come in just a few short weeks and, well, I think you'll find that you have more love to give than anybody else here."

"You really think so, Maggie?"

"No, I don't *think* so. I believe it."

Danny stirred as she applied the iodine swab to his stomach. Her eyes shifted to his face and she watched for any signs of discomfort. His head turned from one side to the other and he grimaced—no doubt from pain.

"Peg? Will you get me some morphine for him, please?" Maggie turned her attention to her hands, which now packed his wound.

She was just about finished the task when Danny let out a slight groan. It took her another minute to wrap the area and clean up his skin. She worked quickly, yet gently, hoping to catch a glimpse of those dark Italian eyes when they opened.

"How about a date?"

Her hands stilled and her heartbeat quickened. A broad smile spread across her face. Danny really was back.

"I don't make it a habit to date my patients," she teased.

"I was talking about the little tart thing."

A soft laugh bubbled from Maggie's stomach, but she played coy. "Oh, that. I'm afraid my friend who gave me those is three thousand miles away."

"Well, then, forget the fruit. About that real date—can you make an exception for me?"

She didn't want to keep up the charade any longer. The bandages dropped from her hands and onto his cot. She threw her arms around his chest and shoulders. "Oh, Danny, you remember. You really remember everything? I was afraid you'd never regain your memory. Oh, how I missed you."

"Maggie. Sweet Maggie. If you only knew how many times I dreamed about you, and wished...wished I could remember your name, who I was, if I even had a family."

Large, crocodile tears streamed down her face and onto his pillow. She held tightly to him, wishing she could never let go. "I didn't know what to do when they told me you'd been killed. I searched months for you. I had no idea you'd been taken prisoner." Her eyes squeezed shut. "I love you, Danny. I love you so much. Don't ever leave me again, you promise me." She used her sternest voice and most pointed look as she came nose to nose with him. Yet love burst from the walls of her heart and leaked from every sense of her body—her touch, her eyes, her lips.

"Did I ever tell you how bossy you are?"

"Do you know what a relief it is to hear you say that? Speaking of relief, how are you feeling?"

"The pain is a bit overwhelming."

"The morphine should take over pretty soon. You'll probably start to feel sleepy again."

"What happened to me?" Danny attempted to lift his chin to his chest, no doubt to peer over his stomach to the wad of bandages wrapped against his skin, but his cut and wounded stomach muscles wouldn't allow him to raise his head. He groaned and his eyes rolled beneath pinched eyelids.

"You were hit in the stomach. The Lord was watching over you, though. The bullet just missed your major organs, but it was lodged pretty good in your abdominal cavity. The doctor was able to retrieve the bullet and stitch you up. If the infection stays at bay, you'll make a full, but somewhat painful, recovery."

"How long have I been out?"

"Two days." Danny began the fight to keep his eyes open. Not able to resist the urge building in her chest, Maggie slowly leaned in and touched her lips to his forehead. A satisfied moan vibrated his chest. "Don't fight it. Sleep is best. Close your eyes." For only a second, she pressed her forehead to his and relished in the moment. This is where she wanted to stay. This was where she belonged.

Dear Grace,

Danny's alive! Maybe the news will have already spread through town by the time this letter reaches you. I wired Danny's parents as soon as I was able to tell them the wonderful news . . .

She couldn't put into words the elation she felt to be able to write this kind of letter. The joy everyone would feel when they learned Danny was alive. Everyone would marvel at his story and rejoice with his family. How she wished she could be there when the news reached them. And Luke...how would Luke react to the news of his best friend's revival and homecoming?

"Knock, knock."

"Come in, Vera. It's me."

"Good. Just the gal I was lookin' for." Vera smacked her gum between her teeth. "Mail call. You've got letters."

"Wonderful. Just place them on my cot. I'll get to them later."

"Um…you might want to read one of them now."

Maggie looked up from her parchment on which she was writing. "What's with the urgency?"

"Well, it seems in the midst of all this joy of her old boyfriend coming back from the dead that Lieutenant Johnson forgot about someone…like her current boyfriend."

Maggie's face fell and a sickening revolt of dread roiled in her stomach. Her lip curled upward in a disgusted fashion, and she looked away. "Oh, Vera. How could I have forgotten?"

"Beats me. I thought when you loved someone you didn't see anyone else." Vera placed a hand on her hip and waited for an explanation.

"Now, Vera, I know what you're getting at, and I—I've put this off for far too long."

"Yes, you have, honey. You need to either let go of the man you lost once or let go of the man who's loved you unconditionally since Danny's death."

"I don't want to hurt either of them."

"Well, you can't juggle them both, kid. Trust me, I've tried and it don't work."

"Heavens, Vera."

"Are you going to tell Danny about Walt?"

"No! I can't let him find out. Whatever happens, Vera, Danny cannot find out about Walt. Especially right now."

"Why not? He's going to ask what you've been up to since he's been gone. Sooner or later it has to come up."

"Just not now while he's still so fragile and susceptible to relapse."

"Look, you're grown up enough to handle your own affairs and I won't be the one to interfere. I'm only warning you that if you don't put one of them to rest soon, it ain't gonna be good for you, kid."

In her heart she knew Vera was right. She was only doing Maggie a favor by warning her of the dangers of keeping secrets. But until she could confront Walt face to face and explain what transpired over the last two months, she couldn't breathe a word to anyone.

CHAPTER TWENTY-EIGHT

E veryone he knew thought him to be dead.

That explosive realization hit Danny like a shell dropping at his feet. Maggie thought he was dead. His parents thought he was dead. Oh, heavens above, how did his mother take the news? He was never one to allow his emotions to get the best of him, but just thinking of his mother grieving the loss of her own child sickened his stomach and stung his eyes. He fought hard to maintain his tough guy composure, but even the news of his own death shook him to his inner core.

He'd been a fool to hand his ID tags and photograph of Maggie to his buddy. It seemed like a good idea at the time, but it sure caused him a world of trouble. He recalled that day—the day he jumped into an unfamiliar land and surrendered his identity to save his buddies...

D-Night, 1944, Normandy, France
2 miles east of Saint-Come-du-Mont

"Check Equipment!" Although the jumpmaster shouted, the thunderous roar of the C-47 SkyTrain's engines muffled his voice, drowning out the harshness of his tone.

The boys of the 101st Airborne Division had an estimated four minutes of life certainty until they reached the drop zone.

With his left hand on the snap, and his snap hooked to the cable, Danny double checked his equipment load. Everything was there: his carbine, his reserve chute, medical kit, leg bag, knife, jump rope. He was ready for this drop.

His cheeks inflated, and he blew out a long breath of air to calm his jittery nerves.

It's just another jump. No different than the hundreds of other jumps we've made.

But really, it wasn't just another jump. He knew that. They all knew that. At this point in his military career as a paratrooper, he had no guarantees after these next 4 minutes...and counting.

Danny exchanged glances with Quincy Easton, or "Easy", as the guys liked to call him. Quincy nodded in Danny's direction. "Good luck, Little Italy. See you at the bottom. Don't let the moon cast a glare on that big nose and give you away."

Danny smiled at the use of his nickname, but wouldn't let Quincy get the last jab. "You too, Easy. Hey, remember to jump out with both feet first and not your head this time, got it?"

Easy glared at him, but the partial red stain on his cheeks told Danny he remembered that harrowing incident in which the paratrooper had somehow lost his balance and plunged head first out of the C-47 and into mid-air, falling up-side down during practice runs. Thankfully, the paratrooper-in-training avoided getting caught in his static lines and made a safe landing.

Easy survived. They'd all survived their training and a few mishaps. The practice runs were over and the real deal awaited just three minutes in their future...and counting. Danny listened to the drone of the plane. That same drone he'd become accustomed to over the last six months. The only difference was tonight the fellas didn't banter back and forth inside the fuselage like they'd done so many times before. Sunlight didn't stream through the small windows. Instead, the air inside the stuffy troop carrier's belly reverberated with twenty heartbeats. Training for battle was over. This was the real test—and no one could secure the return trip home.

"Sound off for equipment check!"

Danny snapped his head up and looked toward the jumpmaster. The boys counted down in their sequence. "Twenty, okay!" "Nineteen, okay!"

Deep breaths. In and out.

"Fourteen, okay!"

The men in his stick continued to sound off with their assigned number. While waiting for his cue, Danny made a mental note of what he needed to remember for the mission ahead. *Welcome* and *Thunder* were the friendly D-night code words. As long as he remembered those two phrases he wouldn't be shot by his own outfit. He patted his jacket's side pocket. His cricket was tucked securely inside. The small clicker would be his tool in identifying and communicating with his men over long distances in the bush after landing.

"Seven, okay!"

His stomach lurched. That was his cue to sound off. "Six, okay!" The effort of calling out his number relieved a smidge of bottled-up tension. His shoulders relaxed, and Danny closed his eyes, inhaling deeply as he did.

Lord, help us tonight. If we die, may we die with dignity and for a cause. But I ask that you grant me the will to survive...so I can make it home to Maggie and Mom.

Maggie. Her name whispered through his mind like a summer breeze. It had been so long since he saw her last, and letters just weren't enough. He ached for the feel of her petite fingers inside his calloused palms. He longed to hear her laugh at his corny jokes, even if they were awful. And his lips burned to say the words he wanted to repeat over and over to her.

Suddenly, the plane jumped, and the boys' knees buckled at the unexpected gravitational shift.

Danny's eyes burst open.

Then they heard it—the screeching sound of metal against metal. Danny's heart accelerated, nearly breaking through his chest.

"What the—" "What'd we hit?" A swell of panic rose in the fuselage. Danny's pulse seemed to match the plane engine's rpm. His neck veins pounded in his throat.

"Settle down, men. We're entering dense flak. Keep calm, and hopefully it'll stop by the time we reach the drop zone. We're over the beachhead."

A flash illuminated the troops' profiles with a red glow. Danny ducked his head to peer out the window, looking for what could have caused the fiery tint. His eyes followed the smoke trail lit up by a burning C-47 SkyTrain.

"It's chalk 26," he announced through a regretful breath.

"Do you see any 'chutes?"

Danny strained to look for the ballooning white sails of paratroopers through the haze and darkness, but nothing appeared. Then a large fireball erupted from the ground.

Danny leaned into his snap and closed his eyes. A dull pain rising up the corridors of his chest made it difficult to breathe. "No 'chutes. They're gone."

Toward the back of the fuselage, the sound of liquid splattering against the cold, metal floor brought everyone's attention to the last man in his stick, Wayne Dresden.

"Awe, Wayne! Come on! Those were my new boots! Use yer helmet next time, would ya?" Percy Layton was the unlucky recipient of mortal fear spilling at his feet.

The air inside the troop carrier grew eerily quiet. Flak and machine gunfire ceased just as quickly as it came. As they flew under the cover of night, a shadow fell over the men inside the SkyTrain. The reality of this moment being their last passed over each man as if the death angel himself hovered above them, making his next selection.

At least they weren't over the ocean. At least if the plane took on heavy damage and the crew had to bail, he'd land on dry, gritty soil. Maybe those horrible nightmares wouldn't come true after all.

In the next seconds, the only sound heard was the drone of the engines. But then the hatch popped open and the jumpmaster hollered, "Go! Go! Go!"

One by one, each man placed his hands on both sides of the door and pushed his way out of the fuselage, leaving no time to think, and his parachute trailing close behind.

Danny moved further up the line until he stood on the edge of the plane's floor, staring down into the blackened earth beneath him. He took one final breath and lunged into hollow darkness. The air rushed against his face, and the load from his leg bag hung heavy around his lower half. He began counting the seconds.

1, 2, 3, 4...

Below him, he could see hundreds of white balloons gracefully floating in the night air. He looked for signs of flak and tracers, but found none. He let out a sigh of relief and relaxed. Maybe their surprise attack would be executed after all.

8, 9, 10...

Then his body yanked and a shock pulsed up his body as his harness pulled taut on the static lines. He looked up to check his 'chute. It was intact and ballooned. All he had to do was keep his count and guide himself safely to the ground, which was quickly coming up to meet him.

34, 35, 36, 37...

He hung in the air peacefully. It was almost as enjoyable as the practice jumps he and the guys performed back at Ramsbury Airfield in England. The kind of jumps where a man could sit back and enjoy the sights around him. Sights like patchwork patterns on the fields below, or how funny it seemed that his commanding officers looked like little ants walking across the airstrip below his booted feet. Or...

Fireworks?

From the corner of his eye, sprays of green, red, and blue followed in dotted lines across the sky. But they weren't fireworks. No, they were...

"Tracers!"

His heart lurched, and his stomach dropped a few inches into his abdomen. Those tracers were following the descent of his fellow men, and the bullets were slowly, yet all too quickly, making their way in *his* direction!

In natural reaction, he kicked his feet to avoid getting hit by bullets. The ground was closing in on him, fast.

Wait! His leg bag! He pulled the cotter pin that held the bag in place. It dropped and dangled by the rope 20 feet below him. Then he heard it hit the ground.

47, 48, 49...

With a thud and a groan, Danny slammed into the ground and rolled. A slight sting started in his feet and worked its way up to his ankles. He made quick work of collapsing his parachute so the enemy wouldn't spot him. While doing so, he prayed that his recovering ankle injured from a sprain received in training wasn't re-injured. Danny pressed his stomach low into the ground, listening for any signs of German soldiers. He spotted the silhouette of one paratrooper bunching up his parachute before he ran for cover.

How long had he been in the air? Nearly 50 seconds, which meant he'd made his descent from an altitude of 1,000 feet.

Danny stumbled to his knees and tried to work the 3-piece harness clip. He couldn't control the shaking in his hands. His thumbs fumbled with the latches and the mechanism wouldn't give. Glancing over his shoulder, he heard another trooper crash into the ground and moan. Finally giving up on the complicated contraption, he pulled his knife from his boot and cut his lines. He wouldn't need his 'chute for the duration of this mission.

Machine gunfire sounded off in the distance.

Shoving the harness to the ground, he abandoned the silk and ran for the nearest hedgerow. The ground crunched beneath him as his boots stomped the grassy terrain under his feet. When he reached the tall thicket of brush, he leaped inside its confines and covered his head.

He'd never felt more alone.

⧉⧉

A little more time than he wanted to allow had passed. Keeping an ear open for unwanted guests, he rose to his knees, pulled out his compass, and checked his coordinates. He was facing north. The two wooden bridges that HQ Company were ordered to take out were approximately six miles inland off the coast of Normandy...Utah Beach to be exact. If they landed in their drop zones, they should be a few short miles from the bridges. Now all he had to do was locate a few men from his stick and set for the Canal de Carentan.

Danny placed the compass back in his pocket, but rushing footsteps made him freeze. The sound was getting closer. Heavy gasps of breath heaved from the individual who rushed toward him. Slowly, Danny lowered himself into the ready position. It could be one of his own guys. Then again, it could be the enemy.

Without warning, the figure jumped into the hedges, knocking into Danny and rolling the two of them on the ground. Danny reached for his knife as the two wrestled. The body tumbled over him, landed on his side, and groaned. Danny pressed his hand down firmly on the chest of the soldier, securing him with the strength in Danny's brawny arms and shoulders. He held the knife close to the man's chest, letting him know he had the upper hand.

The whites of the soldier's eyes grew wide and wild. His hands lifted up in surrender and his breath came so quickly that Danny wondered if the man was hyperventilating.

"Don't kill me. Um...*welcome*?"

Danny's shoulders slumped, and he let out a relived sigh. He knew that high voice. "Geez, Copper, you almost got yourself killed. Why didn't you use the code sooner?" He placed his blade back in its sheath.

Copper scurried to his feet and brushed off his jacket then bent over with his hands on his knees to catch his exasperated breath. "How was I supposed to know this hideout was taken? I can't see a darned thing. Do you know where we are, Italy?"

More gunfire sprayed into the night sky.

"I think I've got a pretty good clue. We need to head northwest. The bridges shouldn't be too far out."

"I'm worried about those machine guns. If they saw us come in like they did, I'm sure the whole coastline has been alerted by now."

That's what Danny feared. But they had a job to do. Whether it put them in harm's way or not, they were sent to carry out an important mission. There was no backing out.

"Come on, Copper. Maybe if we start walking, we'll meet up with the rest of the guys. This is chaos."

More C-47's flew overhead, dropping their cargo of armed soldiers into heavy machine gunfire. In the distance, another explosion erupted on the horizon and Danny wondered if another SkyTrain dropped from the sky. A building, resembling a barn, burned ferociously across the field, casting an orange glow over the countryside. Thankfully, the paratroopers' faces were blackened with war paint. The flat coating would repel any reflection from their skin.

The pair set off into the night. Danny prayed for protection as they trekked across the field toward the French town. Within minutes, they came upon a small farm. A large pine tree stood tall and sturdy to their right. Taking a glance toward the farmhouse, Danny wondered if the French people inside had any idea of what was taking place outside their front door. Thank the good Lord that back home his family and Maggie were safe and had very little threat of the enemy landing outside their own homes.

As they crossed in front of the tree, they heard the small click-clack-click of a cricket from behind the pine.

Danny stopped Copper by holding up his palm and bringing his finger to his lips. Without speaking, he pulled his cricket from his pocket and returned the clicking.

"Oh, thank goodness. It's you guys." A short paratrooper stepped out from behind the tree.

"What stick are you from?" Danny asked.

"Twelve."

"Have you located the rest?"

"No. You're the first two friendlies I've happened upon. Can I join you? I'm lost as all get out."

Danny and Copper exchanged glances then Danny jerked his head, indicating for the man to follow.

"Gee, thanks, fellas. I'm Private Don Hampden."

"Danny Russo. And this here is Copper. Where was your platoon heading?"

"For the footbridge."

"Well, Private Hampden, your plans just changed. You're coming with us."

❧❧

It seemed they'd wandered around for hours. Surely the horizon would start to lighten any minute now, exposing their unwanted attendance on French soil.

"Duck in those hedges." Frustrated, Danny plopped his rear on the ground and slammed his helmet onto the dirt. "We should have reached those bridges by now." Although he kept his voice to a whisper, his sharp tone couldn't be concealed. "We have no navigator. No radio. Geez, I don't even have a charge! Do either of you have charges on you?"

Copper and Don looked at one another. Both regretfully shook their heads.

A pathetic laugh blew from his mouth. His hands rubbed at the fatigue that was settling in his eyes. "So that's it. We've come all this way, walked this long, and we don't even have proper equipment to get the job done. Some soldiers we are."

"Hey, speak for yourself!" Don cut in. "Now I may not be a commissioned officer or some big shot like that, but I do have half a mind! Now I've been thinkin' this through all night. I suppose those planes missed the drop zone. Also seems to me that if our buddies made it to the ground we'd come across someone by now. What if they're all dead?"

"Come on, Don, shut up! Don't you even think for a moment that our battalion has been wiped out." Copper's breath wheezed from his nose. His temper was sparked and if Danny didn't step in now, a fight was inevitable.

"Lay off, Copper." He stepped between the quarreling men and squared Copper's eyes. "Not tonight. Right now we need each other. Don's just giving his opinion, and quite frankly, what he said makes a good deal of sense. We need to keep trekking and hopefully meet up with someone who knows where on earth we are and get this mission over with. Don't let your nerves get the best of you. Not here. Not now. Got it?"

Copper's eyes bore down on Danny's but he found the reserve to back down. "All right, Italy. But only because—" Copper stopped midsentence. His eyes grew wide, terror freezing his jaw in place.

Don heard the impending danger as well because he turned and shouted, "Holy smokes! Watch out!"

All three men craned their heads to the sky above. A screaming, fiery engine barreled toward them. The small crew scrambled for cover, each taking his own path out of the destruction zone.

Danny's heart thundered in his chest. The plane was right on his heels. He could almost feel the heat from the burning fuselage singeing his back. He glanced over his shoulder. The plane's nose loomed a mere thirty feet above his head! He saw a ditch up ahead and pumped his legs as fast as he could to reach it in time. With a mere second to spare, he threw himself into the culvert and covered his head. The C-47 collided with the ground on which they were standing just seconds before. The explosion was enough to rattle Danny's entire body and the earth beneath him. The fireball roared as it reached skyward and the flames crackled in anger.

Had the crew made it out safely?

After the explosions ceased, Danny raised himself to his knees. This night was a complete disaster.

"Hey! Little Italy! You all right?"

He scratched the back of his head with his fingers and panted heavily.

He dodged another misfortune. How many more would he encounter before the mission was accomplished?

•⧉❦⧉•

Two more troopers wandered into the area and joined Danny's patchwork crew. Thankfully, enlisted man, Roy Spears, had two charges on him to blow the bridges.

Gunfire still echoed in the distance. The enemy was well aware there were Americans on their turf. The group continued their cautious walk through the dark countryside. Danny kept one eye on the road ahead of him and one eye over his shoulder. The creeping sensation that someone watched them became stronger over the last few minutes. Danny spotted the outline of tall trees up ahead. At least that would give them a little ground cover.

"Sure would be nice if we stumbled on the colonel." Copper pulled a cigarette from his pocket and attempted to light up.

"Hey! Douse that light!" Danny lunged for the match, shoving Copper backwards.

"Watch it, Italy! That was my last smoke."

"You can't light that thing up here. It'll tip the German's off for sure! You want to be their homing beacon? I sure don't!"

"You owe me a smoke when this thing clears out, Russo. No one messes with my cigarettes."

"Lay off, Copper. Those things will kill ya anyway."

"Hey...Lieutenant?"

Danny paused and faced Don, whose eyes became large and round as he stared up into the branches of the poplar trees.

"What is it Don?"

"I—I think I found the colonel."

Acidic bile bubbled in Danny's stomach. The wavering in Don's voice concluded that it wasn't a good find. Danny swallowed hard and braced himself.

His eyes lifted toward the top branches. Sure enough there was the colonel...his eyes bulged and his head angled in an awfully awkward position.

He swiped at his brow. "It's the colonel all right." Pain crested over his chest. This was a man he'd reported to just hours earlier. Now he was dead. "Can we cut him down?"

Clearly in a state of shock, Copper only stood there with his jaw slack.

"Copper! I said, can we cut him down?"

"Uh...yeah. Let me get my rope and—"

"Halt!"

All five men startled at the sharp, German hiss. They turned toward the voice, already knowing who was standing behind them.

Nazi soldiers stood with lugers ready in their hands. The soldier in charge hollered out German orders.

"Hände hoch oder wir schiessen!"

"What's he saying?" An exasperated edge shook Danny's voice.

"They want us to put our hands behind our heads and stand," Don replied.

"Do we comply?"

"If we don't, they shoot."

"They'll shoot us regardless."

The German called out another order.

"Lieutenant, we better do what we're told—now."

Reluctantly, the American soldiers raised their hands to their heads. The German officers motioned for them to line up. So this was it. This was how the great Danny Russo was to spend his final few minutes in this world—a casualty by German hands. The Nazis were ruthless, not caring if they killed men, women, or children in cold blood. As the boys lined up, the Nazi soldiers surrounded them with their lugers still pointed at their chests. Danny and his men were about to die, or worse, become prisoners of war.

Before Danny had time to think up a plan to get them out of this mess, a sharp blow to his left temple threw him to the ground. With a kick to his stomach and another blow to his head, all grew fuzzy—then all went black.

❧❦

Just a few hours before, Danny awoke over Copper's shoulders. The Germans forced Copper to carry Danny's limp body as they marched to who-knew-where. After coming to and shaking the blur from his vision, Danny's mind began to clear.

As they sat in the crammed rear of a transport's truck bed, Danny tried concocting an escape plan.

To ensure he didn't get caught, he ripped his stripes and insignias from his uniform and found a rusted hole in the bed of the truck. Stuffing a piece of his identity through the hole, he watched it disappear to the speeding ground below him. One last prayer sprinted through his mind...

Help me find my way back, Lord.

The truck rolled to a stop and they were forced out of the transport.

With all six of them standing with their hands pressed behind their heads and German rifles pressed against their sides, they were ordered to march. He knew the only way to save the lives of his buddies was to risk his own. With his plan still formulating in his mind, he waited until they'd walked a little more than two hours and come to a road lined with trenches.

But his plan wouldn't work here. He didn't know an ounce of German. How would he communicate his bogus plans to his captors? He needed to think fast before they ended up being shot and thrown into those live graves stretched out before them.

"Juniper." He called out the order before having a rifle's butt thrust to his stomach. At least he'd gotten the code name for a hand-to-hand combat scheme out of his mouth before the Nazi stole his breath.

As soon as he recovered from the gut-wrenching blow, he lunged for the guard and took him to the ground. The others followed suit and two gun shots rang in their ears. When Danny looked up, two guards lay face down in the dirt.

That's when he gave his dog tags and Maggie's photo to Jumper and told him to run. "Hold these for me until I see you again. Don't give them to anyone unless I don't make it. Now go!"

After Jumper's narrow exit, Danny remembered a sharp blow to his head then waking up in a dank, dark, prison shack.

That's where Al Flemming befriended him and nursed him back to stable health.

But what of Abe and Al? How did the rest of his buddies fare after liberation? And what about the ten months of his life which were non-existent? What about home? Too many unanswered questions surfaced in the swell in his brain, causing a severe headache to pound inside his skull.

Chapter Twenty-Nine

1 May 1945

The whole camp stood in utter silence as all seemed to hold their breath for the impending announcement coming from Army officials. How much more bad news could they bear after hearing the devastating loss of President Roosevelt? Sadness dwelled in Maggie's heart for the man who would not see this war to a victorious end.

However, they'd had their share of false alarms—especially here lately. Several weeks prior, Congress made a statement informing the U.S. citizens that the war in Europe had officially come to an end—but not according to the wounded boys pouring off the fields and into the hospital. Had someone forgotten to inform the enemy?

A glance to her left, Vera and Bonnie were chewing furiously on their nails while Peggy worried her lip. Maggie couldn't keep the jitters away from her own body as she bit down on her diminishing fingernails.

"What's taking so long? Let's just get this over with already so we can get back to work." Vera raked her fingers down her fatigues, obviously agitated and worried.

Whispers and murmurs lifted from the group huddled together outside of headquarters. Maggie shifted her weight to her other foot and folded her arms across her chest. The suspense gnawed at her. Finally, the colonel emerged from HQ and everything around them fell eerily silent.

With a written form in his hand, the colonel held up his massive hand and demanded all eyes and ears on him.

"This just in from the general." He took a moment to read silently over whatever it was that caused concern and defeat to wrinkle across his face. After one swipe of his lip, he continued, "Hitler's dead." Gasps and more murmurings rose from the crowd, but the colonel held his hand up once more to silence them. "He and his fiancé, Eva Braun, were found dead in the Fuhrerbunker inside Berlin yesterday. Eisenhower expects a surrender by the Nazi Party Minister within the week."

Not able to contain the joy they all felt, a roar of cheers went up along with laughter and tears. Nurses hugged one another and soldiers slapped one another on the back. The jubilant crowd broke out in dancing, and garrison caps went flying into the air.

Maggie stood with eyes wide and unyielding, staring into a space somewhere between reality and fantasy. Could it be true this war would finally end? Will they all be going home in just a few short weeks?

"Maggie? Yoo-hoo...earth to Maggie. Can you believe it, kid?"

She blinked out of her trance and zeroed in on Vera. "I—I can't. It's too good to be true." Slowly, the corners of her mouth lifted upward and excitement worked its way into her heart as the news sunk in. With a sudden burst of energy, she threw herself into Vera's arms and shrieked, "We'll be going home! Oh, it's marvelous!"

Bonnie and Peggy joined the duo in celebratory delight. The pop of bottle corks sounded one at a time as blissful men reveled in the moment with rounds of alcohol they'd acquired in the German towns by bartering their cigarettes and chocolates. When the bottle was passed to Maggie, she politely declined the spirited drink and celebrated with praises to God instead.

"Peggy, won't the boys lying in those tents be so glad to hear the news?"

"I can't think of a better time to announce this proclamation than now—whaddya say?"

Maggie's nose scrunched as the brightest smile to ever be displayed on her face broke free. Linking arms with Peggy, they skipped to the tent where Danny rested.

❧❦

"Hey, there she is!" Danny's pulse hammered as soon as Maggie's silhouetted form stepped inside the ward. He touched a hand to his clean shaven face, glad for the chance to clean up before Maggie returned.

"Look at you! You're all spiffed up today." She placed a kiss on his forehead then sat down with a meal tray and rested it on her lap. She leered at him in a way he couldn't place. "You look more like yourself today. It's amazing what a little extra hair can do for a person. I'm glad to see you shaved clean—you look just like I remembered."

He rubbed a hand against his jaw. "Yeah, I figured you've seen the worst of me for long enough. Did I miss any spots?"

Maggie leaned in and took his chin between her fingers and inspected his face. She was close enough he could smell her perfume emanating from her skin. It was a sensation strong enough to force his eyes closed. Right now he longed to take her in his arms and kiss her like the day he'd left her at the train station.

"Handsome as ever. I brought you lunch. Pretend it's a gourmet meal complete with all the trimmings."

All too soon she pulled away. He felt a smidge of disappointment that she didn't linger longer—long enough for him to pull her into that kiss he so desperately wanted.

Before he could read her, she placed his tray on his lap and asked if he needed help cutting his food to which he replied, "Baby, you know me well enough by now. I make a terrible patient. I can cut my own food, but if you want to sit here and nurse me back to health, feel free to spoon-feed me then serve me dessert by sitting right here—" he patted his knee—"and letting me kiss that beautiful mouth of yours."

Instead of laughing freely, she only giggled and shook her head. "Oh, you're back to your old self all right. I can smell the ham on your breath already." With the exception of glancing over at him while she teased, she kept her eyes on her work station. That was Maggie, always keeping a professional stance while at work.

Danny took his knife and cut into his beef. "How about a little company while I eat? If you're nice to me, I'll share."

He heard her sigh and saw her check her wrist watch out of the corner of his eye.

"I wish I could stay longer, Danny. But I only have a few minutes before I start my rounds. I have exciting news to share with you."

"Oh yeah? Well, it's about time someone had something good to share." He bit into a slice of roast beef.

"Hitler is dead. Confirmed today. The colonel just read the bulletin."

His fork clanked to his tray and he struggled to hold his jaw closed. "Truly? So it's over? Have they surrendered?" He found himself leaning so far over his cot that his cup of water spilled over the tray and saturated his blanket. "Oh, geez. Maggie, I'm s—"

She jumped to his aide. "It's all right. I'll clean it up."

"Guess I'm not as suave as I once was."

Her big, brown eyes locked with his for a heartbeat. If he didn't think she could get any more beautiful than she already was, he was wrong. At that moment, all his pain faded away and all he could see was her. It was like seeing her for the first time all over again. She still held his heart captive even after all this time.

She made quick work of tidying up his mess. She removed his tray then went for another blanket. Thankful for her quick return, he didn't waste time seeking out her attention.

"Maggie. Look at me."

Her hands pulled away the moistened, wool blanket and she reached for the fresh one, averting her eyes from his.

"Maggie."

She allowed the fresh blanket to unfold then stretched it over Danny's body.

Now he knew she was keeping her distance. But why?

So he waited.

Her hands tucked the blanket around his feet and she worked her way up his side, stopping when she reached his mid-section. But before she could pull away, he captured her hand.

"Maggie, look at me, please." He tipped her chin.

Her chest heaved up and down and her eyelashes swept upward, revealing those coffee-colored eyes that he adored.

"I still love you, Maggie. Maybe now more than ever, I love you." Would she allow him to swoop in for a tender brush of his lips?

"I—I…we have so much to talk about, Danny."

Was that a little bit of sadness he detected in her voice?

"Well, baby, it looks as though I'm not goin' anywhere for a while. I've got all the time in the world to talk."

"Maybe after my shift. When it's quiet. I have so many questions that are left unanswered. It's been nearly a year, Danny. And then you don't know about—" She stopped herself and cupped a hand over her mouth.

"Know about what?"

❧❧

Of all the places to hold a private conversation, this was not it. Maggie constrained herself against spilling every trifle of news that Danny had missed since his departure. Worse than that, she'd made up her mind to pull away from Danny until she could clear the waters of her love life and make an honest decision.

She cared for two men, but she loved only one.

One had left her, disappearing from her life, and she'd buried him. The other swooped in like her Prince Charming, only instead of riding on his white horse and wearing royal cloth, he'd driven a jeep and worn his formal olive drabs. But still, Walt's merits hung proudly from his uniform in colors of silver, gold, red, and blue. At the time of her mourning, he was very much like royalty. But now the ruse of Walt's knighthood faded. The love she felt for Danny ran through the blood in her veins. She couldn't live without him.

She needed to tell Walt the truth about Danny.

⋙⋘

Under the soft glow of a crescent moon, Maggie supported Danny's side as they walked to a cleared spot, free of brush.

"Easy does it," she said as she lowered him to a wooden chair. "How is the pain?"

"It hurts." His voice was tense and tight, however his eyes were soft and inviting. "But it's worth it."

"I promise, each time you get up and use those muscles again, the better it gets with every passing day."

"It already feels better than that first day."

Her giggle sounded soft, even to her. "The first day's a real brute."

Silence befell them and Maggie rested her eyes as a soft breeze blew in across the countryside. She was glad for the warmer weather that finally moved in.

"Danny? Do you remember…everything?"

From the corner of her eye, his profile shifted in her direction. "All too well."

"What happened to you? What did they do to you?"

His slow intake of breath hissed into the breeze and she caught sight of his hands sliding down his leg and over his knees, as if cleansing them from bad memories.

"Well, it was just like an ambush. They must've seen us land and waited. I know I made sure we weren't being followed, but still, they pounced on us like wildcats."

"I'm so sorry, Danny."

"I didn't remember giving Jumper my tags and your picture until just the other day. I didn't want them to have any reason to trace me back to my unit or…you. And just in case anything happened…I—well, I hoped they'd find their way back." His eyes lingered on her long enough to let her see the depth of his words.

Maggie's eyes drifted shut and the feel of Danny's calloused hand brushed against her cheek. "You kept coming to me, Maggie. Over and over again. I don't know how my mind could ever forget you, but it killed me inside. I knew I belonged somewhere. I just…"

She waited for him to finish the thought, but words seemed to escape him.

"The thought of you being alone and beaten saddens me."

"That's all in the past now."

"But so much time has gone by since then, Danny. What if we're not the same people we once were?"

The first sound of bullfrogs, croaking in the evening, rose from the marshes. Her words seemed to hang somewhere between the distance from her to Danny. She felt his eyes on her, prodding her with questions, looking for answers.

"Are you thinking I've lost my mind?" His silence tore her in two. It was the only question she could think to ask him at the moment.

"I'm thinking I'm scared to death that I may have lost you in the time I was gone."

The edge of his words—although spoken softly—sliced through her guarded heart with speed and extreme precision. She wanted Danny. Loved him more than she could have ever imagined. But would they be able to pick up where they left off as easily as she hoped? There were so many missing pieces.

"Danny, so much has happened since August, 1943. Haven't you once wondered how I got here?"

"Well, yeah, but your letter said you were training—"

"Do you know what I went through to even get to Germany? And the hurdles I've had to jump just to hold things together when it all wanted to fall apart?" She stood to her feet, hands upturned. "And what about your mother, and Grace?"

"Yeah, but Maggie there's time to—"

"And Luke. Heavens sakes, Danny, you don't even know about Luke."

"Luke?" A shadow of deep concern masked his face, and his features hardened. "What about Luke? I don't know *what*, Maggie? Please, tell me."

A tear trickled down her face under the harsh memories of the last year. She wiped the retentions from her eyes and peered down at Danny. "Luke went missing in action right after D-Day—same as you. And just as I started searching for you, Grace began her search for Luke. Nothing was turning up. Weeks, then months, passed without word from either of you. Then one day, the major I'd been working with brought a file to me. Silly me, I thought it was news on Luke. So I opened the file and read through it. That's how I found out you'd been declared dead." Another set of fresh tears leaked from her eyes and her voice wavered. "Heavens, Danny, it felt like—like someone had thrown a lightning bolt through my veins."

"I'm sorry, baby." Danny's hand reached out and invited her into his grasp. She slid into his embrace, careful not to bump his wound. Warmth from his lips pressed into her temple.

"Then another month went by and news came on Luke. He'd been injured and was being held in a hospital in England. He was due back to Georgia right about the time the wire came."

She heard Danny heave a sigh of relief. "Thank the Lord he's alive."

"But he's different now, Danny. He lost his right arm and walks with a limp."

Danny's arms unfolded from around her and his hands covered his face. She could only imagine what thoughts ran through his mind.

"They amputated?"

"They had to, Danny. He would have died."

"I...I can't believe it. We used to wrestle, jump fences, go fishing...Maggie, what's happened to him?"

He would need time to process the shock of the news. She couldn't expect Danny to understand everything all at once. In the next moment, she found herself wrapping her arms around his neck and running her hand through his black locks.

"He's okay, Danny. Grace says he's getting stronger every day."

"Grace?"

He backed away from her. This would be the most difficult thing to tell him.

"Luke and Grace married on New Year's Eve." She tried to put it as gently as possible to take the sting from her words, but his face registered grief and regret.

"And I wasn't there."

"I'm so sorry, Danny."

"I wasn't there for my best friend."

Tears blurred her eyes. "We all thought you were dead."

Beneath the glow of moonlight, she caught the shade of green that now dappled his face. Danny's eyes were distraught.

"Can you take me back inside, Maggie? I'm not feeling so good."

CHAPTER THIRTY

Danny grew distant, often drawing back into his dark corner to sleep. Or maybe it was to mourn.

Maggie tried to put herself in his position. How would it feel to be declared dead and snuffed from the face of the earth? And instead of family members and friends waiting impatiently for a safe return, they go on with life and carry on as if that one never existed. Is that how Danny felt at the moment? Did he feel forgotten, all alone?

The thought plagued her, but not out of wonder. She'd been short with Danny as she tried to sort through her own tangled web of sentiments. Vera was right. Stringing Walt along for so many months had complicated things. It shouldn't surprise her that Danny recoiled his attentiveness.

No matter how many times in the past eighteen months she'd told herself Danny was gone, he still revisited her as she settled into her nighttime dreams. He never truly left her.

Then there was Walt. He gave his love freely to Maggie when she needed it most and did what he could to protect her in this horrid war.

But he wasn't Danny.

So many nights she'd lay awake in her bed and imagine Danny stepping from the Western Rail line and into her arms.

How many times had she looked into Walt's blue eyes and imagined Danny staring back at her?

That's what brought her to Danny's ward at the present time. It was time to see where they would go from here.

She expected Danny to be in the same morose mood she'd left him in last night, but to her surprise, she walked into the ward to find Danny sitting up in bed, reading his Bible. Glad for the change in his complexion and position, she put on her best smile and headed for his cot.

"Hey there, soldier."

Light bounced in his eyes when he smiled up at her. "Hey there, beautiful. I was just doing some reading and a little thinking."

"Not a bad thing to do." She tucked her fatigues behind her knees as she lowered herself to the chair beside his cot and drew imaginary lines over his hand with her forefinger. "Did your Bible reading help?"

"Much. It's amazing how God's word heals a broken spirit. He always knows just what to feed me when I'm starving for His wisdom."

"Me too." She slipped her hand into his. It was time to say those words she'd practiced on the way to his ward. "Danny, through your death I found so much more to life. That's how I got here. I vowed to serve God by serving my country and by helping to make a difference in the lives devastated by war. It didn't always turn out the way I pictured, but God allowed me to plant a seed in each individual I met.

"Do you see what I'm getting at? You inspired me, Danny Russo. You got me here. And through your loss, God showed me that there is so much more to this life than I ever knew. And now that this wretched war is coming to a close, I'm even more excited to see what the future holds. So...where do we go from here?"

His eyes looked past her. He had that far away look as if he had something important to tell her and didn't know how to say it.

"Don't you know, Maggie?"

"Know what?"

"The doc approved my paperwork, and my name was officially reinstated in the United States Army. They're sending me home—didn't they tell you?"

Before he could finish, Maggie stood to her feet and fumbled for his medical record. When the clipboard landed in her grasp, she frantically read over it.

"Discharge set for fourteenth of May? That only gives us nine days together." Her mind whirled and her knees threatened to buckle on her. How could she have missed that order? How could she be separated from Danny...again? "I was hoping to go back *with* you."

"Baby, you know I'd love that more than anything. But I've thought this through this morning. While you're here that gives me time to get back on my feet, find a job, a place to call home, and by the time you return, I can give you that ring I promised you."

"I don't need a ring, Danny."

"Then...is that a yes?"

Was it?

5 May, 1930 Hrs
Hersfeld Airstrip

Major Walter Radford was never so glad to be on the ground. Air travel was not his strong point. Walter found strength in his legs to step off the plane and onto the grass runway. Red flares that served as runway lights seemed to light his path step by step, bringing him closer to the girl he loved.

He was directed to the convoy of army vehicles lined up on a dirt strip where they would take the new arrivals to Weiden. His escort handled his bags for him and placed them in a private vehicle issued just for him. He looked to the passengers under his care and made sure all were well after the long and bumpy ride by air.

Biting down on a sodium bicarbonate tablet to ease the burn in his stomach, he scanned the compound. This was his last leg of his voyage. Just twenty-four more hours, and Maggie would be in his arms forever.

Keep in touch.

She did not want to *keep in touch* as Danny put it. She wanted to be *in* his touch. Within arms-length, just as she was that night curled up against him in the bombed out camp.

She forced the words she didn't want to say out of the hatch. "All right. We'll keep in touch but you better concentrate solely on getting better first." She stood to her feet to hide the tears that formed under her eyelids. "I have to get your paperwork together. Apparently someone around here forgot to tell me about your impending departure."

"Maggie, wait."

Stopping, she blinked back her tears and turned around.

"I hear there's a dance tomorrow night. Am I well enough to go out dancing?"

The moment his question drifted off his tongue, she knew the meaning behind his query and found herself frantically nodding her head yes. She swiped at an escaping tear.

"In that case, can I have the honor of taking you out for a night of dancing?"

A flutter tickled her insides and a tingle danced up her spine. "I'd love to, Danny."

His familiar grin melted her heart. Somewhere beneath skin and bone, the Danny she remembered still lived on. But with each passing day, more weight clung to his famished body and the old Danny Russo was in the beginning stages of being put back together again.

His rustling brought her out of her muse. Danny attempted to stand to his feet. Maggie stepped forward to steady him. "I'm okay. I assure you," he said.

The feel of his hands gliding up and down her arms sent tiny prickles through her body. He took one step closer, leaving her completely breathless.

"I want to sweep you off your feet, Margaret Johnson." His voice was low, soft, deep.

Her body wanted to give out in his arms. She was never so infected with his love like this before. What changed in the last week? She relaxed into his embrace and was ready to let go of all resistance and let him brush her lips with his when a loud crash sounded behind them.

"Maggie! We could use some help over here."

Turning her head and casting a glance over her shoulder, a fatigued soldier gave the nurses a hard time and required the assistance of several medical personnel to hold him down.

"I'm sorry. They need me back there."

Reluctantly, Maggie backed away from Danny and took a moment to catch her breath. "Tomorrow night," she whispered.

✥

Her stomach rolled summersaults all day long as she waited anxiously for six o'clock to come around. She paced at times, tried reading, washed her hair, bathed then finally readied herself by dressing into her formal ANC uniform.

"Ooh, don't you look dazzling," Linda remarked upon entering the tent.

"The best I could without a dancing dress." Maggie spun for Linda who twisted her finger in a circular motion.

"It won't matter. It's you he likes, not your clothes."

"Thanks. That gives me a lot of confidence."

"I thought you already had confidence."

"Not so much."

"No matter. He must be your destined true love. How else would you find each other a half a world away from familiar civilization?"

"Not destiny, Linda. I think it's the Lord working His power."

"If anyone could make a believer out of me, it would be you, my dear. I've never met anyone quite like ya."

"I'll take that as a compliment."

Linda offered a smile, but it quickly faded as she contemplated her next words. "Maggie, have you told Walt yet?"

Maggie's throat grew dry and she swallowed hard. "No, I haven't." Because each time her mind came across Walt's name or face, a deep crater hallowed her chest. She knew breaking their relationship off would devastate him, and she didn't want to be the cause of such pain.

Linda's voice trickled softly onto the still air. "You're a right smart girl, Margaret Johnson. So I know you'll make the right decision. But you can't make that choice final and move on with Danny until Walt knows what your choosing is."

Maggie nodded in understanding. She knew Linda was right. She knew for weeks she had to find some way to tell Walt that she wasn't in love with him. But how would she tell him? In a letter? She couldn't send him a Dear John. It was too tacky.

A crowd of jolly dance-goers passing by the tent broke the silence between Maggie and Linda. Danny was waiting on her.

Linda shooed her from the tent after helping Maggie into her cape. "Go and have a good time."

⁊⸙

At first, Danny thought it was just his nerves wreaking havoc on his stomach, but as the day wore on, the pain became more intense. But he was determined to give Maggie this night. Nothing would keep him away from her, not when she'd waited this long. But just to be sure, he bought an extra morphine syrette off one of the guys and shot a small amount into his leg. He wanted enough of the medication to kill the pain, but not enough to put him to sleep while on the dance floor.

One glance at the clock told him Maggie would be here any minute to walk him to the festivities. Now that the Army had something worth celebrating—such as the eminent surrender of Germany—the whole camp looked forward to tonight's dance.

A nurse greeted a woman behind him, and he turned to see Maggie coming his way.

"Hello, doll."

Her smile was breathtaking.

"Hello."

His eyes swept over her. She looked smart in her formal attire. The navy blue garrison tipped to the side added to her cuteness.

"Wow. I feel like I'm escorting the queen to the ball."

Maggie took his offered arm, which took no coaxing on his part.

"It's just me, silly." She fingered the green of his lapel. "I see the

Army finally issued you some new attire." She didn't have to say her next words. Her upswept gaze told him everything that expelled from her heart. She'd missed him. She loved his uniform. And she loved him.

"You're a sight for sore eyes tonight."

"Thank you. I was thinking the same about you." Her delicate fingers reached up and adjusted his tie. "Tell me, how is the sore area?"

The truth? No, if she knew he was in pain, she'd order him back to bed immediately. She couldn't find out about his discomfort.

"Oh, it's getting better every day. I'm feeling real good and getting around much better than I have the last few weeks."

She smiled and nodded. "Good. Let's keep it that way."

Maggie was as lively as she'd been since his return. It was hard to concentrate on anything else—except when the waves of sharp pain and nausea roiled his stomach. He hoped Maggie wouldn't notice the way he only picked at his food and moved it around on his plate. If she asked later about it, he'd tell her how her beauty affected him like that.

When the band returned from their break, Danny's outstretched hand requested the company of hers. "Will you dance with me?"

"I thought you'd never ask."

He led Maggie around the dance floor. She danced effortlessly and gracefully—just like old times. They fell into their familiar dance routine and she glided into and out of his arms without incident. He appreciated the way she kept herself in check, not bumping into his side that now burned with searing pain.

Nonchalant-like, Danny pressed his hand into the problem area as he led Maggie into and out of a dishrag spin. However, when the cold sweats began, he feared Maggie would know something was up and demand to take him back to the hospital tents for examination.

He made the effort to hide his pain by grimacing only when Maggie's back was facing him, but he made the mistake of grabbing his left side two seconds too late. Maggie stopped in her tracks and placed a hand on his shoulder.

"Danny? Is something wrong?"

He blew out a breath and forced a smile. Nothing was going to keep him from dancing with his girl. "No. I'm fine. I think my uniform is irritating the incision."

The nurse in her turned serious, and a concerned eye went to his abdomen. "Are you sure that's all? Should I check it?"

"No need. I'm all right. It's just when I'm dancing."

"Then why don't we break? I could use a drink right about now."

"A drink right about now sounds wonderful." He made sure the concern in Maggie's eyes faded. When her shoulders relaxed, he knew he was in the clear, but boy was his stomach killing him. It would take some expert acting abilities to keep his discomfort from her.

❧❧

Danny gulped down three cups of punch. Maggie watched his actions and reactions closely the rest of the evening. If he was dehydrated, the first thing he should do is drink as much fluid as his body demanded. Then she would watch for signs of weakness. However, if he broke out in a cold sweat, she'd know a fever worked on him—and that scared her. She'd somehow missed the warning signs with Peter Carlson. She would *not* miss those signs with Danny.

The band slowed and played Kay Kryser's "(There'll Be Bluebirds Over) The White Cliffs of Dover." Couples pulled close, some cheek to cheek, for one of the last slow dances of the night.

Danny pulled Maggie closer to him. All her longings for home melted away in his embrace. Her eyes slid closed and she allowed the sway of their bodies to take her back to Arbor Springs to the place where she first fell in love with the fearless Danny Russo. Being in his arms *was* home. All the times she wished to be back in her small apartment and all she had to do was step into Danny's embrace.

His arms wrapped tighter around her waist. He tensed. But it wasn't a reaction to the chemistry between them. Then his hands fell from her shoulder and grabbed for his stomach.

Maggie lifted her head and stepped back. "What's wrong?"

He gritted his teeth and beads of sweat rolled down his face. "I'm all right."

"No. No, you're not. I think it's time to get you back." She raised a hand to his forehead but he brushed it aside.

"Let's just finish this dance first. Please?"

"Danny, I'm worried about you. You're sweating profusely."

"It's just stuffy in here."

Her fists went to her hips. "You're standing half hunched over. I think the dance is over for you. You're going back to the ward and I'm getting the doctor to look you over. Are you feeling nauseous?"

"Incredibly."

"Oh, Danny. For how long?" Acid burned the walls of her stomach. Not again. Flashbacks flickered behind her eyes as Peter's hunched form haunted her memory. She draped her cape over her shoulders and stood at Danny's side, motioning for the door. Dread curdled her stomach. "Tell me, Danny. How long?" she repeated.

"Two days."

"Two days! Danny! Are you out of your mind?" Fear lapped at her heels until it wrapped its spindly fingers around her waist and constricted her airways. Danny was not well and with his sudden symptoms, she already knew his prognosis wasn't good. She prayed for a miracle while on the way to the hospital ward.

"Here. Strip down and get these on." She handed him long johns. "I'll pull the curtain closed. Call me when you're finished."

A few minutes later, Maggie walked Danny back to his cot, her face a mix of fear, anger, and concern.

"You shouldn't have waited so long to tell me."

"I wanted you to have this night. *I* wanted this night." He'd leaned in and whispered against her ear.

Chills ran down her spine and goose bumps formed on her arms as his breath tickled her ear.

"Maggie, may I request one more item from my list before you send me to the examining table?"

"Danny, I don't know if that's a good—"

"Please? Look, I know I'm in a world of trouble right now, but I need these few minutes with you before—before the doc has me in a coma."

Something squeezed the blood from her heart. She could read between the lines. Danny thought he was going to...

No, she couldn't bring herself to think that way. She swallowed hard and bit back the severity of the situation before tears engulfed her.

She may regret it later, but she nodded her consent.

Not wanting to move too far from the hospital's doors, Maggie led him to a private spot behind the ward that butted up against the supply tent. Most of the camp's members were still lingering at the dance, leaving the rest of the camp deserted.

Danny stopped and pulled Maggie into his chest. He worked hard to hold his discomfort at bay. "Tonight was wonderful, Maggie. Thank you."

"I wouldn't want to spend it with anyone else."

When he cupped her jaw with his hands, she knew she wanted to be his forever.

"You are so beautiful and I'm so in love with *you*. Do you know how long I've wanted to taste your kiss?" He brushed a stray strand of hair behind her ear and gazed deeply into her eyes.

Maggie's breath caught in her throat as she realized he was about to kiss her. When his mouth touched hers, her knees buckled and she fell into his embrace, only catching her balance by wrapping her arms around his neck. The kiss was passionate, intense. It felt so right. Never before had she felt this burst of excitement and adrenaline race through her body or surge through her veins—not even the first time she'd kissed Danny Russo.

Danny's hands encircled her waist, deepening his kiss. He tightened his grip on her, sending shrills of euphoria from the hairs of her head to the curves of her toes. She needed him, wanted him. He could kiss her like this for a hundred years and she'd never tire of his love. She didn't want to let him go.

"Maggie?"

A deep voice cut through the ecstasy of the moment and startled them both. While her arms still clung tightly around Danny's neck, Maggie peered through the shadows to the tall figure standing ten yards away. She knew that voice. Knew that stance.

When he stepped from the shadows, the pole light illuminated his features enough to confirm her worst fear and she gasped in horror.

"W—Walter?"

CHAPTER THIRTY-ONE

She cowered from Walt's gaze and slipped from Danny's grasp, her hands covering her mouth in disbelief. What was Walter doing here? Where had he come from? But there he stood, erect, firm, and not wavering. So much the opposite of what she was feeling right about now.

"Maggie, what's going on here?"

She tried to speak, but the words stopped mid-way up her throat, obstructed by the roiling acid that suddenly forced its way upward. While she struggled for words and breath, she sensed Danny's eyes shift from Walt to her and back again.

"Maggie, I just spent the last 48 hours en route to this installation. Don't I so much as deserve a hello?"

She blinked frantically, hoping to revive her reason and intellect.

When she finally forced her words to her mouth, she was breathless. "Hello, Walt. This is quite a surprise." She pressed a fist into her stomach.

"A surprise indeed. Now I understand the lag in your letters. I hoped for a lot things between us, Maggie, but not once did I imagine I'd find you in the arms of another man." He never moved forward, nor backward, only remained steadfast and firm.

He'd seen her kissing Danny. Her insides ached.

As she wiped at the flush settling on her cheeks, Danny addressed her. "Maggie, what's going on? Who's this?"

She looked between her two men and struggled to determine who she should answer first. Danny settled the question by hunching over in pain and letting out a most ominous moan. Her first thought went to helping Danny.

"Let's get you to the doctor. You've been out here too long." Then she regarded Walt. "Give me a few minutes, Walt. I'll be out soon." She didn't have enough time to wait for a reaction. She shuffled Danny into the ward and motioned for the doctor.

"He's having severe pain in the injured area, Captain. Nausea, headache, profuse sweating—I think he has an infection."

"Only one thing to do then."

She nodded her head, knowing exactly what he meant. She looked down apologetically into Danny's torturous eyes. What lay behind them were a mix of agony, fear, and betrayal. It was enough to break her heart into a million, tiny, glass shards, all slicing into the beat of her heart and bleeding her of every ounce of love Danny had given her. What must he think of her? He must know by now Walt was there for *her*.

"Lieutenant, we need to open him up—now!"

3 hours later

Maggie pulled the mask from her face and slunk down onto a wooden chair. A long, exhausted sigh exited her lungs.

She'd never been more frightened of surgery then tonight. How she kept a steady and unwavering hand through Danny's critical procedure she didn't know. But she did know the only breaths she took were the ones breathing prayers to God Almighty, praying for a miracle. Praying for Danny to make it through surgery.

The infection ate away at much of his muscle, and the risk of damaged organs was the first concern. If the infection had spread to those vital for life, or traveled to his heart, he'd have died in mere minutes. So she prayed. No, she *pleaded* with God to spare Danny's life. When the doctor was certain he'd cleared away most or all of the infection and dead flesh, they sutured him up. Danny's vitals remained steady, and all seemed to be well.

But only time would tell.

Drawing in a shaky breath, she picked herself up and cast off her bloodied apron. She scrubbed at her hands and arms then splashed a handful of cold water over her tired eyes. After patting her face dry with a hand towel, she came face to face with the woman staring back at her in the looking glass. How she'd changed in these last five months. The innocence of a girl's complexion had long melted away and the form of a woman now replaced what was lost. The war did that to her. It stole away the innocence of the fun-loving girl she used to be. But here she was struggling to juggle two wonderful men who didn't deserve the treatment she was giving them at the present time. Did she really believe all this time she could have the both of them and get away with it? Now what would happen to her?

Walt. She still needed to talk to Walt. Would he still be awake at this hour? It was nearly 0100 hours.

She had to try. He'd come several hundred miles, surely he was waiting somewhere outside for her. That was the kind of man he was. So she pinched up her cheeks and tried to disguise the exhaustion and apprehension on her face.

She found him sitting alone at an empty table in the Officer's Club. His cap lay at the place setting beside him and seltzer water sat in a glass in front of him. Good thing he wasn't a drinking man. Maggie shuddered at the thought of facing a man drowning in alcohol.

"Mind if I have a seat?"

Without even glancing at her he answered, "It's free if you want it."

Even the sound of the chair creaking sounded thunderous compared to the silence in the room.

She bounced her eyes from his hands to his profile, hoping he would sense it and look at her, but he only averted her gaze. She didn't know what to say.

"There's a lot we have to talk about, Walt."

He drew in a slow, thought-out breath. "I'll start with the questions. Was that some sort of new life saving technique the Nurse Corps is teaching now? Because it sure looked like your lips were locked tightly onto his, but I'm giving you the benefit of the doubt."

Her hand rested on the stiff fabric of his army greens. "Walter."

But he shrugged away. "What did I do wrong?" His voice shook, and it killed Maggie to hear his heart breaking.

"Nothing. Walt, you...did nothing. I couldn't have known—you couldn't have known. Everything happened so fast, and before I knew it, he was back again and I—"

"Who, Maggie? Who is he?"

She hesitated and bit down on her lip. It sounded crazy, even to her, so how would it sound to Walt?

"Danny. Daniel Russo. My Danny."

His ragged breath seemed to push him backward in his chair. He raked both hands through his dark blond hair. "Just my luck. My girlfriend's lover comes back from the dead. You sure it's even him? How do you know? What if he's an imposter?"

"Walter, it's not. The Army's already made all the changes, made all the contacts, did the blood work, checked dental records, and I know...it's Danny."

"So now you're just gonna up and leave? Forget everything we had together? Shack up with him and leave me here to watch the girl of my dreams find her happy ending with the other guy?"

"You know that's not how I work, Walt. That's not fair. I promised Danny my heart long before I ever met you. Am I supposed to break that promise?"

That question seemed to startle his thinking and he jerked toward her and clutched her hands. "And break the promise you made to me, Maggie? Don't you remember? I asked you to make the same promise to me right before we parted—and you accepted that promise. You moved on in life, left everything else behind because you had me." His large blue eyes stared longingly into hers.

She wanted to pull away from him and run. Run as fast as she could and sit down and bawl her eyes out. She'd managed to juggle two men for two months and then hurt both of them in the same evening. Her heart swelled past the limitations of her own grief and was ready to burst. If she would have just written the letter...

"What letter?"

Did she really say all that out loud?

"Walt, I was going to write and tell you about Danny, but I couldn't bring myself to put it in a letter. It felt so cold and vague. So I wanted to wait and tell you in person..."

"Tell me what?"

She treaded carefully and studied the eagerness in his gaze. She just needed to blurt it out and get it over with and deal with the pain later.

"I can't keep my promise to you, Walt. I just can't." One lone tear slipped from her eye and she casted her eyes downward. "I'm sorry," she whispered.

"Maggie, don't do this to me, darling. Don't do this. I came all the way out here to take you home."

She glanced up. "Home?"

"When I heard the hospital was bombed, I pulled every string in the Army to find a replacement and get you out of here. I even brought her with me. In five hours, you're supposed to be on a plane heading east where an escort will drive you to the docks, and you'll board the Queen Mary back to the States. I was so worried about you, Maggie. I had to come." Placing both hands on the sides of her face, he opened his wounded heart. "Does *he* love you like *that*?"

Maggie closed her eyes and thought back to Danny's story. He'd given up his identity to make sure she was safe from enemy harm. He'd suffered beatings, starvation, and bitter cold temperatures for the sake of the people and country he loved. Just as Christ was bruised, and bled, and died for her, Danny followed Jesus' example of unconditional love and surrendered himself to the enemy to save the lives of others around him.

That precious thought of Jesus dying for her, and Danny suffering for her, squeezed fresh tears from her eyes.

"Yes, Walt. Danny does love me like that...maybe more."

Her eyelashes fell heavy against her cheeks. She didn't want to see Walt's reaction to her confession. Didn't want to see the emotional pain she'd just jabbed into his chest.

The seconds ticked by and he said nothing. Maybe he was comprehending what was happening. Maybe he already knew and now faced the reality. Or maybe he was so angry with her right now that he couldn't stand the sight of her.

The ice in his glass clanked and she glanced up to see him sipping down the rest of his drink. She didn't know why she still sat here at the table with him, but she didn't want to move until they had an understanding.

When he'd cleared his throat, he cocked his head to the side and searched the pocket of his uniform jacket.

"I came here on more than one mission, Maggie. You're worth fighting for and I'm up to the challenge. If I have to work harder to win you back then I will—"

"Walt—"

He held up a palm.

"This war is all but over, and in a few short months, we'll all be heading back to the States for some much needed R&R. You're exhausted, darling, there are black rings under your eyes, your skin is much paler than usual, and you're looking most thin. Let me take care of you and make you a good husband. We'll have a house, raise a family. I can't promise we'll stay in one place and we'll most likely be moved about the country, but that's my career, and I know you won't mind. We're both seasoned in army life. What do you say, Maggie? Will you give me another chance to prove that we belong together?"

He opened a small box and pushed it in front of her. Inside, rested a white gold band with a square diamond mounted in the middle. It was adorned with small rhinestones that glistened, even in the dull lighting.

"Walter, it's beautiful. But I—I can't accept this." She gathered the box in her palm and gently replaced the lid. "I'm truly sorry about everything Walt. I feel like a heel. I didn't know life would turn out this way. And if it hadn't...well, I'm sure we'd be celebrating in each other's arms right now. But Danny was my first true love. And what I've learned from these last two months is that while my heart wasn't quite ready for him two years ago, it is now. And I know that I love him very much. In fact, if I were to go on without him, I'd never be able to live with myself. You don't want a girl like that, do you Walt? A girl who goes to bed each night longing for another man? A girl who sits in your arms and pretends she's sitting in *his*. It wouldn't be fair to you. I couldn't hurt you in that way."

Snatching up the box and shoving it in his pocket, Walt stood to his feet and turned for the door.

"You might be able to live without *me*, Maggie, but I don't know if I can live without *you*."

Something pushed her out of her chair and after him. They'd reached the courtyard when she finally caught up to him and he halted.

"I don't want it to end this way, Walt. Don't leave like this, please."

"How else do you want it to end, Maggie? Do you expect me to stay and cry tears of joy for you? Because I won't be doing that."

"No, of course not. I don't know why I'm here right now."

That was the truth. Why had she follow him out the door when she'd already pledged her love to Danny? Why did it seem so hard to let Walter walk out of her life?

On that notion, Walter turned to her and something sparked in his eyes. "Maybe you do still love me. Of course. We've been apart far too long and the distance has put a wedge between us and distorted our thoughts and feelings. Why else would you care to follow me and still carry this conversation?"

"I—I—I don't know, Walter. I just—"

He inched forward.

"You just...have feelings for me?" Another step closer and she held her breath. "I can see it in your eyes. You still care. There's still some flame of hope." His left hand slid around her waist and to the small of her back. Her heart pounded. "Maggie." His right hand brushed back her hair, traced her jawline and ran down her neck. "Say yes. We'll get married first thing in the morning. In just a few hours, we could be husband and wife." With that, he leaned in for a most passionate kiss, but Maggie's hand pressed firmly against his brawny chest, stopping him.

"No, Walt. Don't. I've already made one mistake in the last twenty-four hours, I can't make another one."

CHAPTER THIRTY-TWO

She found Walter finishing up his breakfast—or at least maybe a quarter of it. She'd been a bawled up bundle of nerves all morning, not finding any room for breakfast herself. She prayed her heart would stop pounding. It was hard enough figuring out what to say, but a shaking voice would only muddle her words together and cause Walter to take pity on her.

She sighed and tapped a finger against her wrist in a nervous compulsion as she stood at the mess entrance contemplating her next move.

Three deep breaths later, her heartbeat slowed its erratic pace and allowed her a small window of passage to clear up her mess. In the next moment, her legs brought her closer to Walt's table, not stopping until she stood at his side...at a comfortable distance.

"Good morning, Walt. I've come to clear things up."

His eyes regarded her in a reserved manner. He no doubt expected her company. Every little mannerism, like his posture and easy position in his seat, the way he brought his coffee tin to his mouth to drink, and even the way his eyes looked for something to focus on other than her face, told her that.

"I saved you a seat, Maggie. Would you like me to grab you a tray of grub?"

Scooting toward the table she answered, "No, thank you. I'm not very hungry this morning."

"Oh? Are you feeling ill?"

His hand reached out for her cheek but she pulled back. "Please, Walt, I'm fine. Don't make this harder than it already is."

"Harder than it already—Maggie, you make it sound like this is good-bye."

"It is, Walt. I'm so sorry. Really, very sorry...for everything. Especially for last night."

His eyes bled with questions, begging her to explain why her decision excluded him. Or why she wouldn't refuse forgetting a man whom she'd already grieved and moved on without.

Walt stood and raked his fingers through his hair. "I'm being shipped to the front in three days."

Maggie jerked her head to look up at him. "To the front?"

"That was the deal. I was to see you were safe, drop off your replacement, and move with the infantry into Berlin. Unless the Germans wave the white flag first."

"Can you talk with the general? Tell him I'm not going and you can go back?"

"It's a done deal. I'm here for your replacement."

"You did that for me?"

Placing his hands on his waist, he hung his head. "Yeah."

Standing to her feet, Maggie took careful steps to meet Walt face to face. She looked up at him, thinking he was still as handsome as she remembered then kissed his cheek. "Thank you. But I can't take that offer. I would feel guilty knowing you pulled strings to move me out."

She watched as Walt's eyes lowered to her scarred wrist. His hand brushed against the pink of her new skin as if he stroked fine china. She could see the memories spilling from his gaze, like the pages of a book spread open for everyone to read. Everything from their first meeting at Walter Reed Campus to their first outing for pie and five cent sodas to their first kiss radiated from his touch.

Her throat constricted, and she swallowed hard against the hurt, but remembering her love for God and the peace He'd given her this morning about her decision, took over and she found new strength.

"You know what, Maggie. It's okay."

Her eyebrows lifted in surprise.

His sigh blew against her cheek, but the warmth of his touch had disappeared and he reached for his cap. "I know you loved Danny long before I came along. And I'm thankful for the time we spent together, but if you're truly happier with him than you are with me, I would only be kidding myself, wouldn't I?" She gave a slight nod. "I loved every minute, Maggie. Every. Single. Minute."

"Maggie!"

Peggy's frantic voice came upon them like a buzz bomb, shrieking as she rushed toward them and landing a bomb at Maggie's feet.

"What is it, Peggy?"

Peggy stopped dead in her tracks when she saw Walt standing beside Maggie. She snapped a quick salute then recovered from her shock. Her gaze moved to Maggie. "It's Danny. He's asking for you." Then her expression grew dismal and she squeezed the flesh on Maggie's arm.

"Maggie, he's not well."

☙❧

Danny's dreams kept rolling around in his head. One minute he was jumping from a C-47, the next he was home eating his mother's delicious pasta supper. But every time he looked out his mother's dining room window, he saw Maggie in another man's arms.

When the anesthesia and medications wore off, and after his sleep melted away into harsh spasms of pain, the real reality of life and dreams came to a crashing halt. Life *had* gone on without him. Somewhere across the ocean, his parents had long ago buried him and now lived with one child less. Worse yet, it seemed Maggie had also moved on—but why didn't she tell him? Why had she allowed him to get so close if she'd given her heart to another?

She lied to him, and that hurt worse than the agony he was going through now.

He clenched his stomach in utter anguish. His current condition wasn't looking good. With a stomach wound like the one he received, and going without treatment for so long, it was a wonder he was here now. Maybe this was God's plan for him all along. Maybe he was destined to die here in Germany. But why torture him and put him through this misery instead of striking death on him in the POW camps? He could die peacefully knowing he was dying for his country under the hand of his enemies, but Maggie, the girl he'd trusted his heart to, he couldn't fathom dying with the knowledge that she'd betrayed him.

He was ready to give up.

☙❧

Fear enveloped Maggie and strangled her, choking the life from her veins. As her legs pumped faster and harder, she prayed God would spare Danny's life once more. It seemed her worst fear had come true. She'd missed something—again. And now Danny's life balanced on a thin thread of hope. She prayed she wasn't too late.

"How bad is he, Linda? Tell me the truth." She grabbed Linda by the shoulders as she entered the post-op ward.

"He's bad, Maggie. Maybe gangrene. Maggie, with a stomach wound, it could—"

Her stomach twisted and bile inched its way up her chest. She closed her eyes and grimaced. "I know, Linda. I know. Don't say it."

231

Her heart plummeted. Tears pooled in her eyes and cascaded down her cheeks. She couldn't lose him now. Not when they stood reunited with each other. Not when she'd finally made a life commitment to love Danny with her whole heart.

She found his cot and kneeled at his side, taking his hand and pressing her lips to his knuckles. "I'm here, Danny. I'm not leaving you."

His blanket shifted. It twisted almost as much as the grimace on his face. He was in a great deal of pain. His hand was hot, and IV's rushed fluid into his dehydrated and sick body. A shudder ran through the hand she was holding, and she noticed only a thin blanket covered his bare chest.

She peeked at the infected incision and brought a hand to her mouth when she saw green fluid oozing from the site. The stench alone turned her belly in all directions and her muscles turned to jelly.

Maggie prayed. She prayed as fervently and hard as she could. She'd given up Walter, and now she risked losing Danny again. *Lord, please, I can't lose* both *of these men. Please heal Danny. Please touch his body and make him well. Give him a full recovery, I ask...*

"Lieutenant Johnson." Maggie's prayer was interrupted by the doctor.

"Captain."

"We have to take him back into surgery now."

"Another?"

"Afraid so. It's our last attempt."

Last attempt.

So now it all came down to a matter of hours. Would this be the last time she ever saw Danny Russo alive?

She pressed her lips against his cheek then whispered into his ear, "I love you, Danny, and I'll be waiting for you when you open your eyes."

∽᷾⌢

When Peggy showed up at the tent with two trays of food, Maggie's eyes quickly filled with tears all over again.

"This is payback." Peggy set Maggie's tray on her cot.

"For what?"

"For not leaving me alone when all I wanted was to sulk on my bed and wallow in my tears and self-pity."

Maggie brushed at moisture gathering on her cheek. "Maybe I should have left you there then."

Peggy smiled then bit into her pork. "Nah. Not in you."

Maggie forced her fork into her mouth, but the food that rolled around on her tongue had no taste. She was only eating to survive the war. Both women ate in a few moments of silence.

"Want to talk about it? I may not be the most comforting woman in the world, but from all those years of silence, I've learned I'm a good listener."

And now Peggy just became her closest confidant. My, how the Lord never ceased to amaze her. She certainly never expected to grow a friend from seeds of hatred, disgust, and ill will, but those seeds had blossomed into beautiful blooms of love and friendship that would hopefully last a lifetime.

Maggie let out a moan. "Oh, Peggy, I've made a mess of things. And I didn't even know it."

"Go ahead and let it out, Maggie. Bleed until you've bled out all your mistakes that way you can replenish your body with a fresh start."

A fresh start. That's what's she wanted. To erase away the last five years of her life and start anew, going back on her errors and correcting them with all the things she knew now. Maybe Mother was right by telling her that age brings wisdom and experience. She could think of a few things she'd learned in the last year that would have caused her a lot less heartache over the last five years.

So she went through her story, from the beginning up to the present. She cried a little, even laughed out of frustration, but confiding in Peggy was good for her soul. Peggy even softened her hard wall and crouched down beside Maggie to offer her small hugs of empathy.

"Peggy, I never realized that giving little pieces of my heart to each man that caught my attention would cause me so much confusion and pain. I feel like such a silly, little school girl." She dabbed at her eyes with a tissue.

"Well, Maggie, what do you really want? A flock of men at your every beck and call, or one man who will always be there for you because you trusted him with all your heart?"

"I'm ready to go back to the States with Danny and fulfill the promise I made to him. I'm ready to throw away everything else I tried to fill my life with and just be married to him alone. But—"

"But what?"

"What if God doesn't give me that chance? What if I return home empty handed?"

"I may be new to this, Maggie, but isn't that kind of thinking the type that doubts what God can do?"

A giggle launched from Maggie's mouth. "My, you're a fast learner, Peggy. You're right. You're absolutely right. I need to pick myself up off the ground and dust off my fatigues. I'm gonna see this fight to the end."

"Well, hey, before you charge the cavalry, can I ask you one question?"

"I'm all ears, Peg."

"Who was the man sitting with you at breakfast?"

CHAPTER THIRTY-THREE

Sunday, 6 May 1945

Danny could've died on the operating table. His early prognosis was bleak and she knew that look in the medical staff's eyes. Her own knowledge of medicine warned her to be prepared for the worst of outcomes, but her heart and love for Danny refused to believe that this complication would take him from her forever.

Gangrene attacked Danny's colon. However, with his appendix removed several years earlier, it was easier for the doctor to pinpoint where the disease headed next. So Danny's doctor cut the dead and diseased tissue and performed a procedure to improve Danny's blood supply to the area.

As she stood with her back turned to his sleeping form, and counting out medical utensils for inventory, she couldn't help but think how they'd come full circle. A glance over her shoulder at his relaxed features, and she thanked God for the peace He'd given her to make Danny the only man in her life. She'd seen how God used those small and unthinkable moments to bring them to this point in their lives. How God put Danny under her care with a case of appendicitis. How Danny's haunting words of love echoed in her mind even after Walter walked into her life. She marveled at how God put small increments of doubt about Walt in her mind months before Danny showed up in the flesh.

"Lieutenant Johnson?" A young corporal snapped a salute.

"Yes, Corporal?"

"A message for you, Lieutenant." He handed her a small slip of paper and saluted his good-bye.

"Thank you." What could it be? She unfolded the parchment and spied Walt's handwriting.

Maggie,
Just one final request. Will you join me for breakfast this morning?
Walt

Her heart sighed. Would he still urge her to change her mind even after the done deal?

She glanced at Danny. He wouldn't be waking up for some time. She'd go and see what Walt wanted, but wouldn't stay. Her place was at Danny's side and she would make that perfectly clear to Walt.

Keeping her head held high and making quick, deliberate steps, she found herself standing at Walt's table.

"Maggie, have a seat."

"Thank you." An awkward silence settled over them, but she waited for Walt to begin.

"How's Lieutenant Russo?"

Always the gentleman.

"I'm afraid we won't know for sure for a while. He pulled through surgery. For that I'm grateful."

"I'm sorry, Maggie."

"You don't have to be sorry, Walt. It's nothing you did."

"What I meant was, I'm sorry for trying to change your mind when it was evident who your heart already belonged to. When I thought over the last year and your search for Danny, I realized just how much he meant...I'm sorry, *means* to you."

He surprised her. She almost didn't know what to say. "Don't be. I'm the one who should apologize to you. I'm sorry I hurt you, Walt. It wasn't my intention."

"I know that now. I did something I hadn't done for a while. I prayed. I thought about you and me and our situation. I guess I knew that you weren't completely happy in our relationship and I denied that. In a way I guess I'm grateful that we had that time apart to think about things."

"So you're not angry?" Hope filled her eyes. Maybe they would end on good terms.

"No. It's better we know our true feelings now rather than later down the road."

"Walter, you're too good for me."

"No. Not good enough, you mean. That's why I'm letting you go. You deserve to be happy. You're a wonderful and strong woman, Maggie. I'm glad for the time God allowed me to spend with you." Walter smiled and squeezed her hand. "Now, I have two days before I leave, can you tell me what there is to do around here?"

A huge burden lifted from her shoulders and she could breathe easier. Maggie relaxed and smiled. "We have a projector. Catch the right night and you may just get the privilege of seeing the same movie you watched three times before you left for the war."

Sharing a laugh as friends felt so good. No pressure, no resistance.

Out of the corner of her eye, Maggie spotted Peggy in the chow line. Knowing Peggy would search for a place to sit, Maggie stood. "I've got to get going. My shift starts in an hour. I haven't had much sleep and could use a few winks."

Walt stood when she rose to leave. "Thank you again, Maggie, for answering my note. I had to tell you all that before I left. Whatever happens in the future, I hope you'll be happy."

"And I wish you well also, Walt." Her eyes strayed to the dirty blonde making her way through mess. "Sit down, Walt, and finish the rest of your breakfast."

As Maggie walked away, she knew she was walking out of his life forever. But as she left through the back door, someone else entered center stage.

Glancing over shoulder, she watched the scene unfold.

Walt hunched over his plate, eating alone at the table and unaware that a beautiful nurse stood five feet away.

"Is this seat taken, Major?"

Peggy never looked more divine than at that moment. Maggie watched as Walter stopped and fumbled to his feet to greet her in proper form.

"No, not at all. Please, sit down."

"Thank you. Do you care for eggs? I can't stand 'em."

"Well, if you're not going to eat them . . ."

She scooped her scrambled eggs onto his plate.

"The name's Walter, by the way."

"Peggy Blizzard. I work with Maggie, and we bunk together."

"Really? Now isn't that interesting."

"The world gets smaller every day, doesn't it?"

Indeed it did. It warmed Maggie's insides to know God would take care of Walt. And by the looks of things, it seemed the good Lord already worked His hand between two lonely hearts.

2 Days Later

The road was dry and dusty. Maggie was tired and irritable. When the chief nurse sent her and one other nurse to a neighboring camp for a supply-pickup, she didn't intend for it to be a two-day trip. She'd missed the celebration with her friends when Germany announced its surrender. She'd also missed Walt's departure—the least she owed him was good-bye. Worse, she feared she wouldn't be there when Danny re-entered the world of the living. However, she had no control over certain things.

Like an army supply truck that decides to break down between safety and peril.

Tired, grouchy, and hungry, Maggie leaned her head against the door window and closed her eyes. A headache drummed on her temples. She must be dehydrated and stressed. Danny was on her mind most of the trip and she wondered how his condition was. Had he gotten worse? Better? What would she find when she returned to the 39th?

As soon as the truck rolled to a stop, Maggie's feet hit the ground and she ran for the hospital ward. She checked for Danny in his usual spot, but he wasn't there. Something squeezed around her heart, and her hands covered her mouth. Surely he hadn't…

"Looking for Lieutenant Russo, Maggie?"

"Vera. Yes. What happened? Is he—"

Vera grabbed hold of her shoulders. "Land sakes, kid, calm yourself down. He was moved. The boy woke up from his long, bedtime nap and was looking better so the doc ordered him to the next ward." A smile crept along Vera's sculpted cheeks. "He was lookin' for ya."

"He was? I have to see him, Vera."

"Linda's got him next tent down."

She was on the move once again. If she could just see him for herself, all her fears and worries would fade away. She barged through the ward doors and scanned the room. Ten beds lined both sides with one long walkway down the center. Recovering soldiers lay with their feet facing her. She scanned each bed until she saw Danny's nose peeking up.

She smiled to herself. *That big, wonderful nose.*

"Danny."

A whole row of heads turned her way when her voice invaded the quiet. She should be used to the lack of privacy but right now she longed for it. A closer look and Danny was the only man in the bunch who didn't regard her.

Not paying any mind to the other boys in the room, she kneeled down at his side.

"Danny?"

"You're back." His voice was flat. Not at all like his normal, cheerful self.

"I'm sorry I was gone. They sent me on an errand and we had engine trouble. But I'm here now."

"Did you use that as your alibi so you and your significant other could spend some quality time together?" His eyes were black as coal and his voice cold as ice.

"Danny…what? What's that supposed to mean?"

This time his cold stare sent icicles spiraling into her chest. "You know what I'm talking about, Maggie. I may be sick and dying, but I'm not stupid, and you can't pull one over on me."

Heat crept up her neck and forehead. The men around them could hear every word coming from Danny's lips. She wished they could go someplace private.

"Who is he, Maggie?"

She didn't expect this reaction from Danny. She hadn't even considered what Danny thought of the exchange between her and Walt. Walt's unexpected arrival threw her whole world off balance. Looking back, she never had a chance to explain anything to Danny—particularly the part about breaking up with Walt *for him.*

"Danny. Let me explain everything. From the beginning."

"What's that going to change, Maggie? Are you in love with him or not? Did he come here for you?"

She stammered on her words, not sure which question to answer first.

"That's what I thought. You were using me the whole time. Now that *he's* back, you don't need me anymore. And why not? Everyone else seems to have forgotten me. Might as well add you to the list too."

"Stop it Danny. That's not fair and you know it." Her fists dug into her sides, and tears burned her eyes, but she refused to let him see them. *Never in front of the boys...*

She charged on. "Walt and I began dating after you...*died.* He was there for me, and before I knew it, we were having a good time as friends. After a while, he wanted more, and I knew it, so I became involved with him, but it was short lived. Walt kept a close leash on me and I wanted out. So I volunteered for the trip into Germany. I told Walt I was reassigned so he wouldn't use his rank to have my orders changed.

"But Danny, I thought of you every night despite the fact that you were gone. I hated not having you to write to or going so long without being in your arms. But what was I supposed to do? I didn't know you were alive."

His eyes shimmered under the dull lighting and she knew he fought back the same tears she was holding back. She wished he'd say something.

"Danny, not one single day passed that I didn't yearn for you."

"Are you or aren't you in love with him?"

She regarded him for a moment, but her answer needed no thought. "No. He and I—we're...over."

"When? Since this morning?" Sarcasm sputtered from his mouth and Maggie loathed his tone.

"No. Four days ago, actually."

"Oh, excuse me. Four days ago. You mean to tell me the whole time we—we were reacquainting with each other you were still involved with that guy? You led me on…made me think…"

"Think what, Danny? That I loved you? Because I do. It's because of you that I didn't tell you about Walt. It killed me to know I had two men in my life, and that I couldn't make a quick and final decision about Walt right then and there. I couldn't write him a Dear John after all he helped me through. Your death being one of them."

She couldn't believe she was having this conversation with Danny. His cold demeanor reminded her of the day she met Peggy Blizzard. Danny was the last person in her little world she thought would turn on her. Why couldn't he understand?

"Will you never forgive me, Danny? Or understand where I'm coming from?"

"Maggie, will you ever understand where *I'm* coming from? Imagine *coming back from the dead* to find that everyone has gone on without you. My best friend got married and I wasn't there to witness it. My mother is probably waking right now to fix Pop and my sisters their breakfast, paying no mind to their dead son and brother. And my girlfriend…well, she decided that a few weeks of mourning for her true love is enough and runs off with some other yank. How's that supposed to make me feel, Maggie? I'm dead to everyone who once knew me." His shaky, pale hand covered his face in frustration. "So just go, Maggie. Move on. I'll manage."

Hot tears bubbled under eyes and pushed to the surface, spilling onto her cheeks and burning holes through her skin. He wanted her gone? Away from him? But what about all the good times they'd shared together? The kiss from the night they danced at the Officer's Club? He was going to throw it all away?

Without a retort, without a sound, she padded out of the ward and found her way to the medical supply tent. She imagined Walter's response to be the malignant and vindictive one, but she never thought Danny would lash out at her the way he did. He wouldn't even listen to reason.

Now she'd lost both men. If Danny wanted her gone, then she'd go. She'd leave his life and never come back.

⤛⤜

Just as the surgery pains came and went, so did Danny's anger toward Maggie. First she'd broken the vow she'd made to him—the vow to wait for his return and take his name as her own. But to hear her say that she'd moved on. . .

How could she forget about him? Like he'd never been there for her. Like he'd never even existed at all.

No, that wasn't true. She'd said so. She even produced his gold cross to prove she'd remembered him. But still, she'd fallen for someone else during his time of imprisonment.

Another stab of finger-tingling pain doubled him over and fueled his odious discord. He wanted to believe Maggie still loved him with every fiber within her, but the horrid reminder of the *other guy* standing in the shadows, looking at her, gnawed at his insides and poisoned his thoughts with unrelenting friction. If the gangrene didn't eat a hole straight through his stomach, surely the venom from the strike to his heart would.

When the burning in his stomach subsided, he reached for the letter on his nightstand. He'd be going home soon. He thought it best to start the letter home to his mother, telling her he was taking the final trip home. He wondered what her reaction might be to the astonishing news of his re-birth. Would she scream with unfathomable elation or would she cry tears of unending joy? Either way, he'd be happy to see her. So happy to wipe the tears from her eyes or join in her laughter.

Home.

He felt sick for the longing to be back in that old town house. The town house with the most beautiful grape arbor in the neighborhood.

Danny's lip shivered under the memory. It'd been so long since he'd slept in a bed—a real bed. He'd been stripped of his name, his pride, his belongings, and his freedom while imprisoned in Germany. He'd been beaten, spat upon, kicked, tortured, cursed, and left for dead. He'd forgotten who he was.

His vision blurred as if he'd just submerged himself under a puddle of water. His Adam's apple bobbed when he swallowed back bitter memories that wanted to purge from his bones. He just wanted to be free. Wanted to go home. He wanted life to go back to the days when all that mattered in life was the best fishing hole. Or seeing the latest picture show. Or stopping at the soda shop for a five cent Coke. And coming home and smelling Mother's delicious, Italian meals. Was that so much to ask? He just wanted a taste of what life used to feel like. How it tasted before the war. Before he lost his identity. Before he lost Maggie.

CHAPTER THIRTY-FOUR

Danny slept peacefully. Even in the midst of his anger and illness, he was perfect. But the sharp sting of his words cut a new wound into her soul every time their argument came to mind. If only he understood that she'd given up her future with Walt to be with him. That she'd never really, fully given up on him. That her dreams were invaded by his charming wit and dashing smile. Was she invading his dreams right now?

Her pain and exhaustion absconded from her body in the form of a tear. Every weakened resolve and every fiber of love that she held for Danny was shoved into the granules of salt hidden within those tears. No matter how many times she'd cried over the last year, they still couldn't hold all her love. She'd never drain herself of the unconditional love she had for Danny. Never.

Lord, I know Danny's the one for me. I know it. I can't lose him again, Father. Please make a way. Please pave it with gold, and lead us back to each other.

Although her heart traveled from her place in the shadows of the ward to where Danny lay, she kept her distance. She made sure he didn't see her lurking behind the canvases, or checking his charts while he slept. She couldn't fully stay away if she wanted to. Her heart was bonded to his. That bond was made stronger through their months of hardship, loss, and struggle to survive. Surely, Danny didn't mean the things he'd said. Surely, he loved her as much as he once did.

Before her mind could protest, her feet began walking. They carried her toward Danny's cot. Her heart thumped harder against her chest. Why did she feel compelled to go to him? What would she say or do?

But those thoughts were quickly cut off as she knelt down to his side. She gingerly reached for his arm, but stopped mid-air and rested her fingers along his cot support instead. Suddenly, a flood of words spilled into her mouth and flowed off her tongue. Sweet as honey, they tasted as they took wing from the tip of her tongue.

"Danny, I've missed you. I know you're angry with me and I'm sorry. Since you won't listen to me in the daylight, maybe these words will find you in your dreams. Every day I kept your cross around my neck. And every night I cradled it in my hand and cried into my pillow for you. Walter never filled that void in my soul. Not like you could. My dream is to grow old with you and you alone, Danny Russo. No one else. No other man could be a better fit for me." Tightness choked her words and prevented her from saying anything else. She sniffed and wiped away silent tears that rolled down her face and dripped from her chin. Leaning in close to his ear, she whispered for him alone, "I love you, Danny." Then left.

1 June 1945

"Won't you say good-bye? You're not just gonna let him leave without saying or doing something, are ya?"

"Vera, he doesn't want me anymore. I'd only kid myself by going to the ward and showing my face." Maggie shoved her foot into her boot with a little more force than necessary. "Ouch. That darned toenail. These boots are utterly too small."

"Don't change the subject now, twinkle toes."

"Vera, I can't push myself on someone when they despise me."

"You did with Peggy. And look where it got you. You two are like best friends now."

"That's different." Maggie buttoned up her fatigues.

"You still love him and you know it."

"I know I do. Thank you for reminding me why it hurts so much." Flinging her hair over her shoulder, Maggie marched out the door, Vera trailing close behind.

"If it's any consolation, he still loves you too."

"How can you know that, Vera?"

"Why else would he be angry with you? Will you stop and listen to me, Maggie?"

"What." Her feet abruptly halted and her arms crossed with irritation.

"That boy is head over heels for you. The only reason he's upset right now is because he loves you dearly. If he didn't, he'd move on without giving you a second glance."

"But he hasn't given me a second glance." Maggie's irritation balanced between annoyance and anger. The more Vera tried to talk to her about Danny the more painful the subject became. It'd been weeks since she'd last seen or talked to Danny. Still, he made no attempt to see her, ask for her, or seek her out in some way, shape, or form. If he asked, she'd run to him without a moment's hesitation.

"Not that you know of, kid. He steals glances your way. He knows the time of day you pass the ward. When the flaps are open, he's staring out that door waiting to catch a glimpse of you."

"Stop, Vera." Her eyes burned with tears. "I don't want to know any more."

"All right. I've tortured you long enough. But listen, kid, don't let that man walk out of your life until you know for sure he isn't the one."

"He should be the one coming after me."

"But you left him, and your new beau showed up at the wrong time. Maybe he needs to be assured of your affections."

Maggie's eyes travelled everywhere but to Vera's. She knew the girl was right, but it didn't make it any easier. Danny was the guy—he needed to be the one chasing after her. She'd tried to explain, tried to reason with him. It was all for nothing.

⊷ი⊶

Danny waited impatiently at the end of his cot. He was going home. Going home for good. Well, after a little R&R at the general hospital, he'd get a clean bill of health and finally get to his mother, father, and sisters again. He longed for their companionship, their hugs, even their relentless kisses. He even looked forward to his mother's fingers pinching his cheeks. But a gaping hole marred the joy of returning home. Aside from his friends and family, he no longer had anyone else to come home to. Every longing dream of returning to a dark haired, brown-eyed girl, waving her hanky in the air as he pulled into the train station, evaporated into thin air. His foolish thoughts dismembered into tiny particles that scattered abroad the atmosphere. A small piece of him hoped he and Maggie would find their way back to each other, but that was impossible. Even if Maggie was still his girl, she wouldn't be there to escort him home. She was bound to the ANC for at least another 6 months. Who knew when she'd find herself back in Maryland?

He chided himself for thinking of her. For caring so much. For dreaming of her every night since their argument. Since he'd told her to go away.

She'd listened.

Except for that day—

"All set, Lieutenant?"

"Yes, ma'am." Danny slowly lifted himself to his feet, stood there a moment, and waited for the dizzy spell to pass.

"Okay to walk there, soldier?"

"I think so."

"I can wheel you, but it'll be a bumpy ride."

"I'd rather walk." A young corporal grabbed Danny's belongings and slung them over his back.

Danny was saying good-bye to so many things today—the war, sleeping in tents and foxholes, his weapons, the countries he'd seen, the ruins of ancient towns, friends, brothers…Maggie.

No, not Maggie. He'd said good-bye to her once. That would have to be enough.

They placed him on a C-47 in a fold out bed. Funny how his return home in a C-47 would be lying down. At least he was returning, not like many of his comrades who never made it onto and back from French soil.

They strapped him down and made sure all the belts were secure. Echoes of footsteps clanked as more men were brought in for evacuation. Each new footstep made him look to see if a petite brunette entered the fuselage.

She's not coming, Danny. Don't beat yourself up over it.

The nurse came around to see if any patients needed air-sickness medication. Danny said he'd be fine in the air and closed his eyes.

The commotion inside quieted, and all that was heard was the flight nurse checking belts and scribbling on her clipboard.

Then hushed whispers.

Fatigue washed over Danny's body. His eyelids fluttered closed. But a shadow hovered over him, causing him to look up.

The glare from the open door only casted a trembling silhouette, but he knew those curves anywhere.

Chapter Thirty-Five

The letter she wrote sat heavy as a one-ton brick in her trouser pocket. Even while Vera made her go-after-Danny-speech earlier that morning, Maggie had already written her final plea to Danny and waited for the right time to hand it over. She first thought to have Bonnie deliver the message to Danny, but pilot, Fred, was ordered to this flight. So while Bonnie and her flyboy boyfriend kissed and talked, Maggie resolved to deliver her message in person.

Her hands melted like butter on a hot day. They steamed from perspiration oozing from her pores. Her nerves decided to jitterbug the whole walk to the plane, and her breathing quickened as if someone chased her down. Sadly, she half hoped Danny was prescribed sedatives before the long journey home so she wouldn't have to look painfully into his eyes.

She braced herself for the confrontation. All the men were loaded on the plane, and the flight was due to take off in fifteen minutes. She could hurry and drop off the letter and leave. No words. No explanation. Or she could hand it off to the flight nurse.

But no . . . the nurse had to tell her it was all right to board the plane and hand the note to Danny herself. What a real pal of a gal.

Now she stared down at the man she loved with her whole heart. A man who was leaving to go to a place she longed for more every passing day. If only she could go with him. If only.

When her shadow loomed over his body, he opened his eyes, finding hers immediately. So much love still rested there. Vera was right in her every assumption. But a cloud impaired the clarity of Danny's eyes, making her feel vulnerable and small. She couldn't handle any more rejection.

"Maggie."

Her name trickled so softly from his tongue. The warm sensation she received from such a small sentiment also brought a weight of hurt. She knew he wouldn't—couldn't—wrap her in his arms and tell her how much he loved her.

But she waited for him to speak first, anyhow.

Just say it, Danny, and I'll come right back to you.

Her hand subconsciously reached for his gold cross as she waited to hear him say the words she hoped would shoot from his mouth. But his eyes spotted the necklace instead.

"You still have it?"

Realizing what he was asking, she glanced down at the gold pendant. "It's never left my neck. Never."

What was going through his mind right now? His hollow eyes left no indication of what he thought or felt. They were...empty.

And all words between them remained left unsaid.

Before tears could trail down her cheeks in front of him, Maggie pressed the folded letter into his hand and bolted out the fuselage.

If he couldn't say anything at all, then she knew his answer.

∽◌∾

It was like having his right hand ripped from his body. It was all his fault. He made her feel insecure, and worst of all, he'd casted her aside just as her parents had done with her feelings.

What kind of man was he? And why did his faults always come to the surface after the damage was done?

He clamped his eyes shut and stared into the black canvas of his mind. One year ago, he would have given a limb to remember an ounce of the life he'd left behind. Now all he wanted to do was erase each painful memory he'd ruined in the last three weeks.

Now that the plane was up in the air, there was no turning back. Part of him wanted it that way. But on the other hand, if he was able, he'd jump at this altitude just to make it back to Maggie and apologize for his stupidity and pride. Now she'd never take him back. Not after the display he'd put on.

But the truth was, her beauty still affected him in ways that took his breath away. Today was no exception. His words became lodged somewhere between his heart and his lips as she stood over him. Her eyes shimmered in the fuselage's dim lighting, revealing her young beauty, and her fear. Would a simple *I'm sorry* have done the trick? He guessed not.

"Nurse? Could you loosen these straps a bit?"

"You promise to stay put?" The nurse eyed him, her hands held firmly at her sides in a don't-mess-with-me manner.

"Yes, ma'am."

"Very well. But I'll have to tighten them again before we land."

"Thank you."

The letter in his left hand begged to be opened. He thought to wait until he boarded the hospital ship, but that would take another day or two. He opted to read it at 30,000 feet.

My Dearest Danny,

If time travel were possible, I'd go back in a heartbeat and change everything from your absence to the present. Words alone cannot describe the way I feel right now. For so long I dreamed and hoped you were alive, but all roads led me to believe the Army was right. You were gone.

Then something happened. I awoke from an awful nightmare and there you were lifting me from a bed of twisted metal and splintered wood. I knew it was you. I knew all along. But you didn't. You never once called me by name. You never came rushing toward me after realizing it was me, Maggie, who you loved and wanted to marry. You told me your name was Joe, and my heart broke.

Nothing made sense, and I feared I really hadn't awaken from that horrid dream. You were more like an apparition sent to haunt me for the choices I'd made and remind me of all I'd lost. That night, sitting in your arms, was like every other evening we spent together. Siting on the porch swing at your parents' house or slow dancing to Glenn Miller. I fit so perfectly in your arms, and I remembered every muscle beneath your skin that tensed when you held me close.

You didn't have those memories at the time, and you were left with unanswered questions when your memory did return. Well, now I have those answers...

Danny's twill patch with his name embroidered into its fibers fell into his hand. He held the soft material between his fingers, running his thumb over the letters that made up his name. It was a simple cloth with just thread weaved into a letter pattern, but it held one magnificent story. It was a small belonging he thought he'd never see again. How had Maggie acquired it?

As you know, the Army has re-instated you back into commission. I thought maybe you'd like to have this patch as a souvenir for all you've endured. Then again, maybe you're wanting to forget it altogether.

Danny, I believe our paths were meant to cross this way. And I believe it was to save me. No one else would have searched for me in that wreckage...at least not until it was too late. But you did and you saved me from more than just a physical demise. You saved me from my own foolish behavior. Danny, all I want is to be one man's girl. Your girl. You're a hero in my eyes.

I still love you with all my heart, Danny. No, even more. Although my heart is breaking and I weep in hiding, I pray one day we'll find each other again.

With my Unending Love,
Maggie

Maggie had poured her heart into this letter. But it didn't settle the uneasiness in his heart. It still ached with deep yearning. He knew why. But he couldn't do anything about it at 30,000 feet above the earth.

CHAPTER THIRTY-SIX

Watching the C-47 SkyTrain leave the ground was like arching a flaming arrow to a floating casket. The further the flying ship sailed from her, the deeper the gash cut into her soul. He was gone.

The burn in her chest returned, and a sob billowed up in her throat. Now more than ever, Maggie longed for home. She'd had her fill of overseas adventures for one lifetime. Now she was ready to cement her feet in her hometown and build her future, and her home, from a little white cottage on the outskirts of town. Forget the night life and dancing sprees. Forget the movies and dinner dates. She just wanted stability and love. And strong arms to chase away all her fears and wrap her close in love and warmth every night.

7 September 1945

Maggie banged a hand against the rear of the ambulance, signaling for it to pull out. The last of the wounded were hauled out and accounted for. Now they were on their way to hospitals in England, and eventually, home.

With hands resting gracefully against her hips, Maggie allowed her gaze to sweep over the quickly crumbling camp. Some of the tents were already lowered and bundled up for closing. Pretty soon the perimeters of the EVAC hospital would return to dust.

Return to dust. Lord, you sure have a way of connecting with my heart.

Memories echoed back in her mind. There certainly were some wonderful times spent at the 39th...and some not so wonderful. Not long ago she longed to return home, wallow in her self-pity, and eat dates. But in the last two months, Maggie learned to be content and found happiness in the work around her. Now it all seemed like a dream, bestowed upon her and drawn away too quickly. What would happen to all those she created friendships with? Where would Vera end up in one year? Married to her high school flame, Allen? Still nursing at the best hospital in Baltimore? And dear, sweet Bonnie. Where would life take her in the next 5 years?

Maggie caught wind that Peggy and Walt finally decided there could be more than friendship in their future. Amazing how the Lord brought people together by tearing others apart. She suspected wedding bells would soon be in their future. Walt and Peggy sure did make a smart match.

Her thoughts drifted home to Mother, Dad, Libby...Grace.

Maggie's eyes slid closed, and she wrapped her arms about her waist. How would Grace look when Maggie finally got to see her best friend again? Would she look as radiant as ever? Would her wifely duties add beautiful years of experience to her perfectly sculpted face? Would she soon hear the pitter patter of tiny feet running around the house?

She tamed her considerations before they moved to Danny. Although she'd found peace in realizing it was over between them, a twinge of pain still lingered in the back of her mind. But now that the 39th was closing down, and she most likely would return to Walter Reed Army Hospital, the Army would first award her with a well-deserved vacation.

Going home sounded wonderful, but her apartment was no longer hers or Grace's. Her parents lived a good six hours from Arbor Springs, and visiting Danny was certainly not an option.

Her hand reached into her trousers for the letter that arrived in yesterday's post. Libby once again put out the invitation for Maggie to visit. Maybe now would be as good a time as any to take her sister-in-law up on that offer and spend the majority of her R&R repairing another broken relationship...after she first visited Grace, of course.

Unfolding Libby's letter, Maggie's eyes scanned the page...

Dear Maggie,

The family anxiously awaits your arrival home. Every day I check with the mailman in hopes that a letter from you will come saying you're heading home. We all rejoiced when the Axis Powers surrendered and signed the peace treaty. I have two homecomings to look forward to now. Yours and my dear Phillip's. Words can't express the nerves that I sit on all day long. Even at work, the time moves too slowly. Each day grows longer than the day before.

Please, as soon as you return, you must come stay with me. It gets awfully lonely here at the apartment all by myself. When I write Phillip, I tell him how the first thing I want to do as a married couple when he returns is find a home. I want a place to call my own and landscape with

gardens and children. I'm ready for that. I pray Phillip is too.
Write me soon. I'll be waiting, as always, to hear back from you.

Love,
Libby

28 September 1945

Civilian clothing never felt so good. And never again would she take a hot shower for granted! Maggie appreciated everything more now that she'd made a re-entry into modern civilization. Goodness, a train ride even felt better now than it had before leaving for Germany. It was warm and comfortable. Not at all cold and gut-jolting like the jeeps she'd ridden in for the last year.

It was all so wonderful, it brought tears to her eyes. That and maybe she still had some left over tears from saying good-bye to the women she'd created life bonds with. They all laughed and cried together as they hugged one another farewell, but all left with the promise of one day reuniting and talking about the *old days*.

At least all left happy. Allen and Vera were finally an item. Walt and Peggy decided to elope in a little chapel that survived the bombing raids in Germany, and little Bonnie and flyboy Fred were engaged. Seemed everyone had found their place in the world and someone to love.

She took a deep breath to ward off any signs of fresh tears. She was happy for the girls and their men, but right now she longed for the tastes of home. Everything else was left behind, a closed chapter in her life. But how did one simply forget the perils that roamed over their heads, lapping at their heels, and then go home as if nothing ever happened?

Maybe coming home would be more difficult than she thought.

The train conductor called their next stop and Maggie prepared herself to exit the train. She was home. Glancing out the window, she caught sight of all the familiar scenes of Arbor Springs. It hadn't changed much—if at all—which is how she hoped it would be.

Her heart fluttered when the train stopped. On wobbly legs, she stood to exit. Her nerves jumped with joy for the people she was anxious to see. Grace and Luke, Libby, Mother, Dad…and the list went on and on. She hoped she could fit all her visits in in just three days.

She adjusted her hat she brought back from Germany and clasped her hands together. Would they all look at her and see she was well? Her eyes shifted to the window, hoping to get a peek at who waited on the platform to greet her.

No sooner had her toes touched the train platform, squeals split the air, followed by quickened footsteps of ladies' heels.

"Margaret!"

"Maggie!"

Tipping up her chin to look beyond the brim of her hat, she caught sight of three of the prettiest women she'd ever laid eyes on.

"Mother! Grace! Libby!" Dropping her bags at her side, she braced herself for the trio of hugs. Tears streamed down her face, but she barely took notice of them as her family's smiling faces came near, crushing her beneath their tight embraces.

"Oh, Margaret, my baby. I was so worried for you. Let me look at you. Let me see how you've changed."

"Mother!" Never in a thousand years did Maggie expect to feel the weight of her mother's arms surrounding her as tightly as they did, or hear those precious words spilling from her lips. But she soaked up the warmth. "Mother, I'm so happy to see you." She gripped her mother's dainty hands and stared deeply into her wrinkled eyes, heavily worn with worry and sleepless nights. "I'm fine. Really. You don't have to—"

"Yes, we do." A man's baritone voice thundered behind her.

"Dad!" She went to lunge herself into his arms, but stopped short, remembering their last, strained meal together.

"We're sorry, Maggie. We were wrong." Before she had time to react, her father's eyes shimmered with moisture and he pulled her into his fatherly embrace. So many years of bitterness and silence melted away with each tear drop shed. The healing began at that instant.

"We have so much to talk about," Dad said to her as he wiped at his eyes with a handkerchief.

Maggie stepped back but kept her hands inside her father's. "We do. I promise, we'll talk about everything."

Patiently waiting behind her, watching every lovely scene unfold was Grace. Dear, sweet Grace and her husband, Luke. Maggie's eyes rested on her dearest friend. They remained silent, their eyes speaking volumes to each other. Maggie nodded, and the two met with a lengthy hug.

"So many days I longed to see you Grace, just to talk. Just to see how you were doing."

"I felt the same way, Maggie. There were so many things to tell you, but none fit to put in a letter."

A smile crept up on Maggie's face. "You mean to tell me you can land a man through letters, but yet you spare me precious details?"

Grace shrugged, tears springing up in her eyes.

"What is it, Grace?"

"These are happy tears. Oh, Maggie, I wanted to tell you sooner."

Maggie arched an eyebrow. "Oh? What is it?"

"Luke and I will soon become a family of three." Her tones were soft, and her cheeks glowed with a beautiful, pink hue.

So that's the reason for the radiance around her.

Maggie held back a squeal and threw her arms around Grace. "That's wonderful! I'm so happy for you. When's the baby due?"

"Spring."

"What a sweet gift, Grace. You must tell me everything that's happened since I've been gone."

Luke stepped up behind Grace and placed his good arm around her shoulders. "Someone's been telling." He threw Maggie a wink.

"Oh, darling, Maggie's my best friend. We tell each other everything."

Luke already sported the proud papa look. He looked just as happy as Grace. Maggie knew he'd make a great father. One-armed or not, he already had enough love and hugs for the child that was on its way.

"Goodness." Maggie's fingers pressed up against her cheekbones. "This is too much excitement for one day. I can't handle all this attention."

Just then Maggie noted Libby hanging behind the homecoming, the girl's meek attitude clearly evident on her face.

"Hi, Libby."

"Maggie, is it ever good to see you."

"Come join the crowd." What was with this girl and her cautious behavior? Surely, Maggie's letters of friendship had reached her by now.

"All right. I was hoping you wouldn't mind my being here."

"Are you kidding? I love the fact that you're here, and I am thoroughly looking forward to spending time with you at your place."

"It'll be good to have the company."

The homecoming crowd shifted to the parking lot. Dad grabbed his daughter's bags and threw them into the trunk of the family car.

Maggie stopped in the middle of the parking lot and stared. "Dad, why the car? I thought we were taking the train back to Pittsburg."

"Ah, you're not the only one moving from place to place."

"What?"

"Wait'll you see, dear."

❧❧

Maggie was unsure how to react to all this unusual behavior. Had she really been away from modern civilization so long that she forgot how to function in the world? Her parents' change of heart and attitude threw her for a loop. She wasn't sure she was even in the right car.

Maggie's Mission

As the Chrysler backed out of the parking spot, Maggie peered out the window toward the crowd of people boarding the train. As much as she'd trained her eye not to look for Danny, a piece of her heart still hoped he'd exceed her expectations and surprise her at the station. She was glad that she hadn't held her hopes up in thinking Danny would ride to her rescue and scoop her up in his arms and take her home to live happily ever after. She'd already lived out that fairy tale once.

Then she realized she was doing it again...caressing the smooth gold surface of Danny's gold cross she still kept hidden around her neck. She'd had every intention of giving it back to him before he left Germany, but her mixed emotions and clouded mind shrouded her good sense. Glancing to Libby, who sat beside her in the backseat, she quickly tucked the necklace back inside her blouse.

Mother's chatter soon started and the car filled with love. It was the family Maggie always wanted. But still, Libby remained quiet and thoughtful, as if visiting a place of her own in the secret hideout of her mind. Maggie yearned to know what went on in that secret place. What made Libby tic? What drew her into her silence?

But those questions would have to wait.

"Where are we going, Dad?"

"Home."

"Home? But we're heading in another direction."

"Margaret, I believe I do know where I live." A gentle look in the rearview mirror told Maggie her father had something up his sleeve. What was this reformed man up to? Was she really looking into the eyes of her father? He was so different. So...loving.

Her questions were soon put to rest when Dad pulled the car into a shaded driveway. A cute, single family home, dressed in white with black shutters, seemed to smile at her. Three large maple trees grew in front of the house and on each side of the driveway, adding privacy to the quaint residence.

Maggie's eyes grew wide with wonder as she stepped from the car and drank in the sight of the home. "It's beautiful. Whose house is this?"

Mother walked into Dad's open arms and both smiled at her. "It's ours."

"Yours?" Maggie's eyes bulged with wonder.

"Maggie, we decided we didn't want to live apart from you any longer. If this is where your heart is, then we want to be part of it too." Dad bent down to kiss Mother on the cheek.

Libby came to Maggie's side. "They are even letting me stay here with them while I wait for Phillip to come home and while I work on our house. So we get to share a room...like real sisters. I couldn't tell you at the train station or it would've spoiled the surprise."

"What do you mean, *your* house?"

"That's the other part of the surprise. Your parents graciously funded the purchase of a cute little home just down the road. It's a fixer upper, but it'll suit us just fine. We'll be neighbors, Maggie!"

"Oh, Libby, I'd like nothing more."

✧✦✧

Her plans had certainly changed. Instead of splitting her time between her parents, Grace, and Libby, Maggie was blessed to see them all as much as she wanted while on leave. But it was today's visit with Grace and Luke that changed her future in a big way.

"I'm thinking the spare bedroom beside our room will work nicely for a baby's nursery. I plan to use the lace curtains that are in there now and add a rocking chair in the corner. Of course we'll use the same buffet that's already in that room, and we'll just move the spare bed to the third bedroom. There's not as much room there, but it'll have to do."

Maggie eyed her friend as she worked diligently on the crocheted blanket that sat in her lap. Grace's demeanor was gentle, content. She'd easily taken on the role as wife and was already fitting the mold to be a wonderful mother.

Maggie's own want for a relationship and home burned deep in her chest. Grace's lovely cottage was filled with tender loving care and gave off a warmth that invited friends to stay put.

Pushing aside her thoughts, Maggie cradled her knee cap with her linked hands and engaged in conversation with Grace.

"I think that room will suit just fine for a baby's nursery. Do you wish for one gender or another?"

"I've thought about it. While a little girl would be fun to dress up and care for, I also think it would be wonderful to have a little Luke. I guess I'm indifferent." A soft laugh hummed from her lips. Then Grace grew silent. A moment later, she checked the clock and placed her crochet hook and yarn in the basket on the floor. Grace's concerned expression focused on Maggie. "How are *you* doing?"

The softness of Grace's touch broke the barriers Maggie fought to keep hidden. But it was just the two of them and Maggie could always tell Grace anything.

"You're talking about Danny."

"Yes."

She took a deep breath. "Do I miss him? Terribly. Do I have regrets?

Many. Do I ever think of him? Every day of my life."

"Have you thought of picking up the telephone and telling him?"

"Many times since I returned home. But I just can't. Twice I've lost him. Opening myself up to being rejected when I've already dealt with the loss is more than I can bear."

The muffled sound of a car door slamming shut caused Grace to pull back her lace curtains and peer outside.

"Maybe you won't need that phone call."

"What do you mean?"

Grace stood and started for the door. "Why don't you come see for yourself?"

Her heart hammered in her chest. Was it...could it be...

Like a shell exploding on the ground, each step she took seemed to land on shaky ground. Her legs trembled, and she feared her knees would knock together. Lightheadedness swirled her thoughts...had she forgotten to breathe?

"You all right, Maggie?"

"I don't know. Is it him?"

When she stepped into the sunlight pouring in from the door, she shielded her eyes and peered outside. Her breath caught in her chest when her eyes rested on a charming Italian and his handsome face.

Leaning against his blue Ford in dark slacks and a button down collared shirt, Danny never looked better. All his weight had returned to his scrawny body and his hair was neatly clipped and slicked back. It *was* him. Whole and healthy. Maggie hoped...

"Go to him, Maggie," Grace urged.

Her feet obeyed and took the steps one at a time. Her eyes pierced his figure and she couldn't look away. He was perfect.

Danny stood with a sheepish grin on his face. As she came closer, something white and fluffy rested in his arms, piquing her interest.

"Hi." His voice was cautious, gentle.

"Hello."

"I'm...glad to see you made it back safely." His hand smoothed over a white, fluffy object resting in his arm.

"Me too. It looks like your mother did a fine job of fattening you up. I think you're back to your pre-war weight."

"Almost. But you know Mother. She'll spoon feed a body if they refuse food. She was pretty shocked to find me in the rough form I was in. Pretty shocked to see me in the flesh even."

"As were we all."

Why was he here? To see her? She wished he would say. The tightness in her throat choked her and she feared tears would soon follow. A subject change was needed.

"What have you got there?"

"She's a kitten. Came with the house. Found her under the porch all alone so I took her in and nursed her back to health."

"What house?"

"The one I bought." He eyed her suspiciously.

"You bought...a house?" On his nod, she understood. "Oh. Congratulations." She swallowed hard. He was here to tell her good-bye for good. He'd found someone else and moved on.

"I bought it for someone special. I didn't expect this little fur ball to come with it."

She tried to smile despite the sound of her heart shattering all over again at the realization of the moment.

"Y—you're getting married." Her voice was flat. When Danny didn't reply, she swallowed back her uneasiness. "When is the big day?"

"I don't know. She hasn't said yes yet."

Maggie didn't want to talk about *her*. Why did he come over here, to torture her and tell her about some other woman who'd stolen his heart? It was cruel.

She turned her attention back on the kitten. "What did you name her?"

"Well—" Danny scratched under his chin— "I need a little help with that, you see. I couldn't see calling her Tank or Colt—she's too dainty for that—so I figured I'd get someone else to pick a name for her."

It was just like Danny to say something to make her giggle even though she wanted to cry. Maggie caught her breath before her quiet laughter turned to tears. "Tank? I thought you had enough of war."

"That's why I need a little help. And I was afraid if I named her that she wouldn't take too kindly to it and turn her claws on me."

"She should be a Snowflake or Annabelle. Or..." A sob wrenched her. "I'm sorry, Danny. I can't do this." Her feet backed away in retreat.

"She's yours if you want her, Maggie. Please don't go."

She halted. "Mine? You found her under *your* house."

"Well, there's a little catch if you take her though. Just a smidge."

"What is it?"

"The house comes with her."

"The house? What are you talking about, Danny?"

He moved closer and reached for her hand. Her heart skipped a few paces in the wake of his touch.

"The house comes with the kitten. You taking the cat means you take the house, and...you take me. If you'll have me."

His name rolled off her tongue with her next breath. Was he asking what she thought he was asking? Her hand fluttered to her mouth. He gently removed it and held it tenderly in his palm.

"The dark-haired angel came to see me again. She's you. You came to visit me every night until I heard you made it into town." He took a step closer. "Marry me, Maggie? I've had a lot of time to think since June—a lot. And I was an idiot. You didn't deserve to be treated like that. Truth was I couldn't stand to think of you with anyone else. But every time I looked at you, I saw *him* standing next to you, winning your heart and stealing it from me. I figured if I let you go before you had the chance to let go of me, it wouldn't hurt as bad. But then that night...you came...and kneeled at my bed. You whispered those words into my ear and I—I didn't know what to say or do."

"You were awake?"

"Guilty as charged."

"And you didn't say anything?"

"I'm sorry. I was irrational and a fool. Maggie, you're the only for one me. You're the only one who knows me inside and out. Coming home and living here without you wasn't the same. And I went to bed every night looking up at the sky and hoping you were watching the same stars I saw. I don't want us to be apart ever again. I know you still love me. I know that because I love you, and I see it in your eyes. You want me as much as I want you."

She couldn't argue that fact. She did want him. She did love him. And she did want to marry him.

"If I agree to take the kitten, can she sleep in the house?"

"Huh?"

Laughter leaked through the corners of her mouth and she pulled Danny in close. Nose to nose they stood.

"I love you with every ounce of fiber in me, Maggie." His arm encircled her waist, the kitten coming between them, caving all Maggie's reservations.

She relaxed into his embrace by cradling his neck in her hands. "I love you too, Danny."

"I have the house and I have the rings. All I need is you." His lips pressed a kiss onto the tip of her nose.

"Then let's make that happen." The feel of his lips against hers righted all the wrongs from the past five months and released all lingering burdens from her shoulders. His kiss was sweet, tender, manly, and everything she wanted it to be. The effect of it left a sweet taste on her lips long after it was broken. "I think my mission is accomplished, Lieutenant Russo."

"Oh, no, Lieutenant Johnson, it's just beginning."

EPILOGUE

14 June 1946

Maggie curled her body up close to Danny's as she slipped in between the sheets. A soft, summer's breeze hooked the curtains and blew across her skin. The glow of the full moon slanted through the window pane, and casted a blue hue over Danny's profile. Why didn't anyone ever embellish on marriage being so sweet?

Her fingers reached up to smooth away a curled tendril that hung over his forehead. He caught her hand before she could pull it away.

"Don't stop."

She smiled in the darkness. "There are no more curls to brush away."

"I can help with that." With one swoop of his hand, Danny tousled his hair into a dark mess.

"What am I going to do with you, Danny Russo?"

"At the moment, I don't care."

"In that case…" She stretched her neck to plant a kiss on his earlobe. He reacted by cradling her in his arms and covering her mouth with his in slow, passionate kisses.

Thump, thump, thump.

"What was that?" Maggie whispered in between breaths.

"I think it came from the front door."

"A caller?"

Danny sat up in bed and listened. Another knock sounded from the porch.

"Someone's at the door."

Maggie's heart thundered. Pulling the covers up close to her chin, she shuddered. "Who do you suppose it is?"

"I don't know. It's awfully odd for someone to call after ten."

"Danny be careful. Wait. Let me go with you."

"No, stay here, Maggie. I'll take care of it."

Danny walked from their bedroom toward the direction of the foyer.

Maggie's Mission

Maggie threw the covers off her body and grabbed her robe to toss over her shoulders. Tying closed her housecoat, she padded quietly through the house. She reached the living room just in time to see Danny throw open the door to a meek little woman whose face was blotched with red marks and a shiner on her cheekbone.

"Libby?" Maggie raced for the door and pulled her sister-in-law inside. But before she could set Libby down on the couch, the girl's legs gave out beneath her. Danny's arms caught her before she hit the floor.

"Libby, honey, what happened to you?"

"Maggie?"

"Yes? What is it, dear?"

"Maggie? Hide me. Don't let him find me, please. I don't have anywhere else to turn."

"Who, Libby? Are you in trouble?"

"Libby." Danny bent down beside her. "Who hit you? Where's Phillip?"

Agony tortured the poor girl's eyes. A mix of blood and tears intermingled on her cheeks and added a sheen to her complexion. But the girl looked famished and sickly. Something was very wrong.

"Libby, you can tell us. Danny and I will protect you."

"He's not the same anymore. He's a monster. You have to believe me."

"I believe you, Libby. But you have to tell me who it is."

Her eyes lazily rolled upward to meet Maggie's gaze. Before Libby's eyes drifted closed, she managed to whisper, "Didn't you know? Phillip."

Author's Note

Thank you for revisiting the Love & War Series with *Maggie's Mission*. This book took nearly 2 years of pouring over research, intensive reading, late-night writing, and revising before going into print.

It was a joy to pen this story of hope and forgiveness as Maggie ventured into peril on the German countryside and learned the value of life, humility, and love's sweet song.

Most of the historical timeline in this novel is true fact. The 39th Evacuation Hospital was indeed a real chain hospital that moved from Belgium into Germany and across the autobahn during the end of the war. EVAC hospitals were expected to pick up and move with the front line on a moment's notice. Nurses were a vital part of the company and also assisted in the breakdown and re-building of these mobile hospitals.

Remember the mention of the 39th boiling used gauze strips for re-use? That was all true. Sometimes new shipments of supplies were delayed, shot down, or just not available. The medical staff "made-do" with what little they did possess. Sometimes this called for procedures that we would cringe at today.

A few more details to make note of were also taken from true-life accounts; the airfield strafing by a Luftwaffe fighter and the hospital bombing despite the fact it bore the Red Cross emblem.

Danny's story was a bit difficult to write in, especially when it came to painting his character without Maggie recognizing him right off the bat. It took months to research POW camps and understand the mental picture of what prisoners experienced in the stalags. Danny's physical appearance needed to be altered just so, creating an emaciated distortion of his former self.

Dysentery was a major problem in these camps. Malnutrition and filthy living conditions were the major contributors to this horrible illness and quickly deteriorated the human body. The disease caused unbearable pain in the abdomen, nausea, vomiting, and diarrhea. Medication and healthier meals were needed to correct the problem, however, this type of treatment was not a common practice in many of the German prison camps.

Much of Danny's story was also taken from true accounts of the D-Night jump. Everything from the plane ride over the English Channel to Danny's jump, and the machine guns strafing the air, is true. Confusion on the ground and missed landings were obstacles that hindered the success of the mission, but only temporarily. The flaming C-47s crashing to the ground were written through the eyes of paratrooper veterans who were there. As was the picture of the German countryside and towns, the dead colonel hanging from the tree, and the fiery German barn.

The march from Oflag 64 to Stalag III A is also a true occurrence in which prisoners were forced to walk through freezing temperatures and snow from Poland to Stalag III A, which was located about 25 miles southeast of Berlin.

Out of the 4,080 men who started on the journey, only 2,800 made it to Stalag III A. Some prisoners were left at camps en route to Luckenwalde. Others were too emaciated and ill to make the trip and were either shot or left to die along the way.

Danny's amnesia and Missing in Action status were events planned from the writing of the first book in this series, *Letters from Grace*. If you recall, Danny's paperwork declared him Killed in Action toward the end of the story. However, Danny's body was never recovered. This was a common occurrence during World War II. Many men were unaccounted for and feared dead. After so many months of MIA status, the Army usually assumed the worst—the soldier had been killed. Many families were visited by the War Department and handed that dreadful Western Union Telegram only to learn months later that their son was still alive. I can't imagine living in such a time as that.

It is my hope, dear reader, that you have found Maggie's story uplifting and satisfying as Danny found his way back to Maggie just as he promised. Now we gear up for the concluding story in the Love & War Series, *Phillip's War*—the story of Maggie's brother and his mental struggle to survive life post-war.

How will Grace and Luke fare as they welcome their first child into the world? Will Danny ever learn of Abe's fate? What is the mystery behind Libby's insecurities? And what is the dark secret Phillip is hiding from his wife?

Find out the answers when *Phillip's War* is released later in 2015!

Blessings,
Rachel

Acknowledgements

This time around, it took a whole new team of supporters to get this project off the ground and launched into action.

Jesus will always be the first who deserves my undying gratitude. His blessings continue to pour down on me and help me survive the ups and downs of publishing. Every morning starts with Him and the strength He gives me to endure another day.

My husband will also always be a huge part of my career. He's been my biggest fan since the day I told him I wanted to be a writer. Since then he's helped with countless dinners, babysitting, and making sure all my needs are met. Thank you, Chris, for always being there, even when things seem to come crashing down on us.

I also owe a great deal of thanks to my oldest daughter, April, who read *Letters from Grace* and became my cheerleader as she pushed me to finish *Maggie's Mission*. I love you, April, for the smart, beautiful, and loving not-so-little-girl you are.

My research team came together as I wrote the story. First on my list is my history-loving cousin. Thank you, Jacob, for all the documentary/war-movie times we spent during the research phase of this project and for the lending of World War II-related, non-fiction works for my research. Your insight and knowledge of World War II and the European Theater of Operations was a vital part of making this book the product it has become. I look forward to many more war conversations and documentary-watching days to come!

To my critique partner and fellow writer, Julie Steele, who spent hours reading over my manuscript and critiquing my work. Julie, without you, this book would be nowhere near done! I have found an absolute gem when it comes to critique partners. Your eye for detail enabled me to push my writing further than I knew could be achieved. It all came together because of you, and I thank you a million times over.

One more tidbit of research became a necessity to create an authentic feel for Danny's prison life ordeal. I owe much gratitude to Lynn Leonard who translated my English lines into German sentences for the capture of Danny and prison camp scenes at the beginning of the book. Lynn, you didn't know me when I first contacted you, and we are still only mere acquaintances, but I thank you from the bottom of my heart for your help in authenticating my German guards and helping me bring them to life.

I once again thank Sarah Sundin for her insight on Army chain hospitals, the medical profession, protocol, and uses for pharmaceuticals during WWII. She's my go-to *gal* when it comes to the ANC.

And the finished product would not be available to the public without the help of my editor for this project. Thank you, Anne-Marie, for your willingness to read, re-read, and make those necessary changes in this novel. A good editor can make or break a book, and I'm so thankful for the mistakes caught by your keen eye. Any mistake found in this book is purely the fault of myself.

None of this would be possible without the help of all these individuals who answered my tedious questions, and poured over my chapters. My words alone cannot express my gratitude to its fullest, but one day I'm sure we'll all meet face to face where I can express my appreciation formally.

Thank you, my friends!

~Rachel

Rachel is the author of the bestselling *Love & War* series. Her debut title, *Letters from Grace*, finaled in Harlequinn Mills & Boon's So You Think You Can Write Contest and semi-finaled in American Christian Fiction Writers' Genesis Contest. Since then, her books have become best sellers. Rachel lives in Central Maryland with her husband, 5 children, and 2 cats.

Learn More About Rachel D. Muller

WWW.RachelDMuller.Com

Facebook: @rmullerbooks | Instagram: @rachelmuller_author | Twitter: @RachelDMuller

READ THE FINAL INSTALLMENT IN THE LOVE & WAR SERIES

"Gripping and thought provoking, *Phillip's War* hits the gold star when it comes to WWII era novels."

—RITA GERLACH, bestselling author of Inspirational Historical Fiction

Phillip can't escape the haunting nightmares born on the bloody islands of battle as he attempts to settle into life away from war. His irrational behavior soon dismantles his marriage to Libby, and when his despair turns volatile, Libby needs an escape.

Will the couple find healing and restore their marriage or will their love sink in the midst of Phillip's inward war?

timelinepress.net   Available Online or In Store

IS LOVING A MAN IN UNIFORM WORTH THE RISK?

America fell in love with Grace Campbell and Luke Brady
as their classic love story unfolded in the sands of time.
Now you can read where the story began in . . .

Letters from Grace

Scarred from the death of her fiancé in World War II, Grace
Campbell must learn to love again. Lieutenant Luke Brady could make
falling in love easy...except he's going to war. There's one thing that can
keep a thread tied between them—letters. But the suave Dr. William
Keller enchants Grace with his charm and proposes marriage. She must
choose between them. Will she settle for comfort and safety or risk
losing everything on the Normandy beaches?

Praise for

Letters from Grace...

"When I finished **Letters From Grace** *I felt that I needed to learn the rest of the story. Therefore I am delighted that Maggie's Mission is now available. I found Rachel Muller's writing style engaging and heartfelt".*
- Susan Bulanda, Award Winning Author.

"In **LETTERS FROM GRACE,** *talented author Rachel Muller proves that nothing--fear, misunderstanding, lack of faith, not even war-- can stand in the way of true love. Readers will identify with the tough choices faced by Muller's characters, and wait with bated breath for the next installment in the Love and War series. Make room for these novels on your "keepers" shelf, because you'll want to read the realistic, heart-pounding stories again and again!"*
- Loree Lough, Bestselling Author

Made in the USA
Middletown, DE
18 December 2022

19180472R00161